Born in Paris in 1947, Christian Jacq first visited Egypt when he was seventeen, went on to study Egyptology and archaeology at the Sorbonne, and is now one of the world's leading Egyptologists. He is the author of the internationally bestselling RAMSES series, THE QUEEN OF FREEDOM trilogy and many other novels on Ancient Egypt. Christian Jacq lives in Switzerland.

Also by Christian Jacq:

The Ramses Series
Volume 1: The Son of the Light
Volume 2: The Temple of a Million Years
Volume 3: The Battle of Kadesh
Volume 4: The Lady of Abu Simbel
Volume 5: Under the Western Acacia

The Stone of Light Series
Volume 1: Nefer the Silent
Volume 2: The Wise Woman
Volume 3: Paneb the Ardent
Volume 4: The Place of Truth

The Queen of Freedom Trilogy
Volume 1: The Empire of Darkness
Volume 2: The War of the Crowns
Volume 3: The Flaming Sword

The Judge of Egypt Trilogy
Volume 1: Beneath the Pyramid
Volume 2: Secrets of the Desert
Volume 3: Shadow of the Sphinx

The Black Pharaoh
The Tutankhamun Affair
For the Love of Philae
Champollion the Egyptian
Master Hiram & King Solomon
The Living Wisdom of Ancient Egypt

About the translator

Sue Dyson is a prolific author of both fiction and non-fiction,
including over thirty novels, both contemporary and historical. She
has also translated a wide variety of French fiction.

The Judge of Egypt Trilogy

Beneath the Pyramid

Christian Jacq

Translated by Sue Dyson

POCKET
BOOKS

LONDON · NEW YORK · SYDNEY · TORONTO

First published in France by Plon under the title
La Pyramide Assassinée, 1993
First published in Great Britain by Simon & Schuster UK Ltd, 2004
This edition published by Pocket Books, 2004
An imprint of Simon & Schuster UK Ltd

Copyright © Librarie Plon, 1993
English translation copyright © Sue Dyson, 2004

This book is copyright under the Berne Convention.
No reproduction without permission.
® and © 1997 Simon & Schuster Inc. All rights reserved.
Pocket Books & Design is a registered trademark of Simon & Schuster Inc

The right of Christian Jacq to be identified as author of this work has been
asserted by him in accordance with sections 77 and 78 of the Copyright,
Designs and Patents Act, 1988.

1 3 5 7 9 10 8 6 4 2

Simon & Schuster UK Ltd
1st Floor
222 Grays Inn Road
London WC1X 8HB

Simon & Schuster Australia
Sydney

A CIP catalogue record for this book is available
from the British Library

ISBN 978-1-47112-711-3

Typeset in Times by SX Composing DTP, Rayleigh, Essex
Printed and bound by CPI Group
(UK) Ltd, Croydon, CR0 4YY

Lo, that which the ancestors predicted has come to pass: crime is everywhere, violence has invaded men's hearts, misfortune besets the land, blood flows, the thief grows wealthy, smiles have faded, secrets have been divulged, trees have been uprooted, pyramids have been desecrated, the world has sunk so low that a few madmen have seized control of the throne, and the judges have been driven away.

But remember respect for the Rule, the righteous succession of days, the happy time when men built pyramids and filled orchards with plenty for the gods, that blessed time when a simple mat provided all that a man could desire and made him content.

Predictions of the sage Ipu-Ur

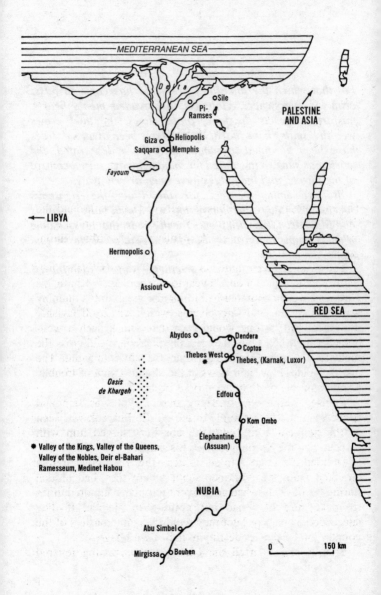

MEDITERRANEAN SEA

Delta

○ Sile

Pi-
Ramses

○ Heliopolis

Giza ○○
Saqqara ○○ Memphis

Fayoum

PALESTINE
AND ASIA

← LIBYA

RED SEA

Hermopolis ○

Assiout ○

Abydos ○   ○ Dendera
                  ○ Coptos
Thebes West ○
          ✴   ○ Thebes, (Karnak, Luxor)

*Oasis
de Khargeh*

Edfou ○

Kom Ombo ○

Élephantine
(Assuan) ○

✴ Valley of the Kings, Valley of the Queens,
Valley of the Nobles, Deir el-Bahari
Ramesseum, Medinet Habou

NUBIA

Abu Simbel ○

Mirgissa ○○ Bouhen

0   150 km

Prologue

The moonless night had cast a veil of darkness around the Great Pyramid, and the group of soldiers who guarded it. In the distance, a desert fox slunk silently into the nobles' burial ground.

The only person permitted to enter the pyramid was the king, Ramses, who visited it once a year to pay homage to Khufu, his glorious ancestor. Rumour had it that the great king's mummy was housed in a gold sarcophagus, which was itself lavishly decorated. But no one would ever dare attack such a well-defended treasure. Only the reigning pharaoh could cross the monument's stone threshold and enter the labyrinth within. The guards would draw their bows at the slightest sign of trouble, bringing instant death to the curious or unwary.

Ramses' reign was a happy one; Egypt was rich and peaceful, a shining example to the world. Pharaoh was seen as the messenger of light, the courtiers served him with respect, and the people glorified his name.

Dressed in coarse linen tunics, the five conspirators emerged from the workmen's hut where they had hidden during the day. They had gone over their plan a hundred times to make sure they had left nothing to chance. If they succeeded, sooner or later they would become masters of the country, and shape its destiny in their own image.

Silently they skirted the Giza plateau, casting fevered

1

glances at the vast pyramid. A direct attack on the guards would be madness. Others before them had dreamed of seizing the treasure, but none had succeeded.

A month earlier, the Great Sphinx had been dug out of a sand drift which had accumulated during several recent storms. The giant monument, shaped like a pharaoh with a lion's body, was only lightly guarded, for it was known as the 'Living Statue', and the terror it inspired was enough to drive away evildoers.

The Sphinx's honour guard consisted of just five former soldiers. Two of them were fast asleep, propped up against the encircling wall facing the pyramids. They would not see or hear anything.

The lightest of the conspirators swiftly scaled the curtain wall, soundlessly strangled the sleeping soldier by the stone beast's right flank, then killed the guard by its left shoulder.

The other conspirators joined their companion. Killing the third guard, who was standing by the stele of Tuthmosis IV between the sphinx's front paws, would not be so easy. He was armed with a spear and a dagger, and was sure to defend himself.

One of the conspirators undressed and walked, naked, towards him.

He stared at her, aghast. This apparition must be one of the demons of the night who prowled around the pyramids, in search of souls to steal! Smiling, she approached him. Terrified, he sprang to his feet and brandished his spear. His arm was shaking. She halted.

'Get back, ghost!' he commanded. 'Leave me alone.'

'I shan't harm you. Let me kiss you.'

The guard could not tear his gaze from the woman's naked body, which gleamed white in the darkness. Hypnotized, he took a step towards her. A noose was suddenly flung about his neck and pulled tight. He dropped his spear, tried in vain to cry out, fell to his knees, and died.

'The way is clear,' she called.

'I'll get the lamps ready,' said one of the men.

The five conspirators stood beside the stele and consulted their map one last time, urging each other to continue despite the fear that racked them. They moved the stele aside, and there before their eyes was the mud seal that marked the position of the mouth of hell, the gateway to the bowels of the earth.

'So it wasn't just a legend.'

'Let's see if there really is a way in.'

Beneath the seal lay a flagstone, with a ring set into it. It took four of them to raise it. A very low, narrow corridor sloped steeply downwards into the depths of the earth.

'Quickly, the lamps!'

They filled dolerite cups with stone-oil, which was very greasy and burnt easily. Pharaoh forbade its use and sale, for the black smoke it produced brought sickness to the craftsmen who decorated temples and tombs, and soiled ceilings and walls. The sages had declared that this 'petroleum', as barbarians called it, was a harmful and dangerous substance; a malign secretion of the rocks filled with harmful vapours. But the conspirators could not have cared less.

Bent double, their heads often bumping against the limestone roof, they drove on deeper into the tunnel, towards the underground part of the Great Pyramid. No one spoke; they were all thinking about the sinister tale of a spirit which would break the neck of anyone trying to violate Khufu's tomb. And could they be sure this tunnel was taking them in the right direction? To mislead would-be thieves, false maps had been circulated; was theirs accurate?

They came up against a stone wall which they attacked with chisels; fortunately, the blocks were quite thin and pivoted easily. The conspirators slipped inside a vast chamber with an earthen floor. The room was about seven cubits high, twenty-eight long, and sixteen wide. In the centre was a well.

'The low chamber . . . We're inside the Great Pyramid!'

They had succeeded.

The long-forgotten passageway* did indeed lead from the sphinx to Khufu's giant monument, whose first chamber lay about sixty cubits below the base. It was here, within this evocation of the earth-mother's bosom, that the first resurrection rites had been carried out.

Now they must climb up a vertical shaft which led to the heart of the pyramid and joined a passage which began beyond the three granite plugs. The lightest of the five climbed up, using projecting rocks as hand- and footholds, and threw down a rope. One of the conspirators almost fainted for lack of air; his companions took him to the great gallery to get his breath back.

The sheer majesty of the place dazzled them. What architect had been mad enough to build such a structure, defying the centuries? According to Ramses' own master craftsmen, no one would ever again achieve such a feat.

One of the men was so overwhelmed that he wanted to give up; but the leader of the conspirators forced him on with a violent shove in the back. Giving up when they were so close to their goal would be stupid, for they now knew that their map was absolutely accurate. One doubt remained: had the stone portcullises been lowered between the great gallery and the corridor leading to the king's chamber? If so, the way would be blocked and they would have to leave empty-handed.

'It's all right – the entrance is clear.'

The five conspirators stooped low and entered the king's chamber, whose lofty ceiling was formed from nine immense blocks of granite. This chamber housed the very heart of the empire, the pharaoh's sarcophagus. It lay upon a silver floor, which maintained the purity of the place.

---

*The existence of this passageway, mentioned in ancient sources, remains a matter for conjecture.

They hesitated.

Up to now, they had behaved like explorers in search of an unknown land. True, they had committed three crimes for which they would have to answer before the court of the afterlife, but they had acted for the good of the country and the people, by preparing the way for a tyrant's overthrow. But if they opened the sarcophagus, if they stripped it of its treasures, they would be violating the eternity not of a mummified man but of a god and his body of light. They would sever their last link with a thousand-year-old civilization in order to bring about a new world which Ramses would never accept.

They were torn between a desire to run away, and a sensation of great well-being. Air entered the pyramid through two channels cut into the north and south walls; and an energy rose up from the floor, imbuing them with some unknown strength. So this was how Pharaoh regenerated himself: by absorbing the power created by the stone and the monument's shape.

'We haven't much time.'

'We ought to leave now.'

'Certainly not.'

Two of the conspirators went over to the sarcophagus, then the third, and then the last two. Together, they lifted off the lid and laid it on the floor.

In the sarcophagus lay a radiant mummy covered with gold, silver and lapis lazuli, a mummy so noble that the looters could not bear to look into its eyes. Furiously, their leader tore off the golden mask; his acolytes seized the gold collar and the scarab, which lay where the heart had been. They took the lapis lazuli amulets and the sky-iron adze, the carpenter's tool that was used to open the mouth and eyes in the otherworld. But these marvels seemed almost derisory compared with the gold cubit symbolizing the eternal law that Pharaoh alone guaranteed.

Most precious of all was a small case in the form of a dove's tail. Inside it lay the Testament of the Gods. This text bequeathed Egypt to Pharaoh, and instructed him to keep the country happy and prosperous. When he celebrated his jubilee, he would be obliged to show the testament to the court and the people, as proof of his rightful kingship. If he could not produce it, sooner or later he would be compelled to abdicate.

By desecrating the pyramid's shrine, the conspirators had disrupted the principal energy centre and disturbed the radiance of the *ka*, the intangible power which animated every form of life. Soon misfortunes and calamities would rain down upon the land. Gradually, injustice would spread through the provinces, and more and more voices would be raised against Pharaoh until they became a destructive flood.

Lastly, the thieves seized a box filled with ingots of sky-iron, a rare metal as precious as gold. It would be used to complete their plan.

All they now had to do was leave the Great Pyramid, hide their booty, and weave their web.

Once safely back outside, before going their separate ways, they took an oath. Anyone who got in their way was to be killed: that was the price of power.

1

After a long career devoted to the art of healing, Branir was enjoying a peaceful retirement at his home in Memphis.

The old doctor was sturdily built and broad-chested, with elegant, silver hair framing a face whose stern appearance belied his kindliness and dedication. His natural nobility had impressed itself on everyone from the humble to the mighty, and no one could remember a single occasion when he been treated disrespectfully.

Branir was the son of a wig maker. He had left the family business to become a sculptor, painter and artist, and one of Pharaoh's master craftsmen had summoned him to the temple at Karnak. During one of the craftsmen's banquets, a stone cutter had fallen ill; instinctively, Branir had treated him with magnetism, snatching him from the jaws of certain death. The temple's own doctors had been quick to recognize his exceptional talent, and Branir had been trained by renowned physicians before beginning his work. Deaf to the court's pleas and uninterested in honours, he lived only to heal the sick.

However, now he was travelling to a small village near Thebes, and not to practise his craft. He had another mission to carry out, one so delicate that it seemed doomed to failure; but he would not give up until he had tried everything.

Branir ordered the bearers to set down his chair close to a

tangled thicket of tamarisk trees. He felt a lump rise in his throat when he saw his home village once again, nestling in the heart of a palm grove. The air and sun were gentle; he watched the peasants at work and listened to the tune a flute player was piping.

An old man and two youths were breaking up clumps of earth in the high fields, turning Branir's thoughts to the season when the annual Nile flood deposited its fertile silt upon the land. The seed was trodden in by herds of pigs and flocks of sheep. Nature had endowed Egypt with untold riches, for this was the gods' beloved country.

Branir continued on his way. At the entrance to the village, he passed a team of placid oxen, and a man squatting outside one of the earthen houses, milking a cow. The old doctor smiled as he remembered the herd of cows he had once looked after; beasts with names like Good Advice, Pigeon, Sun-Water and Happy Flood. He had almost forgotten these simple scenes, this serene, unsurprising way of life, in which a man was simply one among many. Tasks were repeated over and over again, as they had been for centuries, and the Nile waters rose and fell, marking the rhythm of passing generations.

Suddenly, a powerful voice shattered the tranquillity summoning the people to a session of the village court. Nearby, a woman was loudly protesting her innocence, but the man in charge of maintaining order in the village kept a firm grip on her arm.

The court convened in the shade of a sycamore tree. Over it presided Pazair, a twenty-one-year-old judge who had the complete trust of all the village elders. Ordinarily, the elders would have appointed a middle-aged man with plenty of experience, who could answer for his decisions with his possessions if he was rich, and with his life if he had nothing worth seizing. Consequently, there were few candidates for the job of judge, even in a small country village. Any magistrate found to be at fault was punished more severely than a murderer; justice demanded it.

Pazair had had no choice. Because of his strong character and his uncompromising integrity, the elders had elected him by unanimous decision. Although he was very young, he had soon proved his competence by conducting each case with extreme care.

He was a tall man and rather thin, with chestnut hair and a broad, high forehead. His green eyes, flecked with brown, were bright and alert, and he impressed everyone with his serious manner; neither anger nor tears nor attempts at seduction perturbed him. He listened, scrutinized evidence, often investigated and checked witnesses' statements himself, and did not reach a decision until long and patient enquiries had been carried out. The villagers were sometimes astonished by his thoroughness, but they congratulated themselves on his love of truth and his talent for settling differences. Many feared him, knowing that they could not hope for compromise or indulgence from him; but none of his decisions had ever been challenged.

The jurors sat on either side of Pazair. There were eight in all: the village headman and his wife, two farmers, two craftsmen, an elderly widow and the scribe in charge of irrigation. All were over fifty.

The judge opened the court session with prayers to the goddess Ma'at, whose Rule earthly justice must strive to mirror. Then he read out the charge against the young woman. One of her friends accused her of stealing a spade belonging to her husband. In accordance with ancient law, there were no lawyers to act as intermediaries. Pazair asked the accuser to state her grievance clearly, and the defendant to present her defence. The former spoke calmly, the latter with such vehemence that Pazair ordered her to quiet herself.

He asked, 'Did anyone witness the crime?'

'I did,' replied the accuser.

'Where do you think the spade is now?'

'Hidden in her house.'

The accused woman denied the charge again with an energy which impressed the jurors. Her sincerity seemed obvious.

'We shall carry out a search immediately,' declared Pazair.

'You have no right to enter my house,' said the woman angrily.

'Do you confess you're guilty?'

'No! I'm innocent.'

'Lying in court is a serious offence.'

'She's the one who's lying.'

'If she is, she will be severely punished.' Pazair turned to the accuser and looked her straight in the eye. 'Do you still maintain that she stole the spade?' he asked.

She nodded.

The court moved off, following the scribe in charge of dealing with village disputes. The judge carried out the search himself. He found the spade in the cellar, wrapped in rags and hidden behind oil jars.

The guilty woman collapsed in tears. In accordance with the law, the jurors sentenced her to give her victim twice what she had stolen: in other words, two new spades. Moreover, lying under oath carried a sentence of forced labour for life, or even death in a criminal case. She was sentenced to work for several years, unpaid, on the lands of the local temple.

As the jurors were dispersing, Pazair heard someone ask, 'Will the judge grant me an audience?'

He could hardly believe his ears. That voice . . . Surely it couldn't be . . . ? He swung round. 'It *is* you!'

Branir and Pazair embraced.

'What on earth are you doing here?' asked Pazair.

'I have returned to my roots.'

'Let's go and sit down.'

The two men sat down on two low seats in the shade of a

tall sycamore. On one of its sturdy branches hung a goatskin filled with fresh water.

'Sitting here brings back many memories, doesn't it?' said Branir. 'This is where, after your parents died, I told you your secret name, the "Seer, He Who Sees Far into the Distance". The Council of Elders was right to give you that name. What more could anyone ask of a judge?'

'And what a splendid celebration there was! I was circumcised, the village gave me my first official kilt, I threw away my toys, ate roast duck and drank red wine.'

'The boy quickly became a man.'

'Too quickly?'

'Everyone has his own pace. You have youth and maturity in the same heart.'

'You're the one who taught me everything.'

'You know that's not true,' said Branir. 'You taught yourself.'

'You taught me to read and write, you introduced me to the law and let me devote myself to it. Without you, I'd have been a peasant and would have been quite happy tilling my little piece of land.'

'No, you wouldn't. You're a different kind of man; the greatness and the happiness of a country depend upon the quality of its judges.'

'Living a just life,' said Pazair with a sigh. 'It's a daily battle, and no one could ever claim that he always wins.'

'But you want to – that's the most important thing.'

'The village is a haven of peace – today's sad business is an exception.'

'You've been made overseer of the wheat granary, haven't you?'

'The headman wants me to be appointed steward of Pharaoh's field, to prevent disputes at harvest time. The job doesn't tempt me; I hope he fails.'

'I'm absolutely certain he will.'

'Why is that?'

'Because the future holds something very different for you.'

'You intrigue me.'

'I have been entrusted with a mission,' said Branir.

'By the palace?'

'No, by the court of justice at Memphis.'

'Have I done something wrong?'

'On the contrary, for the last two years the inspectors of country judges have been writing highly favourable reports about you. You have just been appointed to the province of Giza, to replace a magistrate who died recently.'

'Giza? But that's so far away!' protested Pazair.

'It's only a few days by boat. You're to live in Memphis.'

Giza! The most famous place in all Egypt, site of the Great Pyramid of Khufu, which was the mysterious energy centre on which the harmony of the entire country depended.

'I'm happy, here in my village. I was born here, I grew up here, I work here. Leaving would be too great a wrench.'

'I supported your appointment, because I believe Egypt needs you. You aren't a man to put your own preferences first.'

'Is the decision irrevocable?'

'No, you can refuse.'

'I need time to think.'

'The body of a man is vaster than a grain store; it is filled with countless answers. Choose the right one, and leave the others locked up.'

Pazair walked towards the riverbank; at this moment, his life hung in the balance. He hated the thought of abandoning his daily routine, the quiet joys of the village and the Theban countryside, and losing himself in a great city. But how could he refuse Branir, the man he revered above all others? He had sworn to answer his mentor's call, no matter what the circumstances.

A great white ibis was striding majestically along the riverbank. Halting, it plunged its long beak into the mud, and turned its gaze on the judge.

'The sacred bird of Thoth has chosen you,' declared the gravelly voice of Pepy the shepherd, who was stretched out in the reeds. 'You have no choice.'

Pepy was a short-tempered seventy-year-old, with no great fondness for human company. As far as he was concerned, being alone with the animals was the pinnacle of happiness. Refusing to take orders from anyone, he wielded his gnarled staff with skill, and was adept at hiding in the papyrus forests whenever the tax collectors descended upon the village like a flock of sparrows. Pazair had given up summoning him before the court. The old man had taken it upon himself to punish anyone who mistreated a cow or a dog, and, in view of this, the judge chose to regard him as a kind of assistant.

'Look at the ibis and mark it well,' stressed Pepy. 'Its stride is the length of one cubit, the symbol of justice. May your conduct also be upright and exact. You're going to leave, aren't you?'

'How do you know that?'

'The ibis is flying up into the sky. It has chosen you.'

The old man stood up. His skin was tanned by the wind and the sun; he wore nothing but a kilt made from reeds. 'Branir is the only honest man I know,' he said. 'He never tries to deceive you or do you harm. When you live in the town, beware of officials, courtiers and flatterers: there is death in their words.'

'I don't want to leave the village.'

'And what about me? Do you think I want to go and look for the goat that's strayed?' Pepy vanished into the reeds.

The black and white bird flew away. Its great wings flapped to a rhythm it alone knew; it was heading north.

When Pazair went back to Branir, the old doctor read the answer in Pazair's eyes, and smiled. He said, 'Be in Memphis

13

at the beginning of next month. You'll stay with me until you take up your post.'

'You aren't leaving already, are you?'

'I no longer practise medicine much, but a few sick people still need my services. I, too, wish I could have stayed longer.'

The chair and its bearers disappeared into the dust of the road.

The headman hailed Pazair, and told him, 'We've got a delicate matter to deal with: three families all claim they own the same palm tree.'

'I know. The dispute has lasted for three generations. Entrust it to my successor; if he doesn't manage to settle it, I'll deal with it when I get back.'

'Get back? You mean you're leaving the village?'

'The government has summoned me to Memphis.'

'And what about the palm tree?'

'Let it grow.'

2

Pazair checked that his travelling bag was in good condition. It was made of leather, and had two wooden poles which he stuck in the ground to hold it upright. When it was full, he would carry it on his back.

What was he going to put into it, apart from a rectangle of fabric for a new kilt, a cloak, and the all-important mat? The mat was made from woven papyrus strips, and could serve as a bed, a table, a carpet, a wall hanging, a screen, or as packaging for precious objects. Its last use would be as a winding-sheet to wrap its owner's dead body. Pazair's mat was very hard-wearing; in fact it was his finest item of furniture. As for his goatskin water-bag, it kept water cool for hours.

Hardly had he opened his travelling bag when a sandy-coloured mongrel rushed up to sniff at it. Brave was three years old, a mixture of greyhound and wild dog. He was long-legged, with a short snout, curly tail and drooping ears which pricked up at the slightest sound; and he was devoted to his master. Although he loved long walks, he did not hunt much and preferred his food cooked.

'We're leaving, Brave.'

The dog looked nervously at the bag.

'We'll walk, and then take the boat to Memphis.'

The dog sat down and waited for the bad news.

'Pepy's made you a collar. He's greased the leather and

stretched it thoroughly. It'll be perfectly comfortable – really it will.'

Brave looked less than convinced, but grudgingly accepted the collar, which was pink, green and white and studded with nails. If another dog or a wild beast tried to seize him by the neck, he would be well protected. Pazair had added a finishing touch with an inscription in hieroglyphs: 'Brave, companion of Pazair'.

The dog gulped down a meal of fresh vegetables, but did not take his eyes off his master. He sensed that this was not the time for play.

Led by the headman, the villagers took their leave of the judge; some wept. They wished him good fortune, and gave him two amulets, one representing a boat and the other a pair of sturdy legs. These would protect the traveller, who must pray to God each morning to preserve the talismans' power.

Pazair picked up his sandals. He did not put them on, for like his fellow countrymen he walked barefoot, using the precious footwear only when he entered someone's home and had washed the dust from his feet. He checked that the leather toe straps and soles were in good condition, put the sandals in his bag, then turned and left the village without a backward glance.

Just as he was setting off along the narrow, winding road which overlooked the Nile, a soft muzzle touched his right hand.

'Way-Finder, you've escaped!' he exclaimed. 'I must take you back to your field.'

The donkey was not listening. Holding out his right hoof for Pazair to take, he began to bray. The judge had rescued him from a brutal peasant who was beating him with a stick because he had chewed through his tether.

Way-Finder had a marked penchant for independence, and the strength to carry the heaviest loads. The animal was well aware that he was worth as much as a good cow or a fine coffin. He had a keen sense of direction, and could easily find his way around the maze of country roads. Often he went from place to place on his own, delivering foodstuffs. Although sober and placid, he would not sleep unless he was by his master's side.

'I'm going a long, long way away,' said Pazair. 'And you wouldn't like Memphis.'

The dog rubbed himself against the donkey's right foreleg. Way-Finder understood Brave's signal and turned sideways on, eager to receive his master's travelling bag.

Gently, Pazair took hold of the donkey's left ear. 'Who is the stubbornest creature in the world?'

With a rueful smile he gave up, and Way-Finder proudly took his place at the head of the little procession, instinctively taking the most direct route to the landing stage.

Under the rule of Ramses, travellers could use the roads and tracks without fear. On their journeys they encountered Pharaoh's messengers and postal officials; and if they needed to, they could ask for help from the guards on patrol. Egypt had come a long way since the days of terror when bandits roamed the land, robbing rich and poor alike. Ramses ensured that public order was respected, for without it happiness was impossible.*

Way-Finder walked sure-footedly down the steep slope that led to the river, as though he knew his master was planning to take the boat for Memphis. The trio boarded the craft, and Pazair paid the fare with a piece of fabric. While the animals slept he gazed out at Egypt, which poets had compared to an immense ship whose high sides were formed by chains of mountains. Hills and tall rock faces towered protectively over the fields. Plateaux bisected by valleys rose up here and there, between the black, fertile, generous earth and the red desert where dangerous forces roamed.

*People travelled a good deal in ancient Egypt mostly on the Nile, though they also used country roads and desert paths. Pharaoh had a duty to guarantee travellers' safety.

Pazair longed to go back to the village, and never leave it again. This journey into the unknown made him uneasy, robbing him of confidence in his own abilities. Only Branir could have persuaded him to accept this appointment, and no promotion could restore the peace of mind that he had lost. Now Pazair felt as though he were heading towards a future which might be beyond his power to control.

Pazair was stunned.

Menes the unifier had created Memphis, the largest city in Egypt.* It was the country's administrative capital, and was known as the 'Balance of the Two Lands'. Whereas the southern city of Thebes was devoted to tradition and the cult of Amon, Memphis, which stood at the junction of Upper and Lower Egypt, looked out towards Asia and the civilizations around the great sea to the north.

The judge, the donkey and the dog disembarked at the port of Perunefer, whose name meant 'Good Journey'. The docks were a hive of activity, with hundreds of cargo boats of all sizes unloading their wares; the goods were taken to immense warehouses, which were guarded and managed with the greatest care. Running parallel to the Nile was a canal, worthy of the builders of the Old Kingdom whose pyramids dominated the nearby plateau. The stone-lined canal allowed boats to travel in safety, and ensured that foodstuffs and raw materials could be transported whatever the season.

The three travellers headed for the northern district where Branir lived. As Pazair crossed the city centre he marvelled at the famous Temple of Ptah, god of craftsmen, and passed by the military zone. This was where weapons were made and warships built. Here, the elite divisions of the Egyptian army were trained; they lived in vast barracks, between arsenals

---

*Menes was the pharaoh who first united the two lands of Upper and Lower Egypt. His name means the 'Stable One'.

filled with chariots, swords, spears and shields.

To the north and south were granaries packed with barley, spelt and other types of grain. The granaries stood alongside the Treasury buildings, which contained gold, silver, copper, fabrics, unguents, oil, honey and other valuable things.

The sheer size of Memphis made the young countryman's head spin. He was sure he'd never find his bearings in this maze of streets and alleyways, this proliferation of districts with names like Life of the Two Lands, the Garden, the Sycamore, Crocodile Wall, the Fortress, the Two Mounds and College of Medicine. Brave seemed unsure of himself and kept close to his master's side, but the donkey went calmly on his way, guiding his two companions through the craftsmen's district, where stone, wood, metal and leather were worked in little shops which opened on to the street. Pazair had never seen so many pots, vases, dinner plates and domestic utensils.

The judge encountered many foreigners: Hittites, Greeks, Canaanites and Asiatics from various little kingdoms. They were relaxed and talkative, decking themselves in lotus garlands and declaring that Memphis was a garden of plenty. They were even able to celebrate their religious rites in temples dedicated to the god Baal and the goddess Astarte, whose presence Pharaoh tolerated.

Pazair asked a weaving-woman for directions, and was reassured to learn that the donkey had not led him astray. The judge noted that the nobles' sumptuous homes were mixed in with the little houses belonging to the common people. Tall porticoes, guarded by gatekeepers, opened on to flower-lined paths leading to two- and three-storey houses.

At last they reached Branir's house. It was delightfully attractive with its white walls, its lintel painted with red poppies, and decorations of cornflowers, perseas and greenery round its windows. A door opened on to a garden where two palm trees grew, shading the little house's terrace. True, the village was a very long way away, but the old doctor had succeeded in preserving a country atmosphere in the heart of the city.

Branir was standing on the threshold. 'Did you have a good journey?' he asked.

'Yes, but the donkey and the dog are thirsty.'

'I'll take care of them. Here is a basin of cool water, so that you can wash your feet, and some bread sprinkled with salt to welcome you.'

Pazair walked down a flight of steps into the first room, where he meditated before a small niche containing the statuettes of the ancestors. Then he continued into the reception room, whose ceiling was supported by two painted columns; the walls were lined with storage cupboards and chests, and there were mats on the floor. The remaining accommodation consisted of a workshop, a bathroom, a kitchen, two bedrooms and a cellar.

Branir invited his guest to climb the staircase up to the terrace, where he had set out cool drinks, accompanied by dates stuffed with honey and sweet pastries.

'I feel lost,' confessed Pazair.

'I'd be astonished if you didn't. A good dinner, a decent night's sleep, and you'll be ready for the investiture ceremony tomorrow.'

'Tomorrow? Why does it have to be so soon?'

'Cases are piling up.'

'I'd have liked time to get used to Memphis.'

'Your enquiries will make you do that. Here's a gift, since you haven't yet taken up your new post.'

Branir handed Pazair a copy of the book that was used to instruct scribes, teaching them how to behave correctly in all circumstances and have proper respect for the hierarchy of beings. At the top were the gods, goddesses, transfigured spirits, Pharaoh and the queen; then the king's mother, the tjaty, the council of wise men, senior judges, leaders of the army and the scribes of the House of Books. These were followed by a multitude of officials, from the director of the Treasury to the man in charge of the canals, and Pharaoh's representatives abroad.

Pazair unrolled the book a little way and read, 'A man with violence in his heart can never be anything but a trouble-maker, nor can a man who does not know when to stop talking. If you want to be strong, become the craftsman of your own words and fashion them, for, in the hands of a man who knows how to use it well, language is the most powerful weapon of all.' As he rolled it up again, he said sadly, 'I'm missing the village already.'

'You'll miss it for the rest of your life.'

'Why was I summoned here?'

'Your own conduct determined matters.'

Pazair slept little and badly, with his dog at his feet and his donkey lying beside his head. Events were moving too quickly, giving him no time to find his balance. Caught in a whirlpool, he had lost his usual points of reference and – in spite of his reluctance – he must embark upon an adventure into the unknown.

Waking at dawn, he washed, cleansed his mouth with natron,* and ate breakfast with Branir, who afterwards took him to one of the best barbers in the city. As they sat on three-legged stools facing each other, the barber moistened Pazair's skin, and covered it with an oily foam before wielding his copper razor with consummate skill.

Dressed in a new kilt and a loose, diaphanous shirt, his body perfumed, Pazair looked fit to face the ordeal.

'I feel as if I'm in disguise,' he confided to Branir.

'Appearances are unimportant, but they shouldn't be neglected. Learn how to handle the tiller so that the tide of days doesn't carry you away from justice, whose practice safeguards a country's balance. Be worthy of yourself, my son.'

---

*A natural compound of carbonate of soda and bicarbonate of soda.

3

Pazair followed Branir into the Ptah district, which lay in the southerly part of the ancient, white-walled citadel. Although the young man was happy about the fate of the donkey and the dog, he was less sure about his own.

Not far from the palace stood several government buildings, whose entrances were guarded by soldiers. The old doctor spoke to an officer, who disappeared for a few moments before returning with a senior judge, the tjaty's delegate.

'I am happy to see you again, Branir,' he said. 'So this is your pupil.'

'Pazair is very nervous.'

'That is quite understandable, given his age. Is he ready to take up his new duties nevertheless?'

Pazair cut in, 'You need have no doubt of it.'

The judge frowned. 'I shall take him from you now, Branir. We must proceed with the investiture.'

The old doctor's warm smile gave his pupil the courage he still lacked. Whatever the difficulties might be, he would do Branir credit.

Pazair was shown into a small, rectangular room with bare white walls. The judge invited him to sit down on a mat, facing the court, which comprised himself, the governor of the province of Memphis, an official from the administration secretariat, and a senior priest of Ptah. All four men wore heavy wigs and full-skirted kilts. Their faces were unreadable, devoid of emotion.

'You are in the place where "the evaluation of difference"* is carried out,' announced the judge, who was in charge of the justice system. 'Here, you will become a man unlike others, a man who has been called to judge his fellow men. Like your colleagues in Giza province, you will carry out enquiries, preside over the local courts under your jurisdiction, and refer matters to your superiors when they exceed your scope. Do you promise to do these things?'

'I promise.'

'Are you aware that your word, once given, cannot be taken back?'

'I am.'

'Let the court proceed, according to the commandments of the Rule, and judge the future judge.'

The governor of Memphis said in solemn, measured tones, 'Which jurors will you call upon to make up your court?'

'Scribes, craftsmen, guards, experienced men, respectable women, widows.'

'How will you intervene in their deliberations?'

'I shall not. Each juror will speak without being influenced, and I shall respect each one's opinion in making my judgment.'

'In all circumstances?'

'There is only one exception: if a juror is found to be corrupt. In such a case I would immediately halt the trial in progress and have the juror charged.'

'How must you act when a crime has been committed?' asked the administration official.

'I must carry out a preliminary investigation, document

---

*The expression is used in the *Book of the Dead* for distinguishing the just from the unjust.

23

everything that happens in the case and give the information to the tjaty's office.'

The priest of Ptah placed his right arm across his chest, with his closed fist touching his shoulder. He said, 'No act will be forgotten, when you are judged in the afterlife; your heart will be laid upon the scales and weighed against the Rule. In what form has the law been passed down to us?'

'There are forty-two provinces and forty-two rolls of the law; but its spirit was not written down and must not be. Truth can only be passed on orally, from the master's mouth to the disciple's ear.'

The priest smiled, but the tjaty's deputy was not yet satisfied. He asked, 'How would you define the Rule?'

'Bread and beer.'

'What does that mean?'

'Justice for all, great or small.'

'Why is the Rule symbolized by an ostrich feather?'

'Because it is the means of communication between our world and the world of the gods. The feather is the rectrix, the rudder that determines both the direction of a bird's flight and the direction a human being will take. The Rule, the breath of life, must remain in men's lungs and drive evil from their hearts and bodies. If justice disappeared, wheat would no longer grow, rebels would seize power and festivals would no longer be celebrated.'

The governor stood up and placed a block of limestone in front of Pazair. 'Lay your hands upon this white stone,' he said.

The young man did so. His hands were steady.

'Let it bear witness to your oath. It will remember for ever the words you have spoken, and will be your accuser if you betray the Rule.'

The governor and the administration official stood on either side of the judge.

'Stand up,' ordered the tjaty's deputy. 'Here is the ring that bears your seal,' he said. He handed Pazair a rectangular plaque attached to a ring which the young man slipped on to the middle finger of his right hand. The flat surface of the gold plaque was inscribed, '*Judge Pazair*'. 'Documents upon which you place your seal will be official and you will bear responsibility for them. Do not use that ring lightly.'

The judge's accommodation was on the southern outskirts of Memphis, halfway between the Nile and the western canal and south of the Temple of Hathor. The young man, who had been expecting an imposing place, was cruelly disappointed: the government had allocated him only a small, two-storey house.

Sitting fast asleep on the doorstep was a sentry. Pazair tapped him on the shoulder, and he awoke with a start.

'I would like to go in,' said Pazair.

'The office is closed.'

'I am the judge.'

'I doubt that – he's dead.'

'I am Pazair, his successor.'

'Pazair? Oh yes, that's right. Iarrot, the scribe to the court, gave me your name. Have you got proof of your identity?'

Pazair showed him the seal ring.

'My job was to watch this place until you arrived. Now I'm done here.'

'When will I see Iarrot?'

'I've no idea. He's sorting out a tricky problem.'

'What kind of problem?'

'The wood for heating. It's cold in Memphis in winter, but last year the Treasury refused to deliver wood to this office because the request hadn't been submitted in triplicate. Iarrot has gone to the records office to sort things out. I wish you good luck, Judge Pazair; you certainly won't get bored here in Memphis.' And the sentry went on his way.

Slowly, Pazair pushed open the door of his new domain.

The office was quite a large room, filled with cupboards and chests laden with tied or sealed papyrus scrolls. The floor was covered in a suspicious layer of dust. Pazair did not hesitate to tackle this unexpected peril. Despite the dignity of his office, he seized a stiff broom and swept the dust away.

Next, the judge drew up a list of the contents of the archives: land registry and tax documents, reports, complaints, notes relating to accounts and the payment of salary in grain, baskets or fabrics, letters, lists of employees . . . his duties covered widely diverse areas.

The largest cupboard contained all the essential materials a scribe needed: palettes with hollows for red and black ink, cakes of solidified ink, pots, bags of powdered pigments, bags for brushes, scrapers, adhesives, stone pestles, linen strings, a tortoise shell for mixing, a clay baboon representing Thoth, the master of hieroglyphs, limestone shards for rough notes, clay, limestone and wooden tablets. Everything was of good quality.

A small acacia-wood chest contained an extremely precious object: a water clock. The little vase, shaped like a truncated cone, was graduated inside, according to two different scales, with twelve notches; water flowed out through a hole at the bottom of the clock, and in this way the hours were measured. No doubt the scribe must have deemed it necessary to keep a check on the amount of time spent at his place of work.

One thing needed to be done straight away. Pazair picked up a fine reed brush, dipped the tip into a water pot, and let a drop fall on to the palette he was going to use. He murmured the prayer all scribes recited before writing: 'Water from the ink pot for your *ka*, Imhotep.' That was how they venerated the creator of the first pyramid, who was a designer of buildings, a doctor, an astrologer and the model for all those who practised hieroglyphs.

The judge climbed up to his official living quarters on the

first floor. They had been empty for a long time. Pazair's predecessor, who preferred to live in a little house on the edge of the city, had neglected to look after the three rooms, which were occupied by fleas, flies, mice and spiders.

The young man was not discouraged. He felt he had the skills he needed for this particular battle. In the country, homes often had to be cleansed and unwelcome guests driven away.

After obtaining the necessary ingredients from local traders, Pazair set to work. He sprinkled the walls and the floor with water in which he had dissolved natron, then followed this with a layer of pulverized charcoal, mixed with the *bebet* plant,* whose strong smell drove away insects and vermin. Finally, he mixed incense, myrrh, cinnamon and honey, and burnt the mixture; the fumes would both purify the house and make it smell nice. To acquire these expensive ingredients, he had got himself into debt and had spent most of his next salary.

Worn out, he unrolled his mat and lay down on his back. Something bothered him and kept him awake: the seal ring. But he did not take it off. Pepy the shepherd was right: he no longer had a choice.

*Inula graveolens.

4

The sun was already high in the sky when Iarrot's heavy step sounded outside the office. A rather large man, he had a florid, veined complexion and podgy cheeks, and wherever he went he swung his stick to the rhythm of his stride. It was a special walking stick, inscribed with his name – indicating that he was an important person, worthy of respect. Iarrot was a self-satisfied forty-year-old with a young daughter who was the cause of all his woes. Each day, he argued with his wife about how to bring up the child whom he did not wish to displease for any reason whatever. The house echoed to the sound of their quarrels, which were becoming more and more violent.

To his great surprise, he found a workman mixing plaster with crushed limestone to make it whiter. As he watched, the man checked its quality by pouring it into a limestone cone, then filled in a hole on the front wall of the judge's house.

'I did not order any work to be done,' said Iarrot angrily.

'Ah, but I did. What's more, I'm doing it without delay.'

'On whose authority?'

'I am Judge Pazair.'

'But . . . but you're so young!'

'Are you by any chance Iarrot?'

'I am indeed.'

'The day is already well advanced.'

'Yes, that's true. I was delayed by family problems.'

'Are there any urgent cases?' asked Pazair, continuing with his plastering.

'Just one. A complaint from a man who owns a building company. He had bricks, but no donkeys to transport them. He accused the donkey hirer of sabotaging his building site.'

'It's been sorted out.'

'How?'

'I saw the donkey hirer this morning. He will pay damages to the builder and will transport the bricks first thing tomorrow; we have avoided a court case.'

'And you're a . . . plasterer, too?'

'Only a very modest amateur. Our budget is rather small, so in the majority of cases we shall have to manage by ourselves. What else?'

'You are expected to attend a re-count of livestock.'

'Won't the specialist scribe suffice?'

'The master of the estate, Qadash the tooth doctor, is convinced that one of his employees is stealing, and has asked for an investigation. Your predecessor delayed it as long as possible – to tell you the truth, I can well understand why. If you like, I'll find reasons for delaying it still more.'

'That won't be necessary. By the way, do you know how to handle a broom?'

Iarrot gaped. The judge handed him one.

Way-Finder was happy to smell the country air again. He trotted along briskly with the judge's materials, while Brave scampered about, chasing a few birds out of their nests. As usual, Way-Finder had listened carefully when the judge told him that they were going to Qadash's estate, which was two hours' walk from the Giza plateau, and lay to the south; the donkey had set off in the right direction.

Pazair was warmly welcomed by the estate steward, who was only too happy to greet a competent judge at last, one who wanted to resolve a mystery which was making the oxherds' lives a misery. Servants washed Pazair's feet and gave him a new kilt, promising to wash the one he was wearing, while two small boys fed the donkey and the dog. Qadash was informed of his arrival, and a platform was hastily erected, topped off by a red and black canopy with columns in the shape of lotus stems. Pazair and the scribe of the herds waited beneath it, shaded from the sun.

Qadash arrived, holding a long staff in his right hand. Servants followed, carrying his sandals, his parasol and his armchair; girls played the tambourine and the flute, and young peasant women presented him with lotus flowers.

He was about sixty, with a mass of white hair. He was tall, with a prominent nose criss-crossed with blue veins, a low forehead, high cheekbones and rheumy eyes, which he wiped frequently. Pazair was astonished by the redness of his hands; doubtless the man suffered from poor circulation of the blood.

Qadash regarded him suspiciously. 'So you're the new judge?'

'At your service. It's good to see that the peasants are happy when the owner of the estate has a noble heart and a firm grip on the reins of power.'

'You will go far, young man, if you respect the great.' Qadash was richly dressed. A kilt pleated at the front, a cat-skin corselet, a seven-string necklace of blue, white and red pearls, and row upon row of bracelets gave him an air of pride.

'Let's sit down,' he suggested.

He lowered himself into his painted wooden armchair, and Pazair sat down on a cube-shaped seat. In front of him and the scribe of the herds were small, low tables, designed to hold their writing materials.

'According to your declaration,' Pazair reminded him, 'you possess one hundred and one head of cattle, seventy sheep, six hundred goats and the same number of pigs.'

'Correct. At the time of the last count, two months ago, there was an ox missing. Now, my animals are very valuable; even the thinnest one could be exchanged for a linen tunic and ten sacks of barley. I want you to arrest the thief.'

'Have you conducted your own investigation?'

'That is not my line of work.'

The judge turned to the scribe of the herds, who was seated on a mat, and asked, 'What did you write in your registers?'

'The number of animals I was shown.'

'Whom did you question?'

'No one. My job is to write things down, not question people.'

Pazair could not draw anything more out of him. Irritated, he took from his basket a sycamore tablet covered with a fine layer of plaster, a sharpened reed brush and a water pot, in which he prepared some black ink. When he was ready, Qadash signalled to the head oxherd, who tapped the enormous lead ox on the neck and began leading the procession of animals past the platform. The ox moved forward slowly, followed by his heavy, placid fellows.

'Splendid, aren't they?' said Qadash.

'You must congratulate the men who rear them,' advised Pazair.

'The thief must be a Hittite or a Nubian – there are too many foreigners in Memphis.'

'Isn't your name of Libyan origin?'

Qadash did not hide his annoyance very well. 'I have lived in Egypt for a long time and I belong to the best society – isn't the wealth of my estate proof of that? I have treated the most famous members of court, you know. You should remember your place.'

The animals were accompanied by servants carrying fruit, bunches of leeks, baskets of lettuces and vases of perfume. Evidently this was not a simple re-count; Qadash wanted to dazzle the new judge and show him the extent of his fortune.

Brave had slipped silently under his master's chair and was watching the animals go past.

'Which province are you from, Judge?'

'I am the one conducting the investigation.'

Two yoked oxen passed the platform; the older one lay down on the ground and refused to go any further.

'Stop playing dead,' said the oxherd. The beast looked at him fearfully, but did not move.

'Beat him,' ordered Qadash.

'One moment,' ordered Pazair, stepping down from the platform.

He stroked the ox gently and, with the oxherd's help, encouraged it to get it back on its feet. Reassured, it stood up. Pazair went back to his seat.

'What a sensitive soul you are,' commented Qadash sarcastically.

'I detest violence.'

'Isn't it necessary from time to time? Egypt had to fight against the invader, and men died for our freedom. Would you condemn them?'

Pazair concentrated on the procession of animals; the scribe of the herds counted. At the end of the count, there was indeed one ox missing as the owner had claimed.

'This is intolerable!' roared Qadash, his face turning purple. 'People are stealing from me on my own lands, and no one will denounce the guilty party!'

'Your animals must be marked.'

'Of course.'

'Summon the men who applied the marks.'

There were fifteen of them. The judge questioned them one after the other, and kept them separate so that they could not talk to each other.

'I have identified your thief,' he announced when he had finished.

'Who is it?'

'Kani.'

'I demand that the court be convened immediately.'

Pazair agreed. He chose as his jurors an oxherd, a woman who looked after the goats, the scribe of the herds and one of the estate guards.

Kani, who had made no attempt to escape, came freely up to the platform, and looked the furious Qadash straight in the eye. The accused man was short and heavy-set, with deeply lined brown skin.

'Do you admit your guilt?' asked Pazair.

'No.'

Qadash struck the ground fiercely with his walking stick. 'Punish this insolent thief immediately!'

'Be quiet,' ordered Pazair. 'If you cause a disturbance, I shall halt the court proceedings.'

Angrily, Qadash turned away.

'Kani, did you mark an ox with Qadash's name?' asked Pazair.

'Yes.'

'That animal has disappeared.'

'It escaped from me. You'll find it in a neighbouring field.'

'Why were you so careless?'

'I'm a gardener, not a cowherd, and my real work is irrigating small patches of ground. All day long I carry a yoke on my shoulders, and empty heavy jars of water on to the fields. Even in the evening I can't rest; I must water the most delicate plants, maintain the irrigation channels, reinforce the banks of earth. If you want proof, look at the back of my neck; you'll see the scars of two abscesses. That's a gardener's complaint, not a cowman's.'

'Why did you change your occupation?'

'Because Qadash's steward caught me when I was delivering vegetables. I had to take care of the oxen and abandon my garden.'

Pazair summoned witnesses, and established that Kani was telling the truth. The court acquitted him, and the judge ordered that, as compensation, the runaway ox should become his property and Qadash must give him a large quantity of food in exchange for the working days he had lost.

The gardener bowed before the judge, and Pazair saw deep gratitude in his eyes.

'Compelling this peasant to work for you is a serious offence,' he reminded Qadash.

Blood rose to the man's face. 'I'm not responsible! I knew nothing about it. Punish my steward – he deserves it.'

'You know what the punishment is: fifty strokes of the stick and demotion to the status of a peasant.'

'The law is the law.' Qadash bowed briefly, and went back to his house.

When the steward was brought before the court, he did not deny his guilt. He was convicted, and the sentence was carried out on the spot.

When Judge Pazair left the estate, Qadash did not come to say goodbye.

5

Brave was asleep at his master's feet, dreaming of a feast, while Way-Finder, who had breakfasted on fresh forage, was acting as a sentry outside the office. Inside, Pazair had been hard at work since dawn, studying the current cases. The mass of difficulties did not overwhelm him. On the contrary, he was determined to make up for lost time and leave no loose ends.

Iarrot arrived in the middle of the morning, looking dishevelled.

'You seem rather depressed,' commented Pazair.

'Another argument with my wife – she's unbearable. I married her so that she could prepare tasty meals for me and now she's refusing to cook. Life's becoming impossible.'

'Are you considering divorce?'

'No, because of my daughter. I want her to become a dancer, but my wife has other plans, which I won't agree to. Neither of us will give in.'

'I fear that is something of a stalemate.'

'So do I. Did your investigation at Qadash's estate go well?'

'I'm just putting the final touches to my report. The ox was found, a gardener acquitted and the steward convicted. In my opinion, Qadash was at least partly responsible, but I can't prove it.'

'Leave him well alone,' said Iarrot. 'He has influential friends.'

'Are his customers rich?'

'He has treated the most famous mouths, but malicious gossips say that he's lost his touch and that it's better to avoid him if you want to keep healthy teeth.'

Brave growled; his master stroked him and he stopped. On first acquaintance, the dog seemed not to like the scribe much.

Pazair applied his seal to the papyrus containing his conclusions about the matter of the stolen ox. Iarrot marvelled at the fine, regular hieroglyphs; the judge wrote without the slightest hesitation, expressing his thoughts clearly.

'Surely you didn't implicate Qadash, did you?' asked the scribe.

'Of course I did.'

'That's dangerous.'

'What are you afraid of?'

'I don't know.'

'Be more precise,' said Pazair.

'Justice is so complex . . .'

'I don't agree. On one side there is the truth, on the other, falsehood. If you give in to the latter, even to the tiniest degree, justice no longer reigns.'

'You talk like that because you're young. When you've got a bit of experience, your opinions will be less clear-cut.'

'I hope not. In my village, many people put that argument to me, but I find it worthless.'

'You're ignoring the weight that important people carry.'

'Is Qadash above the law?'

Iarrot gave a sigh. 'You seem intelligent and brave, Judge Pazair. Don't pretend not to understand.'

'If the ruling classes are unjust, the country will rush headlong to its ruin.'

'They'll crush you like the others. Be content to resolve the problems put to you, and refer delicate matters to your superiors. Your predecessor was a sensible man, who knew how to avoid traps. You've been given a fine promotion; don't spoil it.'

'I was given this appointment because of my methods, so why should I change them?'

'Make the most of your opportunities without disturbing the established order.'

'The only order I know is the order of the Rule.'

Annoyed, the scribe said, 'You're running full tilt towards a precipice!' He tapped himself on the chest. 'Don't say I didn't warn you.'

'Tomorrow, you are to deliver my report to the provincial government.'

'As you wish.'

'One detail puzzles me. I don't doubt your zeal, but are you the only person I have working for me?'

Iarrot seemed embarrassed. 'In a way, yes.'

'What is that supposed to mean?'

'There's a man called Kem . . .'

'What does he do?'

'He's a guard officer. It's his job to make the arrests you order.'

'An important role, I'd have thought.'

'Your predecessor didn't have anybody arrested. If he suspected someone of being a criminal, he referred the case to a higher jurisdiction. Kem gets bored in the office, so he goes out on patrol all the time.'

'Am I to have the privilege of meeting him?'

'He comes here from time to time. Don't be under any illusions: he's a hateful man. I'm afraid of him. Just don't expect me to say anything unpleasant to him.'

Re-establishing order in my own office isn't going to be easy, thought Pazair. He reached for more papyrus and saw that there was not much left.

'Where do you get papyrus?' he asked.

'From Mahu, the best maker in Memphis. His prices are

high, but the papyrus is excellent and never wears out. I can recommend him.'

'Just reassure me on one point, Iarrot. Is that recommendation completely free of self-interest?'

'How dare you!'

'My mind was wandering.'

Pazair examined the recent complaints; none seemed serious or urgent. Then he moved on to the list of personnel he was to control and the appointments he was to approve; a mundane administrative task which required him simply to add his seal.

Iarrot sat down, his left leg bent underneath him, and the other raised in front of him; with a palette under his arm and a reed pen tucked behind his left ear, he washed brushes as he watched Pazair.

'Have you been at work long, Judge?' he asked

'Since dawn.'

'That's very early.'

'A village custom.'

'A . . . daily custom?'

'My master taught me that one day's negligence was a catastrophe. The heart cannot learn unless the ear is open and the mind alert. What better way to achieve such a state than through good habits? If we fail, the monkey dozing inside us starts dancing, and the shrine is deprived of its god.'

The scribe's tone darkened. 'That's not a very pleasant life.'

'We are the servants of justice.'

'About my hours of work—'

'Eight hours a day,' cut in Pazair, 'with six days' work to be followed by two rest days, and between two and three months' annual holiday, including the various festivals.* Are we in agreement?'

Iarrot nodded. He understood that, although the judge had not pressed the point, he must make an effort to be more punctual.

*The usual working pattern for Egyptians.

One brief report interested Pazair. The head of the guards at the Sphinx in Giza had just been transferred to the docks. This was a brutal downturn in the man's career: he must have committed a serious offence. No such offence was mentioned, contrary to usual custom, but the head provincial judge had placed his seal upon the document. All it now lacked was Pazair's seal, since the soldier resided within his area of jurisdiction. A mere formality, which he could have carried out without thinking.

'The post of head of the guards at the Sphinx is a coveted one, isn't it?'

'There's no lack of candidates,' agreed Iarrot, 'but the current post-holder puts them off.'

'Why?'

'He is an experienced soldier, with a remarkable service record, and he's a brave man, too. He guards the Sphinx with immense diligence, although that old stone lion is impressive enough to take care of its own defence. Who would think of attacking it?'

'So his is a prestigious post, it would seem.'

'Absolutely. The head guard recruits other veterans, to ensure that they have a small, regular income, and the five of them take charge of the night watch.'

'Did you know he'd been transferred?'

'Transferred? Is this a joke?'

'Here is the official document.'

'That's very surprising indeed. What has he done wrong?'

'That's exactly what I was wondering. The report doesn't say.'

'Don't worry about it. It's probably a military decision whose logic we don't understand.'

In the street, Way-Finder gave the special bray that signalled danger. Pazair got to his feet and went out. He found himself face to face with an enormous baboon, which its master was holding on a leash. With their aggressive eyes, massive head and broad torso covered in a cape of fur, baboons had an unchallenged reputation for ferocity. It was common for a wild beast to succumb to their blows and bites, and lions had been seen to run away at the approach of a troop of enraged baboons.

The creature's master, a Nubian with bulging muscles, was as impressive as the animal itself.

'I hope you're holding him securely,' said Pazair.

'This guard baboon* is at your service, Judge Pazair, as am I.'

'You must be Kem.'

The Nubian nodded. 'People around here are talking about you. They say you stir things up a lot, for a judge.'

'I don't much care for your tone of voice.'

'You'll have to get used to it.'

'Certainly not. Either you show me the respect due to a superior, or you resign.'

The two men stared at each other for a long time; the judge's dog and the guard's baboon did the same.

'Your predecessor left me free to do as I pleased,' said Kem.

'I shall not.'

'You're making a mistake. By walking through the streets with my baboon, I deter thieves.'

'We shall see. What is your service record?'

'I must warn you, my past is a dark one. I belonged to the corps of archers in charge of guarding one of the fortresses in the Great South. Like many young men in my tribe, I signed on for the love of Egypt. I was happy for several years, but then, without intending to, I stumbled on gold-trafficking among the officers. The senior officers wouldn't listen to me, and I killed one of the thieves, my direct superior, in a brawl. At my trial I was sentenced to have my nose cut off. This one

---

*An impressive police baboon can be seen arresting a thief on a bas-relief from the tomb of Tepemankh, now in the museum at Cairo.

is made of painted wood – I'm not afraid of blows in the face any more. However, the judges recognized my loyalty, which is why they gave me this job. If you want to check, you'll find my details in the records at the army offices.'

'Very well, let's go there.'

Kem had not been expecting this reaction. While the donkey and the scribe guarded the office, Pazair and Kem headed for the administrative centre of the armed forces accompanied by the baboon and the dog, who continued to eye each other warily.

'How long have you lived in Memphis?' asked Pazair.

'A year,' replied Kem. 'I miss the south.'

'Do you know the man in charge of guarding the Sphinx at Giza?'

'I've met him two or three times.'

'Does he seem trustworthy to you?'

'He's a famous soldier – even at my fortress we'd heard of him. You don't give such a prestigious post to just anyone.'

'Is it dangerous?'

'Not in the least. Who would attack the Sphinx? It's a guard of honour, whose members' chief duty is to stop the monument being buried in the sand.'

Passers-by stepped aside when they saw the quartet; everyone knew how swiftly the baboon could react, sinking its teeth into a thief's leg or breaking his neck before Kem had time to intervene. When those two were on patrol, evil intentions evaporated into thin air.

'Do you know where he lives?'

'He has an official residence, near the main barracks.'

'My idea was a bad one. Let's go back to the office.'

'Don't you want to check my details?'

'It was his details I wanted to look at; but that won't get me any further. I shall expect you tomorrow, at dawn. What is your baboon's name?'

'Killer.'

At sundown, the judge closed the office and took Brave for a
walk on the banks of the Nile. Ought he to persevere with this
insignificant case, which he could close by putting his seal to
it?

6

At sundown, the judge closed the office and took Brave for a
walk on the banks of the Nile. Ought he to persevere with this
insignificant case, which he could close by putting his seal to
it? Obstructing a mundane administrative procedure seemed
rather nonsensical. But was it really mundane? Through
contact with nature and animals, a countryman develops keen
intuition. Pazair had such a strange, almost worrying, feeling
about the case that he decided to carry out an investigation,
no matter how brief, so that he wouldn't later regret
approving the transfer.

Brave was a playful dog, but he didn't like water. He
trotted a good distance from the river, where cargo vessels,
fast sailing ships and small boats were passing by. Some
people were sailing for pleasure, others delivering goods, or
on a journey. Not only did the Nile feed Egypt, but it also
provided her with an easy, rapid means of travelling around.

Large boats, with experienced crews, were leaving
Memphis and heading for the sea; some were undertaking
long expeditions to unknown lands. Pazair did not envy them;
their fate seemed cruel to him, since it carried them far from
a land which he loved down to its last grain of sand: every
field, every hill, every desert track, every village. All
Egyptians feared dying in a foreign land; the law stated that
their bodies should be repatriated, so that they could live out

eternity in the company of their ancestors, and under the gods' protection.

Brave whined; a lively little green monkey had just splashed his hindquarters with water. The mortified dog shook himself and bared his teeth in annoyance; scared, the little joker leapt into the arms of its mistress, a young woman aged around twenty.

'He's not a bad dog,' said Pazair, 'but he hates getting wet.'

'My monkey is well named: Mischief is always playing jokes, especially on dogs. I do try to reason with her, but it does no good.'

The woman's voice was so sweet that it calmed Brave, who sniffed her leg and licked it.

'Brave!' said Pazair.

'Let him be. I think he's adopted me, and that makes me happy.'

'Will Mischief accept me as a friend?'

'Come closer and find out.'

Pazair was rooted to the spot: he dared not step forward. In the village, a few girls had hung around him, but he had paid them no attention because, absorbed in his studies and learning his trade, he had had no time for love trysts or feelings. Practising law had made him mature for his age, but faced with this woman he felt completely defenceless.

She was beautiful. As beautiful as a spring dawn, an unfolding lotus bud, a sparkling wave upon the Nile waters. She was a little shorter than he, with light brown hair, a gentle, open face, a direct gaze and eyes of summer blue. Round her slender neck she wore a necklace of lapis lazuli; on her wrists and ankles were cornelian bracelets. Her linen robe disclosed glimpses of firm, high breasts, shapely flanks and long, slender legs. Her feet and hands were delightfully delicate and elegant.

'Are you afraid?' she asked, surprised.

'No – no, of course not.'

Approaching her would mean seeing her at close quarters, breathing in her perfume, almost touching her . . . He didn't dare.

Realizing that he wasn't going to move, she took three steps towards him and held the monkey out to him. With a trembling hand he stroked its brow, and in return Mischief scratched his nose with a nimble finger.

'That's her way of showing you're a friend.'

Brave did not protest; a truce had been concluded between the dog and the monkey.

'I bought her in a market where Nubian wares were on sale. She seemed so unhappy, so lost, that I couldn't resist.'

There was a strange object on her left wrist. Pazair couldn't help staring at it.

'Does my portable clock intrigue you?* I need it for my work. My name is Neferet, and I'm a doctor.'

Neferet, the Beautiful, the Perfect, the Complete. What other name could she possibly have had? Her golden skin seemed unreal; each word she spoke was like one of those enchanting songs heard at sunset in the countryside.

'May I ask your name?' she said.

It was unforgivable. By not introducing himself, he was displaying inexcusable bad manners. 'It's Pazair – I'm one of the provincial judges.'

'Were you born here?'

'No, in the Theban region. I've only just arrived in Memphis.'

'I was born down there, too!' She smiled with delight. 'Has your dog finished his walk?'

'Oh, no. He's tireless.'

---

*Egypt invented the first kind of watch, a portable water clock, which was used only by specialists (such as astronomers and doctors) who needed to be able to calculate time.

'Shall we walk together? I need some air – I've had a very tiring week.'

'Are you practising already?'

'Not yet; I am finishing the fifth year of my studies. First, I learnt how to prepare remedies, using plants and other ingredients. Then I worked as an animal doctor at the temple in Dendera. I was taught how to check the purity of the sacrificial animals' blood, and how to treat all sorts of animals from cats to cattle. Mistakes were severely punished: we were beaten with the rod, just as the boys were.'

Pazair winced at the thought of such tortures being inflicted on such a delightful body.

'Our old teachers' strictness is the finest education there is,' she assured him. 'Once the ear on your back has been opened, you never forget your lessons again. Next, I studied and practised a variety of specialist treatments: of the eyes, the stomach, the anus, the head, the hidden organs, the liquids dissolved in the humours and surgery. After that I was admitted to the medical school at Sais, where I was given the title of "attendant to the sick".'

'What will you do when you finish your training?'

'I could be a specialist, but that's the lowest rung of the ladder – I'll have to make do with that if I can't practise general medicine. A specialist sees only one aspect of sickness, a limited manifestation of the truth. A pain in a specific place doesn't mean that you know where the problem comes from. A specialist can make only a partial diagnosis. Becoming a general practiser is the true ideal of the doctor, but the standards that must be met are so high that most people give up.'

'Is there anything I can do to help you?'

'Thank you, but I must face my teachers alone.'

'I hope you succeed,' said Pazair.

They walked across a carpet of cornflowers where Brave was romping about, and sat down in the shade of a red willow.

'I've talked a great deal,' she said ruefully. 'I'm not usually like that. Are you the sort of person who attracts confessions?'

'They're part of my job. Thefts, late payments, contracts of sale, unjust taxes, slanders and a thousand other offences – they're what I deal with all the time. It's up to me to make enquiries, check witness statements, reconstruct the facts and arrive at a judgment.'

'What a huge responsibility!'

'Well, yes, but so is your profession. You love to heal, I love to see justice done; to do less than our utmost would be treason.'

'I hate taking advantage of circumstances, but . . .'

'Don't worry about that. Please tell me what the problem is.'

'One of my suppliers of herbs has disappeared. He's a rough-and-ready fellow, but honest and skilful. I and a few of my colleagues reported him missing recently. Perhaps you could speed up the search?'

'Of course I will. What's his name?'

'Kani.'

'Kani!'

'Do you know him?'

'He was forcibly conscripted by the steward on Qadash's estate. Yesterday, he was released, so there shouldn't be any further problems.'

'Was that your doing?'

'I carried out the investigation and passed judgment.'

She kissed him on both cheeks. Pazair, who was not a dreamer by nature, felt as if he had been transported to one of the paradise gardens reserved for righteous souls.

'Qadash,' said Neferet. 'Do you mean the famous tooth doctor?'

'That's right.'

'He used to be very good, they say, but he should have retired a long time ago.'

The green monkey yawned and curled up on Neferet's shoulder.

'I must go,' said Neferet. 'I've really enjoyed talking to you. We'll see each other again, I expect. And thank you with all my heart for saving Kani.'

She didn't walk, she danced; her step was light, her whole being radiant. Pazair stayed under the red willow for a long time, engraving deep into his memory every small movement she had made, every glance, every nuance of her voice.

Brave laid his right paw on his master's knee.

'You understand, don't you?' said Pazair. 'I've fallen madly in love.'

7

Kem and Killer were waiting at the agreed meeting place.

Pazair greeted Kem and asked, 'Have you decided whether to take me to see the head guard of the Sphinx?'

'I am yours to command.'

'I don't care for that tone of voice any more than the other one. Irony is just as offensive as defiance.'

The comment touched the Nubian on the raw. 'I'm not going to bow the knee to you.'

'Just do your job well and we'll get on fine together.'

The baboon and his master stared fixedly at Pazair; both pairs of eyes were full of suppressed rage.

'Let's go,' said Pazair calmly.

It was early morning, and the narrow streets were coming to life. Housewives were chatting, water carriers were distributing their precious burden, craftsmen were opening their shops. Seeing Killer, the crowd quickly parted to let them through.

The guard lived in a house similar to Branir's, but less attractive. On the doorstep, a little girl was playing with a wooden doll, but when she saw Killer she took fright and ran back inside, howling.

Her mother emerged immediately, and said angrily, 'Why are you scaring my child? Take that monster away.'

'Are you the wife of the head of the Sphinx's guard?' asked Pazair.

'What right have you to ask?'

'I am Judge Pazair.'

The young man's serious expression and the baboon's menacing appearance convinced the woman to calm down and be more polite.

'He doesn't live here any more. My husband's a former soldier, too – the army gave us this house.'

'Do you know where he's gone?'

'I met his wife when she was moving out, and she seemed upset. She said something about a house in the south of the city.'

'That's rather vague. Didn't she say whereabouts in the south?'

'I've told you all I know.'

The baboon strained at its leash. The woman recoiled and pressed herself back against the wall.

'She really said nothing more?'

'No, nothing, I swear!'

Since Iarrot had to take his daughter to her dancing class, Pazair gave him permission to leave the office in the middle of the afternoon. In return, he promised to deliver the reports of the cases the judge had dealt with to the provincial government headquarters. In only a few days, Pazair had sorted out more problems than his predecessor had done in six months.

When the sun went down, Pazair lit several lamps. He wanted to be rid of a dozen tax disputes, all of which he had resolved in favour of the taxpayer. All, that is, except one, which concerned a ship owner called Denes. The head provincial judge had written a note on the document: 'File. No further action.'

Taking Way-Finder and Brave with him, Pazair set off to visit Branir, whom he had not had a chance to consult since taking up his post. On the way, he pondered the curious fate of the senior guard who had left a prestigious post and lost his official house. What was hidden in this swarm of little irritations? Pazair had asked Kem to track the ex-soldier down. Pazair would not approve the transfer until he had questioned the man.

Brave kept scratching his right eye. Pazair examined it and saw that it was inflamed. Branir would know how to treat it.

The lamps were lit in Branir's house; he liked to read at night, when the sounds of the city had ebbed away. Pazair pushed open the front door, stepped down into the entrance hall and halted in astonishment. Branir was not alone. He was talking to a woman whose voice the judge recognized immediately. Her, here!

Brave slipped through his master's legs, went over to the old doctor and asked to be stroked.

'Pazair!' said Branir. 'Come in.'

Shyly, the judge accepted the invitation. He had eyes only for Neferet, who was sitting on the floor in front of Branir. Between her index finger and thumb she held a linen thread, at the end of which a small diamond-shaped piece of granite was swinging to and fro.*

'This is Neferet, my best pupil. My dear, this is Judge Pazair. Now that the introductions have been made, will you take a little cool beer?'

'Your best pupil . . . ?'

'We've already met,' she said with an amused smile.

Pazair thanked his lucky stars; seeing her again filled him with joy.

'Neferet will soon have to take the final test before she can practise her art,' Branir explained, 'so we're repeating the dowsing exercises she'll have to use to help her make her

---

*A pendulum. Dowsing rods are also known, and we know that certain pharaohs, such as Seti I, were great practitioners of this art, able to find water in the desert.

diagnosis. I'm convinced she'll be an excellent doctor, because she knows how to listen – someone who knows how to listen will act wisely. Listening is better than anything. There is no greater treasure. It is the gift of the heart.'

'A knowledge of the heart is the doctor's secret, isn't it?' asked Neferet.

'That's what will be revealed to you if you are judged worthy.'

'I'm tired,' she said. 'I'd like to go home and rest.'

'Then you must.'

Brave scratched his eye again, and Neferet noticed.

'I think he's in pain,' said Pazair.

The dog let Neferet examine him. 'It's nothing serious,' she said when she'd finished. 'A simple eye lotion will cure it.'

Branir went and fetched it for her; eye infections were common and there were plenty of remedies. This one acted instantly. Brave's eye became less swollen as soon Neferet applied the lotion. For the first time, Pazair was jealous of his dog. He tried to think of a way of keeping Neferet here, but had to be content with wishing her goodbye as she left.

Branir poured out some excellent beer, which had been made the previous day.

'You look tired,' he said. 'You must have a great deal of work to do.'

'I came up against a man called Qadash.'

'Ah yes, the tooth doctor with the red hands. He's a tormented man – and he's more malicious than he seems.'

'I think he's guilty of forcing a peasant to work on his estate.'

'Can you prove it?'

'No. That's merely my opinion.'

'Be conscientious in your work. Your superiors won't forgive a lack of precision.'

There was a pause while Pazair absorbed the warning. Then he asked, 'Do you often give Neferet lessons?'

'I'm passing on all my knowledge to her, for I have total confidence in her.'

'She was born in Thebes, she told me.'

'She's the only daughter of a locksmith and a weaving-woman. It was when I was treating them that I got to know her. She asked me a thousand questions, and I encouraged her budding vocation.'

'A woman doctor . . . Won't she meet all sorts of obstacles?'

'She's as brave as she is gentle. There'll be enemies as well as obstacles. For instance, the head doctor at court hopes she'll fail, and she knows it.'

'He'll be a formidable opponent.'

'She knows that, too. But one of her great strengths is her determination.'

'Is she married?' asked Pazair casually.

'No.'

'Betrothed?'

'There's nothing official, as far as I know.'

Pazair spent a sleepless night. He couldn't stop thinking about Neferet, hearing her voice, smelling her perfume, dreaming up a thousand and one plans for seeing her again, without finding a satisfactory one. And the same worry kept recurring again and again: was she indifferent to him? He had detected no signs of attraction in her, only a polite interest in his work. Even justice took on a bitter taste. How could he go on living without her? How could he bear her absence? Never had Pazair thought that love could be such a torrent, capable of bursting its banks and flooding his entire being.

Brave saw how upset his master was and lavished affectionate looks on him, but he knew his affection was no longer enough. Pazair reproached himself for making his dog unhappy. He wished he could have been content with Brave's unclouded friendship, but he could not resist Neferet's eyes, or her limpid face, or the whirlpool into which she had drawn him.

What was he to do? If he kept silent, he was condemning himself to suffer. But if he told her he loved her he risked rejection and despair. He must persuade her, charm her – but what could he possibly offer her? He was only a minor local judge with no money.

The sunrise did not calm his torment, but prompted him to lose himself in his work. He fed Brave and Way-Finder, and left them to guard the office, for he was sure Iarrot would be late. Armed with a papyrus basket containing tablets, a case of brushes and prepared ink, he headed for the docks.

There were several boats at the quayside; the sailors were unloading them themselves, under the direction of an officer. After positioning a gangplank in the forward part of the boat, they balanced poles on their shoulders, hung bags and baskets from them, then walked down the slope. The strongest men were carrying heavy bundles on their backs.

Pazair asked the officer, 'Where can I find Denes?'

'The owner? He's everywhere.'

'Do the docks belong to him?'

'Not the docks, no, but an awful lot of boats do. He's is the most important carrier in Memphis, and one of the richest men in the city.'

'Is there any chance I might meet him?'

'He only stirs himself when a really big cargo comes in. Go to the central dock. One of his largest vessels has just berthed.'

The boat was indeed large – about a hundred cubits long – and could carry more cargo than a whole donkey caravan could. She was flat-bottomed, and made of many carefully hewn planks, put together like bricks; the ones on the edges of the hull were very thick and bound together with leather strips. A sizeable sail had been hoisted on a three-legged mast, which could be lowered and was firmly braced. The captain, a crusty fifty-year-old, was ordering his men to drop the round anchor.

When Pazair tried to step aboard, a sailor barred his way. 'You're not a member of the crew.'

'I am Judge Pazair.'

The sailor stood aside, and the judge crossed the gangplank and climbed up to the captain's cabin.

'I should like to see Denes,' he said.

'Denes?' snorted the captain. 'Here, at this hour? Surely you're not serious?'

'I have here a properly drawn-up complaint.'

'About what?'

'Denes is levying a tax on unloading boats which don't belong to him, which is illegal and unjust.'

'Oh, that old story! That's an owner's privilege, and the government turns a blind eye to it. Every year there's another complaint. It's unimportant: you can throw it in the river.'

'Where does he live?'

'In the largest house behind the docks, beside the entrance to the palace quarter.'

Without his donkey, Pazair found it rather difficult to find his way around. Without Kem's baboon, he had to confront large gatherings of gossips, in heated discussions around strolling merchants.

Denes's immense house was surrounded by high walls, and the impressive entrance was guarded by a porter armed with a staff. Pazair introduced himself and asked to be admitted. The porter called a steward, who took the request to his master, returning for the judge ten minutes later.

Pazair scarcely had time to savour the beauty of the garden, the charming boating-lake and the sumptuous flower beds, for he was taken directly to Denes, who was about to have his breakfast in a vast hall with four pillars and walls decorated with hunting scenes.

The ship owner was about fifty years old, a massive man,

heavily built, with a square, rather coarse face fringed by a narrow white beard. He was sitting in a deep, lion-footed chair, and one servant was hurriedly anointing him with fine oil, while a second trimmed his fingernails, a third did his hair, a fourth rubbed his feet with scented ointment and a fifth told him what there was for breakfast.

'Judge Pazair,' said Denes. 'What favourable wind blows you to me?'

'A complaint.'

'Have you had breakfast? I haven't had mine yet.'

Denes sent away the servants. Two cooks immediately entered, bearing bread, beer, a roast duck and some honey-cakes.

'Help yourself, Judge,' he said.

'Thank you, but no.'

'A man who doesn't eat a hearty breakfast won't have a good day.'

'A serious accusation has been made against you.'

'I'm astonished to hear it.' Denes's voice lacked nobility. Sometimes it tended towards the shrill, betraying a nervousness which contrasted with his rather dignified, aloof bearing.

'You have been levying an unjust tax on unloading, and you are suspected of levying an illegal tax on the people who live on the riverbanks by two state landing stages you often use.'

'They're old customs – don't worry about them. Your predecessor attached no more importance to them than the head provincial judge did. Forget about all that and have a slice or two of duck.'

'I'm afraid I can't forget about it.'

Denes stopped eating. 'I haven't time to bother about this. Go and see my wife. She'll soon convince you that you're fighting a losing battle.'

The ship owner clapped his hands, and a steward appeared.

'Take the judge to the lady Nenophar's office,' and with that Denes went back to his breakfast.

Nenophar had a statuesque figure and a petulant manner. She dressed in the height of fashion, and was wearing an impressive black wig with heavy tresses, a turquoise pectoral, an amethyst necklace, expensive silver bracelets and a long dress adorned with green pearls. She owned vast, productive lands, several houses and twenty or so farms, and was a successful businesswoman, whose team of agents sold large quantities of products in Egypt and Syria. She also managed the royal storehouses, inspected the Treasury and was steward of fabrics at the palace.

Despite her success, she had succumbed to the charms of Denes, who was much less wealthy than she was. Considering him a poor manager, she had put him in charge of shipping goods. Her husband travelled a good deal, supported a huge network of relatives, and indulged in his favourite pastime – debating endlessly over a good wine.

Nenophar looked disdainfully at the young judge who had dared to venture into her domain. She had heard that this peasant had taken the place of the recently deceased judge, with whom she had been on excellent terms. No doubt he was paying her a courtesy visit: a good opportunity to tell him what was what.

He was not handsome, but he had a certain attraction; his face was fine-featured and serious, his gaze deep. She noted with displeasure that he did not bow as an inferior should do before his betters.

'I believe you have only just been appointed to Memphis?' she said.

'That is correct.'

'Congratulations. The post promises a brilliant career. Why did you wish to speak with me?'

'Regarding a tax which has been wrongfully levied and which—'

'I'm aware of it – as is the Treasury.'

'Then you will agree that the complaint is well-founded.'

'It's issued every year and cancelled immediately. I have an acquired right to the money.'

'That is not in accordance with the law – still less with justice.'

'You should be better informed about the extent of my offices. As a Treasury inspector, I myself cancel this kind of complaint. The country's business interests mustn't suffer because of an outdated legal case.'

'You are exceeding your rights.'

'Those are fine words, but they're meaningless. You know nothing about life, young man.'

'Please do not speak to me with such familiarity,' said Pazair. 'Must I remind you that I am questioning you officially?'

Nenophar did not take the warning lightly. A judge, no matter how junior, did not lack for powers.

She said, 'Have you settled in well in Memphis?'

Pazair did not reply.

'I've heard that your house isn't very comfortable. As you and I shall necessarily become friends, I could rent you a pleasant house at a very reasonable rate.'

'I am quite content with the accommodation allocated to me.'

A fixed smile appeared on Nenophar's lips. 'This complaint is ridiculous, believe me.'

'You have acknowledged the facts.'

'But you can't contradict your superiors!'

'If they are wrong, I shall not hesitate for a moment.'

'Be careful, Judge Pazair. You aren't all-powerful.'

'I am well aware of that.'

'Are you determined to examine this complaint?'

'I shall summon you to my office.'

'Please leave.'

Pazair bowed and obeyed.

In a fury, Nenophar burst into her husband's apartments, where she found Denes trying on a new pleated kilt.

He asked, 'Have you put the little judge firmly in his place?'

'No, I haven't, you idiot. He's as uncooperative as a wild animal.'

'You're very pessimistic. Let's give him some presents.'

'There's no point. Instead of preening yourself, do something about him. We must bring him to heel as a matter of urgency.'

8

'That's it over there,' announced Kem.

'Are you sure?' asked Pazair in astonishment.

'There's no doubt about it. That's definitely his house.'

'How can you be certain?'

The Nubian smiled fiercely. 'Tongues loosen when people see Killer. When he shows his teeth, even the dumb find their voices.'

'Those methods—'

'Are effective. You wanted a result and you've got one.'

The two men gazed around. They were in the great city's most miserable district. People had enough to eat, as they did everywhere in Egypt, but many of the hovels were dilapidated, and their cleanliness left something to be desired. This was where Syrians lived when they were looking for work, together with peasants who had come to Memphis and quickly been disillusioned, and widows with only a pittance to live on. It certainly wasn't wasn't a fitting home for the senior guard of Egypt's most famous sphinx.

'I'm going to question him,' said Pazair.

'This isn't a very safe place. You shouldn't go alone.'

'As you wish.'

In amazement, Pazair saw doors and windows slammed shut as they walked past. Hospitality, which was so dear to the hearts of Egyptians, seemed to have no place in this enclave. The baboon was on edge, and moved forward with jerky steps, while Kem kept a constant watch on the roofs.

'What are you afraid of?' asked Pazair.

'Archers.'

'Why should someone try to kill us?'

'You're carrying out an investigation, and if we have ended up here, it's because the matter is a shady one. If I were you, I'd give up.'

The palm-wood door looked solid. Pazair knocked. They heard someone moving around inside, but no one answered.

'Open the door. I am Judge Pazair.'

Silence fell. Forcing entry to a home without authorization was a crime; the judge wrestled with his conscience.

'Do you think your baboon . . . ?' he asked tentatively.

'Killer is on oath. His food is provided by the government, and we must answer for his actions.'

'Theory sometimes differs from practice.'

'Fortunately,' agreed the Nubian.

The door did not hold out for long. Pazair was astonished by Killer's strength – it was a good thing he was on the side of the law.

The two small rooms were in pitch darkness, because of mats slung across the windows. There was a beaten-earth floor, a chest for linen, another for crockery, a mat for sitting on and a few toiletries. This was a modest home, but clean.

In a corner of the second room crouched a small, white-haired woman, dressed in a dark-brown tunic.

'Don't hit me,' she pleaded. 'I didn't say anything, I swear I didn't!'

'Don't be afraid,' said Pazair. 'I want to help you.'

She accepted the judge's hand, and stood up. Suddenly, her eyes filled with terror. 'The monkey! He'll tear me to ribbons!'

'No, he won't,' Pazair reassured her. 'He's a guard baboon. Now tell me, are you the wife of the senior guard of the Sphinx?'

'Yes,' she said in a tiny, scarcely audible voice.

Pazair invited her to sit down on the mat and sat down opposite her.

'Where is your husband?'

'He's . . . he's gone on a journey.'

'Why did you leave your official house?'

'Because he was dismissed.'

'I am dealing with the matter of his transfer,' explained Pazair. 'The official documents don't mention his dismissal.'

'Perhaps I'm wrong.'

'What's happened?' asked the judge gently. 'Please understand that I'm not your enemy. If I can help you, I shall.'

'Who sent you?'

'Nobody. I making enquiries on my own initiative, so as not to make a decision when I don't understand what's going on.'

The old woman's eyes became moist with tears. 'Do you really mean that?'

'I promise you – on the life of Pharaoh.'

'My husband is dead.'

'Are you certain?'

'Some soldiers told me. They assured me that he'd be buried properly, and they ordered me to leave my home and come and live here. I shall have a small pension until I die, as long as I keep silent.'

'What were you told about how he died?'

'That it was an accident.'

'I must know the truth.'

'What does it matter?'

'Let me take you somewhere safe.'

'No,' she said. 'I shall stay here and wait for death. Now go, I beg you.'

Nebamon, head doctor to the Egyptian court, was justly proud of himself. Although in his sixties, he was still a very handsome man; the list of his feminine conquests would continue to grow for a long time yet. Laden with titles and marks of honour, he spent more time at receptions and banquets than in his consulting room, where ambitious young doctors worked for him. Weary of other people's sufferings, Nebamon had chosen an entertaining and lucrative speciality: beauty. Lovely ladies often wished to have a flaw or two removed so as to remain delectable and make their rivals turn pale with jealousy. Only Nebamon could restore their youth and preserve their charms.

He was dreaming of the magnificent stone gateway which, as a mark of Pharaoh's favour, would decorate the entrance to his tomb; the king himself had painted the uprights dark blue, to the great envy of the courtiers who dreamt of such a privilege. Fawned upon, rich and famous, Nebamon treated foreign princes, who were happy to pay very high fees. Before agreeing to accept them as patients, he made extensive enquiries, and he granted consultations only to patients with benign illnesses which were easy to treat. A failure would have tarnished his reputation.

A scribe announced the arrival of Neferet.

'Show her in.'

The young woman had angered Nebamon by refusing to join his team. Her refusal still rankled, and he was set on revenge. If she acquired the right to practise, he would see that she had no power or influence and that she was distanced from the court. Some claimed that she had a real instinct for medicine, and that her talent with the pendulum enabled her to be both quick and accurate, so he would give her one last chance before declaring war and condemning her to a life of mediocrity. Either she would obey him, or he would break her.

Neferet bowed and said, 'You summoned me.'

'I have a proposition for you.'

'I'm leaving for Sais the day after tomorrow.'

'I am aware of that, but your services won't be needed for long.'

Neferet was really very beautiful. Nebamon dreamt of having a delicious young mistress like her, one he could show off in the best society. But her natural nobility and the brightness that radiated from her prevented him from paying her those few stupid compliments which were ordinarily so effective. Seducing her would be difficult, but particularly exciting.

'My patient is an interesting case,' he continued, 'a woman of the middle rank, from a large, quite well-off family with a good reputation.'

'What is the matter with her?'

'Her husband demands that she reshape those parts of her body he doesn't like. Certain curves will be easy to alter – we shall simply remove some fat here and there in accordance with the husband's instructions – and to slim her thighs and cheeks and dye her hair will be child's play.'

Nebamon did not add that he had already received his fee of ten jars of unguents and rare perfumes: a fortune which made failure unthinkable.

He turned on all his charm. 'I'd be delighted if you would work with me on this, Neferet – you have a very steady hand. Moreover, I'd write an extremely favourable report, which would be useful to you. Will you see my patient?'

Without giving Neferet time to reply, he went to an inner door and fetched the lady Silkis into the room.

Silkis hid her face in her hands. 'I don't want anyone to look at me,' she said in the voice of a scared child. 'I'm too ugly.'

Her body was well hidden under a loose robe, but it was clear she had quite ample curves.

'What food do you like?' asked Neferet.

'I . . . I don't really pay much attention.'

'Do you like cakes?'

'Very much.'

'It would help if you didn't eat so many of them,' said Neferet with a gentle smile. 'May I examine your face?'

This gentleness overcame Silkis's reticence; she let her hands drop. True, her doll-like face was a bit pudgy, but it certainly didn't inspire horror or disgust.

'You look very young,' said Neferet.

'I'm twenty.'

'Why don't you accept yourself as you are?'

'My future husband's right, I'm hideous. I'll do absolutely anything to please him.'

'Isn't this going too far?'

'He's so strong – and I've promised.'

'Couldn't you persuade him he's mistaken?'

Nebamon was furious. 'It is not for us to judge our patients' motivations,' he snapped. 'Our role is to meet their wishes.'

'I refuse to make this young woman suffer for no good reason.'

'Leave the room!'

'With pleasure.'

'You're making a big mistake behaving like this, you know.'

'I believe I'm being faithful to the doctor's ideal.'

'You know nothing, and you'll have nothing! Your career is finished.'

Iarrot gave a little cough.

Pazair looked up. 'Is there a problem?'

'It's a summons.'

'For me?'

'Yes. The Judge of the Porch wants to see you immediately.'

In front of the royal palace, and also in front of each temple, stood a wooden porch where a judge dispensed justice. He heard complaints, distinguished truth from falsehood, protected the weak and saved them from the powerful.

At the palace, the judge sat in some state. The porch was held up by four pillars and backed on to the front of the palace. It was large, four-sided and at its far end lay the audience chamber. When the tjaty went to see Pharaoh, he always spoke first with the Judge of the Porch, whose firmness of character and forthright way with words were known to everyone.

A summons from him must be obeyed immediately. Pazair laid down his brush and palette and set off at once.

When he got there, the audience chamber was empty. The Judge was seated on a chair of gilded wood, and his expression was decidedly frosty.

'Are you Judge Pazair?'

The young man bowed respectfully. Coming face to face with the most senior judge in the province was nerve-racking. This abrupt summons to see him did not augur well.

'You have made a stormy start to your career,' commented the Judge. 'Are you satisfied?'

'I shall never be that. My dearest wish has always been that people would become wise and judges' offices would disappear, but that childish dream is beginning to fade.'

'I have heard a great deal about you, although you have not been in Memphis long. Are you fully aware of your duties?'

'They are my whole life.'

'You get through a lot of work, and quickly, too.'

'Not enough for my liking. Once I have a better understanding of the difficulties of my task, I shall be more effective.'

'"Effective"? What do you mean by that?'

'Dispensing the same justice to all. Is that not our ideal and our rule?'

'No one would disagree with that.'

The Judge's voice had grown hoarse. He got to his feet and paced up and down. 'I did not care for your comments regarding Qadash.'

'I suspect him of wrongdoing.'

'Where is the proof?'

'As I made clear in my report, I have not found any, which is why I have not begun proceedings against him.'

'In that case, why this pointless attack?'

'To draw your attention to him. You probably know more about him than I do.'

Angry, the Judge stopped in his tracks. 'Be careful, Judge Pazair! Are you insinuating that I am withholding information?'

'That's the last thing I mean. If you consider it necessary, I shall continue my enquiries.'

'Never mind about Qadash. Why are you persecuting Denes?'

'In his case, the offence is flagrant.'

'Wasn't the complaint against him accompanied by a recommendation?'

'Indeed it was: "File. No further action." That's why I dealt with it as a priority. I have sworn to resist such practices with my last scruple of strength.'

'Are you aware that I am the author of that . . . recommendation?'

'A great man must lead by example, not benefit from his wealth to exploit humble folk.'

'You are forgetting the economic necessities.'

'The day they take precedence over justice, Egypt will be condemned to death.'

The Judge of the Porch was shaken by the retort. In his youth, he had himself uttered opinions like that, and with the same fervour. Then difficult cases had come along, promotions, necessary compromises, arrangements, concessions to people of high rank, middle age . . .

He asked, 'What are you accusing Denes of?'

'You know that.'

'Do you think his behaviour justifies convicting him?'

'The answer is obvious.'

The Judge could hardly tell Pazair that he had just spoken with Denes and that the ship owner had asked him to dismiss the young man. He said, 'Are you determined to continue your enquiry?'

'Yes, I am.'

'Do you know that I can send you back to your village within the hour?'

'Yes.'

'And that doesn't alter your point of view?'

'No.'

'Are you impervious to all reason?'

'This is a crude attempt at influencing the law. Denes is a cheat, and he's benefiting from privileges he doesn't deserve. His case comes within my jurisdiction, so why should I neglect it?'

The Judge thought for a moment. Ordinarily, he would have dismissed the young man on the spot, in the absolute belief that he was serving his country, but Pazair's stance had brought back many memories. He could see himself in this young judge who so wanted to do his duty without fear or favour. The future would destroy Pazair's illusions, but was he wrong to attempt the impossible?

'Denes is a rich and powerful man, and his wife is a famous businesswoman. Thanks to them, goods are transported regularly and efficiently. What is the point of disrupting that system?'

'Don't cast me in the role of the accused. If Denes is found guilty, cargo boats will still sail up and down the Nile.'

After a long silence, the Judge of the Porch sat down again. 'Carry out your duties as you see fit, Pazair.'

9

For two days, Neferet had been meditating in a room at the famous Sais medical school, in the Delta, where would-be doctors faced an ordeal whose nature had never been revealed. Many failed. In a country where people often lived to eighty, the authorities were determined to recruit only worthwhile members.

Would the young woman realize her dream as she struggled against evil? She would experience many defeats, but would never give up fighting suffering. But she still had to satisfy the demands of the medical court at Sais.

A priest brought her dried meat, dates, water and some medical papyri which she read over and over again; some of the ideas were starting to get mixed up in her head. Wavering between anxiety and confidence, she took refuge in meditation, gazing out at the vast orchard of carob trees that surrounded the school.*

As the sun was setting, the Keeper of the Myrrh, who specialized in cleansing and purifying buildings, came to find her. He took her to the workshop and presented her to several of his colleagues. In rapid succession they required Neferet to make up a prescription, to prepare remedies, to evaluate the

---

*The carob fruit, a pod containing sugary juice, was seen by the Egyptians as the perfect embodiment of sweetness.

good and ill effects of a drug, to identify complex substances, and to relate in detail how plants, gum-resin and honey were gathered. Several times she was severely taxed and had to dig deep into the recesses of her memory.

At the end of an examination lasting five hours, four of the five voted in her favour. The fifth explained why he had not: Neferet had made a mistake over two doses. Ignoring her tiredness, he demanded to question her again. If she refused, she would have to leave Sais.

Neferet met the challenge. Without departing from her usual sweetness of character, she submitted to her opponent's attacks. And he was the first to yield.

She received no praise or congratulations, but was simply told she might withdraw. She went to her room and fell asleep as soon as she lay down on her mat.

The examiner who had so sorely taxed her awoke her at dawn. 'You have the right to continue,' he said. 'Are you willing to do so?'

'I'm at your disposal.'

'You have half an hour to wash and have breakfast. I warn you, the next trial is a dangerous one.'

'I'm not afraid.'

'Take time to think while you wash and eat.'

In half an hour he returned and escorted her to the workshop. On the threshold he repeated his warning and said, 'Don't take my words lightly.'

'I don't, but I shan't withdraw.'

'Very well. Take this.' He handed her a forked stick. 'Go into the workshop and prepare a remedy using the ingredients you will find there.'

Neferet went in, and he closed the door behind her. On a low table were phials, small dishes and jars. In the furthest corner, under the window, lay a basket with a lid. The weave was sufficiently open for her to see the contents as she approached it.

She recoiled in horror: a horned viper. Its bite was fatal, but the venom provided the base for very effective remedies against severe bleeding, nervous conditions and heart problems. So she understood what was expected of her.

Taking a deep breath, she reached out a steady hand and lifted the lid. The viper was wary, and did not come out of its lair immediately. Neferet stood absolutely still, concentrating hard, watching as it eventually slithered over the rim of the basket and away across the ground. The snake was as long as a man's arm and moved fast; the two horns jutted menacingly from its head.

Neferet gripped her stick with all her strength, moved to the left of the snake, and prepared to try to pin its head in the fork of the stick. For a split second she closed her eyes; if she failed, the viper would climb the stick and bite her. She struck.

The snake writhed furiously: she had succeeded. She knelt down, and seized it behind its head. She would make it spit out its precious venom.

On the boat carrying her home to Thebes, Neferet had had little time to rest. Several doctors had pestered her with questions on their respective specialities which she had practised during her studies.

Neferet adapted well to new situations, and didn't falter in even the most unexpected circumstances. She accepted whatever the world threw at her, and the differences between people; and took little interest in herself, concentrating instead on gaining a deeper understanding of the powers and the mysteries. She preferred being happy, of course, but adversity did not daunt her: through it all, she sought for the future joy that was hidden beneath the unhappiness. Not for a moment did she hate the men who had treated her so badly; as she saw it, they were building and proving the solidity of her vocation.

It was a real pleasure to see Thebes again. The sky seemed bluer than in Memphis, the air softer and smoother. One day she would come back to live here, close to her parents, and would once again walk in the countryside where she had spent her childhood. She thought of her monkey, which she had entrusted to Branir, hoping that the little creature would respect her old master and cause less mischief.

When Neferet reached the temple enclosure, behind whose high walls several shrines had been built, two shaven-headed priests opened the gate to allow her in. Here, in the domain of the goddess Mut, whose name meant both 'Mother' and 'Death', doctors were inaugurated.

The High Priest greeted her and said, 'I have received the reports from the school at Sais. If you wish, you may continue.'

'I do.'

'The final decision does not belong to human beings. Gather your thoughts, for you are about to appear before a judge who is not of this world.'

The priest fastened a cord with thirteen knots around Neferet's neck and told her to kneel.

'The doctor's secret,'* he said, 'is knowledge of the heart; from it visible and invisible vessels lead to every organ and every limb. Because of that, the heart speaks throughout the body. When you examine a patient by placing a hand on his head, the nape of his neck, his arms, his legs, or some other part of his body, seek first of all the heart's voice and rhythm. Be sure that it is solidly based, that it does not move from its proper place, that it does not fade and that it dances as it should. Know that a network of channels pervades the body and that they carry subtle energies, as well as air, blood, water, tears, sperm or faecal matter. Make sure that the

*The text called *The Doctor's Secret* was known by all practising doctors and formed the basis of their craft.

vessels and the lymph are pure. When illness arises, it reveals a disorder of the energy; beyond the effects, look for the cause. Be honest with your patients and give them one of the three possible diagnoses: an illness which I know and which I shall cure; an illness which I shall fight; an illness against which I can do nothing. Now go towards your destiny.'

The temple was silent.

Sitting back on her heels, with her hands on her knees and her eyes closed, Neferet waited. Time no longer existed. She was calm, in control of her anxiety. She had absolute trust in the brotherhood of physician-priests who, since Egypt's earliest days, had consecrated the vocation of healers.

Two priests helped her to her feet. Before her, a cedar-wood door swung open; it led into a shrine. The two men did not accompany her. Outside herself, beyond fear and hope, Neferet entered the dark, oblong chamber.

The heavy door closed behind her.

Immediately, Neferet sensed a presence: someone was crouching in the gloom, watching her. Her arms taut at her sides, her breathing laboured, she refused to yield to her fear. Alone, she had made it this far; alone, she would defend herself.

Suddenly, a ray of light shone down from the temple roof and lit up a diorite statue leaning against the far wall. It represented the goddess Sekhmet walking forward, the terrifying lion goddess who, at the end of each year, tried to destroy humanity by sending forth hordes of evil vapours, sicknesses and harmful germs. They scoured the earth, trying to spread misfortune and death. Only doctors could counter the formidable goddess, who was also their patron; she alone taught them the art of healing and the secret of remedies.

Neferet had often been told that no mortal being could look into Sekhmet's face on pain of losing their life. She ought to have lowered her eyes, turned her face away from the extraordinary statue, the furious face of the lioness,* but she confronted it.

Neferet looked straight at Sekhmet. She prayed to the goddess to make clear her vocation, to enter the very depths of her heart and to judge it true. The ray of light grew stronger, lighting up the whole of the stone figure, whose power overwhelmed the young woman.

Then a miracle happened: the terrifying lioness smiled.

The College of Doctors at Thebes had assembled in a vast pillared hall with a large pond at its centre.

The High Priest approached Neferet. 'Is it your firm intention to heal the sick?'

'The goddess witnessed my oath.'

'What one recommends to others one must first apply to oneself.' He presented her with a cup filled with a reddish liquid. 'Here is a poison. After drinking it, you will identify it and make your diagnosis. If it is correct, you will have recourse to the right antidote. If it is wrong, you will die and the law of Sekhmet will have saved Egypt from a bad doctor.'

Neferet accepted the cup.

'You are free to refuse to drink, and to leave this assembly.'

Slowly, she drank the bitter liquid, already trying to work out what it was.

Followed by weeping women, the funerary procession passed along the temple enclosure and headed towards the river. An ox hauled the sledge on which the sarcophagus was laid.

From the temple roof, the High Priest and Neferet watched the game of life and death. She was worn out, and savoured the sun's caress on her skin.

---

*The Arabs were so terrified by this statue, which they called the 'Ogress of Karnak', that they did not destroy it. It can still be admired today in one of the shrines of the Temple of Ptah.

The High Priest said, 'You will feel cold for a few hours more, but the poison will leave no trace in your body. Your speed and accuracy greatly impressed all my colleagues.'

'Would you have saved me if I had been wrong?'

'No, because he who cares for others must be pitiless with himself. As soon as you have recovered, you will return to Memphis to take up your first post. On your path, you will find many obstacles. A healer as young and gifted as you will arouse a good deal of jealousy. Don't be blind or naive.'

Swallows played in the sky above the temple. Neferet thought of her mentor, Branir, the man who had taught her everything and to whom she owed her life.

10

Pazair was finding it more and more difficult to concentrate on his work: he saw Neferet's face in every hieroglyph.

Iarrot brought him a pile of clay tablets. 'Here's the list of the craftsmen taken on at the weapons workshops last month. We must check that none of them has ever been convicted of a crime.'

'What's the quickest way to find out?' asked Pazair.

'Consult the registers at the main prison.'

'Could you deal with it?'

'Not until tomorrow – I must go home now, because I'm organizing a birthday party for my daughter.'

Pazair smiled. 'Enjoy yourself.'

Once the scribe had left, he re-read the document he had drawn up summoning Denes and notifying him of the charges. It swam in and out of focus before his eyes. It was no good: he was too tired. He fed Way-Finder, who then lay down in front of the office door, and went out for a walk with Brave. His steps led him into a quiet area, near the scribes' school where the country's future elite learnt their craft.

The sound of a door slamming shattered the silence. This was followed by shouts and snatches of music, in which he heard a flute and a tambourine. The dog's ears pricked up; intrigued, Pazair halted. The argument was turning nasty, with threats giving way to blows and cries of pain. Brave, who hated violence, presssed close against his master's leg.

About a hundred paces from where Pazair was standing, a young man in a fine scribe's outfit climbed the school wall, jumped down into the alleyway and ran full pelt towards him, shouting the words of a bawdy song. As he ran though a ray of evening sunlight, the judge glimpsed his face.

'Suti!' he exclaimed.

The fugitive stopped in his tracks and turned round. 'Who called my name?'

'Apart from me, there's no one here.'

'There soon will be: they're after my hide. Come on, we'd better run for it.'

Pazair accepted the invitation. Brave was delighted and galloped alongside. The dog was astonished at the two men's lack of stamina when, ten minutes later, they stopped to get their breath back.

'Suti, is it really you?' panted Pazair.

'It really is – and you're really Pazair! Come on. One final effort and we'll be safe.'

The trio took refuge in an empty warehouse on the banks of the Nile, far from the area where armed guards patrolled.

'I was hoping we'd meet again soon,' said Pazair, 'but in rather happier circumstances.'

'Oh, these circumstances are absolutely wonderful, I assure you! I've just escaped from that prison.'

'Prison? The great Memphis scribes' school?'

'I'd have died of boredom there.'

'But when you left the village five years ago, you said wanted to become a scholar.'

'I'd have said anything if it got me the chance to explore the city. The only wrench was leaving you – you were my only friend among all those peasants.'

'We were happy there, though, weren't we?'

Suti stretched out on the ground. 'There were some good moments, you're right. But we've grown up. Enjoying myself in the village, living real life, that wasn't possible. I was always dreaming of Memphis.'

'And has your dream come true?'

'At first I was patient. I studied and worked and read and wrote and listened to the teachings that open up the spirit – what a bore! Fortunately, I soon started frequenting ale-houses.'

'Those places of debauchery?' said Pazair reproachfully.

'Don't moralize.'

'But you loved books even more than I did.'

'Ah, books and wise maxims! I've had my ears battered by them for the last five years. Do you want me to play teacher, too? "Love books as you love your mother, for nothing surpasses them; the books of the sages are pyramids, and the writing case is their child. Listen to the advice of those who are wiser than you, and read their words, which live on in books. Become a learned man; be neither lazy nor idle, but store knowledge in your heart." I recite the lessons well, don't I?'

'Very well.'

'They're just mirages for blind men.'

Pazair looked at him curiously. 'What happened this evening?'

Suti burst out laughing. The restless, boisterous boy, the life and soul of the village, had become a man of impressive stature. His hair was long and black, his face open, his gaze direct, and when he spoke there was pride in his voice. It was as though an all-consuming fire burnt inside him.

'I organized a little celebration.'

'At the school?'

'Of course. Most of my fellow students are dull, sad and characterless. They needed to drink some wine and beer and forget their precious studies. We played music, we got drunk, we threw up and we sang. Even the most dedicated students were wreathed in flower garlands and banging tambourines

77

on their bellies.' Suti sat up. 'These little pleasures annoyed the masters in charge, and they came bursting in armed with clubs. I defended myself, but my comrades denounced me. I had to run away.'

Pazair was appalled. 'You'll be expelled.'

'Good. I wasn't meant to be a scribe. Never harm anyone, never worry them, never leave them in poverty and suffering – I'm going to leave that ideal world to the sages. I'm burning for adventure, a great adventure.'

'What sort of adventure?'

'I don't know yet – no, that's not right, I do know: the army. I shall travel and discover other lands, other peoples.'

'You'll be risking your life,' warned Pazair.

'It'll be all the more precious to me, after the danger. Why spend all your time guarding your life when death will destroy it anyway? Believe me, my friend, we must live from day to day and take pleasure where we find it. We're less than the butterflies; let's at least find out how to fly from flower to flower.'

Brave growled.

'Someone is coming,' said Pazair. 'We must go.'

'My head's spinning.'

Pazair stretched out an arm and Suti used it to help himself to his feet.

'Lean on me,' said Pazair.

'You haven't changed, have you? You're still a rock.'

'You're my friend. I'm your friend.'

They left the warehouse, walked along its side and entered a maze of little streets.

'Thank you. They won't find me now.' The night air had sobered Suti up. 'I'm not a scribe any longer. What about you? What do you do?'

'I hardly dare tell you.'

'Are the authorities looking for you?'

'Not exactly.'

'Are you a smuggler?'

'Not that either.'

'You rob honest folk, then!'

'I'm a judge.'

Suti stopped, took Pazair by the shoulders and looked him in the eye. 'You're playing a joke on me.'

'I couldn't if I tried.'

'That's true, you couldn't. A judge . . . By Osiris, that's unbelievable! Do you have guilty people arrested?'

'I have that right.'

'Are you a junior or a senior judge?'

'A junior one, but in Memphis. Come home with me – you'll be safe there.'

'Aren't you breaking the law?'

'No one has lodged a complaint against you.'

'Supposing they had?'

'Friendship is a sacred law. If I betrayed it, I'd be unworthy of my office.'

The two men embraced.

'You can always count on me, Pazair,' said Suti fervently. 'I swear it on my life.'

'I know. That day in the village, when we mixed our blood, we became more than brothers.'

'Tell me, do you have guards answering to you?'

'Two, a Nubian and a baboon, each as fearsome as the other.'

'You're giving me the shivers.'

'Don't worry; the school will be content with expelling you. But try not to commit any serious crimes – those would be outside my jurisdiction.'

'It's so good to see you you again, Pazair!'

Brave bounded around Suti, who challenged him to a race, much to the animal's joy. Pazair was delighted that they liked each other. Brave had good judgment and Suti had a big heart. True, Pazair didn't approve of the way he thought or the way he lived his life, and feared his friend might lead him into regrettable excesses; but he knew that Suti had criticisms of him. By joining forces, they would discover many truths about each other's nature.

The donkey seemed to approve of Suti and allowed him to enter Pazair's house. The young man did not tarry in the office, whose papyri and tablets brought back bad memories, but climbed straight up to the upper floor.

'It's no palace,' he remarked, 'but at least the air's breathable. Do you live here alone?'

'Not entirely. I have Brave and Way-Finder to keep me company.'

'I was talking about women.'

'I'm overwhelmed with work, and—'

'Pazair, my friend, don't tell me you're still . . . chaste?'

'I'm afraid so.'

'We'll soon put that right. I'm certainly not chaste any more. In the village I had no luck with girls, because there were always nosy old women on the lookout. Here in Memphis, it's paradise!

'I made love for the first time with a little Nubian girl who'd already had more lovers than she had fingers. When pleasure overwhelmed me, I thought I was going to die of happiness. She taught me how to caress her, to wait for her moment of pleasure, and how to get my strength back so that we could play games which no one lost.

'My second woman was betrothed to the school gate-keeper, but before becoming a faithful wife she wanted to sample a boy who was scarcely out of his teens. Her appetite almost wore me out. She had magnificent breasts, and buttocks as beautiful as islands in the Nile before the flood. She taught me delicate arts, and we had lots of fun together.

'Next, I enjoyed the company of two Syrian girls in an ale-house. There's no substitute for experience, Pazair; their hands were as soft as balm and even their feet could make me shiver just by brushing my skin.'

Suti burst out laughing again. Pazair couldn't maintain even a shred of dignity, and joined in his friend's happiness.

'I'm not boasting,' said Suti, 'but it would be quite a job to list all my conquests. I can't help myself – I just can't resist the warmth of a woman's body. Chastity is a shameful ailment which must be dealt with energetically. First thing tomorrow, I shall take charge of your case.'

'Well . . .'

A malicious glint appeared in Suti's eyes. 'You aren't refusing, are you?'

'My work, all those cases . . .'

'You were never any good at lying, Pazair. You're in love, and you're saving yourself for your sweetheart.'

'I'm usually the one who makes the accusations.'

'It's not an accusation. Personally I don't believe in undying love, but anything's possible with you – you being a judge and my friend at the same time proves that. So what's this marvel called?'

'I . . . She doesn't know anything. I'm probably just fantasizing.'

'Is she married?'

'Surely you're not thinking of—'

'Oh yes I am. My list of conquests doesn't contain a good wife. I won't force anyone, for I do have some morals, but if the chance presents itself I won't turn it down.'

'The law punishes adultery.'

'Only if it notices. In love, apart from frolics the most important quality is discretion. I shan't torture you about your intended. I shall find everything out by myself, and if necessary I shall give you a hand.' Suti lay down on a mat and tucked a cushion beneath his head. 'Are you really a judge?'

'You have my word.'

'In that case, I could do with a bit of advice.'

Pazair had been expecting something like this; he called

upon Thoth, in the hope that the offence Suti had committed would come within his jurisdiction.

'It's a stupid story,' said his friend. 'I seduced a young widow last week. She's about thirty, with a lithe body and delicious lips . . . She'd had the misfortune to be mistreated by her husband, whose death was a godsend. She was so happy in my arms that she entrusted me with a little business deal: trading a sucking-pig at the market.'

'She owns a farm?'

'No, just a poultry yard.'

'What did you exchange the pig for?'

'That's the problem: nothing. The poor beast was roasted during our little celebration tonight. Usually, I'd be sure my charm would do the trick, but my widow's a bit of a miser and very much attached to her inheritance. If I go back empty-handed, I'm liable to be accused of theft.'

'Is there anything else?'

'Oh, nothing much, just a few debts here and there. The pig's my main worry.'

'Sleep well.' Pazair stood up.

'Where are you going?'

'Down to the office to consult a few documents. I'm sure there must be a solution.'

11

Suti didn't like getting up early, but he had to leave Pazair's house before dawn – his friend had to pour a jar of cold water over his head to wake him up. Pazair's plan seemed excellent, although it carried a few risks.

Suti reached the town centre, where the great market was being set up. Peasants and their womenfolk came here to sell country produce in a clamour of haggling and debate. Soon the first customers would start arriving. He slunk between the stalls and crouched down a short distance from his target, an enclosure filled with poultry. The prize he wanted to win was indeed there: a superb cockerel.*

The young man waited until his prey came within his grasp, then made a grab for its neck, gripping it so swiftly that it made no sound. The undertaking was hazardous: if he was caught, prison beckoned. Of course, Pazair had not chosen this particular trader at random; the man had been convicted of fraud, and should have paid his victim the value of a cockerel. The judge had not reduced the punishment, simply altered the procedure a little. Since the victim was the government, Suti was acting in its place.

*The Egyptians regarded the cockerel not as the king of the poultry yard but as a rather stupid creature, too concerned with its own importance.

Stuffing the cockerel under his arm, he headed for the young woman's farm. She was feeding her hens.

'I've got a surprise for you,' he announced, producing the fowl.

She was delighted. 'He's superb! You've done a good deal there.'

'It wasn't easy, I must confess.'

'I'm not surprised: a cockerel like that is worth at least three sucking-pigs.'

'When love guides a man, he can be persuasive.'

She set down her bag of grain, took the cockerel and put him in with the hens. She said, 'You're very persuasive, Suti. I can feel a gentle heat rising up within me, and I'd love to share it with you.'

'How could I refuse an invitation like that?'

Locked in a passionate embrace, they made their way to the widow's bedroom.

Pazair felt ill: listless and lacking his usual energy. Sluggish and drowsy, he could no longer find consolation even in reading the great ancient authors who had once enchanted his evenings. He had managed to hide his despair from Iarrot the scribe, but he could not hide it from Branir.

'You're not ill are you, Pazair?'

'It's nothing. I'm just tired, that's all.'

'Perhaps you oughtn't to work quite so hard.'

'I feel as if I'm being buried in cases.'

'You're being tested, to find out your limits.'

'They've already been passed.'

'Not necessarily. Supposing overwork isn't the reason why you aren't yourself?'

Pazair did not reply; he just looked gloomy.

'My best pupil has succeeded,' said Branir.

'Do you mean Neferet?'

'She passed the trials, in both Thebes and Sais.'

'So she is a doctor now.'

'Indeed she is, to our great joy.'

'Where will she practise?'

'To begin with, in Memphis. I have invited her to a modest celebration at my house tomorrow evening, to celebrate her success. Will you join us?'

Denes ordered his bearers to set down his travelling chair before the door of Pazair's office. The magnificent chair was painted blue and red, and had dazzled passers-by. However delicate the coming meeting might prove, it was unlikely to be as trying as his recent argument with his wife. Nenophar had accused her husband of being simple-minded, useless and no better than a sparrow,* because his attempt to influence the Judge of the Porch had proved utterly futile.

Denes had ridden out the storm and tried to justify himself, pointing out that his tactics usually resulted in total success. Then why, demanded his wife, had the judge refused to listen to him this time? Not only was he not transferring the new little judge, but he had even authorized him to send out a properly drafted summons, as though Denes were any common citizen of Memphis! It was all because of Denes's lack of perspicacity that the two of them found themselves reduced to the level of suspects, subject to the ill will of a judge with no future, who had come up from the provinces determined to ensure that the law was observed to the letter. Since Denes was so brilliant at business discussions, let him charm Pazair and have the court case stopped!

Their large house had rung with Nenophar's shouts for a long time. She could not bear to be thwarted. Besides, bad news spoilt her complexion.

Way-Finder barred the entrance to the judge's office.

---

*Because of its perpetual agitation and its tendency to flock, the sparrow was considered a symbol of evil.

When Denes tried to elbow the donkey out of his path, it bared its teeth.

He leapt back. 'Get that animal out of my way,' he ordered.

Iarrot emerged from the office, and pulled the beast's tail; but Way-Finder never obeyed anyone but Pazair. Denes skirted round the donkey at a distance so as not to soil his expensive clothes.

Pazair was studying a papyrus. 'Please be seated,' he said.

Denes looked around for a chair, but found none of them to his liking. 'You must admit, Judge Pazair, I am being very accommodating in responding to your summons.'

'You had no choice.'

'Must a third party be present?'

Iarrot got to his feet, ready to leave. 'I'd like to go home early. My daughter—'

'Scribe, you are to take notes when I tell you to.'

Iarrot huddled in a corner of the room, hoping that his presence would be forgotten. Denes would not allow himself to be treated like this without retaliating. If he carried out reprisals against the judge, the scribe would be caught up in the whirlwind.

'I am very busy, Judge Pazair,' said Denes. 'You were not on the list of meetings I had arranged for today.'

'But you were on mine.'

'We should not clash head-on like this. You have a small administrative problem to resolve, and I want to be rid of it as quickly as possible. Why don't we come to an understanding?' Denes used his most conciliatory voice. He knew how to talk to people on their own level and flatter them. Then, when their attention wandered, he struck the decisive blow.

'You are digressing.'

'I beg your pardon?'

'We are not discussing a business transaction.'

'Allow me to tell you a little story. A disobedient goat left the herd, where he was safe, and ran off. A wolf threatened him. When he saw its jaws opening, he declared, "Lord Wolf, I shall no doubt provide you with a feast, but before that happens I could entertain you. For example, I can dance. Don't you believe me? Play the flute, and you'll see." The wolf was in a playful mood, and agreed. The goat's dance alerted the dogs, who charged at the wolf and made it run away. The wild beast admitted its defeat; I am a hunter, he thought, and I played at being a musician. Too bad for me.'*

'What is the moral of your tale?'

'Every man must know his own place. When you try to play a role you aren't familiar with, you run the risk of making a mistake you will bitterly regret.'

'You impress me,' said Pazair.

'I am glad. Shall we leave it there?'

'In the land of fables, yes.'

'You're more understanding than I thought. You won't be stuck in this pathetic office for long. The Judge of the Porch is a good friend of mine. When he knows that you have handled the situation with tact and intelligence, he will consider you for an important post. If he asks for my opinion, it will be very favourable.'

'It is good to have friends.'

'In Memphis, it's essential – you're on the right path.'

Nenophar's anger had been unjustified; she feared that Pazair was not like other men, but she was wrong. Denes knew plenty of others like him: apart from a few priests, hidden away in temples, their only goal was to further their own interests.

Denes turned away from the judge and made ready to leave.

'Where are you going?' asked Pazair.

*This fable is a classic. Aesop took his inspiration from Egyptian fables, which were also embodied in the work of La Fontaine.

'To meet a boat which is arriving from the South.'

'We have not quite finished.'

The ship owner turned back.

'Here are the charges: exacting an unjust levy and a tax not prescribed by Pharaoh. The fine will be a heavy one.'

Denes turned white with anger. 'Have you gone mad?' he hissed.

'Write this down, scribe: "Insulting a magistrate".'

Denes turned on Iarrot, tore the tablet from his hands and trampled it underfoot. 'Don't you do any such thing!'

'Destroying materials belonging to the forces of law,' observed Pazair. 'You are making matters worse for yourself.'

'That's enough!'

'You will need this papyrus. Written on it, you will find the legal details of the case and the size of the fine. Do not fail to pay, or a police record will be opened in your name at the main prison.'

'You are nothing but a young goat, and you will be eaten alive.'

'In your story, it was the wolf who lost.'

When Denes stormed across the office, Iarrot hid behind a wooden chest.

When Pazair reached Branir's house, he found it decorated with wreaths of flowers.

The old doctor was putting the finishing touches to a delicious meal. He had taken the roes from female grey mullet and, following a traditional recipe, washed them in lightly salted water before pressing them between two planks and drying them in the fresh air. He was also going to grill sides of beef, and serve them up with a purée of beans. The menu would be completed by figs and cakes, not forgetting a fine wine from the Delta.

'Am I the first to arrive?' asked Pazair.

'Help me set the table.'

'I attacked Denes head-on. My evidence is rock solid.'

'What sentence have you given him?'

'A heavy fine.'

Branir frowned. 'You've made a formidable enemy.'

'I applied the law.'

'Be careful.'

Pazair had no time to protest: the sight of Neferet made him forget Denes, Iarrot, the office and all his cases.

She wore a pale-blue dress with straps that left her shoulders bare, and had lined her eyes with green kohl. At once frail and reassuring, she lit up her host's home.

'Am I late?' she asked.

'Not at all,' said Branir. 'You gave me time to finish cooking. The baker has just delivered fresh bread, so now we can sit down to eat.'

Neferet had slipped a lotus flower into her hair; Pazair could not take his eyes off her.

'I am thrilled by your success,' said Branir. 'As you're a doctor now, I give you this talisman. It will protect you as it has protected me – wear it always.'

'But what about you?'

'At my age, demons no longer have any hold on me.'

He placed a fine gold chain around the young woman's neck. On it was suspended a magnificent turquoise.

'This stone,' he said, 'came from the mines of the goddess Hathor, in the Eastern desert. It keeps the soul young and the heart joyful.'

Neferet bowed before her master, her hands clasped in a sign of veneration.

'I would like to congratulate you, too,' said Pazair, 'but I don't know how.'

'The thought alone is enough.' She smiled.

'And I should like to give you a modest gift.'

He presented her with a bracelet of coloured pearls. Neferet took off her right sandal and slipped her bare foot through the bracelet, which she fastened round her ankle.

'Thank you,' she said. 'I feel prettier now.'

Those few words gave Pazair an insane hope: for the first time, he felt that she had noticed he existed.

The meal was a friendly one. Relaxed now, Neferet talked about some aspects of her difficult traning, though she was careful not to divulge any secrets. Branir assured her that nothing had changed since his young days. Pazair picked at his food, but devoured Neferet with his eyes and drank in her words. In the company of his mentor and the woman he loved, he spent an evening of utter happiness, shot through with flashes of anxiety: would Neferet reject him?

While Pazair worked, Suti took the donkey and the dog for walks, made love with the owner of the poultry yard, went off in search of new, rather promising, conquests, and revelled in the bustling life of Memphis. He was discreet, and did not annoy his friend very much – he had not slept at his house once since that first evening. Pazair had proved intractable on only one point: drunk with the success of his sucking-pig 'exchange', Suti had mentioned that he would like to repeat it. The judge was adamantly opposed. Suti's mistress was proving generous, so he didn't press the point.

The baboon's massive bulk loomed up, filling the doorway. Almost as tall as a man, it had a head like a dog and the teeth of a wild beast. Its arms, legs and belly were white, while its shoulders and back were covered in reddish fur. Behind the baboon stood Kem.

'There you are at last,' said Pazair.

'The investigation was long and difficult. Has Iarrot gone out?'

'His daughter's ill. What have you found out?'

'Nothing.'

'What do you mean, "nothing"? That's unbelievable.'

The Nubian fingered his wooden nose, checking that it was

securely in place. 'I consulted my best informants. No one knows anything about the guard's death. I was constantly referred back to the commander of the guards, as if everyone was acting on orders.'

'Then I shall go and see him.'

'I wouldn't advise it. He doesn't like judges.'

'I shall try to be pleasant.'

Mentmose, the guards' commander, had two houses, one at Memphis, where he lived most of the time, and the other at Thebes. He was short and fat with a round face, and inspired confidence in people; but his pointed nose and nasal voice belied his affable appearance.

Mentmose was a bachelor. Since his youth, he had thought only of his career and the honours it could bring him. Luck had served him in the form of a succession of opportune deaths. Just as he was destined to become overseer of canals, the official in charge of his province's security had broken his neck falling off a ladder and, although Mentmose had no special qualifications, he was swift in putting himself forward, and obtained the post.

Profiting skilfully from his predecessor's work, he soon forged himself an excellent reputation. Some men would have been content with this promotion, but he was devoured by ambition, and now thirsted for the command of the river guards. Alas, the post was held by an enterprising young man beside whom Mentmose looked unimpressive. But the inconvenient fellow had drowned during a routine operation, leaving the field free for Mentmose, who had applied immediately, with the support of numerous relatives. He was chosen over other candidates who were better qualified but less adept at strategy, and had continued to apply his proven method: taking the credit for other people's efforts and deriving personal benefit from them.

Although he already held high rank in the security guards, he dreamt of attaining the highest position, but that was completely out of reach because the incumbent was a vigorous, middle-aged man who had known nothing but success. His only failure proved to be an unfortunate chariot accident as a result of which he died, crushed beneath the wheels. Naturally, Mentmose put himself forward immediately and was successful, despite note-worthy opponents. He was particularly skilful at displaying himself and his service record to best advantage.

Once he had reached the pinnacle of success, Mentmose was determined to remain there, so he surrounded himself with second-rate men, who were incapable of replacing him. As soon as he detected a strong personality, he sent him away. Working away in the shadows, manipulating individuals without their realizing it, and plotting intrigues: these were his favourite pastimes.

He was studying the list of appointments to the desert guards when his steward announced the arrival of Judge Pazair. Ordinarily, Mentmose referred junior judges to his subordinates, but this one interested him – after all, he had got the better of Denes, whose fortune normally enabled him to buy anyone. The young judge would soon meet his downfall, falling victim to his own illusions, but perhaps Mentmose could derive some advantage from his youthful zeal. The fact that he was bold enough to inconvenience the commander of the guards was proof of his determination.

Mentmose received Pazair at his home, in the room where he displayed his decorations, gold collars, semi-precious stones and staves of gilded wood.

'Thank you for seeing me,' said Pazair.

'I am devoted to assisting justice. Are you enjoying yourself here in Memphis?'

'I must speak with you about a strange matter.'

Mentmose ordered his steward to serve the finest beer and gave instructions that he was not to be disturbed.

'What is it?'

'I cannot ratify a transfer without knowing what has become of the person concerned.'

'That is indeed true. Who is the person?'

'The former head of guards of the Sphinx at Giza.'

'Isn't that an honorary post, reserved for former soldiers?'

'In this case, the ex-soldier has been sent away.'

'Has he committed a serious crime?'

'There is no mention of it in my documents. What's more, the man was forced to leave his official house and take refuge in the poorest part of town.'

Mentmose seemed annoyed. 'That is indeed strange.'

'There is something more serious. His wife, whom I have questioned, says her husband is dead, but she has not seen his body and does not know where he is buried.'

'Why is she so sure he's dead?'

'Soldiers told her – and they also ordered her to keep silent if she wished to receive a pension.'

Mentmose slowly drank a cup of beer. He had been expecting to hear about the Denes case, instead of which he was being told of an unpleasant enigma. 'A remarkably quick and efficient enquiry, Judge Pazair. Your growing reputation is well deserved.'

'I intend to continue.'

'How?'

'We must find the body and discover the cause of death.'

'Yes, you're right.'

'Your help will be vital. Being in charge of the guards in the towns and villages, on the river and in the desert, you can easily facilitate my investigations.'

'Unfortunately that won't be possible.'

'I'm surprised you should say that. Why not?'

'Your information is too vague. Besides, at the heart of this matter we have an ex-soldier and a group of soldiers – in other words, the army.'

'I know, and that's why I am asking for your help. If you

93

ask for explanations, the military authorities will be obliged to respond.'

'The situation is more complicated than you realize. The army sets great store by its independence from the guards. I'm not accustomed to trespassing on its ground.'

'And yet you know it well.'

Mentmose waved a hand airily. 'Merely exaggerated rumours,' he said. 'But I fear you may be setting out on a dangerous journey.'

'I cannot leave a death unexplained.'

'I agree with you.'

'What do you advise me to do?'

Mentmose thought long and hard. This young judge wasn't going to back down, and manipulating him would certainly not be easy. It would take time and study to discover his weak points and use them wisely.

Eventually he said, 'Go and see the man who appointed the veterans to their honorary positions: General Asher.'

12

The shadow-eater* moved like a cat in the night, soundlessly avoiding obstacles, sliding along walls and melting into the shadows. No one saw or suspected anything.

The poorest part of Memphis was slumbering. Here, there were no porters or watchmen as there were outside wealthy people's homes. Face hidden beneath a wooden jackal mask,† the shadow-eater slipped into the house belonging to the senior guard's wife.

All orders were obeyed without question – it was a long time since the last vestiges of emotion had drained from that black heart. Like a human falcon,‡ the shadow-eater loomed up out of the darkness, deriving strength from it.

The old woman awoke with a start. The horrific sight took her breath away. She let out a terrible cry and collapsed, stone dead. The killer had not even needed to use a weapon or disguise the crime. The loose-tongued woman would speak no more.

General Asher punched a novice soldier hard on the back, and the lad collapsed into the dust of the parade ground.

*An Egyptian expression meaning 'assassin'.
†The type of mask worn by priests playing the parts of the gods when celebrating rituals.
‡An Egyptian expression corresponding to our 'werewolf'.

'That's what sluggards deserve,' sneered the general.

An archer stepped forward from the ranks. 'He committed no offence, sir.'

'You talk too much. Leave the exercise immediately. Fifteen days confined to barracks, followed by a long spell in a southern fortress will teach you discipline.'

The general ordered the men to run for an hour with their bows, quivers, shields and food bags on their backs; when they left on campaign, they would encounter tougher conditions. If one of the soldiers halted, exhausted, Asher would grab him by the hair and force him to start running again – any man who failed to do so would rot in a cell.

Asher had enough experience to know that ruthless training was the only path to victory: every suffering endured, every action mastered, gave the fighter a better chance of survival. After a colourful career on the battlefields of Asia, Asher, a hero famed for his exploits, had been appointed Steward of the Horses, officer in charge of recruits, and training officer at the main barracks in Memphis. With a savage joy, he carried out this last office for the last time. From now on – his new appointment had been officially confirmed the previous day – he would be free of its onerous duties. As Pharaoh's emissary to foreign countries, he would pass on royal orders to the elite garrisons posted at the borders, act as charioteer to His Majesty, and fulfil the role of standard-bearer at the king's right hand.

Asher was a small man, of unpleasant appearance: the hair on his head was close-cropped, while that on his shoulders was stiff, black and thick. He had a broad chest and short, muscular legs. A scar ran across his chest from shoulder to navel, a reminder of the sword blade that had almost ended his life. Laughing uncontrollably, he had strangled his attacker with his bare hands. His deeply lined face was reminiscent of a rat's.

After spending this last morning at his favourite barracks,

Asher's thoughts were turning to the banquet that had been organized in his honour. He was heading for the washrooms when an officer came up to him.

'Forgive me for bothering you, General, but a judge would like to speak with you.'

'Who is he?'

'I've never seen him before.'

'Send him away.'

'He claims it is urgent and serious.'

'Why does he want to see me?'

'It's confidential. He says it doesn't concern anyone but you.'

'Very well. Bring him here.'

Pazair was brought to the central courtyard where the general was standing, his hands crossed behind his back. To his left, recruits were exercising to develop their muscles; to his right, archers were busy at target practice.

'What is your name?' asked Asher.

'Pazair.'

'I detest judges.'

'What do you have against them?'

'They stick their noses into everything.'

'I am making enquiries about a man who has disappeared.'

'That is not possible in regiments under my command.'

'Not even in the Sphinx's honour guard?'

'The army is still the army, even when it is taking care of its former soldiers. The Sphinx has been guarded without fail.'

'According to his wife, the former head guard is dead, and yet the authorities are asking me to authorize his transfer.'

'Then authorize it. One does not argue with the authorities' directives.'

'In this case, I must.'

The general's voice rose to a roar. 'You are young and inexperienced. Get out of here.'

'I am not under your command, General, and I want to know the truth about this guard. You appointed him to his post, did you not?'

'Be very careful, little Judge. It is not wise to cross swords with General Asher.'

Pazair stood his ground. 'You are not above the law.'

'You don't know who I am. One more false move, and I'll crush you like an insect,' and Asher marched off, leaving Pazair alone in the middle of the courtyard.

His reaction puzzled the judge. Why was he so vehement if he had nothing to be ashamed of?

As Pazair was leaving by the barracks gate, the archer who had been placed under close arrest hailed him. 'Judge Pazair?'

'What do you want?'

'Perhaps I can help you. What are you looking for?'

'Information about the former head guard of the Sphinx.'

'His military records are filed in the barracks record office. Follow me.'

'Why are you doing this?'

'If you find firm evidence against Asher, will you charge him?'

'Without hesitation.'

'Then come with me. The keeper of the records is a friend of mine, and he hates the general, too.'

The archer and the keeper of the records spoke briefly.

'To consult the barracks records,' said the keeper, 'you'd need authorization from the tjaty's office. I shall leave the office for a quarter of an hour, just long enough to go and get something to eat from the mess. If you're still here when I get back, I'll have to raise the alarm.'

Five minutes to understand the filing system, another three to find the right papyrus scroll, the rest to read the document, memorize it, put it back into its case and then disappear.

*

Back in his office, Pazair thought over what he had read. The head guard's career had been exemplary, with not a single blot on his record. The end of the papyrus offered an interesting piece of information: the man had headed a squad of four men, the two oldest posted by the sphinx's flanks, the other two at the base of the great ramp leading to the pyramid of Khufu, inside the enclosure. Since Pazair now had their names, he could question them and probably obtain the key to the enigma.

Kem came in, scowling. 'She's dead.'

'Who are you talking about?'

'The guard's widow. I patrolled in that area this morning, and Killer sensed that something was wrong. The door of the house was ajar. I found her body.'

'Any traces of violence?'

'None at all. She succumbed to old age and grief.'

Pazair asked Iarrot to check whether the army would take care of the funeral arrangements; if not, the judge would defray the costs himself. Although he might not have been responsible for the poor woman's death, he had caused her anxiety in her final days.

'Have you made any progress?' asked Kem.

'Decisive progress, I hope – although General Asher gave me no help at all. Here are the names of the four guards commanded by the missing man. Obtain their addresses.'

Iarrot arrived just as the Nubian was leaving.

'My wife is persecuting me,' grumbled Iarrot, who looked crestfallen. 'Yesterday, she refused to make dinner. If things go on like this, she'll soon be barring me from her bed. Fortunately, my daughter's dancing better than ever.'

Muttering as he worked, he sulkily filed away tablets with bad grace. 'Oh, I almost forgot,' he said. 'I investigated the craftsmen who want to work at the weapons workshops. Only one interests me.'

'A criminal?'

99

'A man mixed up in an illegal trade in amulets.'

'But has he ever been convicted of anything?'

Iarrot's face took on a look of smug satisfaction. 'It should interest you. He's a jobbing carpenter. He used to be employed as a steward on Qadash's land.'

Pazair managed to enter Qadash's waiting room, not without some difficulty. He sat down next to a small man with a tense expression. His black hair and moustache, lustreless skin and long, dry face dotted with moles lent him a sombre, rather repellent, look.

The judge greeted him. 'Waiting's difficult, isn't it?'

The little man nodded.

'Are you in a lot of pain?'

He replied with a vague wave of the hand.

'This is my first attack of toothache,' said Pazair. 'Have you ever been treated by a tooth doctor before?'

Qadash appeared. 'Judge Pazair! Are you in pain?

'Unfortunately, yes.'

'Do you know Sheshi?'

'I don't have that honour.'

'Sheshi is one of the most brilliant inventors at the palace – he has no rivals when it comes to creating new things. I order medicated plasters and fillings from him, and he has just suggested an innovation to me. Don't worry, I shan't be long.'

Qadash's manner was ingratiating, as though he were greeting a long-standing friend. If this fellow Sheshi remained as uncommunicative as he had been up to now, his conversation with the doctor was liable to be brief. Indeed, it was no more than ten minutes before Qadash came and escorted the judge into his office.

'Sit down on this folding chair and lean your head back.'

'He doesn't say much, your inventor.'

'He's a rather reserved fellow, but very upright, a man you can count on. What's the trouble?'

'A sort of generalized pain.'

'Let's have a look.'

Using a mirror to reflect a ray of sunlight, Qadash examined Pazair's teeth. 'Have you consulted anybody before?'

'Only once, in the village. A travelling tooth doctor.'

'I can see a tiny speck of decay. I shall stabilize the tooth with an effective filling: terebinth resin,* Nubian earth, honey, grains of millstone, green eye drops and fragments of copper. If it becomes loose, I shall bind it to the neighbouring molar with gold wire . . . No, that won't be necessary. You have sound, healthy teeth. From now on, take care of your gums. To prevent inflammation, I shall prescribe you a mouthwash composed of colocynth, gum, aniseed and the cut fruits of the sycamore; you must leave it outside for one whole night so that it becomes impregnated with dew. You must also rub your gums with a paste made from cinnamon, honey, gum and oil. And don't forget to chew plenty of celery. Not only is it good as a tonic and an appetizer, but it also strengthens the teeth. Now, let's talk seriously. Your teeth did not need urgent treatment. Why were you so eager to see me?'

Pazair stood up, glad to escape from the dentist's diverse array of instruments. 'About your steward.'

'I dismissed that useless idiot.'

'I mean the previous one.'

Qadash washed his hands. 'I don't remember him.'

'Try harder.'

'No, really . . .'

'Are you by any chance a collector of amulets?†

*The terebinth is a pistachio tree which yields a resin used in medicine and in ritual ingredients.

†Figurines, most often made of faience, representing the gods, symbols like the cross of life or the heart, etc. The Egyptians liked to carry them to protect themselves from harmful forces.

Although carefully washed, the dentist's hands remained red. 'I have a few, as everyone does, but I don't attach much importance to them.'

'The most beautiful ones are very valuable.'

'I expect they are.'

'Your former steward was interested in them – he even stole a few especially fine specimens. Which is what worries me. Could it be that they were stolen from you?'

'There are more and more thieves, since there are more and more foreigners in Memphis. Soon, this town will no longer be Egyptian. With his obsession with probity, the tjaty is the man chiefly responsible. Pharaoh has such trust in him that no one can criticize him – you even less than others, since he is your superior. Fortunately, your humble position in the government means you won't have to meet him.'

'Is he so daunting?'

'He's impossible. Judges who forgot that have been dismissed, but they had all committed offences. By refusing to expel foreigners under the pretext of justice, the tjaty is causing the country to decay. Have you arrested my former steward?'

'He tried to get work at the weapons workshops, but a routine check revealed his past. It's an unfortunate story to tell the truth: he sold amulets stolen from a workshop, was denounced and dismissed by the successor you chose.'

'Whom was he stealing for?'

'He doesn't know. If I had the time, I'd investigate; but I don't have any leads and there are so many other matters occupying me. The main thing is that you did not suffer from his misdeeds. Thank you for attending to me, Qadash.'

Mentmose had summoned his principal colleagues to his home; this working meeting would not be mentioned in any official document.

He summed up their reports on Judge Pazair. 'No hidden

vices, no illicit passions, no mistress, no network of relatives
. . . You have drawn me a portrait of a demi-god. Your
enquiries have proved fruitless.'

'His spiritual father, a man called Branir, lives in
Memphis, and Pazair often goes to his house.'

'An old retired doctor, inoffensive and without power.'

'He used to have the ear of the court,' objected an officer.

'He lost it long ago,' replied Mentmose sarcastically. 'No
one's life is free from shadows – and that applies to Pazair as
much as to anyone else.'

'He devotes himself to his work,' said another officer, 'and
does not flinch in front of characters like Denes or Qadash.'

'A judge with integrity and courage? Whoever would
believe in such a fairytale? Work harder and bring me back
something more believable.'

When the men had gone, Mentmose went outside and
stood beside the lake where he liked to fish, and pondered
deeply. He had the unpleasant feeling that he was not in
control of this elusive, formless situation, and was afraid he
might make a mistake which would tarnish his own
reputation.

Was Pazair an innocent, lost in the maze of Memphis, or
truly an uncommon individual, determined to forge ahead
irrespective of dangers or enemies? Whichever was the case,
he was doomed to failure.

There remained a third, extremely worrying, possibility:
that the little judge was an emissary sent by someone else,
some devious courtier at the head of a plot in which Pazair
was simply the visible part. Furious at the idea that the man
dared to defy him on his own territory, Mentmose called for
his steward and ordered him to prepare his horse and chariot.
He felt a burning desire to go into the desert and hunt hares.
Killing a few terrified creatures would relax his over-
stretched nerves.

13

Suti's right hand slid back up his mistress's back, stroked her neck, slid back down again and caressed her bottom.

'Again,' she purred.

The young man did not need to be asked twice. He loved giving pleasure. His hand became more insistent.

'No . . . I don't want to.'

Suti went on, slyly. He knew his companion's tastes and satisfied them unreservedly. She pretended to resist, then turned over and slid her legs apart to welcome in her lover.

'Are you pleased with your cockerel?' he asked some time later.

'The hens are delighted. You are an absolute godsend, my darling.'

Overwhelmed with pleasure, the young widow prepared a hearty lunch and made him promise to return the following day.

As night was falling, and after he had slept for two hours at the port in the shade of a cargo vessel, he went to Pazair's house. The judge had lit the lamps, and was sitting on the floor writing, with his dog at his side. Way-Finder allowed Suti to pass and in return he stroked the donkey.

'I'm afraid I need you,' said the judge.

'An affair of the heart?'

'I very much doubt it.'

'It's not to do with the guards, though, is it?'

'I'm afraid it is.'

'That's interesting. Can I know more, or are you sending me out blind?'

'I have set a trap for a tooth doctor named Qadash.'

Suti gave an admiring whistle. 'He's a famous man! He only treats rich people. What's he done?'

'His behaviour intrigues me. I ought to have used Kem, but he is busy elsewhere.'

'Can I do a little burglary?'

'Don't even think of it! Just follow Qadash if he leaves his house and behaves strangely.'

Suti climbed up into a persea tree. From there, he had a good view of the front door of the Qadash's house and the back entrance. He was not unhappy to be out on this restful evening. Alone at last, he could enjoy the night air and the beauty of the sky. After the lamps were extinguished and silence fell once again over the great house, a silhouette slipped out by way of the stable door. The man wore a cloak, but the white hair and profile definitely belonged to the man Pazair had described.

It was easy to follow him. Although wary, Qadash walked slowly and did not turn round. He headed for a district which was being rebuilt. Former government buildings which had fallen into disrepair had been demolished, and piles of bricks obstructed the roadway. Qadash walked round a mountain of debris and disappeared. Suti climbed up it, taking care not to dislodge any bricks and so betray his presence. Once he reached the top, he spotted a fire, round which three men were standing. One of them was Qadash.

They took off their cloaks and revealed that they were naked, save for leather sheaths hiding their penises; each wore three feathers in his hair. Brandishing a short staff made of jet in either hand, they danced and pretended to attack each other. Qadash's partners were younger than he was, and they sprang about, shouting like wild men. Although he found it difficult to keep up, Qadash joined in with gusto.

The dance lasted for more than an hour. Then, suddenly, one of the actors took off the leather sheath and revealed his manhood. His friends immediately did the same. As Qadash was showing signs of tiredness, they gave him palm wine to drink before leading him into a new frenzy.

Pazair listened attentively to Suti's account.

'That's strange,' he said.

'You don't know Libyan customs,' said Suti. 'That kind of celebration is typical.'

'What do they hope to achieve?'

'Virility, fertility, the ability to seduce women. As they dance, they acquire new energy. Qadash seems to find it difficult.'

'So he must feel his powers are waning.'

'From what I saw, he has reason to to. But there's nothing illegal in what they did, is there?'

'Basically, no. But this man claims to hate foreigners, yet hasn't forgotten his Libyan roots and indulges in customs which the members of polite society, whom he treats, would strongly disapprove of.'

'Have I at least been useful?'

'Invaluable.'

'Next time, Judge Pazair, send me to spy on women dancing.'

Using their powers of persuasion, Kem and his baboon combed every inch of Memphis and its suburbs, to trace the four men who had been guards at the Sphinx.

The Nubian did not speak to the judge until Iarrot had left; he did not trust the scribe. When Killer entered the office, Brave hid under his master's chair.

'Any problems?' asked Pazair.

'I have their addresses.'

'I trust you got them without using of violence?'

'Not even a trace of it.'

'First thing tomorrow, we shall question them.'

'They've all disappeared.'

Pazair laid down his brush in astonishment. When he had refused to ratify that mundane administrative document, he had never imagined that he was lifting the lid on a cauldron full of mysteries.

'Where have they gone? Do you know?'

'Two have left to live in the Delta, two in the Theban region. I have the names of the villages.'

'Pack your travelling bag.'

Pazair spent the evening at Branir's house. On his way there, he had the feeling he was being followed. He slowed his pace, and turned round two or three times, but saw no further trace of the man he thought he had glimpsed. No doubt he had been mistaken.

Sitting opposite Branir, on the terrace of his flower-covered house, he savoured a cup of cool beer and listened to the breath of the great city as it dozed off to sleep. Here and there, lights indicated people who liked to stay up late, or busy scribes still at work.

In Branir's company, the world came to a halt. Pazair would have loved to hold on to this moment like a jewel, keep it safe in the palm of his hand, and prevent it from dissolving into the blackness of time.

'Has Neferet received her posting yet?' he asked.

'Not yet, but it should come any day now. She is staying in a room at the medical school.'

'Who makes the decision?'

'An assembly of doctors, led by the head physician, Nebamon. Neferet will be given a post that is not too taxing,

107

then the difficulty will be increased as she gains experience. You seem rather sombre, Pazair. Anyone would think you'd lost your love of life.'

Pazair outlined the facts. 'A good many disturbing coincidences, wouldn't you say?'

'What is your theory?'

'It's too soon to have one. A crime has been committed – I'm sure of that. But what sort of crime, and how serious? I'm worried, perhaps without reason. Sometimes I wonder if I should go on, but I cannot take responsibility, however small, unless it is in full agreement with my conscience.'

'The heart devises plans and guides the individual; as for the personality, it retains what has been gained and preserves what the heart sees.'*

'My personality won't be weak. I shall explore what I have uncovered.'

'Never lose sight of Egypt's happiness. Pay no attention to your own well-being. If your actions are righteous, they will come back to you many times over.'

'If we tolerate a man's disappearance without question, if an official document is as good as a lie, does that not threaten Egypt's greatness?'

'You're right to be worried.'

'If your spirit is with mine, I shall confront the most fearsome dangers.'

'You don't lack courage, but be more clear-sighted and be careful to avoid certain obstacles. Confronting them head-on will only wound you. Go round them, learn to use your opponent's strength. Be as supple as a reed and as patient as granite.'

'Patience is not my strong point,' said Pazair.

'Build yourself, as an architect works his raw material.'

---

*Branir is passing on to his pupil the words of the sages. These words were collected together as maxims, in the text known as *Teachings*.

'Do you advise me not to go to the Delta?'

'You have made your decision.'

Nebamon looked most impressive in his robe of pleated linen with its coloured fringes. Haughty and beautifully groomed, he opened the plenary session in the great hall at the Memphis medical school. Ten renowned physicians, none of whom had ever been found guilty of the death of a patient, were about to appoint the young, newly qualified doctors to their first posts. Ordinarily these decisions were made in a spirit of benevolence and did not lead to arguments. And this time, too, the task would be swiftly carried out.

'Now for the case of Neferet,' said one of the doctors. 'She has received glowing reports from Memphis, Sais and Thebes. It is said she has a brilliant, even exceptional, gift.'

'Yes, but she's a woman,' objected Nebamon.

'She isn't the first.'

'Neferet is intelligent, I admit, but she lacks stamina. Experience may well prove too much for her theoretical knowledge.'

'She has passed through numerous training courses without faltering,' a doctor reminded him.

'During training, the students have tutors,' said Nebamon smoothly. 'When she's alone with the patients, she may lose her footing. Her capacity for resilience worries me; I cannot help wondering if she has taken a wrong decision in following our path.'

'What do you suggest?'

'A rather severe trial and difficult patients. If she overcomes the difficulties, we shall congratulate ourselves. If not, we shall learn from it.'

Without raising his voice, Nebamon received his colleagues' assent. He was about to give Neferet the most unpleasant surprise of her budding career. When he had broken her, he would pick her up out of the ditch and take her back into his fold, grateful and submissive.

Neferet was devastated, and felt like going off on her own to weep.

Hard work did not daunt her, but she had not expected to be placed in charge of a military hospital, where sick and wounded soldiers were treated on their return from Asia. Thirty or more men were stretched out on mats. Some were on the point of death, others were delirious, some incontinent. The officer responsible for health in the barracks had not given the young woman any instructions; he had simply left her there. He was obeying orders.

Neferet pulled herself together. Whatever the cause of this punishment might be, she must do her job and take care of these unfortunate men. After examining the barracks' medical stores, she began to feel more confident. The most urgent task was to ease severe pain. She crushed roots of mandragora to extract a potent substance which served as both an analgesic and a narcotic. Then she mixed scented dill, date juice and grape juice, and boiled the result in wine. For four consecutive days, she would give the sick men this potion to drink.

She called to a young recruit who was cleaning the barracks' courtyard. 'You're going to help me.'

'Me? But I—'

'I'm appointing you my orderly.'

'The commander—'

'Go and see him immediately, and tell him that thirty men are going to die if he refuses to let you help me.'

The commander gave his permission. He did not care for the cruel game in which he had been forced to participate.

When the new recruit entered the hospital, he almost fainted.

Neferet comforted him, and told him, 'Raise their heads

gently so that I can pour the remedy into their mouths. Then we shall wash them and clean the room.'

To begin with, the lad closed his eyes and stopped breathing; but, reassured by Neferet's calm demeanour, he forgot his disgust and was happy to see that the potion took effect quickly. Shouts and moans died down; several soldiers fell asleep.

One of the less seriously ill grabbed Neferet's leg as she gave him his medicine.

'Let go of me,' she ordered.

'Certainly not, my beauty – I'm not letting a prize like you escape me. I'm going to give you pleasure.'

The orderly let go of the patient's head, which fell back heavily on to the ground, and knocked him out with a punch. The man's grip slackened, and Neferet freed herself.

'Thank you,' she said.

'Weren't you afraid?'

'Of course I was.'

'If you want, I'll give them all the same sleeping draught.'

'Only if it's necessary.'

'What's wrong with them?'

'They've got dysentery.'

'Is it serious?'

'It's an illness which I know and which I shall cure.'

'In Asia, they drink stagnant water. I'd rather sweep the barracks.'

As soon as everywhere was perfectly clean, Neferet gave her patients potions based on coriander, to calm their spasms and purify the intestines. Then she crushed pomegranate roots with brewer's yeast, filtered the result through fabric and let it rest for a whole night. The yellow fruit, filled with bright red pips, produced a remedy which was effective against diarrhoea and dysentery.

Neferet treated the most acute cases with a clyster made

from honey, fermented vegetable matter, sweet beer and salt, which she introduced into the anus with a copper horn. Five days of intensive treatment produced excellent results. Cow's milk and honey, the only foods she allowed, finished the job of putting the patients back on their feet again.

Nebamon was in a very good mood when he arrived to inspect the barracks' health facilities six days after Neferet had taken up her post. He pronounced himself satisfied, and decided to finish off his inspection with the dysentery cases in the hospital. The young woman would be exhausted and at the end of her tether. She would beg him to grant her another post and would agree to work in his team.

A recruit was sweeping the floor of the infirmary, whose door stood wide open. A draught of fresh air was purifying the room, which was empty and whitewashed.

'I must be mistaken,' said Nebamon to the recruit. 'Do you know where Doctor Neferet is working?'

'First office on your left.'

He found her writing names on a papyrus.

'Neferet, where are the patients?'

'Convalescing.'

'That's impossible!'

'Here is the list of patients, the types of treatment used, and the dates when they left the hopsital.'

'But how . . . ?'

'I must thank you for entrusting me with this task, which has enabled me to check how well our medicine works.' She spoke without animosity, with a gentle light in her eyes.

'I think I have made a mistake,' said Nebamon.

'What do you mean?'

'I'm an idiot.'

'That's not what people say.'

'Listen to me, Neferet . . .'

'You shall have a complete report first thing tomorrow.

Will you be kind enough to notify me about my next post as quickly as possible?'

Mentmose was in a fury. In the great house, not one servant would dare move until his anger had been appeased.

During periods of extreme tension, his head seethed, and he scratched himself until he drew blood. At his feet lay shreds of papyrus, the miserable remains of his subordinates' reports, which he had torn up.

Nothing.

No consistent evidence, no notorious faults, no hints of malpractice: Pazair was behaving like an honest – and therefore dangerous – judge. Mentmose was not in the habit of underestimating his opponents. This one belonged to a formidable breed and would not be easy to thwart. No decisive action could be taken until he had an answer to one question: who was manipulating Pazair?

14

The wind swelled the broad sail of the single-masted boat as it sailed through the watery expanses of the Delta. The pilot steered the vessel with skill, making use of the current, while his passengers, Judge Pazair, Kem and Killer, rested in the cabin at the centre of the deck; their luggage was stowed on the roof. At the prow, the captain sounded the depth of the water with a long pole and gave orders to the crew. The eye of Horus, which was drawn on the prow and on the poop, protected the boat on its journey.

Pazair emerged from the cabin and leant over the rail, gazing out at the countryside, which he was seeing for the first time. How far away the valley was, with its fields tightly enclosed by two deserts. Here, the river divided into branches and canals, irrigating towns, villages, palm groves, fields and vines. Hundreds of birds – swallows, hoopoes, white herons, crows, larks, sparrows, cormorants, pelicans, wild geese, ducks, cranes and storks – flew across a soft blue sky, dotted here and there with clouds. The judge felt as though he were looking at a sea filled with reeds and papyrus; on mounds which stood clear of the water, thickets of willow and acacia protected single-storey whitewashed houses. Surely this must be the primordial marsh the old authors had spoken of, the earthly incarnation of the ocean which surrounded the world and from which the new sun emerged each day.

Men hunting hippopotamus signalled to the boat to change direction. They were pursuing a male, and had wounded it. It had just dived, and there was a risk that it would surface again suddenly and overturn a boat, even a sizeable one. The monster would fight fiercely for its life.

The captain did not ignore the warning; he chose to take 'the waters of Ra', which formed the easternmost branch of the Nile, leading in a north-easterly direction. Close to Bubastis, the city of the goddess Bastet, whose symbol was a cat, he directed the boat into the 'channel of gentle water', along Wadi Toumilat, towards the Bitter Lakes; the wind was blowing hard. To the right, beyond a pool where buffalo were bathing, was a hamlet, sheltered by tamarisk trees.

The boat tied up and the gangplank was thrown down. Pazair, who was not a good sailor, swayed as he walked down it. At the sight of Killer, a group of children ran away. Their cries alerted the peasants, who came to deal with the new arrivals, brandishing pitchforks.

'You have nothing to fear. I am Judge Pazair, and my companions represent the guards.'

The pitchforks were lowered, and the judge was taken to the village headman, a grumpy old man.

'I would like to speak with the ex-soldier who returned home a few weeks ago.'

'That will be impossible on this earth.'

'Is he dead?'

'Some soldiers brought back his body. We buried him in our burial ground.'

'What did he die of?'

'Old age.'

'Did you examine the body?'

'It was mummified.'

'What did the soldiers say to you?'

'They weren't very talkative.'

Exhuming a mummy would have been sacrilege. Pazair

and his companions got back on the boat and left for the village where the second ex-soldier lived.

'You'll have to walk across the marsh,' said the captain. 'There are dangerous islets around there, and I must keep well out from the bank.'

The baboon did not like the water. Kem talked to it at length and managed to persuade it to venture along a path he had opened up in the reeds. The monkey was anxious and kept turning round, darting glances to right and left. The judge strode impatiently ahead, towards little houses clustered together at the top of a mound. Kem watched the animal's reactions carefully. It was confident in its own strength, and would not behave like this without good reason.

Killer let out a loud cry, knocked over the judge and seized the tail of a small crocodile which was slithering along in the muddy water. Just as the reptile opened its mouth, he pulled it backwards. The 'great fish', as the river folk called it, was quite capable of ambushing sheep and goats which came down to drink in the pools and killing them.

The crocodile struggled, but it was too young and too small to resist the fury of the baboon, which plucked it out of the mud and hurled it several paces away.

'Thank him,' Pazair told the Nubian. 'I predict promotion for him.'

The village headman was sitting on a low chair with a sloping seat and a rounded back, nicely settled in the shade of a sycamore tree. He was enjoying a copious meal of poultry, onions and a jug of beer, which had been arranged in a flat-bottomed basket.

He invited his guests to share the food. Killer, whose heroic deed was already the talk of the marshes, tore eagerly at a chicken thigh with his teeth.

'We are looking for a former soldier who has come to live out his retirement here,' said Pazair.

'Alas, Judge, all we have seen of him is his mummy. The

army took charge of transporting the body, and paid the costs of burial. Our burial ground is modest, but eternity there is as happy as anywhere else.'

'Were you told the cause of his death?'

'The soldiers didn't say much, but I demanded to know. An accident, apparently.'

'What kind of accident?'

'That's all I know.'

On the boat taking him back to Memphis, Pazair could not conceal his disappointment. 'A total failure: the head guard has vanished, two of his men are dead, and the other two have probably been embalmed too.'

'Then you won't be setting out on another journey?' asked Kem.

'I must. I want to set the record straight.'

'I shall be happy to see Thebes again.'

'What do you think of all this?'

'That the fact that these men are dead is preventing you from discovering the key to the mystery – and so much the better.'

'Don't you want to know the truth?'

'When it's too dangerous, I'd rather not. The truth has already cost me my nose, and now it could rob you of your life.'

When Suti came home at dawn, Pazair was already at work, his dog at his feet.

'Didn't you sleep? Nor did I. I need some rest. My poultry keeper's wearing me out – she's insatiable and wants to try absolutely everything. I've brought some hot-cakes; the baker has just made them.'

Brave was the first to be fed; then the two friends had breakfast together. Although he was half-dead for lack of sleep, Suti saw that Pazair was deeply troubled.

'Either you're tired, or something is seriously worrying you. Is it something you can't resolve?'

'I can't talk about it.'

'Not even to me? It must be really serious.'

'I'm floundering, but I'm certain I've stumbled upon a criminal matter.'

'What is it? A murder?'

'Probably.'

'Be careful, Pazair. Crimes like that are rare in Egypt. Shouldn't you let sleeping dogs lie? You might annoy some important people.'

'That comes with the job.'

'Doesn't crime come under the tjaty's jurisdiction?'

'Provided it is proven.'

'Whom do you suspect?'

'I know only one thing for certain: soldiers have been involved in a plot. Soldiers who must be under the command of General Asher.'

Suti whistled admiringly. 'You're aiming high! A military plot?'

'I'm not ruling it out.'

'What's it for?'

'I don't know.'

'I'm your man, Pazair.'

'What do you mean?'

'I am seriously intending to enlist in the army. I shall swiftly become an excellent soldier, an officer – perhaps a general. In any case, a hero. I shall find out everything about Asher. If he's guilty of something, I shall find out, and then you'll find out, too.'

'It's too risky,' said Pazair.

'No, it's exciting. At long last, the adventure I've been dreaming of! And what if the two of us end up saving Egypt? If you mention military plots, you're really saying that a section of the army is planning to seize power.'

'That's a fine plan, Suti, but I'm not yet sure if the situation is that desperate.'

118

'What do you know about it? Tell me what to do.'

A charioteer officer, accompanied by two archers, arrived at Pazair's office towards the middle of the morning.

The man was curt but polite. 'I am here to regularize a transfer which was submitted to you for approval.'

'Are you referring to the former head of the Sphinx's guard?'

'I am.'

'I refuse to place my seal upon it before he has appeared before me.'

'My orders are to take you to where he is, in order to bring an end to the matter.'

Suti was sound asleep, Kem was on patrol, and Iarrot had not yet arrived. Pazair dismissed all thoughts of danger. What organized body, even the army, would dare make an attempt on a judge's life? He agreed to climb into the officer's chariot after stroking Brave, whose eyes were full of anxiety.

The vehicle sped out of Memphis and set off along a road which skirted the fields and plunged into the desert. There towered the pyramids raised by the pharaohs of the Old Kingdom, surrounded by magnificent tombs bearing witness to the genius of painters and sculptors.

The step-pyramid at Saqqara, the work of Djoser and Imhotep, loomed over the countryside; its gigantic stone steps formed a staircase to the heavens, enabling the king's soul to climb up to the sun and descend to earth. Only the top of the monument was visible, for a thick wall with a single carefully guarded gate hid it from the outside world. Within the great inner courtyard, Pharaoh would experience the rites of regeneration when his powers waned.

Pazair breathed in great lungfuls of the desert air, which was sharp and dry; he liked this red earth, this sea of burnt rocks and yellow sand, this void filled with the voices of the ancestors. Here, a man was stripped of all but the essentials.

119

'Where are you taking me?'

'We've arrived.'

The chariot halted before a house with tiny windows, far from all habitation; several sarcophagi were leaning against the wall. The wind raised clouds of sand. Not a single small tree or flower was visible; in the distance, there was nothing but pyramids and tombs. A rocky hill blotted out any view of the palm groves and fields. On the fringes of death, at the heart of solitude, the place seemed utterly abandoned.

'It's here.'

The officer clapped his hands.

Intrigued, Pazair got down from the chariot. The place was ideal for an ambush, and no one knew where he was. He thought of Neferet; to die without revealing his love for her would haunt his soul eternally.

The door of the house creaked open. A thin man appeared on the threshold. His skin was very white, his face and hands endlessly long and his legs frail. His thick black eyebrows joined above his nose; his thin lips seemed devoid of blood. There were brownish stains on his goatskin apron.

His dark eyes stared at Pazair. The judge had never encountered eyes like them before; their gaze was intense, glacial, as sharp as a blade. He resisted it.

'Djui is the official embalmer,' explained the lieutenant charioteer.

The man bowed his head.

'Follow me, Judge Pazair.

Djui stood aside to allow the officer to pass, followed by the judge, who entered the embalming workshop where Djui mummified bodies on a stone table. Iron hooks, obsidian knives and sharpened stones hung on the walls; on shelves, there were pots of oil and unguents, and sacks filled with natron, which was vital for embalming. In accordance with the law, the embalmer had to live outside the town; he belonged to a feared caste, made up of wild, silent men.

The three men began walking down the steps that led to an immense cellar. They were worn and slippery. Djui's torch flickered. On the ground lay mummies of varying sizes. Pazair shivered.

'I have received a report concerning the former head guard of the Sphinx,' explained the officer. 'You were sent the request for transfer in error. He has died as a result of an accident.'

'A terrible accident, indeed.'

'What makes you say that?'

'Because it killed at least three men, maybe more.'

The officer shrugged. 'I don't know about that.'

'How did the accident happen?'

'I don't know the exact details. The head guard was found dead and his body was brought here. Unfortunately, a scribe made a mistake; instead of ordering his burial, he requested a transfer. It was a simple administrative error.'

'What about the body?'

'I wanted to show it to you, so as to put an end to this regrettable matter.'

'Mummified, of course?'

'Of course.'

'Has the body been placed in the sarcophagus?'

The officer looked at the embalmer, who shook his head.

'Then the final rites have not yet been celebrated,' concluded Pazair.

'That is true, but—'

'Then show me this mummy.'

Djui led the judge and the officer into the depths of the cave. He pointed out the head guard's body, which was standing upright in an alcove, wrapped in bandages. It bore a number written in red ink.

The embalmer presented the officer with the label which would be fixed on to the mummy.

'All that remains is for you to affix your seal,' the officer told Pazair.

Djui stood behind Pazair. The light flickered more and more.

'Ensure that this mummy remains here, Officer, and in this condition. If it disappears, or if anybody damages it, I shall hold you personally responsible.'

15

'Can you tell me where Neferet is working?' asked Pazair.

'You seem preoccupied,' commented Branir.

'It's very important,' said Pazair. 'I may have obtained material proof, but I can't do anything with it unless I have the help of a doctor.'

'I saw her last night. She has overcome an epidemic of dysentery and cured thirty soldiers in less than a week.'

'Soldiers? What job was she given?'

'Nebamon was trying to bully her.'

'I'll beat him senseless.'

'Is that really in accordance with the duties of a judge?'

'That bully deserves to be punished.'

'He was only exercising his authority,' Branir pointed out.

'You know that's not true. Tell me the truth: what new ordeal has that useless idiot subjected her to?'

'It seems he has mended his ways. Neferet is working at the Temple of Sekhmet, creating new remedies and potions.'

Near the Temple of Sekhmet, workshops processed hundreds of plants which were used as the basis for prescribed preparations. Daily deliveries guaranteed the freshness of the potions, which were sent out to doctors in towns and in the countryside. Neferet was supervising, making sure that the prescriptions were properly made up. Compared to her previous post, this was a step backwards. Nebamon had presented it to her as a compulsory phase and a time of rest before taking care of the sick again, and, ever professional, the young woman had not protested.

At noon, they all left the workshop and went to eat in the communal dining room. Colleagues chatted easily about new remedies, and lamented their failures. Two specialists were talking to Neferet, who was smiling. Pazair was certain they were paying court to her.

His heart beat faster; he plucked up the courage to interrupt them. 'Neferet?'

She stopped. 'Were you looking for me?'

'Branir told me about the injustices you suffered. They revolt me.'

'I was happy to be able to cure people. The rest is unimportant.'

'I need your help.'

'Are you ill?'

'I have a delicate enquiry which entails the involvement of a doctor. A simple expert opinion, nothing more.'

Kem drove the chariot with a steady hand; Killer crouched down, trying not to look at the road. Neferet and Pazair stood side by side, their wrists tied to the shell of the vehicle with leather straps, to prevent them falling out. As the chariot ran over bumps in the road, their bodies were jolted together. Neferet seemed not to notice, but Pazair felt a joy that was as secret as it was intense. He wished that this short journey could be endless and that the road could get worse and worse. When his leg touched Neferet's he did not move it away; he was afraid she'd rebuke him, but no rebuke came. Being so close to her, smelling her perfume, believing that she accepted this contact . . . the dream was sublime.

Two soldiers were on guard outside the embalmer's workshop.

'I am Judge Pazair. Let us pass.'

'Our orders are clear: nobody comes in. The place has been requisitioned.'

'No one may resist the law. Are you forgetting that we are in Egypt?'

'Our orders—'

'Stand aside.'

The baboon moved forward and bared its teeth; it stood on its hind legs, its eyes staring and its arms bent, ready to spring. Little by little, Kem slackened the chain.

The two soldiers gave in. Kem kicked open the door.

Djui was sitting on the embalming table, eating dried fish.

'Take us downstairs,' ordered Pazair.

Kem and Killer searched the darkened room suspiciously while the judge and the doctor went down into the cellar, lit by Djui's torch.

'What a horrible place,' whispered Neferet. 'And I love the air and the light so much.'

'To be honest, I'm not very comfortable, either.'

The embalmer walked down the staircase with his usual speed, not missing his footing once.

The mummy had not been moved; Pazair could see that no one had touched it.

'Here is your patient,' he said. 'I shall unwrap him under your directions.'

The judge took off the bandages carefully, revealing an amulet in the shape of an eye, placed on the mummy's forehead. There was a deep wound to the neck, undoubtedly caused by an arrow.

'There's no need to go any further. In your opinion, how old was this man?'

'About twenty,' replied Neferet.

Mentmose was wondering how to resolve the press of animals and vehicles that was making the daily lives of

Memphis's citizens so difficult: too many donkeys, too many oxen, too many chariots, too many itinerant vendors, too many people chattering, all clogging up the narrow streets and blocking the flow of traffic. Every year he drew up decrees, each one less practicable than the last, and did not even bother submitting them to the tjaty. All he did was promise improvements which nobody believed would ever happen. From time to time, an influx of guards quietened frayed tempers. A street would be unblocked for a few days by a ban on stopping animals or carts, those who infringed the ban would be fined, and then bad habits would once more regain the upper hand.

Mentmose made sure his subordinates felt the weight of responsibility, and was careful not to give them the means to eliminate the problems. By remaining above the hurly-burly and plunging his colleagues into it, he preserved his own excellent reputation.

When Judge Pazair's arrival was announced, he emerged from his office to greet him in the waiting room. Little niceties like that made a good impression.

The judge's sombre face did not augur well.

'I have an extremely busy morning,' said Mentmose, 'but I am at your disposal.'

'I consider that essential.'

'You seem shaken.'

'I am.'

Mentmose scratched his forehead. He took the judge into his office, sending away his personal scribe. Tense, he sat down on a fine chair with feet in the shape of a bull's hooves. Pazair remained standing.

'I'm listening,' said Mentmose.

'A charioteer officer took me to see Djui, the official army embalmer. He showed me the mummy of the man I have been looking for.'

'The former Sphinx guard? Then he really is dead?'

'That's what they tried to make me believe, anyway.'

'What do you mean?'

'As the final rites had not been celebrated, I unwrapped the upper part of the mummy under the direction of Doctor Neferet. The body is that of a man of about twenty who was killed by an arrow. It is clearly not the body of the former soldier.'

Mentmose looked thunderstruck. 'That's unbelievable!'

'What is more,' the judge continued imperturbably, 'two soldiers tried to stop me entering the embalming workshop. When I came out, they had disappeared.'

'What is the chariot officer's name?'

'I don't know.'

'That's a serious omission.'

'Don't you think he'd have lied to me?'

On second thoughts, Mentmose agreed. He asked, 'Where is the body?'

'At Djui's house – he's guarding it. I shall draw up a detailed report, which will include witness statements from Doctor Neferet, the embalmer and my guard, Kem.'

Mentmose frowned. 'Are you satisfied with Kem?'

'His conduct is exemplary.'

'His past hardly speaks in his favour.'

'He helps me most effectively.'

'Don't trust him.'

'Let us get back to the mummy.'

Mentmose detested this type of situation, in which he was not master of the game. 'My men will go and fetch it and we shall examine it. We must find out who the man was.'

'We must also know if we are in the presence of a death resulting from a military engagement or from a crime.'

'A crime? Surely you don't think . . . ?'

'For my part, I am continuing my enquiries.'

'In what direction?'

'I am sworn to silence.'

'Are you defying me?'

'That is an ill-chosen question.'

'I am as lost as you are in this muddle. Shouldn't we work together?'

'I consider it more important for justice to be independent.'

Mentmose's anger made the walls of his headquarters shake. Fifty senior officials were dismissed that very day, and deprived of numerous benefits. For the first time since he had attained the summit of power, he had not been correctly informed. Such a failure cast a damning light on his system. But he would not allow himself to be struck down without fighting back.

Alas, the army seemed to have instigated these manoeuvres, the reasons for which remained beyond his comprehension. Advancing into that territory carried risks Mentmose would not run. If General Asher, whose recent promotions had rendered him untouchable, was the mastermind, there was no chance of striking him down.

Giving the little judge free rein presented many advantages. He would involve no one but himself and would, with all the zeal of youth, take virtually no precautions. He ran the risk of forcing open forbidden doors and infringing laws he did not know existed. By following his tracks, Mentmose could exploit the results of his enquiries while remaining in the shadows. It was as good as making an ally of him, until the day when he no longer needed him.

One irritating question remained: why had this drama been staged? Whoever was behind it had underestimated Pazair, believing that the strangeness of the place, its stifling climate and the oppressive presence of death would prevent the judge from examining the mummy closely, and would induce him to leave after placing his seal upon it. The result had in fact been the opposite: far from losing interest in the matter, Pazair was even more determined to resolve it.

Mentmose tried to reassure himself: the disappearance of one humble ex-soldier, the holder of an honorary post, wasn't going to topple the state! No doubt it was just a petty crime, committed by a soldier who was being protected by some senior military man – probably Asher or one of his acolytes. That was the line of enquiry that ought to be pursued.

16

On the first day of spring, Egyptians honoured the dead and also their own ancestors. As the mild winter drew to a close, the nights became suddenly cool because of the gusty desert wind. In all the great burial grounds, families venerated the memory of the dead by laying flowers in the shrines of their tombs, which opened on to the outside world.

There was no stark frontier between life and death, and so the living feasted with the departed, whose souls entered the flames of lamps. The darkness was filled with light, celebrating the meeting of this world with the world beyond. At Abydos, the sacred city of Osiris where the mysteries of resurrection were celebrated, the priests placed little boats on the tops of the tombs, representing the journey towards paradise.

After lighting sacred lamps in all the main temples at Memphis, King Ramses headed for Giza. He prepared to enter the great pyramid alone, as he did on the same day each year, and meditate before the sarcophagus of Khufu. At the heart of the immense monument, the pharaoh was nourished with the power he needed to unite the Two Lands of Upper and Lower Egypt, and make them prosper. He would gaze upon the builder's golden mask and gold cubit, which provided him with inspiration. When the time came for his regeneration ritual, he would lift up the Testament of the Gods and display it to the country.

The full moon shone down upon the plateau where the three pyramids stood.

Dressed only in a simple white kilt and broad gold collar, Ramses arrived at the outer wall of Khufu's monument, which was guarded by handpicked soldiers. The guards bowed and drew back the bolts. The king passed through the gate and began climbing the sloping walkway, which was paved with limestone flags. Soon, he would reach the Great Pyramid's entrance, whose secret mechanism was known only to Pharaoh.

This encounter with immortality affected the king more intensely with each year that passed. Without the vital energy the rites provided, Pharaoh could not carry out the exhausting task of ruling Egypt.

Slowly, Ramses climbed up to the great gallery and entered the sarcophagus chamber. Not even in his worst nightmare would he have dreamt that the country's energy centre could be transformed into a sterile hell.

Down at the docks, everyone was celebrating the feast day: the boats were decorated with flowers, beer flowed freely, sailors danced with bold-eyed girls, and itinerant musicians entertained the large crowds. Pazair had taken Brave for a short walk, and was retreating from the hubbub when a familiar voice hailed him.

'Judge Pazair! Surely you're not leaving already?'

From the midst of a crowd of revellers Denes's square, bearded face emerged. The ship owner jostled his way through the throng and joined the judge. 'What a beautiful day,' he said. 'Everyone's having fun and forgetting their cares.'

'I don't care for the noise.'

'You're too serious for your age.'

'It's difficult to change the way we are.'

'Life will take care of that.'

'You seem very cheerful.'

'Business is good,' said Denes. 'My cargoes arrive on time, my men obey me without question. What is there to complain about?'

'It seems you don't bear grudges.'

'You did your duty – I can't hold that against you. And besides, there's the good news.'

'What good news?'

'Because this is a feast day, several minor sentences have been annulled by the palace. It's an old Memphis custom, which had more or less fallen into disuse. I'm lucky enough to be one of the beneficiaries.'

Pazair turned pale. He could not conceal his anger. 'How did you contrive that?'

'I told you, it's the festival, just the festival. In the document you drew up, charging me, you forgot to specify that my case was not to be eligible for clemency. Play the game, Pazair. You've won, and I haven't lost.' Denes tried hard to make Pazair share his good humour. 'I'm not your enemy, Judge. In business, we sometimes pick up bad habits. My wife and I think you were right to teach us a lesson, and we shall learn from it.'

'Do you truly mean that?'

'I do. Forgive me, but I must go now – someone's waiting for me.'

Pazair was mortified. He had been impatient and vain, in such a hurry to see justice done that he had neglected the letter of the law. He turned to go, but found his way blocked by a military parade led by the triumphant General Asher.

Mentmose sat at his desk, looking confident and very much at his ease. 'The reason I summoned you here, Judge Pazair,' he said, 'is to tell you the results of my enquiries. The mummy you found is that of a young recruit killed in Asia during a skirmish. He was hit by an arrow and died instantly. Because of a similarity in names, his case was confused with that of the Sphinx's head guard. The scribes responsible claim it wasn't their fault. No one tried to mislead you. We thought there was a conspiracy, when in fact it was merely incompetence. You look sceptical, but you needn't be. I've checked every point.'

'I don't doubt your word.'

'I'm glad to hear it.'

'Nevertheless, the guard still hasn't been found.'

'That is strange, I agree. Perhaps he's in hiding, trying to escape some army disciplinary matter?'

'Two veterans who were serving under him died in an "accident".' Pazair emphasized the last word.

Mentmose scratched his head. 'What's suspicious about that?'

'The army ought to have a record of the incident, and you ought to have been informed.'

'Not at all. That sort of incident isn't my concern.'

Pazair tried to drive Mentmose into a corner. According to Kem, Mentmose was quite capable of orchestrating this affair in order to carry out a vast purge of his own administrative staff, certain members of which were beginning to criticize his methods.

'Aren't we over-dramatizing the situation?' asked Mentmose. 'The whole affair's just a chain of unfortunate circumstances.'

'Two ex-soldiers and the wife of the head guard are dead, and he himself has disappeared. Those are the facts. Couldn't you ask the military authorities to send you their report on the . . . accident?'

Mentmose stared at the end of his writing brush. 'That would be considered highly undesirable. The army doesn't like interference from the civilian security forces.'

'Then I'll attend to it myself.'

The two men took leave of each other with glacial politeness.

'General Asher has just left on a mission abroad,' an army scribe told Pazair.

'When will he be back?'

'That's a military secret.'

'Whom should I see, in his absence, to obtain a report on the accident that occurred recently at the Great Sphinx?'

'I can certainly help you. Oh, I almost forgot. General Asher entrusted me with a document which I was to send you. As you're here, I shall hand it to you in person. You must sign the register.' He handed Pazair a papyrus scroll.

Pazair removed the linen tie that kept the papyrus rolled up, and began to read. The text related the regrettable circumstances leading to the deaths of the head guard and his four men, following a routine inspection. The five had climbed on to the head of the Sphinx, to check that the stone was in good condition and identify any damage caused by sandstorms. One of them, in a moment of clumsiness, had slipped and dragged his companions down with him. The four ex-soldiers had been buried in their home villages, two in the Delta, two in the south. As for the head guard's body, because of his honorary position, it had been kept in an army shrine and would receive long, careful embalming. On his return from Asia, the general himself would lead the funeral ceremonies.

Pazair signed the register, confirming that he had indeed received the document.

'Is there anything else I can help you with?' asked the scribe.

'Thank you, but there's nothing more.'

Pazair wished he hadn't accepted Suti's invitation. Before enlisting, his friend wanted to celebrate the event in the most famous ale-house in Memphis. The judge thought constantly of Neferet, of the sun-bright face that lit up his dreams. Lost among the gleeful revellers, Pazair had no interest in the naked Nubian dancing girls or their supple bodies.

The customers sat on soft cushions, with jars of wine and beer lined up in front of them.

'You don't touch the girls,' explained Suti, beaming all over his face. 'They're here to excite us. Don't worry, Pazair, the lady of the house provides an excellent contraceptive made from crushed acacia thorns, honey and dates.'

Everyone knew that acacia thorns contained an acid which destroyed the fertile power of sperm, and from their earliest amorous trysts adolescents used this simple means of devoting themselves safely to pleasure.

About fifteen young women, veiled in diaphanous linen, came out of the small bedrooms that led off the central room. They were heavily made up, with lips painted red and eyes accentuated with kohl, and wore lotus flowers in their loose hair. Heavy bracelets jingled at their wrists and ankles as they approached their delighted guests. Couples formed instinctively and disappeared into the bedrooms, each one screened from the next by curtains.

As Pazair had rejected offers from two delightful dancers, he remained alone with Suti, who did not want to leave him on his own.

Then another woman appeared: Sababu, the owner of the ale-house. She was about thirty, and was naked save for a heavy wig of blonde ringlets and a belt of shells and coloured pearls. They clinked together as she danced slowly and played the lyre. Suti gazed in fascination at her tattoos, a lily on her left thigh, close to her pubis, and the god Bes above the black fleece of her sex – this one was designed to drive away venereal diseases. Sababu was more fascinating than even the most beautiful of her girls. Flexing her long, smooth legs, she danced slowly and lasciviously to the rhythm of the music.

Her skin was freshly oiled, surrounding her with an enchanting perfume.

When she approached the two men, Suti could not control his passion.

'I like you,' she told him, 'and I think you like me too.'

'I can't desert my friend.'

'Leave him be. Can't you see he's in love? His soul is not here. Come with me.'

She led Suti into the largest bedroom. She sat him down on a low bed, covered with multicoloured cushions, knelt down and kissed him. He made to take her by the shoulders, but she pushed him away gently.

'There's no hurry – we have all night. Learn to hold back your pleasure, to make it grow in your belly, to savour the fire that flows through your blood.' She took off her belt of shells and lay down on her stomach. 'Massage my back.'

Suti played the game for a few seconds, but then, inflamed by the sight of her wonderful body, the touch of her perfumed skin, he could restrain himself no longer. Seeing how intense his desire was, Sababu stopped resisting him. Covering her in kisses, he made ardent love to her.

'You pleased me a lot. You aren't like most of my clients – they drink too much and get flabby and soft.'

'Not to pay homage to your charms would be a sin against the spirit.'

Suti caressed her breasts, attentive to her least reaction. Thanks to her lover's knowledgeable hands, Sababu was rediscovering long-forgotten sensations.

'Are you a scribe?' she asked.

'Soon I shall be a soldier, but before becoming a hero I wanted to have the sweetest of adventures.'

'In that case, I must give you everything.'

Using the lightest touch of her lips and tongue, Sababu reawakened Suti's desire. Their bodies joined once again, and for a second time they cried out together in pleasure.

Afterwards they lay gazing into each other's eyes, while they got their breath back.

'You have seduced me, my ram,' said Sababu, 'for you adore making love.'

'Is there any illusion more beautiful than this one?'

'And yet you're very real.'

Suti put his arm round her. 'How did you become the owner of an ale-house?

'Because I despise false nobles and so-called great men. They say fine words, but they're hypocrites – really they're just like you and me, ruled by the demands of their sex and their passions. If you only knew . . .'

'Tell me.'

'Would you steal away my secrets?'

'Why not?'

Despite her experience, and all the men whose bodies she had known, handsome and ugly, Sababu could not resist her new lover's caresses. He awoke in her the will to avenge herself against a world which had so often humiliated her.

'When you are a hero,' she said, 'will you be ashamed of me?'

'Certainly not! I'm sure you've had lots of famous men as lovers.'

'You're right about that.'

'You must have some amusing stories to tell.'

She laid a slender finger on the young man's mouth. 'Only my private journal knows about them. It ensures my peace.'

'You write down the names of your clients?'

'And their habits and their confidences.'

'It must be an absolute treasure house.'

'If I'm left in peace, I shan't use it. When I am old, I shall read over my memories again.'

Suti rolled over on top of her. 'I'm still curious. At least give me one name.'

'No, I can't.'

'Just for me.'

The young man kissed her nipples. She shivered with pleasure.

'One name, just one,' he pleaded.

'He's known as a model of virtue. When I divulge his vices, his career will be at an end.'

'What's his name?'

'Pazair.'

Suti flung himself off Sababu's gorgeous body. 'What have you been told to do?'

'Spread rumours.'

'Do you know him?'

'I've never even seen him.'

'Yes you have.'

'What?'

'Pazair's my best friend. He's here, this very evening, but all he thinks of is the woman he loves and the cause he's defending. Who told you to smear his name?'

Sababu was silent.

'He's a judge,' Suti went on, 'the most honest judge in Egypt. Don't tell any more lies about him. You're powerful enough not to have to worry if you stop.'

'I can't promise anything.'

17

Pazair and Suti sat side by side on the banks of the Nile, watching the birth of the day. Vanquishing the darkness, the new sun sprang forth from the desert, turned the river to blood, and made the fish leap for joy.

'Are you really serious-minded?' asked Suti.

'Whatever are you accusing me of?' asked Pazair in surprise.

'A judge who's over-fond of debauchery is liable to find his mind gets clouded.'

'You're the one who dragged me into that ale-house. While you were fooling around, I was thinking about my cases.'

'About your beloved, more like.'

The river sparkled. Already, the bloody hue of dawn was fading, to be replaced by the golden tones of early morning.

Suti went on, 'How many times have you been to that pleasure house?'

'You must have been drinking.'

'So you've never met Sababu before?'

'Never.'

'And yet she was ready to tell anyone who'd listen that you're one of her best customers.'

Pazair turned pale, not so much because, if the story got about, his reputation as a judge would be tarnished for ever, but because of what Neferet would think of him.

'She's been bribed to do it!' he exclaimed.

'Exactly.'

'By whom?'

'Our love-making was so good that she took a liking to me. She told me about the plot she's mixed up in, but not who's behind it. But if you ask me the ringleader's easy to identify: those methods are absolutely typical of Mentmose.'

'I shall defend myself.'

'There's no need. I persuaded her to keep her mouth shut.'

'Let's not deceive ourselves,' said Pazair. 'The first chance she gets, she'll betray us both.'

'I'm not so sure. That girl has morals.'

'Allow me to be sceptical.'

'In certain circumstances, a woman does not lie.'

'All the same, I want to speak to her.'

Shortly before noon Pazair arrived, with Kem and Killer, at the door of the ale-house. A young Nubian girl hid in fright under a pile of cushions; one of her colleagues, who was less easily scared, dared to face the judge.

'I would like to see the owner,' he said.

'I'm just one of her girls, and—'

'Where is the lady Sababu? Don't lie to me. If you do, you'll be sent to prison.'

'But if I tell you, she'll beat me.'

'And if you don't, I'll charge you with obstructing justice.'

'I haven't done anything wrong.'

'No, and you haven't been charged yet. So tell me the truth.'

'She's gone to Thebes.'

'Did she leave an address?'

'No.'

'When is she coming back?'

'I don't know.'

So Sababu had chosen to run away and hide. From now on,

the judge would be in danger if he made the slightest mistake. Someone was lurking in the shadows, plotting against him. Someone – probably Mentmose – had paid Sababu to destroy his good name, and to save herself she wouldn't hesitate to denounce him. The judge owed his temporary safety only to Suti's powers of seduction.

Sometimes, mused Pazair, debauchery was not entirely reprehensible.

After long reflection, Mentmose took a decision which would have weighty consequences: he would ask Tjaty Bagey for a private audience. Nervously, he rehearsed his declaration several times in front of a copper mirror, trying out different facial expressions. Like everyone else, he knew the tjaty's reputation for intransigence. Bagey was sparing with his words, and loathed wasting his time. His office obliged him to hear all petitions, wherever they came from, so long as they were well-founded; but anyone who wasted time, lied, or falsified the facts would live to regret it bitterly. Face to face with the tjaty, every word and every gesture counted.

Mentmose went to the palace in the late morning. At seven o'clock, Bagey had spoken with the king, then given instructions to his principal colleagues and consulted the reports that had arrived from the provinces. Next, he had held his daily audience, to deal with the numerous matters that other courts had been unable to resolve. Before eating a frugal lunch, the tjaty would consent to a few personal meetings, if urgency demanded it.

He received Mentmose in an austere office whose spartan decor scarcely matched the grandeur of his rank: it contained only a chair, a mat, some storage chests and papyrus cases. A visitor would have thought he was in the presence of a simple scribe, if Bagey had not been wearing his grand robe and collar of office.

Tjaty Bagey was sixty years old, a tall, stooping, stiff-bodied man with a long face, prominent nose, curly hair and blue eyes. His hands were those of an artist, slender and elegant. He had never taken part in any sports; his skin reacted badly to the sun. After working as a craftsman, he had become first a teacher of writing, then an expert in geometry, renowned for his great thoroughness.

In time he had come to the notice of the palace, which had appointed him in succession head geometrician, senior judge of the province of Memphis, Judge of the Porch and finally tjaty. Many courtiers had tried in vain to catch him out. Feared and respected, Bagey belonged to a long line of great statesmen who, since the days of Imhotep, had kept Egypt on the right path. If he was sometimes criticized for the severity of his judgments and the inflexibility with which they were applied, no one could say that they were not well thought-out.

Up to now, Mentmose had confined himself to obeying the tjaty's orders and taking care not to displease him. This meeting made him nervous.

The tjaty was tired, and seemed half asleep. 'I'm listening,' he said. 'Be brief.'

'It's not that simple—'

'Then simplify it.

'Several ex-soldiers have been killed in an accident, falling off the Great Sphinx.'

'Tell me about the official enquiry.'

'The army carried it out.'

'Any anomalies?'

'There don't seem to be. I haven't looked at the official documents, but—'

'But your contacts have informed you of the contents. That is somewhat irregular.'

Mentmose had been afraid the tjaty might take that line. 'These are old customs.'

'They must be changed. If there's nothing amiss, why are you here?'

'It's about Judge Pazair.'

'Is he unworthy to be a judge?'

Mentmose's voice became more nasal. 'I'm not accusing him of anything, it's just that his conduct worries me.'

'Does he not respect the law?'

'He's convinced that the disappearance of the head guard, a former soldier with an excellent reputation, took place in peculiar circumstances.'

'Has he any proof?'

'No, none. I have the feeling that this young judge wants to stir things up so that he can make a reputation for himself. I find such an attitude deplorable.'

'I'm delighted to hear it,' said Bagey. 'Regarding the basic facts of the case, what is your opinion?'

'Oh, my opinion is of little value.'

'On the contrary. I am eager to know it.'

A trap yawned before Mentmose. He had a horror of committing himself one way or the other, for fear of taking a firm stance which might be criticized.

The tjaty opened his eyes. His cold blue gaze pierced Mentmose's soul.

Mentmose said, 'It seems unlikely that there's any mystery about the deaths of those unfortunate men, but I don't know enough about the matter to be definite about it.'

'If the head of Memphis's security guards himself has doubts, why should a judge not do so too? It is not his first duty to accept received opinions.'

'Of course,' murmured Mentmose.

'Incompetent people are not appointed in Memphis. Pazair was undoubtedly noticed because of his good qualities.'

'Indeed, Tjaty, but the atmosphere of a great city, ambition, too much power . . . The young man may carry too great a responsibility.'

'We shall see,' declared Bagey. 'If he does, I shall dismiss him. In the meantime, we shall allow him to continue. I am relying on you to assist him.' Bagey leant his head back and closed his eyes again.

Convinced that the tjaty was watching him through closed eyelids, Mentmose stood up, bowed and left. He would vent his anger on his servants.

Kani was sturdily built, with sun-browned skin. He arrived at Pazair's office just after dawn, and sat down outside the closed door, next to Way-Finder. Kani dreamt of owning a donkey. It would help him to carry heavy loads and relieve his back, which was worn out from the weight of the jars he used for watering the garden. Way-Finder listened attentively while Kani talked to him of days that were always the same, of his love for the earth, of the care he took when digging the irrigation channels, of his pleasure at seeing the plants flourish.

His confidences were interrupted by the sound of Pazair's brisk footsteps.

'Kani, did you want to see me?'

The gardener nodded.

'Come in.'

Kani hesitated. The judge's office scared him, as did the city. Far from the countryside, he felt ill at ease. Too much noise, too many nauseating smells, too many blocked horizons. If his future had not hung in the balance, he would never have ventured into the narrow streets of Memphis.

'I got lost ten times,' he explained.

'Are you having more problems with Qadash?'

'Yes.'

'What is he doing now?'

'I want to leave, and he won't let me.'

'Leave?'

'This year my garden produced three times more vegetables than the stipulated quantity, so I'm entitled to become an independent worker.'

Pazair nodded. 'That is certainly the law.'

'Qadash says it isn't.'

'Describe your piece of ground to me.'

Nebamon received Neferet in the shady gardens of his sumptuous home. Sitting under a blossoming acacia tree, he drank pink wine while a servant fanned him.

'Beautiful Neferet, how glad I am to see you.'

The young woman was primly dressed and wearing a short wig in the old style.

'You look very severe today,' said Nebamon. 'Isn't that dress long out of fashion?'

'You interrupted me in my work. Why did you summon me here?'

Nebamon told his servant to leave. Sure of his own charm, and convinced that the delightful setting would enchant Neferet, he had decided to offer her one last chance.

'You don't like me much, do you?' he said.

'Please answer my question.'

'Enjoy this lovely day, this delicious wine, the paradise we are living in. You are beautiful and intelligent, with a greater gift for medicine than the best-qualified of our doctors. But you have neither fortune nor experience, and without my help you'll vegetate in a village. At first, your moral strength will enable you to overcome the ordeal; but once you reach maturity you will regret your much-vaunted purity. A career cannot be built on idealism, Neferet.'

Arms folded, the young woman gazed silently across the garden to the small lake, where ducks were flapping among the lotus flowers.

'You will learn to love me,' Nebamon went on, 'and the way I conduct my affairs.'

'Your ambitions are no concern of mine.'

'You would make a worthy wife for Pharaoh's head doctor.'

'Don't deceive yourself.'

'I know a great deal about women.'

'Are you sure of that?'

Nebamon's charming smile hardened. 'Don't forget that I control your future.'

'My future is in the gods' hands, not yours.'

Nebamon rose to his feet, his expression grim. 'Leave the gods aside, and pay attention to what I say.'

'Don't rely on it.'

'This is my final warning.'

'May I return to my work?'

'According to the reports I have just received, your knowledge of preparing remedies is thoroughly inadequate.'

Neferet kept her composure. Unfolding her arms, she stared into her accuser's eyes and said, 'You know very well that isn't true.'

'The reports are quite clear.'

'Who wrote them?

'Men who value their jobs and deserve to be promoted for their vigilance. If you cannot prepare complex remedies, I cannot allow you to become part of an elite body. You know what that means, don't you? It will be impossible for you to progress in the medical profession. You will stagnate, unable to use the best that the workshops produce – they answer to me, and you will be denied access to them.'

Neferet said angrily, 'You are condemning sick people to death.'

'You are to refer your patients to more competent colleagues. When you can no longer bear the meaninglessness of your life, you will come crawling back to me.'

Denes's travelling chair was set down in front of Qadash's house while Pazair was speaking to the door keeper.

'Have you got toothache?' asked the door keeper.

'No, it's a legal problem.'

'You're lucky – I've got receding gums. Is Qadash in trouble with the law?'

'No,' said Pazair. 'It's just a simple detail which needs sorting out.

The dentist with the red hands greeted his two clients, and asked, 'Who shall I start with?'

'Denes is your patient. As for me, I wish to speak to you about Kani.'

'My gardener?'

'Not any more. His work gives him the right to independence.'

'Rubbish! He's my employee and that's how he'll stay.'

'Place your seal upon this document.'

'I refuse.' Qadash's voice was unsteady.

'In that case, I shall instigate court proceedings against you.'

Denes intervened. 'Let's not lose our tempers. Let the gardener leave, Qadash; I'll find you another one.'

'It's a question of principle,' protested Qadash.

'A good compromise is better than a bad court case. Forget about Kani.'

With bad grace, Qadash followed Denes's advice.

Sekhem was a small town in the Delta, surrounded by wheat fields; its college of priests was devoted to the mysteries of the god Horus, the falcon whose wings were as vast as the skies.

Neferet was received by the High Priest, a friend of Branir, whom she had told about her exclusion from the official body of doctors. The priest allowed her to enter the shrine containing a statue of the jackal-headed god, Anubis, who had revealed the secrets of mummification and opened the gates of the afterlife to the souls of the righteous. He transformed inert flesh into a body composed of light.

Neferet walked round the statue. On the pillar at its back

she found a long text in hieroglyphics, a treatise on the treatment of infectious diseases and the purification of lymph. She engraved it in her memory. Branir had decided to instruct her in a healing art to which Nebamon would never have access.

It had been an exhausting day. Pazair was relaxing, enjoying the peaceful evening on Branir's terrace. Brave, who had watched over the office all day, was also taking a well-deserved rest. The dying light crossed the sky and reached the very edges of the horizon.

'How is your investigation going?' asked Branir.

'The army's trying to snuff it out. What's more, someone's plotting against me.'

'Who's behind all this?'

'I can't help suspecting General Asher.'

'You mustn't have preconceived ideas.'

'I can't make any more progress because I'm being smothered under a mass of administrative documents which have to be dealt with straight away. This sudden increase is probably due to Mentmose. I was planning to go to Thebes, but I had to give up the idea.'

'Mentmose is a dangerous man. He's destroyed many people's careers to strengthen his own.'

'At least I've made one man happy – Kani the gardener. He's become a free worker and has already left Memphis for the South.'

'He used to supply me with medicinal plants. An awkward character, but he loves his work. No doubt Qadash objected to your involvement?'

'He listened to Denes's advice and bowed before the law.'

'He had no choice,' said Branir drily.

'Denes claims he has learnt his lesson.'

'He's first and foremost a businessman.'

'Do you think he really has turned over a new leaf?'

'Most men act in their own best interests.'

After a pause, Pazair asked, 'Have you seen Neferet lately?'

'Nebamon is still trying to keep his hold over her. He asked her to marry him.'

Pazair froze. Brave raised concerned eyes to his master's face. 'Did she refuse?'

'Neferet is gentle and loving, but no one will force her to act against her will.'

'She did refuse, didn't she?'

Branir smiled. 'Can you imagine Nebamon and Neferet as a couple, even for a moment?'

Pazair could not hide his relief. Reassured, the dog went back to sleep.

'Nebamon wants to force her into submission,' Branir went on. 'On the basis of false reports, he has declared her incompetent and expelled her from the body of qualified doctors.'

Pazair clenched his fists. 'I shall discredit those reports.'

'You'd have no chance of winning. A lot of doctors and remedy makers are in Nebamon's pay, and will uphold their lies.'

'She must be desperate.'

'She has decided to leave Memphis and set herself up in a village near Thebes.'

18

'We're going to Thebes after all,' Pazair told Way-Finder.

The donkey greeted the news with satisfaction, but when Iarrot saw the preparations for the journey, he was worried.

'Will you be gone long?' he asked.

'I don't know.'

'Where can I reach you if I need to?'

'Just put the cases to one side for me.'

'But—'

'And do try to be punctual. Your daughter won't suffer if you are.'

Kem lived near the workshops where weapons were made. He had an apartment in a two-storey building containing ten two- and three-roomed apartments. Today was his rest day, so Pazair hoped to find him at home.

The baboon opened the door, its eyes unblinking.

The main room was full of knives, spears and slingshots. Kem looked up from the bow he was repairing.

'What are you doing here?' he asked.

'Is your travelling bag packed and ready?'

'I thought you'd decided not to go.'

'I've changed my mind.'

'I'm at your command.'

*

Slingshot, spear, dagger, club, cudgel, axe, rectangular wooden shield: Suti had wielded all these weapons for three days with great dexterity. He had shown the assurance of an experienced soldier, and had drawn grudging admiration from the officers charged with training the recruits.

At the end of the trial period, the candidates for the military life were gathered together in the great courtyard of the main barracks in Memphis. On one side were stables containing horses, which observed the spectacle with curiosity; in the centre was an enormous reservoir of water.

Suti had visited the stables. They were built on pebbled pavements criss-crossed with channels along which dirty water could run away. The horsemen and charioteers pampered their charges, seeing that they were well-fed, clean and beautifully groomed, and had the best possible living conditions. The young man also approved of the soldiers' living quarters, which were shaded by a row of trees.

But he remained allergic to discipline. Three days of orders and being shouted at by junior officers had destroyed his taste for uniformed adventure.

The recruitment ceremony took place according to strict rules. First, an officer addressed the volunteers and tried to persuade them to enlist by describing the joys that awaited them in the army. Security, respectability and a comfortable retirement featured among the main benefits. Bearers held aloft the standards of the principal regiments dedicated to the gods Amon, Ra, Ptah and Set. A royal scribe got ready to register the names of the men enlisting. Behind him stood baskets piled high with food; the generals were hosting a banquet, with ample supplies of beef, poultry, vegetables and fruit.

'What a fine life we're going to have,' whispered one of Suti's companions.

'Not me.'

'Aren't you enlisting?'

'I prefer freedom.'

'You're mad. According to the captain, you have the best chance of promotion of any of us. You'd get a good posting straight away.'

'I'm looking for adventure, not slavery.'

'I'd think carefully if I were you.'

A messenger from the palace hurried across the courtyard, carrying a papyrus. He showed it to the royal scribe, who stood up and issued a few brief orders. In less than a minute all the gates of the barracks had been closed.

Murmurs rose from the ranks of volunteers.

'Quiet!' ordered the officer who had given the speech. 'We have just received orders. By Pharaoh's decree, you are all enlisted. Some will join provincial barracks, others will leave tomorrow for Asia.'

'It must be a state of emergency or a war,' said Suti's companion.

'I don't give a damn.'

'Don't be a fool. If you try to run away, you'll be treated as a deserter.'

That argument carried weight. Suti weighed up his chances of getting over the wall and disappearing into the neighbouring streets: they were non-existent. He was no longer at the scribes' school, but in a barracks full of archers and spear throwers.

One by one, the conscripted men walked past the royal scribe, whose welcoming smile had been replaced by an expression of cold efficiency.

'Suti . . . excellent results. Posting: Asian army. You are to be an archer, alongside the officer commanding the corps of charioteers. You leave tomorrow at dawn. Next.'

Suti saw his name written down on a tablet. Now desertion was impossible, unless he spent the rest of his life abroad and never saw Egypt or Pazair again. He was condemned to become a hero.

'Will I be under General Asher's command?' he asked.

The scribe looked up in annoyance. 'I said: next.'

Suti was given a shirt, a tunic, a cloak, a breastplate, leather leg-protectors, a cap, a small two-edged axe, and a long acacia-wood bow, thick at its centre and tapering towards the ends. It took great strength to draw, and could shoot arrows a hundred paces in a straight line, or two hundred in an arc.

'What about the banquet?' he asked the supply officer.

'Here is some bread, a pound of dried meat, some oil and some figs. Eat, drink some water from the tank, and get some sleep. Tomorrow, you'll be eating dust.'

On the boat on which Pazair and Kem travelled south, all talk was of Ramses' decree, which had been spread abroad by many heralds. Pharaoh had ordered that all the temples were to be purified, that lists were to be made of all the country's treasures and grain reserves, that offerings to the gods were to be doubled and that a military expedition was to be sent into Asia.

Rumour had multiplied these measures, and there was talk of imminent disaster, armed disturbances in the towns, rebellion in the provinces and an impending Hittite invasion. Like the other judges, Pazair must ensure that public order was maintained.

'Wouldn't it have been better to stay in Memphis?' asked Kem.

'Our journey won't take long. The village headmen will tell us that the two ex-soldiers were killed in an accident, and have already been mummified and buried.'

'You don't sound very optimistic.'

'Five men fell to their deaths: that's the official version.'

'But you don't believe it.'

'Do you?'

'What does that matter? If war's declared, I'll be called up again.'

'Ramses is advocating peace with the Hittites and the Asian princedoms.'

'They'll never give up their plans to invade Egypt,' said Kem.

'But our army's too strong for them.'

'Then why this Asian expedition and these extreme security measures?'

'I'm puzzled, too. Perhaps the problem's to do with internal security.'

'The country is rich and happy, the king is loved by his people, everyone has enough to eat, and the roads are safe. There's no threat of unrest.'

'I agree, but Pharaoh seems to think somewhat differently.'

The air whipped their cheeks. The sail had been lowered, and the boat was using the current. Dozens of other boats were sailing up and down the Nile, obliging the captain and his crew to be permanently watchful.

Not long after they had passed Meidum, a fast boat belonging to the river guards caught up with them, and ordered them to slow down. A guard grabbed the rigging and jumped on to the deck.

'Is Judge Pazair among the passengers?' he asked.

'Yes, here I am.'

'I must take you back to Memphis.'

'Why?'

'A complaint has been lodged against you.'

Suti was the last man up and dressed. The officer in charge of the barrack room ordered him to hurry and make up for lost time.

The young man had been dreaming of Sababu, of her caresses and her kisses. She had shown him undreamt-of paths to ecstasy, which he was determined to explore again before too long.

Watched enviously by the other recruits, Suti climbed into

a war chariot, driven by an impressively muscular officer aged about forty.

'Hold on tight, my lad,' he advised Suti.

Scarcely had Suti slipped his left wrist into a retaining strap when the officer whipped his horses into a gallop. The chariot was the first one to leave the barracks and head north.

'Have you fought before, youngster?'

'I've fought scribes, sir' said Suti.

'Did you kill them?'

'I don't think so.'

'Don't worry, I'm going to offer you much better fare.'

'Where are we going, sir?'

'Straight to the enemy. We cross the Delta, follow the coast, and then come up against the Syrians and the Hittites. I think this decree's a splendid one. It's a long time since I trampled on one of those barbarians. Draw your bow.'

'Aren't you going to slow down?'

'A good archer can hit his target even in the worst conditions.'

'What happens if I miss?'

'I'll cut your retaining strap and send you tumbling down into the dust.'

'Sir, why are you so ruthless?'

'Ten Asian campaigns, five wounds, two Golden Fly awards for bravery, congratulations from Ramses himself – is that enough for you?

'There's no room for error?'

'Either you win or you lose,' said the officer. 'Now, instead of talking, hit that acacia over there, that one in the distance.'

Becoming a hero was going to be be more difficult than Suti had realized. He took a deep breath, drew his bow as far as it would go, forgot the chariot, the jolting and the bumpy road. The arrow shot up into the sky, described a graceful arc, and plunged into the trunk of the tree, which the chariot passed at top speed.

'Well done, young lad!'

Suti let out a long sigh. 'How many archers have you thrown into the dust, sir?' he asked.

'I've stopped counting – I loathe amateurs. This evening I'll buy you a drink.'

'In the tent?'

'Officers and their assistants are allowed to go to the inn.'

'And . . . what about women?'

The officer gave Suti a hearty thump on the back. 'You were born to be in the army, my lad. After the wine, we'll have a little game or two with the women, which will empty our purses.'

Suti kissed his bow. Luck hadn't deserted him after all.

Pazair sat in his office, brooding. He had underestimated his enemies' capacity to strike back. On one hand, they wanted to stop him leaving Memphis and making enquiries in Thebes; on the other, they wanted to have him dismissed, so as to put an end to his investigations once and for all. So Pazair had indeed stumbled upon a murder – or, rather, upon several.

Alas, it was too late now to do anything about them. Just as he had feared, Sababu, acting under Mentmose's instructions, had accused him of debauchery. The governing body of judges would condemn Pazair for leading a dissolute life, which was incompatible with his office.

Kem came in, his head hanging low.

'Have you found Suti?' asked Pazair.

'He's been conscripted into the army fighting in Asia.'

'Has he left?'

'Yes, as an archer on a war chariot.'

'So the only witness who can prove my innocence is out of reach.'

'I could take his place.'

'No, Kem. It would be shown that you weren't at Sababu's ale-house, and you'd be convicted of perjury.'

'I hate seeing you slandered like this.'

'I was wrong to lift the veil that's been hiding these crimes.'

'If no one, not even a judge, can tell the truth, what's the point of living?'

Pazair was touched by the Nubian's concern, and said, 'I shan't give up, but I shall have to find proof.'

'They'll find a way to silence you.'

'I shan't let them.'

'I'll be right beside you, and so will Killer.'

The two men embraced.

The case was heard under the wooden porch in front of the palace, two days after Pazair's return. It was heard so quickly because of the accused man's position: if a judge was suspected of breaking the law, the case required immediate investigation.

Pazair had not hoped for indulgence on the part of the Judge of the Porch, but he was stunned by the sheer extent of the plot when he saw the members of the jury: Denes and Nenophar, Mentmose, a scribe from the palace and a priest from the Temple of Ptah. His enemies were in the majority, and, if the scribe and the priest were their allies, perhaps unanimous.

The Judge of the Porch sat at the back of the audience chamber, wearing a pleated kilt, his head shaven, his expression cold. At his feet lay a sycamore-wood cubit, signifying the presence of Ma'at. The jurors sat on his left; to his right was a clerk. Behind Pazair were many onlookers.

'Are you Judge Pazair?' began the Judge of the Porch.

'I am. I officiate at Memphis.'

'And your staff includes a scribe named Iarrot?'

'It does.'

'Bring forward the accuser.'

An alliance between Iarrot and Sababu? Pazair would

never have foreseen that. So he had been betrayed by his closest colleague.

But the woman who stepped into the audience chamber was not Sababu but a short, heavily built brunette with an unattractive face.

'You are the wife of Iarrot the clerk?' asked the Judge.

'I am indeed,' she replied, in a bitter, rather stupid voice.

'Set out your accusations. And remember that you are speaking under oath.'

'My husband drinks beer – far too much beer, especially in the evenings. For a week now, he's been insulting me and beating me in the presence of our daughter. She's afraid, the poor child. I've been hit; a doctor has seen the marks.'

'Do you know Judge Pazair?'

'Only by name.'

'What do you ask of the court?'

'That my husband and his employer, who is responsible for his morals, are sentenced. I want two new dresses, ten sacks of grain and five roasted geese. Twice that, if Iarrot starts beating me again.'

Pazair was astounded.

'Bring forward the principal defendant,' ordered the Judge.

Iarrot obeyed, shamefacedly. His face even redder than usual, he presented his defence. 'My wife provokes me, and she refuses to cook my meals. I didn't mean to hit her – it was an unfortunate reaction. You must understand that I work very hard for Judge Pazair. The hours are dreadful, and there are so many cases to deal with that there really ought to be another scribe.'

'Would you object to that, Judge Pazair?'

'Those statements are untrue. We do indeed have a lot of work, but I have respected Iarrot's situation, accepted his family problems, and allowed him to vary his working hours.'

'Are there any witnesses who can confirm what you say?'

'People who live in the area, I suppose.'

The Judge of the Porch turned to Iarrot. 'Are we to call them, and do you dispute what Judge Pazair has said?'

'No . . . no, I don't. But all the same, I wasn't entirely in the wrong.'

'Judge Pazair, did you know that your clerk was beating his wife?'

'No.'

'You are responsible for your employees' moral standards.'

'I do not deny that.'

'Through negligence, you omitted to check Iarrot's moral character.'

'I had no time to do so.'

'Negligence is the only correct term.'

The Judge of the Porch had Pazair at his mercy. He asked the main participants if they wished to speak again; only Iarrot's agitated wife repeated her accusations.

The jury convened.

Pazair felt almost like laughing. Being condemned because of a domestic dispute – who could have imagined it? Iarrot's spinelessness and his wife's stupidity were unforeseen traps, which his adversaries were making the most of. The legal niceties would be respected, and he would be dismissed without the need for recourse to violence.

The jury's deliberations lasted less than an hour.

The Judge of the Porch announced the outcome, his expression as sour as ever.

'By unanimous decision, Iarrot the clerk is found guilty of bad conduct towards his wife. He is sentenced to give the victim what she asks for and to receive thirty strokes of the rod. If he offends again, a divorce will be immediately pronounced, with him as the guilty party. Does the accused protest against the sentence?'

Iarrot was only too happy to have escaped so lightly – the law dealt severely with brutes who mistreated women – and bared his back for punishment. He whimpered and snivelled under the rod; afterwards, a guard took him away to the local hospital.

The Judge of the Porch continued, 'By unanimous verdict, Judge Pazair is acquitted. The court advises him not to dismiss his scribe but to give him a chance to mend his ways.'

Mentmose merely acknowledged Pazair with a nod; he was in a hurry, as he was sitting on another jury which had been convened to judge a thief.

Denes and his wife – the latter wearing a many-coloured dress which was the talk of Memphis – offered the young judge their congratulations.

'It was a grotesque accusation,' said Nenophar emphatically.

'Any court would have acquitted you,' said Denes. 'We need judges like you in Memphis.'

'That's true,' agreed Nenophar. 'Business can only develop in a peaceful, just society. Your steadfastness impressed us greatly – my husband and I admire men of courage. From now on, we shall consult you if there are any legal problems in the way we conduct our business.'

19

After a swift and uneventful journey, the boat carrying Judge Pazair, Way-Finder, Brave, Kem, Killer and a few other passengers, came within sight of Thebes. Everyone fell silent.

On the left bank stood the holy temples of Karnak and Luxor. Behind high walls, sheltered from unworthy eyes, a small number of men and women worshipped the gods night and day, beseeching them to remain upon the earth. Acacias and tamarisks shaded the rows of stone rams leading to the huge pillared gateways that led into the temples.

This time, the river guards had not intercepted the boat. Pazair was to see his native province again; since he had left, he had endured trials, had been toughened up and, above all, had found love.

Neferet had not been out of his thoughts for an instant. He had lost his appetite, and was having more and more trouble concentrating; at night, he kept his eyes open, hoping to see her emerge from the darkness. His distraction was plunging him deeper and deeper into a void which was eating him away from the inside. Only the woman he loved could cure him, but could she understand his sickness? Neither gods nor priests could give him back his taste for life, no triumph could drive away his pain, no book could calm it.

Thebes, the city where Neferet was hiding, was his last hope.

Pazair was disheartened and no longer had any faith in his investigation: the plot had been woven perfectly. Whatever his suspicions, he would not reach the truth. Just before leaving Memphis, he had learnt that the head guard of the Sphinx had been buried, because, as General Asher's mission in Asia had no time limit, the military authorities had thought it best not to defer the funeral ceremonies. Was it really the guard's body in the tomb, or was it another corpse? Was the missing man still alive, hidden somewhere? Pazair would never know.

The boat tied up, just before the temple at Luxor.

'We're being watched,' said Kem quietly. 'A young fellow up in the bows. He was the last one to embark.'

'Let's see if he follows us – we can lose him in the town.'

The man did indeed follow them.

'Do you think he's one of Mentmose's men?' asked Kem.

'Probably.'

'Do you want me to get rid of him for you?'

'I've got a better idea.'

The judge headed for a main guard post, where he was greeted by a fat official whose office was filled with baskets of fruit and pastries.

'You were born in this region, weren't you?' the official asked.

'Yes, in a village on the west bank. I've been appointed to Memphis, where I had the privilege of meeting your superior, Mentmose.'

'And now you've come back.'

'Only for a short stay.'

'Business or pleasure?'

'I'm looking into the wood tax.* My predecessor left me some incomplete and rather obscure notes on this vital point.'

---

*Wood was quite a rare material in Egypt, so its value was considerable.

The fat man swallowed a few raisins. 'Is Memphis short of firewood?'

'Not at all. The winter was mild, and we didn't use up all our reserves. But I'm not sure that the rota of branch cutters is being managed properly – there are too many Memphites, and not enough Thebans. I'd like to consult your lists, village by village, in order to identify the people who are defrauding the system. Some don't want to collect small sticks, brush-wood and palm fibres and carry them to the sorting and redistribution centres. It's time to take action, don't you think?'

'Indeed, indeed.'

The official had had a letter from Mentmose, alerting him to Pazair's arrival and describing the judge as formidable, keen and over-curious. In place of that daunting individual, the fat man found a pernickety man preoccupied with minor details.

'The respective quantities of wood provided by the North and South speak volumes,' continued Pazair, 'and at Thebes the dried tree stumps aren't being correctly cut. Is there an illegal trade?'

'It's possible.'

'Please be good enough to register the object of my investigation locally.'

'I'll see to it.'

When the fat man received a visit from the young guard charged with following Pazair, he told him of the conversation. The two agreed that the judge had lost his original motivation and was sinking into routine. This sensible attitude would spare them a great deal of trouble.

The shadow-eater was wary of the monkey and the dog, perceptive creatures which could sense evil intentions, and spied on Pazair and Kem from a distance.

By giving up following them, the young guard – who was

no doubt one of Mentmose's men – had made the task easier. If the judge got close to his goal, the shadow-eater would have to take action; otherwise, observation would be enough.

The orders were quite clear, and the shadow-eater never disobeyed orders. No one would be killed unless it was absolutely necessary. It was Pazair's persistence that had led to the death of the head guard's wife.

After the incident at the Sphinx, the ex-soldier had taken refuge in the little village on the west bank where he had been born. He would spend a happy retirement there, after his loyal service in the army. The story of the accident suited him perfectly. At his age, why should he fight a battle that was lost from the outset?

Since his return, he had repaired the bread oven and taken on the job of baker, much to the villagers' satisfaction. After ridding the grain of its impurities by sieving it, the women broke it up on the millstone and crushed it in a mortar, using long-handled pestles. This produced a coarse flour, which was then refined several times. The women then moistened it, producing a dough to which they added yeast. Some used a wide-necked jar to knead the dough, while others laid it out on a flagstone, angled to make it easier for the water to run off.

The baker then stepped in, baking the simplest loaves on hot coals and the more elaborate ones in an oven made of three vertical stone slabs covered by a horizontal slab, under which the fire was lit. He also used perforated moulds for cakes and stone platters, on which he placed the dough, to prepare round or oblong loaves, or hotcakes. Sometimes he shaped it into little animals, which the children loved.

He had forgotten the sounds of fighting and the cries of the wounded. The song of the flames was sweet to him, and he loved the softness of hot loaves. He still had the authoritarian nature of a military man, though. When he was heating the platters, he drove away the women and would allow no one near him but his assistant, a sturdy lad of fifteen, his adopted son, who would succeed him.

This morning the boy was late. The baker was getting annoyed, when he heard footsteps on the paved floor of the bakery. He turned round.

'I'm going to— Who are you?'

'I'm here to take your assistant's place. He has a bad headache.'

'You don't live in the village.'

'I work with another baker, half an hour from here. The headman of the village told me to come.'

'Very well. Then help me.'

The oven was deep, so the baker had to lean his head and shoulders inside in order to push the maximum number of moulds and loaves right to the back. His assistant held on to his hips, so as to pull him back out if anything went wrong.

The ex-soldier thought he was safe, but the shadow-eater knew that this very day Judge Pazair was to visit the village. He would find out the baker's true identity and would interrogate him. The shadow-eater had no choice. He seized the baker by his ankles, lifted them off the ground, and pushed him deep inside the oven.

The entrance to the little town was deserted. Not one woman stood at her front door, not one man dozed under a tree, not a single child was playing with a wooden doll. Pazair was certain that something unusual had happened, and he told Kem to stay where he was. The baboon and the dog looked around in all directions.

Pazair hurried down the main street, which was lined with single-storey houses.

Every inhabitant was gathered round the bakery oven. People were shouting, jostling each other, and calling upon the gods. A young lad was explaining for the tenth time that he had been knocked unconscious as he came out of his house on his way to work. He blamed himself for the terrible accident to his adoptive father, and was weeping copiously.

Pazair pushed through the crowd. 'What has happened?' he asked.

'Our baker has just died in the most horrible way,' replied the village headman. 'He must have slipped and fallen into his oven. Usually, his assistant holds on to his legs to prevent such a thing happening.'

'Was he an ex-soldier who recently returned from Memphis?'

'He was indeed.'

'Was anyone present when this . . . accident happened?'

'No. Why are you asking all these questions?'

'I am Judge Pazair, and I came here to question the unfortunate man.'

'What about?'

'That is not important.'

A hysterical woman seized Pazair's arm. 'It was the night demons who killed him, because he agreed to deliver bread – our bread – to Hattusa, the foreign woman who rules the harem.'

The judge pushed her gently aside, but she went on, 'It your job is to see that justice is done, avenge our baker and arrest that she-devil!'

Pazair and Kem ate their lunch in the countryside, beside a well. Killer delicately peeled some sweet onions. He was beginning to accept the judge's presence, and to be less aggressive. Brave feasted on fresh bread and cucumber, while Way-Finder munched fodder.

Edgily, the judge hugged a goatskin bag of fresh water. 'One accident and five dead men! The army lied, Kem. Its report was falsified.'

'It could be a simple administrative error.'

'No, it's a murder, another murder.'

'There's no proof. The baker had an accident – it's happened before.'

'A murderer got here before us, because he knew we were coming to the village. No one should have found the fourth guard, no one should have taken an interest in this matter.'

'Don't look into it any further. What you've unearthed is probably a settling of scores between soldiers.'

'If justice gives up, violence will rule in Pharaoh's place.'

'Isn't your life more important than the law?'

'No,' said Pazair.

'You're the most single-minded man I've ever met.'

How wrong the Nubian was! Pazair could not drive Neferet from his thoughts, even in these moments of high drama. Following this last murder, which had confirmed that his suspicions were well-founded, he ought to have been concentrating on his investigation. Instead, love, as strong as the south wind, had swept away all his resolution. He stood up and leant against the well, his eyes closed.

'Do you feel ill?' asked Kem.

'It will pass.'

'The fourth guard was still alive until a little while ago,' Kem reminded him. 'What about the fifth?'

'If we could question him, we'd solve the mystery.'

'I'm sure his village isn't far away.'

'We shan't go there.'

The Nubian smiled. 'At last you're seeing reason.'

'We shan't go because we're being followed and someone will get there before us. The baker was murdered because we came here. If the fifth guard is still in the land of the living, we'll condemn him to death if we carry on like this.'

'Then what do you suggest?'

'I don't know yet. For the moment, we shall return to Thebes. The person or persons watching us will think we are straying from the right path.'

*

Pazair examined the results of the previous year's wood tax. The fat official opened up his archives and guzzled carob juice. It was obvious that the little judge was of no account. While Pazair consulted large numbers of accounting tablets, the Theban official wrote a letter to Mentmose, reassuring him that the young man was not going to ruffle any feathers.

Despite the comfortable room he had been provided with, Pazair spent a sleepless night, torn between the obsessive desire to see Neferet again and the need to continue his enquiries. To see her again, even though she was indifferent to him; to continue his enquiries, even though the matter was already dead and buried.

Sensing his master's turmoil, Brave lay down next to him. The dog's warmth gave him the energy he needed. Pazair stroked the dog, thinking of the walks he had taken along the Nile when he was a carefree young man; he'd then been convinced he was going to lead a peaceful existence in his village, where life followed the rhythm of the seasons.

Destiny had seized him like a merciless bird of prey. If he gave up his mad dreams – Neferet, the truth – would he regain his peace of mind?

He lied to himself in vain. Neferet would be his only love.

Dawn brought him a glimmer of hope. There was one man who might be able to help him.

So he went to the quayside, where a large market was held each day. As soon as the foodstuffs had been unloaded from the boats, the sellers laid them out on their little stalls. Men and women ran open-air shops selling a wide variety of foods, fabrics, clothes and a thousand and one other things.

Under the reed awning of one stall, some sailors were drinking beer and ogling the pretty housewives as they came to see what was new. A fisherman, sitting in front of a plaited reed basket containing Nile perch, exchanged some fine fish for a small pot of unguent. A pastry cook bartered cakes for a necklace and a pair of sandals, while a grocer swapped beans for a broom. Each transaction involved much haggling before a compromise was reached. If the debate centred on the weight of the goods, the matter was referred to a scribe with a set of scales.

At last, Pazair saw him.

As he had thought, Kani was there, selling chickpeas, cucumbers and leeks.

The baboon suddenly pulled at its leash with unexpected force and hurled itself on a thief whom nobody had noticed stealing two succulent lettuces. The monkey sank its teeth into the offender's thigh and he, roaring with pain, tried in vain to fight off his attacker. Kem intervened so that Killer did not rip the flesh to shreds, and the thief was handed over to two guards.

'You're always coming to my rescue, Judge,' remarked the gardener.

'I need your help, Kani.'

'In two hours I'll have sold everything. We'll go to my house then.'

The vegetable garden was bordered by cornflowers, mandragora and chrysanthemums. Kani had created neat beds for each type of vegetable: beans, chickpeas, lentils, cucumbers, onions, leeks, lettuces, fenugreek. At the far end of the garden was a palm grove, protecting it from the wind; to its left were a vineyard and an orchard. Kani delivered most of his produce to the temple and sold his surplus at the market.

'Are you happy with your new life?' asked Pazair.

'The work's as hard as ever, but at least I'm reaping the rewards. The steward at the temple likes me.'

'Do you grow medicinal plants?'

'Come with me.'

Kani showed Pazair his proudest creation: a bed of

simples, curative herbs and plants from which remedies could be made. Purple loosestrife, mustard, pyrethrum, pennyroyal and camomile were just a few examples.

'Did you know that Neferet is living in Thebes?' asked Pazair.

'Oh no, Judge, not now. She has an important job in Memphis.'

'Nebamon dismissed her from it.'

Intense anger showed in Kani's face. 'He dared . . . that crocodile dared!'

'Neferet no longer belongs to the official body of doctors and no longer has access to the great medicinal workshops. She must confine herself to a village and send seriously ill patients to more highly qualified colleagues.'

Kani almost pawed the ground in his fury. 'That's shameful, unjust!'

'You could help her.'

The gardener looked up questioningly. 'How?'

'If you supply her with rare and expensive medicinal plants, she'll be able to prepare remedies and cure her patients. We'll all fight to restore her reputation.'

'Where is she?'

'I don't know.'

'I'll find her,' said Kani determinedly. 'Is that what you wanted me to do?'

'No.'

'Then what is it?'

'I'm looking for a man who used to be in the Sphinx's honour guard. He's returned to his home, on the west bank, to live out his retirement. He is in hiding.'

'Why?'

'Because he has a secret. If he talks to me, his life will be in danger. I was going to speak to one of his fellow guardsmen, who had become a baker, but he was killed in an accident.'

'What do you want me to do?'

'Find him. Then I shall act – with the utmost discretion. Someone's watching me, so if I search for the man myself, he'll be murdered before I can speak to him.'

'Murdered!' echoed Kani.

'I shan't conceal the gravity of the situation, or the risks you'll be running.'

'You're a judge, so can't you—'

'I have no proof, and I'm involved in a matter which the army has covered up.'

'But what if you're wrong?'

'When I hear the guard's testimony – if he's still alive – all doubts will be dispelled.'

'I know the towns and villages on the west bank very well.'

'Be very careful,' warned Pazair. 'The murderer kills without hesitation and doesn't care about losing his soul.'

Kani smiled and said, 'Just this once, allow me to be the judge.'

At the end of every week, Denes held a reception to thank the captains of his cargo boats and a few senior officials who were especially willing to sign shipping, loading and unloading permits. Everyone loved the splendour of the vast garden, with its lakes and its aviary full of exotic birds. Denes went from one guest to another, exchanging friendly words and asking after their families, while Nenophar strutted about.

This evening, the atmosphere was less cheerful than usual. Ramses' decree had caused anxiety among the ruling elite. Some suspected others of having confidential information and keeping it to themselves. Denes, flanked by two colleagues whose business he was planning to absorb after buying up their boats, greeted a rare guest: Sheshi. He spent most of his life in the most secret workshop at the palace, and had little time for fraternizing with the nobility. A short man, with a sombre, rather unattractive face, he was said to be skilful and modest.

'Your presence honours us, dear friend,' said Denes.

171

A half-smile twitched on Sheshi's lips.

'What was the outcome of your latest experiments? Mum's the word, of course, but everyone's talking about them. They say you've created an extraordinary fusion of metals that will enable us to make unbreakable swords and spears.'

Sheshi shook his head doubtfully.

'Ah, obviously it's a military secret. Well, do your best to succeed. With what's in store for us . . .'

'What does that mean?' asked another guest.

'If Pharaoh's decree is to be believed, a fine old war. Ramses wants to crush the Hittites and rid us of the Asian princelings who are always rebelling against us.'

'But Ramses loves peace,' objected the captain of a merchant vessel.

'That may be the official position, but his actions speak differently.'

'That's very worrying.'

'Not at all,' said Denes. 'Who and what is there for Egypt to fear?'

'Some people are saying the decree shows that Ramses' power is weakening.'

Denes burst out laughing. 'Ramses is the greatest of all and he will remain so. Let's not turn a minor incident into a tragedy.'

'All the same, we ought to check our food reserves.'

Nenophar cut in, 'It's obvious what ought to be done: prepare for a new tax and fiscal reform.'

'Rearmament has to be financed,' added Denes. 'If he wanted to, Sheshi could tell us about it, and justify Ramses' decision.'

All eyes were turned on Sheshi, but he said nothing.

Ever the accomplished hostess, Nenophar guided her guests to a pavilion where refreshments were being served.

Mentmose took Denes by the arm and led him aside. 'Your problems with the law are over, I hope?'

'Pazair didn't press the point. He's more reasonable than I thought. He's young and full of ambition, certainly, but there's nothing wrong with that, is there? You and I both went through that stage, before we became leading citizens.'

Mentmose frowned. 'His whole personality . . .'

'It will improve with time.'

'You're an optimist.'

'No, a realist. Pazair is a good judge.'

'And an incorruptible one, according to you.'

'An incorruptible and intelligent judge who respects those who observe the law. Thanks to men like him, business is prosperous and the country is at peace. What more could anyone want? Believe me, dear friend, you should look favourably upon Pazair's career.'

'That's valuable advice.'

'There'll be no malpractice from him.'

'That's certainly an important point.'

'But you still have reservations.'

'He sometimes alarms me a bit. He doesn't seem to appreciate subtlety.'

'That's just his youth and inexperience,' said Denes. 'What does the Judge of the Porch think of him?'

'He agrees with you.'

'You see!'

The news Mentmose had received from Thebes by special messenger confirmed what Denes said. Mentmose need not have worried for nothing: the judge was concerned merely with the wood tax and the honesty of those paying it.

Perhaps he ought not to have alerted the tjaty so soon. But one could never take too many precautions.

20

Going on long country walks with Way-Finder and Brave, consulting documents in the government offices, drawing up an accurate list of those liable to pay the wood tax, inspecting villages, having administrative discussions with headmen and landowners. That was how Pazair spent his days in Thebes.

Each day ended with a visit to Kani, and each day the gardener's head hung low, and Pazair could tell that he had found neither Neferet nor the fifth ex-soldier.

A week passed. The officials in Mentmose's pay sent him routine reports about the judge's activities. Kem simply patrolled the markets and arrested thieves. Soon it would be time to return to Memphis.

Pazair crossed a palm grove, took an earthen track beside the irrigation channel, and went down the steps leading to Kani's garden. When dusk approached, Kani tended his medicinal plants, which needed regular careful attention. He slept in a hut after spending part of the night watering the plants.

The garden was deserted.

Surprised, Pazair walked round it, then tried the door of the hut. It was open. He sat down on a low wall and watched the sun go down. The full moon turned the river to silver. As time passed, anxiety clutched at his heart. Perhaps Kani had identified the fifth guard. Perhaps he had been followed. Perhaps . . . Pazair reproached himself for involving the gardener in an investigation that was beyond his skill. If something bad had happened to Kani, he would consider himself chiefly responsible.

Even when he felt the cool air of night on his shoulders, the judge did not move. He would stay there until dawn, and then he would know Kani wasn't coming back. Teeth clenched, muscles aching, Pazair deeply regretted his actions.

A boat was coming across the river.

Pazair got up and ran to the bank. 'Kani!'

The gardener moored the boat to a stake, and slowly climbed up the slope.

'Why are you so late back?' asked Pazair.

'Are you shivering?'

'Yes, I'm cold.'

'The spring wind makes people ill. Let's go into the hut.'

The gardener sat down on a tree stump, his back propped against the wooden wall, and Pazair sat on a tool chest.

'Any news of the guard?'

'No, still nothing.'

'Were you in any danger?'

'Never. I buy rare plants here and there, and I gossip with the old folk.'

Pazair asked the question that was burning on his lips. 'What about Neferet?'

'I didn't see her, but I know where she's living.'

Sheshi's workshop occupied three large rooms in the basement of a building attached to the barracks. The regiment lodged there contained only support soldiers who built earthworks. Everyone thought Sheshi worked at the palace, but he carried out his real research in these discreet surroundings. To outward appearances, there were no particular security measures, but anyone who tried to walk down the staircase into the basement would be roughly intercepted and questioned.

Sheshi had been recruited by the palace because he was exceptionally knowledgeable about the resistance of materials. Originally a bronze worker, he had continually sought better ways of handling raw copper, which was vital for manufacturing stone-cutters' chisels. Because of his success and dedication, he had been promoted again and again. The day he had provided remarkably good tools to cut stone blocks for Ramses' Temple of a Million Years, his reputation had reached the ears of the king.

Sheshi had summoned his three principal colleagues, all of them mature and experienced. Lamps with smokeless wicks lit the basement. Slowly and meticulously, Sheshi set out the papyri on which he had noted down his latest calculations.

The three men waited uneasily. His silence did not augur well, even though it was usual for him not to say very much. This sudden and urgent summons was not at all like him.

The little man turned his back on the others and asked, 'Which one of you talked?'

No one replied.

'I shall not repeat my question.'

'It has no meaning.'

'When I was at a reception, a prominent citizen talked about new fusions of metals and new weapons.'

'That's impossible! Whoever says that is lying to you.'

'I heard it myself. Now, who talked?'

Once again, the question was met with silence.

'Even if the information spread abroad is incomplete, and therefore inaccurate, my trust has been betrayed.'

'You mean—'

'I mean that you're all dismissed.'

Neferet had chosen the poorest, most isolated village in the Theban region, which lay on the fringes of the desert. It was poorly irrigated, and its inhabitants suffered from a higher than usual incidence of skin diseases. The young woman was neither sad nor downcast, though; she was happy to have escaped from Nebamon's clutches, even if she had given up a promising career in return for her freedom. She would care for the poorest people with whatever means she had, and she would be content with a solitary life in the country. When a hospital boat went downriver to Memphis, she would go and see Branir. He knew her, and would not try to change her mind.

On only the second day after her arrival, Neferet had cured the most important person in the village, a man who specialized in fattening geese and who suffered from an irregular heartbeat. A long massage and manipulation of his spine had swiftly put him back on his feet. The cure was thought miraculous, and Neferet had become the heroine of the village.

The peasants asked her to advise them on how to fight the enemies of harvests and orchards, notably grasshoppers and crickets, but she preferred to fight another plague, which seemed to her to be at the root of the villagers' skin problems: flies and mosquitoes. Their abundance was explained by the presence of a stagnant pool which had not been drained for three years. Neferet had it dried out, advised all the villagers to cleanse and fumigate their houses, and treated the bites with loriot fat and applications of fresh oil.

The only patient who caused her concern was an old man with a worn-out heart. If his condition worsened, he would have to go to the hospital in Thebes – there'd be no reason for it if only she had certain rare plants she needed.

She was tending the old man at his bedside when a small boy came to tell her that a stranger had arrived and was asking questions about her.

Even here, Nebamon would not leave her in peace! Now what was he accusing her of? What failure was he going to have her judged guilty of? She must hide. The villagers would keep silent, and the emissary would go away again.

Pazair sensed that the villagers were lying and that they knew the name Neferet, despite their silence. The isolated village feared any intrusion; most of the doors closed in his face.

He was about to give up and leave when he saw a woman heading for the rocky hills.

'Neferet!' he called.

She turned, saw him, and came back towards him. 'Judge Pazair, what are you doing here?'

'I want to speak with you.'

The light of the sun shone out of her eyes. The country air had bronzed her skin. Pazair wanted to reveal his feelings to her, pour out his heart, but he could not say a single word.

She said, 'Let's go up to the top of that little hill.'

He would have followed her to the ends of the earth, to the bottom of the sea, to the heart of darkness. To walk beside her, to sit down next to her, to hear her voice, were intoxicating joys.

'Branir told me what happened,' he said when they were settled. 'Do you want to lodge a complaint against Nebamon?'

'It would be no use. Many doctors owe their careers to him and would testify against me.'

'I'll charge them with perjury.'

'There are too many of them, and, anyway, Nebamon would stop you.'

Despite the gentle spring warmth, Pazair shivered. He could not suppress a sneeze.

'Have you caught a chill?' she asked.

'I spent the night out of doors, waiting for Kani to come back.'

'Kani the gardener?'

'He's the one who found you. He lives in Thebes, and is tending his own garden there. Here's your chance, Neferet: he produces medicinal plants, and knows how to grow even the rarest ones.'

'You mean I could set up a workshop here?'

'Why not? You have all the necessary knowledge of medicines. Not only could you treat serious illnesses, but your reputation would be restored.'

'I have little appetite for beginning that struggle again. I'm content with my current situation.'

'Don't waste your gifts. Do it for the sick.'

Pazair sneezed again.

'Shouldn't we attend to you first? The treatises say that a spring wind breaks the bones, shatters the skull and hollows out the brain. I must prevent that disaster.'

Her smile, which was utterly free of irony, delighted him.

'Will you let Kani help you?' he asked.

'He's stubborn. If he's made his mind up, I can't stop him. Let us deal with this emergency first: a cold is a serious ailment. I'll put palm juice into your nostrils and then, if that doesn't work, mother's milk and aromatic gum.'

The cold grew worse. Neferet took the judge into her modest house in the centre of the village. He was developing a cough, so she prescribed him natural sulphur of arsenic, which the country people called "that which makes the heart blossom".

'We must try to stop it getting worse. Sit down on this mat and don't move.'

She gave instructions without raising her voice, which was as gentle as her gaze. Pazair hoped that the chill would last a long time and that he'd have to stay as long as possible in this humble room.

Neferet mixed sulphur of arsenic, resin and the leaves of antiseptic plants, crushed them and reduced the whole to a paste, which she heated. She spread it out on a stone which she placed in front of the judge, then covered it with an upturned pot with a hole in the bottom.

'Take this reed,' she told her patient. 'Place it in the hole and breathe through the nose and mouth alternately. The inhalation will relieve your symptoms.'

Pazair would not have minded if it failed, but the treatment worked. The congestion was reduced, and he breathed more easily.

'No more shivers?' she asked.

'No, but I feel rather tired.'

'For a few days, I advise you to eat rich, rather fatty foods, red meat and plenty of fresh oil on your food. A little rest would also do you good.'

'I can't rest.'

'What brings you back to Thebes?'

He wanted to cry out, 'You, Neferet, only you,' but the words wouldn't come. He was certain that she could sense his passion, and waited for her to give him a chance to open his heart, for he dared not shatter her peace with a madness she would undoubtedly deplore.

Instead, he said, 'Perhaps one crime, perhaps several.'

He sensed that she was troubled by the drama, even though she was not involved in it. Had he the right to involve her in this affair, whose true nature he himself did not know?

'I trust you unreservedly, Neferet, but I don't want to burden you with my worries.'

'You're bound to secrecy, aren't you?'

'Yes, until I formulate my conclusions.'

'Murders . . . would those be your conclusions?'

'My firm personal belief.'

'But it's many years since a murder was committed!'

'Five ex-soldiers, who formed the honour guard to the Great Sphinx, were supposed to have died in a fall from its head during an inspection. An accident: that's the army's official version. One them actually survived and was hiding in a village on the west bank, where he was working as a baker. I wanted to question him, but when I got there he really was dead – another "accident". Mentmose is having me followed as if I were a criminal because I am carrying out an investigation. I'm lost, Neferet. Forget everything I've told you.'

'Do you want to give up?'

'I have a keen love of truth and justice. If I give up, I'll destroy myself.'

'Can I help you?'

A different fever filled Pazair's eyes. 'If we could talk from time to time, I'd feel braver.'

'A chill can have side effects and they should be carefully watched. Several more consultations will be necessary.'

21

The night at the inn was as pleasurable as it was exhausting. Suti indulged himself with slices of grilled beef, aubergines in cream sauce, an abundance of cakes, and a superb forty-year-old Libyan woman who had fled her own country and now entertained Egyptian soldiers. How lustily she laughed as she bent her body into unbelievable positions. The chariot officer had not lied: one man was not enough for her. Although Suti had always considered himself the most energetic of lovers, he was obliged to make a tactical withdrawal and pass the baton to his superior officer.

When the chariot set off next morning, Suti could hardly keep his eyes open.

'You'll have to learn how to do without sleep, my lad. Don't forget that the enemy will attack when you are tired. Now, I've a piece of good news for you. We're to be the vanguard of the vanguard – the first blows struck will be ours. If you want to be a hero, you're in luck.'

Suti clutched his bow to his chest.

The chariot ran along the King's Walls, a series of formidable fortresses built along Egypt's north-eastern frontier by the sovereigns of the Middle Kingdom, and constantly improved upon by their successors. It was well named, for it was in effect a huge wall stretching from the ocean shore to Iunu. The fortresses were linked by visual signals, and the system prevented invasion attempts by sand-travellers* or Asiatic peoples.

The King's Walls housed both permanent garrisons of soldiers, experienced in watching the borders, and customs officials. No one entered or left Egypt without giving their name and the reason for their journey; traders had to state the nature of their merchandise and pay a tax. The border guards turned back undesirable foreigners, and people were not allowed to pass until their documents had been carefully scrutinized by an official from the capital. As Pharaoh's stele proclaimed, 'Anyone who crosses this border becomes one of my sons.'

The chariot officer presented his papers to the commander of a fortress whose sloping walls were surrounded by ditches. Archers were stationed on the battlements, and lookouts in the towers.

As he did so, he looked around and commented, 'The guard's been reinforced.'

Ten armed men surrounded the chariot.

'Dismount,' ordered the commander of the guard post.

'Are you joking?'

'Your documents aren't in order.'

The officer gripped the reins tightly, ready to whip his horses into a gallop. Spears and arrows were aimed at him.

'Dismount immediately.'

He turned to Suti. 'What do you think, youngster?'

'There'll be better battles to fight, sir.'

They stepped down.

'Your documents don't bear the seal of the first fort of the King's Walls,' said the commander. 'You'll have to turn back.'

'We are already late.'

*Like the Libyans, the Bedouin were permanent troublemakers whom the Egyptians had been fighting since the earliest dynasties. In ancient times, they were known as 'sand-travellers'.

'Rules are rules.'

'Couldn't we discuss this?' asked the officer.

'Very well. In my office – but don't get your hopes up.'

The discussion was brief. The officer left the office at a run, leapt into the chariot and galloped off along the road to Asia. The wheels squeaked, sending up a cloud of dust.

'Why the hurry, sir?' asked Suti. 'Everything's been settled now.'

'Well, more or less. I hit that idiot hard, but he may wake up sooner than I planned – that kind of stubborn fool has a hard head. I put our documents in order myself. In the army, youngster, you have to know how to improvise.'

The next few days of the journey were peaceful. Lengthy periods were spent travelling, caring for the horses, checking equipment, sleeping under the stars, stocking up on food in small towns where the officer contacted an army messenger or a member of the secret services. Their job was to inform the main body of the forces that there was nothing to halt their progress.

The wind turned, and became biting.

'Spring in Asia is often cold,' said the officer. 'Put your cloak on.'

'You seem on edge, sir.'

'Danger's coming. I can scent it, like a dog. How much food have we got?'

'Enough flat cakes, meatballs, onions and water for three days.'

'That should be enough.'

The chariot entered a silent village; there was no one in the main square. Suti's stomach knotted up.

'Don't panic, youngster. They may be in the fields.'

The chariot advanced very slowly. The officer snatched up a spear and looked around him with a practised eye. He halted before the official building where the military representative and interpreter were billeted. It was empty.

'The army won't get our report, so it'll know something serious has happened. A rebellion, most likely.'

'Are we going to stay here, sir?'

'I'd rather go on. Why? Wouldn't you?'

'That depends,' said Suti.

'On what?'

'Where's General Asher?'

'How do you know about him?'

'He's famous in Memphis. I'd like to serve under him.'

'Then you really are in luck. He's the one we're to join up with.'

'Do you think he evacuated this village?'

'Certainly not.'

'Then who did, sir?'

'The sand-travellers. They're the vilest, most fanatical and deceitful people. Raiding, pillaging, taking hostages, that's their strategy. If we don't wipe them out, they'll bring ruin to Asia, to the peninsula between Egypt and the Red Sea, and to all the surrounding provinces. They're willing to form an alliance with any invader, they despise women as much as we love them, and they spit on beauty and the gods. I'm not afraid of them, but I dread them, with their ragged beards, their turbans and their long robes. Always remember, youngster, they're cowards: they strike from behind.'

'Do you think they killed all the villagers?'

'Probably.'

'Then General Asher's isolated, sir, cut off from the main army.'

'He may be.'

Suti's long black hair danced in the wind. Despite his solid build and powerful torso, the young man felt weak and vulnerable. 'Sand-travellers between him and us. How many, do you think?'

The officer shrugged. 'Ten, a hundred, a thousand . . .'

'Ten I can deal with. A hundred, I'm not so sure.'

'A thousand, youngster, that's the number for a real hero. You're not thinking of deserting me, I hope?'

The chariot set off again, the horses galloping towards the entrance to a ravine bordered by vertical cliffs. A tangle of bushes grew out of the rock, leaving only a narrow way through.

The horses whinnied and reared; the officer calmed them.

'Sir, they can sense something's wrong,' said Suti.

'So can I, lad. The sand-travellers are hiding in the bushes. They'll try to slash the horses' legs with axes, bring us down, slit our throats and cut off our testicles.'

'If you ask me, the price of heroism is too high.'

'Thanks to you, we shan't run much risk. An arrow into each bush, a good gallop, and we'll win.'

Suti swallowed. 'Are you sure about that?'

'Why? Aren't you? Just don't think about it too much.'

The officer shook the reins, and the horses leapt forward into the ravine. Suti had no time to be afraid; he let fly one arrow after another. The first two landed in empty bushes, but the third pierced the eye of a sand-traveller who fell out of the bush with a cry of pain.

'Keep it up, youngster,' shouted the officer.

His hair standing on end and his blood turned to ice, Suti aimed at each bush, turning to right and left with a speed he would have thought himself incapable of. The sand-travellers fell, wounded in the belly, the chest, the head.

The exit from the ravine was blocked by a barrier of stones and tree roots.

'Hold on tight, lad, we're going to jump it!'

Suti stopped firing and gripped the edge of the chariot. Two enemies he hadn't been able to shoot hurled their axes at the Egyptians.

At full speed, the two horses leapt over the barricade at its lowest point. The roots scratched their legs, and a stone broke the spokes of the right wheel, while another made a hole in the right side of the shell. For a moment, the chariot swayed, but with a final effort the warhorses cleared the obstacle.

The chariot raced on for some time before slowing down. Tossed about, dazed, barely keeping his balance, Suti hung on to his bow. At last, panting, covered in sweat and with foam on their muzzles, the horses halted at the foot of a hill.

The officer collapsed over the reins; there was an axe buried between his shoulder blades.

'Sir!' Suti tried to lift him up.

'Remember, youngster, cowards always attack from behind.'

'Don't die, sir!'

'Now you're the only hero.'

The officer's eyes closed, and he stopped breathing.

For a long time, Suti held the body tightly. Never again would the officer fight, urge him on, attempt the impossible. Suti was alone, lost in a hostile country, he, the hero, whose praises could be sung only by a dead man.

Suti buried the officer, taking care to fix the place in his memory. If he survived, he would come back for the body and return it to Egypt. There was no crueller destiny, for a child of the Two Lands, than to be buried far from his homeland.

Turning back meant going through the ravine again; going on meant the risk of meeting more enemies. But he chose the second option, hoping he'd soon be able to make contact with General Asher's soldiers – assuming they hadn't all been wiped out.

The horses were rested enough to continue. Suti picked up the reins and drove off. If there was another ambush, he would not be able to drive the chariot and use his bow at the same time. His throat tight, he followed a stony track which ended at a dilapidated hovel. He grabbed his sword and jumped down. Smoke was coming out of a rudimentary chimney.

'Come out of there!' he shouted.

On the threshold there appeared a wild-looking young

woman dressed in rags, with dirty hair. She was brandishing a rough knife.

'Don't be afraid,' he said. 'Put the knife down.'

The woman looked too frail to put up a fight, and Suti wasn't afraid of her. But when he drew close, she threw herself at him and tried to plunge the blade into his heart. He dodged aside, but felt a burning pain in his left upper arm. Maddened, she struck again. He disarmed her with a kick, then overpowered her and pushed her to the ground. Blood trickled down his arm.

'Calm down, or I'll tie you up.'

She struggled like a fury. He turned her over and knocked her out with a blow to the nape of the neck. His relationships with women, as a hero, were taking a turn for the worse. He carried her into the hovel, whose single room had a floor of beaten earth, filthy walls, miserable furniture and a hearth covered with soot. Suti laid down his pathetic prisoner on a tattered mat, and bound her wrists and ankles with rope.

Suddenly, exhaustion overcame him. He sat down with his back to the chimney breast and his head in his hands, and began to shake all over.

The place's filth repelled him. Behind the house was a well. He filled jars, washed his wound, and then cleaned the room. When he'd finished, he looked down at the woman and said thoughtfully, 'You could do with a good wash, too.'

He threw some water over her, and she awoke and started screaming in rage. The contents of another jar silenced her cries. When he took off her dirty dress, she started wriggling like a snake.

'I don't want to rape you, you silly girl!'

Could she understand what he meant? She submitted. Standing up, naked, she seemed to enjoy the wash. When he dried her, she almost smiled. Without its layer of dirt and grease, her hair was fair, which surprised him.

'You're pretty. Have you ever been kissed?'

From the way she parted her lips and moved her tongue, Suti realized that he was not the first.

'If you promise to be good, I'll untie you.'

Her eyes pleaded with him. He took off the rope which bound her feet, stroked her calves, her thighs, and placed his mouth upon the golden curls of her sex. Her body arched like a bow. Once her hands were free, she embraced him.

Suti had slept for ten dreamless hours. Then his wound started to hurt, and he awoke with a start and went outside.

She had stolen his weapons, cut the chariot reins and chased the horses away. No bow, no dagger, no sword, no boots, no cloak. The chariot would sink uselessly into the mud where it stood in the rain, which must have been pouring down for hours. The hero, reduced to the status of an idiot fooled by a madwoman, could do nothing but walk north. In rage, he kicked the chariot to pieces so that it would not fall into enemy hands.

Dressed in nothing but a plain kilt, and laden like a mule, Suti walked through continuous rain. In a bag, he had some stale bread, a piece of chariot-shaft bearing the officer's name, a couple of pitchers of fresh water and the tattered mat. He crossed a pass, walked through a pine forest and slithered down a steep slope ending in a lake, which he skirted.

The mountains were becoming inhospitable. After a night spent in the shelter of a rock which protected him against the east wind, he climbed a slippery path and ventured into an arid region. His food stocks were exhausted, and he began to suffer from thirst.

As he was taking a few mouthfuls from a stagnant pool, Suti heard branches crack. Several men were coming. He crawled away and hid behind the trunk of a giant pine tree.

Five men were pushing a prisoner, his hands bound behind his back. Their leader, a short man, seized him by the hair and forced him to kneel. Suti was too far away to hear what he said, but the tortured man's cries soon shattered the calm of the mountains.

One against five, and without weapons . . . Suti had no chance of saving the luckless man.

The torturer rained blows upon the prisoner, interrogated him, beat him again, then ordered his men to drag the prisoner to a cave. After a final interrogation, he slit the man's throat.

When the murderers had gone, Suti stayed still for over an hour. He thought of Pazair, of his love of justice and his idealism. How would he have reacted to this barbarism? He did not know that, so close to Egypt, there was a lawless world where human life had no value.

He forced himself to go down to the cave, though his legs almost gave way beneath him as the dying man's cries echoed in his head. The tortured man's soul had fled. To judge from his kilt and general appearance, he was an Egyptian, probably a soldier from Asher's army who had fallen into rebel hands. Suti dug him a grave with his bare hands, inside the cave.

Shocked and exhausted, he continued on his way, putting himself in the hands of destiny. If he came face to face with the enemy, he would no longer have the strength to defend himself.

When two helmeted soldiers hailed him, he collapsed onto the damp earth.

A tent. A bed, a cushion beneath his head, a blanket. Suti sat up.

The point of a knife forced him to lie down again, and a voice said, 'Who are you?'

The questioner was an Egyptian officer, with a deeply furrowed face.

'My name's Suti, and I'm an archer in the corps of charioteers.'

'Where have you come from?'

He related everything that had happened.

'Can you prove that?'

'In my bag there's a piece of the chariot, with my officer's name on it.'

'Tell me again what happened to him.'

'The sand-travellers killed him, I buried him.'

'You ran away, didn't you?'

'Of course I didn't! I killed a good two dozen of them with my arrows.'

'When did you enlist?'

'At the beginning of the month.'

'Barely a fortnight, and you're already an elite archer!'

'It's a gift.'

'I believe in training, not gifts. Why don't you tell me the truth?'

Suti threw back the blanket. 'It *is* the truth.'

'You killed your officer, didn't you?'

'You're mad!'

'A long stay in a prison cell will straighten out your ideas.'

Suti ran towards the way out. Two soldiers seized his arms, and a third punched him in the belly and knocked him out with a blow to the back of the neck.

'We were right to take care of this spy,' said the officer. 'He'll sing like a bird.'

22

Sitting at a table in one of Thebes' busiest taverns, Pazair steered the conversation towards Hattusa, one of Ramses' diplomatic wives. She was a daughter of the Hittite emperor, and was named after her birthplace, the capital of the Hittite empire. When a peace treaty was concluded with the Hittites, Pharaoh had married the princess as a pledge of his sincerity. She had been placed in charge of the harem at Thebes, and lived a life of luxury there.

Inaccessible and invisible, Hattusa was highly unpopular. Many rumours surrounded her: she was said to practise evil magic, to be in league with the demons of night, and to have refused to appear at major festivals.

'It's because of her,' claimed the tavern keeper, 'that the price of ointments has doubled.'

'How is she responsible for that?'

'She has vast numbers of attendant ladies, who spend all day making themselves look beautiful. The harem uses an incredible amount of high-quality unguents, buys them at inflated prices and makes the price rise. It's the same with oil. When are we going to be rid of the foreigner?'

No one spoke up in Hattusa's defence.

Luxuriant plants and flowers surrounded the buildings that made up the harem on the east bank of Thebes. The palaces were served by a canal whose abundant water irrigated several gardens reserved for elderly and widowed ladies of the court, a large orchard, and a flower-filled park where spinning and weaving women relaxed.

Like other Egyptian harems, the Theban one contained many workshops, schools of dancing, music and poetry, and a centre for producing aromatic herbs and beauty products. Specialists worked in wood, enamels and ivory. Superb linen dresses were made and sophisticated flower arrangements created.

Always bustling with activity, the harem was also an educational centre for the training of Egyptians and foreigners destined for senior government posts. Alongside elegant ladies decked with dazzling jewellery were craftsmen, teachers and managers whose job was to ensure that the residents received ample fresh food.

Judge Pazair arrived early in the morning at the main palace. His status enabled him to get past the guards and speak to Hattusa's steward, who passed on the judge's request to his mistress. To the steward's surprise, she did not reject it.

The judge was shown into a four-pillared room whose walls were decorated with paintings of birds and flowers. Many-coloured floor tiles added to the room's charm. Hattusa was sitting on a gilded wooden throne, while two maids bustled around her with pots and spoons of make-up, and boxes of perfume. Their mistress's morning toilette concluded with the most delicate operation of all, the adjustment of the wig and the replacement of any defective curls with false locks of hair.

At thirty years old, the Hittite princess was radiant and haughty. She sat gazing at her beauty in a mirror whose handle was shaped like a lotus stem.

'A judge in my apartments so early in the morning. I'm curious. Why have you come here?'

'I would like to ask you a few questions, my lady.'

She put down the mirror and dismissed her attendants. 'Will a private conversation suit you?'

'Perfectly.'

'A little entertainment at last! Life in this palace is so boring.'

With her very white skin, long slender hands and black eyes, Hattusa was at once alluring and disturbing. Mischievous, sharp-tongued and quick-witted, she showed no mercy to those who spoke to her, and took pleasure in pointing out their weaknesses, be they faults in speech, clumsiness or physical imperfections.

She looked Pazair up and down. 'You aren't the most handsome man in Egypt, but a woman could fall in love with you and remain faithful. Impatient, passionate, idealistic . . . you're a collection of serious defects. And you are so serious, almost sombre – so much so that it ruins your youthfulness.'

'Will you permit me to question you, my lady?'

'An audacious move! Are you aware of your impudence? I am one of the wives of the great Ramses, and could have you dismissed within the hour.'

'You know very well that that is untrue. I would defend my cause before the tjaty's court, and you would be charged with abusing your power.'

'Egypt is a strange country. Not only do its inhabitants believe in justice, but they actually respect it and see that it is put into practice. The miracle won't last, of course.'

Hattusa picked up her mirror and examined the curls of her wig, one by one. 'If your questions amuse me, I'll answer them.'

'Who delivers fresh bread to you?'

The Hittite's eyes widened in astonishment. 'You're worrying about my bread?'

'To be precise, about the baker on the west bank who wanted to work for you.'

'Everyone wants to work for me. My generosity is well known.'

'And yet the common people dislike you.'

'The feeling is mutual. The common people are stupid here, as they are elsewhere. I am a foreigner, and proud to remain so. I have dozens of servants at my feet because the king has entrusted me with the running of this harem, the most prosperous of all.'

'My lady, please tell me about the baker.'

'See my steward – he'll tell you. If this baker has delivered any bread here, you'll know about it. Why is it so important?'

'Are you aware of an incident which occurred near the Great Sphinx at Giza?'

'What are you hiding, Judge Pazair?'

'Nothing vital, my lady.'

'This game is as boring as festivals and courtiers. The only thing I want is to go home. It would be amusing if the Hittite armies crushed your soldiers and invaded Egypt – a splendid revenge! But I shall probably die here, the wife of the most powerful king in the world, a man I've seen only once on the day when our marriage was sealed by diplomats and jurors in order to ensure our peoples' peace and happiness. Who cares about my happiness?'

'Thank you for your help, my lady.'

'It is for me to bring this audience to an end, not you.'

'I did not mean to offend you.'

'You may leave.'

Hattusa's steward told Pazair that he had indeed ordered bread from an excellent baker on the west bank, but none had been received.

Puzzled, Pazair left the harem. In accordance with his usual practice, he had tried to follow up even the smallest clue, even if it meant annoying one of the greatest women in the kingdom.

Was she somehow mixed up in the plot? It was yet another question with no answer.

The mayor of Memphis's assistant opened his mouth in panic.

'Relax,' advised Qadash. He had not hidden the truth: the molar would have to come out. Despite his intensive treatment, he had not been able to save it.

'Open wider.'

True, Qadash's hand might not be as steady as it had once been, but it would continue to prove his talent for a long time to come. After numbing the man's mouth, he moved on to the first phase of the extraction, positioning his pincers round the tooth.

His grip was imprecise and shaky, and he cut the gum, but pressed on regardless. But he had lost his nerve and did not manage the operation well; and when he tried to get the roots out, he caused heavy bleeding. Hurriedly he seized a drill, placed the pointed end in a hole in a block of wood, and rotated it fast until it produced a spark. As soon as the flame was sufficiently large, he heated a lancet and cauterized the wound.

The mayor's assistant left the surgery with a painful, swollen jaw, and did not thank the tooth doctor. Qadash had lost an important client who would be sure to blacken his name.

He was at a crossroads. He would not admit that he was getting old, or accept that he must give up his craft. True, dancing with the Libyans gave him comfort and a passing revival of his flagging energy, but that was no longer enough. The solution was so near and yet so far!

Qadash must use other weapons, perfect his technique, demonstrate that he was still the best.

Another kind of metal: that was what he needed.

The ferry was pulling away from the bank. Pazair made a huge leap, and landed on the loose boards of the flat-bottomed boat, which was crammed with people and animals.

The ferry travelled continuously between the two banks and, though it was a short crossing, people on board exchanged news and even made business deals. A restless ox jostled him with its hindquarters and pushed him against the woman next to him, who turned her back on him.

'I beg your pardon,' he said.

She did not reply, and covered her face with her hands.

His interest caught, Pazair looked at her more closely. 'You're Madam Sababu, aren't you?'

'Leave me alone.'

In a plain brown dress and maroon shawl, and with her hair untidy, Sababu looked like a pauper.

'There are a few things we need to talk about.'

'I don't know you. Go away.'

'Remember my friend Suti? He persuaded you not to smear my name.'

Terrified, she hurled herself towards the side of the boat.

Pazair seized her arm and held her back. 'The Nile flows dangerously fast here. You might drown.'

'I can't swim.'

Children jumped onto the bank as soon as the ferry arrived. They were followed by donkeys, oxen and peasants. Pazair and Sababu were the last to disembark. He was still holding her by the arm.

'Why won't you leave me alone? I'm just a simple serving woman, I—'

'That's a ridiculous defence. Now, be honest. Didn't you tell Suti I was one of your regular clients?'

'I don't understand.'

'I am Judge Pazair – remember?'

She tried to run away, but he held her fast, and said, 'Be sensible.'

'You're frightening me.'

'You tried to destroy me.'

She burst into tears. Somewhat embarrassed, he let go of her. She might be an enemy, but her distress moved him.

'Who gave you the order to slander me?' he asked.

'I don't know.'

'You're lying.'

'I'm not. One of his men contacted me.'

'A guards officer?'

'How should I know? I don't ask questions.'

'How were you paid?'

'By being left in peace.'

'And why are you helping me now?'

She gave a wan smile. 'Because I have many memories of happy days. My father was a country judge – I adored him. When he died, I couldn't bear to stay in my village and I moved to Memphis. I went from one bad encounter to another and eventually became a prostitute – a rich, respected prostitute, mind you. I was paid to obtain confidential information on the men who visited my ale-house.'

'Paid by Mentmose – am I right?'

'You can draw your own conclusions. I've never sullied the name of a judge, and out of respect for my father's memory I spared you. If you're in danger, that's too bad for you.'

'Aren't you afraid of reprisals?'

'My memories protect me.'

'What if the man who employs you isn't worried by that threat?'

She lowered her eyes. 'That's why I left Memphis and hid here. Because of you, I've lost everything.'

'Did General Asher ever come to your ale-house?'

'No.'

'The truth will out, I promise you.'

'I don't believe in promises any more.'

'Trust me.'

She look up at him again. 'Why do they want to destroy you, Judge?'

'I'm investigating an accident at Giza. The official report says that five men from the Sphinx's honour guard died there.'

'I haven't heard anything about it.'

His attempt had failed. Either she knew nothing, or she was keeping her mouth shut.

Suddenly, she clutched her left shoulder and gave a cry of pain.

'What is the matter?' he asked.

'I suffer badly from rheumatism. Sometimes I can't move my arm at all.'

Pazair did not hesitate. She had helped him, and now he must help her.

Neferet was treating a donkey foal with a wounded foot when Pazair introduced Sababu to her. The prostitute had promised the judge to conceal her identity.

'Neferet,' said Pazair, 'I met this woman on the ferry. She has a bad pain in her shoulder. Can you do anything?'

Neferet washed her hands carefully. 'Have you had this pain long?'

'More than five years,' replied Sababu aggressively. 'Do you know who I am?'

'A sick person whom I shall try to cure.'

'I am Sababu, a prostitute and the owner of an ale-house.'

Pazair went white with horror.

Neferet, however, was unmoved. She said, 'The frequency of sexual relations and the company of partners of dubious cleanliness may be the causes of your illness.'

'Examine me,' said Sababu, and she took off her dress. Underneath, she was naked.

Pazair didn't know where to turn; he wished the ground would open up and swallow him. Neferet would never forgive this insult. He was a prostitute's client – that was the revelation he was offering her. It would be as ridiculous as it would be pointless to deny it.

Neferet felt the shoulder, traced the line of a nerve with her finger, detected the energy points and checked the curve of the shoulder blade.

'It's serious,' she pronounced. 'The rheumatism has already caused deformity. If you don't look after yourself, you'll lose the use of your arm.'

Sababu's arrogance vanished. 'What . . . what must I do?'

'First, you must stop drinking alcohol. Next, each day you must drink a tincture of willow bark. Finally, you must receive a daily application of a balm made from natron, white oil, terebinth resin, oliban, honey and the fat of hippopotamus, crocodile, silurid fish and grey mullet. Those are expensive things, and I haven't got them. You must consult a doctor in Thebes.'

Sababu put on her clothes.

'Don't waste any time,' advised Neferet. 'The disease seems to be progressing rapidly.'

Mortified, Pazair accompanied the prostitute to the entrance to the village.

'Am I free to go?' she asked.

'You broke your word.'

'It may surprise you, but sometimes I have a horror of lying. And lying to a woman like that would be impossible.'

When she had gone, Pazair sat down in the dust beside the road. His naivety had led him to disaster. In an unexpected way, Sababu had at last fulfilled her mission; he felt broken. He, the honest judge, would be seen in Neferet's eyes as a prostitute's accomplice, a hypocrite, a dissolute man.

Sababu of the good heart, Sababu who respected judges and her father's memory, Sababu who had not hesitated to betray him at the first opportunity. Tomorrow, she would sell him to Mentmose – if she hadn't done so already.

Legend had it that those who drowned received the mercy of Osiris when they appeared before the court of the afterlife. The Nile waters purified them. He had lost his beloved, his

good name, his ideals . . . The thought of suicide attracted
him.

He felt a hand on his shoulder.

'Is your cold better?' asked Neferet.

He dared not move. 'I'm sorry.'

'What for?'

'That woman . . . I swear to you that—'

'You brought a sick woman to me. I hope she'll get
treatment soon.'

'She was meant to ruin my reputation, but claims she
stopped before any harm was done.'

'A prostitute with a heart of gold?'

'That's what I thought.'

'Why should anyone blame you for that?'

'I went to Sababu's ale-house with my friend Suti, to
celebrate his enlistment in the army.'

Neferet did not take her hand away.

'Suti's a wonderful person,' he went on, 'with inexhausti-
ble energy. He adores wine and women, wants to become a
great hero, defies all restraint. He and I are friends for life,
friends until death. While Sababu was entertaining him in her
room, I stayed outside, thinking about my investigation. I beg
you to believe me.'

'I'm worried about one of my patients, an old man. He
must be washed and his house cleansed. Will you help me?'

23

'Get up.'

Suti dragged himself out of the cell where he had been locked away. Although dirty and famished, he had passed the time singing bawdy songs and thinking about the wonderful times he had spent in the arms of beautiful Memphis women.

'Step forward.'

The soldier giving the orders was a mercenary. A former pirate, he had left that adventurous life and joined the Egyptian army because it offered its soldiers such a comfortable retirement. He wore a pointed helmet, carried a short sword, and was completely lacking in feeling.

'Are you the one called Suti?'

The young man was slow to respond, so the mercenary hit him in the stomach. Although bent double, Suti did not kneel.

'You're proud and sturdy,' said the soldier. 'They say you fought the sand-travellers, but I don't believe it myself. When you kill an enemy, you cut off his hand and present it to your superior officer. I think you ran away like a frightened rabbit.'

'With a piece of shaft from my chariot?'

'You got that from pillaging. You say you were an archer. Well, we're going to check that.'

'I'm hungry.'

'We'll see about that later. A real warrior can go on fighting even when he's utterly exhausted.'

The man took Suti to the edge of a wood and handed him a heavy bow. The upper surface was coated with horn, the back with bark. The bowstring was an ox tendon covered with linen fibres, stopped by knots at either end.

'Target at a hundred paces, on the oak tree right in front of you. You have two arrows to hit it.'

When he drew the bow, Suti thought the muscles in his back were going to rip. Black dots danced before his eyes. He must maintain the right pressure, load the arrow, aim, forget what was at stake, visualize the target, become the bow and the arrow, fly through the air, sink into the heart of the tree.

He closed his eyes and fired.

The mercenary walked forward a little way. 'Almost in the centre.'

Suti picked up the second arrow, drew the bow again and aimed at the soldier.

'That is very unwise.' The mercenary dropped his sword.

'I told the truth,' insisted Suti.

'All right, all right!'

The young man let the arrow fly, and it plunged into the target, just to the right of the previous one.

The soldier breathed again. 'Who taught you how to handle a bow?'

'It's a gift.'

'Down to the river with you, soldier. Wash and dress and get something to eat.'

Equipped with a bow made of his favourite acacia wood, boots, a woollen cloak and a dagger, and properly fed and washed, Suti appeared before the commander of the hundred or so footsoldiers. This time, the officer listened to him attentively and made detailed notes.

He told Suti, 'We're cut off from our bases and from General Asher. He's encamped three days' march from here, with an elite force. I'm sending two messengers south, so that the main army can move more quickly.'

'Is there a rebellion?'

'Two Asian princelings, an Iranian tribe and some sand-travellers have formed an alliance. Their leader is an exiled Libyan called Adafi. He is the prophet of a vengeful god, and has decided to destroy Egypt and mount the throne in Ramses' place. Some say that he's a puppet, others that he's a dangerous madman. He favours surprise attacks, and takes no account of treaties. If we stay here we'll be slaughtered. But between us and Asher is a well-defended fort. We're going to attack it and take it.'

'Have we got any chariots?'

'No, but we've got several ladders and a wheeled tower. What we didn't have until now was a really good archer.'

Pazair had tried to talk to her ten times – no, a hundred times. But he had confined himself to lifting an old man, laying him down under a palm tree out of the wind and sun, cleaning his house and helping Neferet. He was on the alert for any sign of disapproval, any condemnatory look. But she was absorbed in her work, and seemed indifferent.

The previous evening, he had gone to see Kani, whose investigations were continuing. Kani was very careful, but he had visited most of the villages and talked to dozens of peasants and craftsmen. There was no trace of an ex-soldier who had returned from Memphis. If the man did indeed live on the west bank, he was well hidden.

When they had finished cleaning the old man's house, Pazair told Neferet, 'In about ten days' time, Kani will bring you the first consignment of medicinal plants.'

'The headman has allocated me an abandoned house on the edge of the desert. I shall be able to see my patients there.'

'What about water?'

'A channel will be dug as soon as possible.'

'And what are your quarters like?'

'They're small, but clean and pleasant.'

'Yesterday Memphis, today this forgotten place.'

Neferet smiled. 'Here, I have no enemies. There, it was war.'

'Nebamon won't rule over the doctors for ever.'

'That's for destiny to decide.'

'One day you'll be restored to your rightful status.'

'What does that matter? Now, you never told me how your cold is.'

'The spring wind doesn't agree with me.'

'You must have another inhalation.'

Pazair yielded. He loved to hear her preparing the antiseptic paste, kneading it and spreading it on the stone before covering it with the pot. Whatever she did, he adored.

Pazair's bedchamber had been searched from top to bottom. Even his mosquito net had been torn down, rolled into a ball and thrown on the wooden floor. His travelling bag had been emptied, his tablets and papyri strewn everywhere, his mat trampled on, and his kilt, tunic and cloak torn to bits.

Pazair knelt down and searched for clues. But the burglar had not left a single trace behind him.

He went and lodged a formal complaint with the fat official, who was astounded and outraged.

'Do you suspect anyone?'

'Yes, but I daren't say anything.'

'Please!'

'I was followed.'

'Did you identify the person?'

'No.'

'Can you describe him?'

'No, I can't.'

'That's a pity,' said the official. 'Finding the culprit won't be easy.'

'I quite understand.'

'I and all the other guard posts in the province have

received a message for you. Your scribe is looking everywhere for you.'

'Why?'

'He doesn't say. He asks you to return to Memphis as quickly as possible. When will you leave?'

'Well . . . tomorrow.'

'Would you like an escort?'

'Kem will be quite enough.'

'As you wish, but be careful.'

'Who would dare attack a judge?'

The Nubian was armed with a bow, arrows, a sword, a club, a spear and a wooden-framed shield covered in ox skin; in other words, he carried all the usual weapons of a dedicated officer, ready to deal with tricky situations. Killer was happy with just his teeth.

'Where did all these weapons come from?' asked Pazair.

'The traders in the market bought them for me. One by one, my baboon arrested every member of a band of thieves who have been running wild for more than a year. The merchants wanted to thank me.'

'Did you get permission for them from the Theban guards?'

'They've been listed and numbered, and everything's in order.'

'There's a problem in Memphis, and we must go back. Any news of the fifth soldier?'

'Not a whisper in the market,' said Kem. 'Have you discovered anything?'

'No, nothing.'

'He must be dead, like the others.'

'Then why was my room searched?'

'I don't know,' said Kem, 'but I shall stick closer to you than a flea.'

'Don't forget you're under my command.'

'My duty is to protect you.'

'If I think it necessary. Wait for me here, and be ready to leave.'

'At least tell me where you're going.'

'I shan't be long.'

The wind was changing, and spring was becoming gentle and warm. Soon the sandstorms would begin, forcing people to take refuge in their homes for several days at a time. Everywhere, nature was flourishing.

Neferet was treated almost like a queen in her village. For the little community, having the benefit of a doctor's services was a priceless gift. Her smiling authority worked miracles; both children and adults listened to her advice and no longer feared illness.

She was very strict about the rules of cleanliness, which everyone knew but which were sometimes neglected. Hands must be washed frequently, particularly before meals, bodies must be washed every day, and feet before entering a house. The mouth and teeth must be purified, hair cut and body hair shaved regularly, and she advocated the use of ointments, creams and deodorants based on carob. Both rich and poor used a paste made from sand and fat; when added to natron, it cleaned and disinfected the skin.

At Pazair's urging, Neferet agreed to go for a walk beside the Nile.

'Are you happy here?' he asked.

'I think I'm useful.'

'I admire you a lot.'

'There are other doctors who deserve your admiration more than I do.'

'I've got to leave Thebes straight away. I've had a message from my scribe, Iarrot, saying I've been recalled to Memphis.'

'Because of this strange case?'

'Iarrot didn't say.'

'Have you made any progress?'

'We still haven't found find the fifth soldier, and we would have done if he had a regular job on the west bank. My investigation has reached a dead end.'

'Will you come back?' asked Neferet.

'As soon as I can.'

'You're worried, aren't you?'

'My room was searched.'

'To make you drop the case?'

'Someone thought I had a vital document. Now they know I haven't.'

'Aren't you taking too many risks?'

'Because of my incompetence, I'm making too many mistakes.'

'Don't be so hard on yourself. You've done nothing you need regret.'

'I want to put right the injustice that's been done to you.'

'You'll soon forget me.'

'I shan't – ever.'

She smiled, touched. 'Youthful promises are blown away by the evening breeze.'

'Mine aren't.' Pazair stopped, turned to her, and took her hands. 'I love you, Neferet. If you only knew how much I love you . . .'

Anxiety filled her eyes. 'My life is here, yours is in Memphis. Fate has decreed it.'

'I don't care about my career. If you love me, nothing else matters.'

'Don't be childish.'

'You are my happiness, Neferet. Without you, life is meaningless.'

She gently withdrew her hands. 'I need time to think, Pazair.'

He longed to take her in his arms, to hold her so tightly that no one could part them. But he must not shatter the fragile hope contained in her reply.

The shadow-eater watched Pazair's departure. The judge was leaving Thebes without having spoken to the fifth soldier, and was not taking away any compromising documents. The search of his room had revealed nothing.

The shadow-eater had not found the man, either. But he had had one small success: the soldier had been living in a small town to the south of the city, where he planned to set himself up as a repairer of chariots. Panicked by the baker's death, he had disappeared, and neither the judge nor the shadow-eater had managed to track him down. He knew he was in great danger, so he would hold his tongue.

Reassured, the shadow-eater decided to take the next boat for Memphis.

24

Tjaty Bagey had pains in his legs, which felt heavy and were so swollen that his ankle bones were all but invisible. He put on broad-fitting sandals with loose straps, but had no time for any other treatment. The more he stayed sitting in his office, the worse the swelling became, but the service of Egypt gave no scope for rest or absence.

His wife, Nedyt, had rejected the large official house outside the city that Pharaoh granted the tjaty, and Bagey had gone along with her decision, for he preferred the town to the country. Although at the pinnacle of government, he had not made himself rich: his duty came before his own prosperity. So they lived in a modest house in the centre of Memphis, watched day and night by guards. The tjaty of the Two Lands enjoyed perfect security; never in the entire history of Egypt had a tjaty been assassinated or even attacked.

Nedyt had found her husband's rise to power difficult to bear. Disadvantaged by being plain, short and plump, she refused to appear in society or attend official banquets. She longed for the days when Bagey had occupied an obscure post with limited responsibilities. Back then, he had come home early, helped her in the kitchen and had time to pay attention to his son and daughter.

As he walked to the palace, the tjaty's thoughts turned to his children. His son had originally been a carpenter, but his laziness had come to the attention of his master. As soon as he was told, Bagey had had the lad dismissed from the workshop and punished him by making him prepare rough bricks. Pharaoh had considered the decision unjust, and had reprimanded the tjaty, saying he was too strict with his own family. A tjaty must be careful not to favour his own, but to do the opposite was equally bad.* So Bagey's son had risen to become a checker of baked bricks. He had no other ambition; his only passion was playing board games with other lads of his own age.

Bagey was better pleased with his daughter. She was not attractive but her manners and behaviour were excellent, and she hoped one day to enter the temple as a weaver. Her father would not offer her any help; she must succeed by her talents alone.

When he reached his office, the tjaty was tired. Instead of sitting at his desk, he sat down on a low seat, slightly curved towards the centre, made of plaited cords in a fish-scale pattern. Before his daily meeting with the king, he must read the reports received from the various government secretariats. His back hunched and his feet aching, he had to force himself to concentrate.

His personal scribe interrupted him. 'I'm sorry to disturb you, Tjaty.'

'What is it?'

'A messenger from the Asian army has arrived with a report.'

'Summarize it for me.'

'General Asher's regiment has been cut off from the main body of our troops.'

'A rebellion?'

---

*There is a case of a tjaty who was dismissed from his post because, out of fear of being accused of favouritism, he had been unjust towards those close to him.

'Yes, by Adafi the Libyan, two Asiatic princelings and some sand-travellers.'

'Them again! Our informers have let themselves be caught off guard.'

'Are we to send reinforcements?'

'I shall consult His Majesty immediately.'

The king took the matter very seriously. He gave orders for two new regiments to leave for Asia, and the main army to move forward more quickly. If Asher had survived, he must wipe out the rebels.

Since the proclamation of the decree about security measures, the tjaty no longer knew where to turn to apply Pharaoh's instructions. Thanks to his efficient management, it would only take a few months to draw up an inventory of Egypt's wealth and her various reserves; but his emissaries would have to question the high priest of each temple and the governor of each province, draw up an impressive body of accounts and ensure that there were no mistakes. The king's demands had provoked an undercurrent of hostility, so Bagey, who was considered the one really responsible for this inquisition, would have to pour oil on troubled waters and calm numerous angry officials.

By late afternoon, Bagey had received confirmation that his instructions had been carried out to the letter. The garrison at the King's Walls was already on permanent alert, and from tomorrow its size would be doubled.

At the encampment, the evening was a sombre one. Tomorrow, they would attack the rebel fort in order to break through and try and establish a link with General Asher. The attack promised to be difficult. Many men would not be returning home.

Suti ate with the oldest soldier, a warrior who had been born in Memphis. He would be directing operations using the wheeled tower.

'In six months' time, my lad,' he said, 'I'll have retired. This is my last Asian campaign. Here, eat some of this fresh garlic. It'll purify your blood and stop you catching a chill.'

'It would go down better with a little coriander and some good wine.'

'We'll have a feast after our victory. Usually we eat well in this regiment. We often get beef and cakes, and quite fresh vegetables, and plenty of beer. In the old days, soldiers stole food all over the place, but Ramses forbade it and expelled the thieves from the army. I've never stolen from anybody. They'll give me a house in the country, a bit of land and a serving woman. I shan't pay many taxes and I can pass on my property to anyone I choose. You were right to sign on, lad: your future's assured.'

'As long as I get out of this hornets' nest alive.'

'Don't worry, we'll demolish that fort. But make sure you watch your left. Male death comes from that side, female from the right.'

'Hasn't the enemy got any women?''

'Oh yes, and brave ones, too.'

Suti decided that he'd watch both his left and his right – and he'd remember his back as well, as his chariot officer had told him to.

The Egyptian soldiers threw themselves into a wild dance, whirling their weapons above their heads, and pointing them skywards to ensure a favourable outcome and the courage to fight to the death. According to established custom, the battle would take place one hour after dawn. Only sand-travellers attacked without warning.

The old soldier stuck a feather in Suti's long black hair, and told him, 'It's the custom, for elite archers, and it represents the feather carried by the goddess Ma'at. With her help, your heart will be brave and your aim true.'

The footsoldiers, led by the former pirate carried the

ladders. Suti climbed into the siege tower alongside the old man, and ten men pushed it towards the fort. The artificers had built a rough and ready earthen track, which enabled the wooden wheels to turn without too much difficulty.

'To the left,' ordered the old soldier.

The ground levelled out. Enemy archers fired from the battlements of the fort. Two Egyptians were killed, and an arrow just missed Suti's head.

'Now it's your turn, lad.'

Suti drew his horn-handled bow. If fired in a sweeping arc, his arrows could travel more than two hundred paces. Pulling back the bowstring as far as it would go, he concentrated hard, breathed out and let go.

A sand-traveller toppled from the battlements, shot through the heart. This success wiped away the footsoldiers' fear, and they ran straight at the enemy. When they were some hundred paces from their goal, Suti changed weapons. With his acacia-wood bow, which was more accurate and less tiring to use, he was able to make every arrow count, and he cleared half the battlements. Soon, the Egyptians were able to put up their ladders.

When the tower was no more than twenty paces from its objective, Suti's companion fell, an arrow in his belly. The tower speeded up and bumped against the walls of the fort. While his comrades were leaping onto the battlements and forcing their way inside the fortifications, Suti bent over the old soldier.

The wound was clearly mortal, but the old man raised his head a little and gasped, 'You'll have a fine retirement, my lad, just you see . . . I was just unlucky.' His head lolled on his shoulder.

The Egyptians used a battering-ram to force open the gate; and the ex-pirate finished off the remains with his axe. Their opponents ran about in panic and disarray. The local princeling jumped on his horse and rode down the Egyptian officer who demanded his surrender. This unleashed a furious onslaught by the Egyptians, who gave no quarter.

While the fort was being set on fire, a fugitive clad in rags escaped from the conquerors' watchful gaze and fled towards the forest. Suti ran off in hot pursuit, and grabbed the tattered tunic, which ripped and came away in his hand.

It was a woman, young and comely. The very one who had robbed him.

Although naked, she kept running. To the accompaniment of his fellow soldiers' laughter and shouts of encouragement, Suti brought her down. She was terrified, and struggled long and hard. When she grew quiet, he picked her up, tied her hands and covered her with the remains of her pitiful dress.

'She belongs to you,' declared a soldier.

The few survivors, hands on heads, had abandoned their bows, shields, sandals and cudgels. According to the sacred texts, they had lost their souls and their names, and been drained of their sperm. The victors seized bronze dishes, oxen, donkeys and goats, burnt down the barracks, the furniture and fabrics. Nothing remained of the fort but a heap of charred rubble.

The former pirate came up to Suti. 'Our commander's dead, and so is the soldier in charge of the tower. You're the bravest of us, and a fine archer, you must take command.'

'But I'm a raw recruit.'

'You're a hero. We all agree that without you we'd have failed. Lead us north.'

Suti gave in, and agreed. He told the men to question the prisoners and to treat them properly. During the questioning, they established that the instigator of the rebellion, Adafi, had not been among the troops in the fort.

When they set off northwards, Suti marched at the head of the column, his bow in his hand. His prisoner walked beside him.

'What's your name?' he asked.

'Panther.'

Her beauty fascinated him. She was wild, with blonde hair, eyes like burning coals, a superb body and alluring lips. Her voice was warm and enchanting.

'And where are you from?'

'Libya. My father was one of the walking dead.'

'What do you mean?'

'In a raid, his skull was smashed open by an Egyptian sword. He should have died then, but he didn't. He was taken prisoner and worked as a farm labourer in the Delta. He forgot his language and his people and became an Egyptian. I hated him so much that when he did die I didn't even go to his funeral. I took up the fight in his place.'

'Why do you hate us?'

The question surprised Panther. 'We've been enemies for two thousand years!' she exclaimed.

'Wouldn't it be a good idea to arrange a truce?'

'Never!'

'I shall try to persuade you.'

Suti's charm was not entirely ineffective. Panther grudgingly raised her eyes to his, and asked, 'Am I to be your slave?'

'There aren't any slaves in Egypt.'

A soldier gave a shout of warning, and everyone flung himself to the ground. On the crest of a hill, the bushes were moving. A pack of wolves emerged, looked at the travellers, then continued on their way. Much relieved, the soldiers gave thanks to the gods.

'I'll be rescued,' declared Panther.

'Don't rely on anyone but yourself.'

'I'll betray you at the first opportunity.'

'Honesty's a rare virtue. I'm beginning to like you.'

She retreated into sulky silence.

They marched for two hours across stony terrain, then followed the bed of a dried-up river. His eyes glued to the rocky escarpments, Suti watched for the slightest sign of trouble.

When ten Egyptian archers barred their way, they knew that they were safe at last.

Pazair arrived at his office at about eleven o'clock in the morning, and found the door shut.

'Go and find Iarrot,' he told Kem.

'With Killer?'

'With Killer.'

'What if he's ill?'

'Bring him to me within the hour, no matter what state he's in.'

Kem hurried off.

When Iarrot arrived, red-faced and with swollen eyes, he explained in a whining voice, 'I was resting after an attack of indigestion. I took some cumin seeds in milk, but I still felt sick. The doctor told me to drink an infusion of juniper berries and take two days off work.'

'Why did you bombard Thebes police with messages for me?'

'Because of two emergencies.'

The judge's anger abated. 'What are they?'

'First, we've run out of papyrus. Second, checks have been made on the granaries under your jurisdiction. According to the note from the authorities, half the grain reserves are missing from the main store.' Iarrot lowered his voice. 'An enormous scandal is in the offing.'

The priests presented the first harvested grain to Osiris and offered bread to the goddess of harvests. Afterwards, a long procession of people carrying baskets of the precious foodstuff set off towards the grain stores, singing, 'A happy day is born for us.' They climbed steps leading to the grain stores' roofs, some of which were rectangular and others cylindrical, and emptied their treasures through a skylight which was closed by a trapdoor. A door at the foot of the building enabled the grain to be removed.

The overseer of the granaries greeted the judge coldly.

'The royal decree obliges me to check the grain reserves,' said Pazair.

'A specialist scribe has already done so for you.'

'What did he find?'

'He didn't tell me,' said the overseer. 'That concerns you alone.'

'Have a long ladder put up against the front of the main granary.'

'Must I repeat myself? A scribe has already checked.'

'Are you defying the law?'

At once, the overseer became less hostile. 'I'm only thinking of your safety, Judge Pazair. Climbing up there is dangerous, and you aren't used to doing such things.'

'So you don't know that half your reserves has disappeared?'

The overseer gaped at him in horror. 'What a disaster!'

'Have you any explanation?'

'Vermin – it must be.'

'Controlling vermin is your main responsibility, is it not?'

'I delegate the task to the health officials – they're the ones to blame.'

'Half the reserve,' said Pazair thoughtfully. 'That's an enormous quantity.'

'When you get vermin—'

'Put up the ladder.'

'It's pointless, I assure you. Besides, that's no job for a judge.'

'When I place my seal on the official report, you will be responsible before the law.'

Two workers brought a long ladder and leant it against the front of the grain store. Uneasily, Pazair climbed up; the rungs creaked, and it was not as stable as he might have wished. When he was halfway up, it swayed.

'Hold it steady!' he ordered.

The overseer looked around, as if seeking a means of escape, but Kem laid a hand on his shoulder and Killer crouched down beside his legs.

'Do as the judge says,' advised the Nubian. 'You wouldn't want an accident to happen, would you?'

They held the ladder firmly. Reassured, Pazair continued his climb. He reached the top, sixteen cubits above the ground, pushed across a latch, and opened the trapdoor. The store was full to bursting.

'That's unbelievable!' gasped the overseer when Pazair told him. 'The man who checked lied to you.'

'Or you were both involved,' suggested Pazair.

'Oh no, Judge! I've been deceived, you can be sure of that.'

'I find it difficult to believe you.'

The baboon growled and bared its teeth.

'He hates liars,' said Kem.

'Keep that creature under control,' quavered the overseer.

'I can't control him at all when a witness annoys him.'

The overseer hung his head. 'He promised me a rich reward if I backed up what he said. We were going to steal the grain that was supposed to be missing, and make a fine profit. Since the crime didn't actually take place, will I be able to keep my job?'

Pazair worked late. He drew up a document dismissing the overseer, added supporting arguments, and searched in vain among the lists of officials for the man who had checked the grain reserves. No doubt he had given a false name, but he would have to be found before the overseer was formally dismissed. Thefts of grain did happen occasionally, but theft on such a large scale as this was unheard of. Was it a single act, limited to one store in Memphis, or a sign of widespread corruption? If the latter, that would justify Pharaoh's surprising decree. The king was counting on the judges to re-establish equity and righteousness. If everyone acted justly, whether his office be humble or important, evil would soon be eliminated.

In the flame of the lamp, he saw Neferet's face, her eyes, her lips. At this hour of the night, she would be asleep. Was she dreaming of him?

25

Accompanied by Kem and Killer, Pazair took a fast boat to the largest papyrus plantation in the Delta, which was run by Mahu under authorization from the king. In the mud and swamps, the plants with the tufted leaves and three-sided stems could grow to a height of twelve cubits and form dense thickets. The parasol-shaped flowers grew in tight clumps, crowning the precious plant.

The woody roots were used to make furniture; the fibres and bark to make mats, baskets, nets, cables, ropes and even sandals and kilts for the poorest folk. As for the spongy sap which flowed copiously beneath the bark, it underwent special treatment to become Egypt's famous papyrus, which was the envy of the world.

Mahu was not content to let nature take its course, so on his immense estate he had cultivated papyrus to increase production and export a portion of it. For every Egyptian, the verdant stems symbolized youth and vigour; the goddesses' sceptres were shaped like papyrus stems, and temple pillars were stone representations of the plant.

A broad path had been opened up through the thickets. Pazair encountered naked peasants carrying heavy bales on their backs. They chewed the tender shoots of the papyrus, drank the juice and spat out the pulp. In front of the large warehouses where the material was kept dry in wooden cases or in terracotta pots, specialists were carefully washing selected fibres, before spreading them out on mats or planks.

The sections, which were a little less than a cubit long, were cut lengthways, and laid out in two layers, one on top of the other at right angles. Other skilled workers covered the whole arrangement with a damp cloth and struck it repeatedly with a wooden mallet. At last came the delicate moment when the strips of papyrus must stick together as they dried, without the addition of any other substance.

'Magnificent, isn't it?'

The stocky man who addressed Pazair had a round, moon-shaped head, and black hair smoothed down with balm. He was heavily built, with plump hands and feet, yet he seemed full of energy, almost agitated. He hitched up his kilt and adjusted his fine linen shirt. Although he bought his clothes from the finest weaver in Memphis, they always seemed too small, too large or too loose.

He went on, 'I'm honoured that you should visit me, Judge Pazair. My name is Mahu. I am the owner of this estate.'

'I'd like buy some papyrus,' said Pazair.

'Come and see my finest specimens.'

Mahu led him into the warehouse where he kept his best papyri, in rolls made up of about twenty sheets, and unrolled one.

'Look at this splendid example. See how finely made it is, and what a wonderful shade of yellow. None of my competitors has succeeded in matching it. One of the secrets is the time it is exposed to the sun, but there are many other important points – on which my lips are sealed.'

Pazair touched the end of the roll. 'It's perfect.'

Mahu did not conceal his pride. 'I made it for the scribes who copy out the ancient *Words of Wisdom** and add to them. The palace library has ordered a dozen like this for next

---

*Collections of maxims, passed on from generation to generation.

month. I also supply papyri for copies of the *Book of Going Forth by Day*, which are placed in tombs.'

'Your business seems to be flourishing.'

'It is indeed, as long as I work night and day. But I'm not complaining – I love my work. Providing a basis for texts and hieroglyphs is vital work, isn't it?'

'My funds are limited. I can't afford such beautiful papyri.'

'I can provide some which aren't so fine, but are still of excellent quality. Their strength is guaranteed.'

The judge was happy with the goods, but the price was still too high.

Mahu scratched the back of his neck. 'I like you very much, Judge Pazair, and I hope the feeling is mutual. I love justice, for it is the key to happiness. Will you allow me the pleasure of giving you this consignment?'

'I'm touched by your generosity, but I'm afraid I can't accept.'

'But I insist.'

'Any gift, in any form, would be classed as corruption. If you will allow me time to pay, it must be noted down and registered.'

'Very well, then. I've heard that you have no hesitation in attacking important merchants who don't respect the law. That's very brave.'

'It's simply my duty.'

'In Memphis recently, traders' moral standards have tended to decline. I assume Pharaoh's decree will stop this worrying development.'

'My colleagues and I will use it to do so, though I know little of Memphite morals.'

'You'll soon get used to them. These last few years, competition between merchants has been rather fierce, and they've been happy to deal one another severe blows.'

'Have you suffered any?'

'Yes, like everyone else. But I fight back. At first, I was employed as an accounting assistant on a large estate in the Delta, where papyrus was poorly exploited. My salary was tiny and I toiled night and day. I suggested improvements to the owner of the estate, and he accepted them, and raised me to the rank of accountant. I'd have been happy to go on the way I was, but I had some bad luck.'

The two men left the warehouse and walked along the flower-lined path which led to Mahu's house.

'May I offer you a drink? I'm not trying to corrupt you, I assure you.'

Pazair smiled. He could tell that the man wanted to talk, so he said, 'You said you had some bad luck. What happened?'

'It was rather humiliating. I'd married a woman older than myself, from Elephantine; we got on well, despite a few minor squabbles. I usually got home late from work, but she accepted that. One afternoon, I took sick – overwork, probably – and had to be taken home. My wife was in bed with the gardener. At first I wanted to kill her, then I wanted to have her tried for adultery, but . . . the punishment's very heavy.* I made do with a divorce, which was pronounced immediately.'

'It must have been very painful for you.'

'I was deeply hurt, and I consoled myself by working twice as hard. The estate owner offered me a piece of land which no one wanted. Using a system of irrigation which I devised myself, I made it pay: the first harvests were a success, prices were good, and my customers were happy – and the palace noticed me! I was overwhelmed to become a supplier to the court. I was granted the marshes which you crossed to get here.'

'Congratulations.'

'Hard work is always rewarded. Are you married?'

'No.'

---

*Adultery was considered a serious offence, for it represented a betrayal of a promise, and marriage rested on mutual trust.

'I risked trying it again, and I'm glad I did.' Mahu swallowed a pastille made from oliban resin and aromatic reeds from Phoenicia, a mixture which sweetened the breath. 'I'll introduce you to my young wife.'

The lady Silkis was terrified of seeing her first wrinkle appear. So she had procured some oil of fenugreek, which smoothed and freshened the skin. The perfumier separated pods and seeds, prepared a paste and heated it. The oil rose to the surface. Carefully, Silkis smeared her face with a paste made from honey, red natron and northern salt, then massaged the rest of her body with powdered alabaster.

Thanks to Nebamon's skill, her face and her body had been made more slender, according to her husband's wishes. She felt she was still too heavy and a little on the plump side, but Mahu didn't criticize her for her voluptuous thighs. Before welcoming him for a substantial lunch, she painted her lips with red ochre, smoothed a gentle cream over her cheeks, and lined her eyes with green kohl. Then she rubbed her scalp with an antiseptic lotion containing beeswax and resin, which prevented the appearance of white hairs.

Silkis looked in the mirror and was satisfied with her reflection. She put on a wig made from perfumed locks of real hair. Her husband had given her this little treasure on the birth of their second child, a boy.

Her serving-woman announced the arrival of Mahu and a guest. In panic, Silkis snatched up her mirror again. Would Mahu think she looked attractive enough, or criticize a flaw she hadn't noticed? She had no time to re-do her make-up or change her dress.

Nervously, she went out of her bedchamber.

'Silkis, my darling,' said Mahu, 'this is Judge Pazair, from Memphis.'

The young woman smiled, with respectable modesty and shyness.

'We entertain many buyers and experts on papyrus making,' Mahu went on, 'but you're our first judge. It's a great honour.'

A serving woman brought beer, which had been kept cool by the large jars in which it was stored. She was followed by two children, a little red-haired girl and a small boy who looked like his father. They greeted Pazair, then ran to Mahu, clamouring for his attention.

'Ah, these children,' said Mahu. 'We adore them, but sometimes they're exhausting.'

Silkis agreed with a nod. Fortunately, her confinements had been straightforward and had not spoiled her body, thanks to long periods of rest. She hid a few rebellious curves under a full dress of fine linen, discreetly decorated with little red fringes. Her earrings, which were ornamented with ivory, had been imported from Nubia.

Pazair was invited to sit down on a chair made from papyrus.

'Original, isn't it?' said Mahu. 'I like new things. If people like the design, I shall start selling it.'

Pazair marvelled at the layout of the house. It had ten rooms, all dimly lit – Silkis feared the sun, for it reddened her skin – and was laid out in a long line, very low, without a terrace because, said Mahu, 'I suffer from vertigo. But come, Judge, and sit under this canopy, where we'll be sheltered from the heat.'

'Do you like Memphis, Judge?' asked Silkis.

'I preferred my village.'

'Where do you live?'

'Above my office. My quarters are a bit cramped, and since I took up my post there has been no shortage of cases to investigate. Documents are building up so fast that in a few months I shall be crowded out.'

'That's easily put right,' said Mahu. 'One of my best business contacts is the official responsible for storing documents at the palace. He's the person who allocates space in state warehouses.'

'I wouldn't want to take advantage.'

'You won't. You're bound to meet him sooner or later, and sooner would be better, that's all. I'll give you his name, and you can sort it out.'

Pazair drank a little more of his beer. It was delicious.

'This summer,' said Mahu, 'I'm going to open a papyrus warehouse near the weapons workshops. Delivery to government secretariats will be much faster.'

'Then your new premises will come under my jurisdiction.'

'I'm delighted to hear it. If I'm any judge of character, your controls will be thorough and effective, and that will help to establish my reputation firmly. Despite all the opportunities that come up, I loathe fraud – quite apart from anything else, you always get caught red-handed sooner or later. Egypt does not like fraudsters. As the proverb says, "A lie finds no ferry and will not cross the river."'

'Have you heard anything about an illegal trade in grain?' asked Pazair.

'When the scandal breaks, there'll be some severe sentences.'

'Who's involved?'

'All I know is that there are rumours that part of the harvest stored in the granaries is being stolen by certain people for their own profit. Just rumours, as I say, but they're persistent.'

'Haven't the authorities investigated?'

'Yes, but without success. But to more pleasant matters. Will you stay and have lunch with us?'

'I don't want to cause any inconvenience.'

'My wife and I would love to have you.'

Silkis leant forward and smiled her agreement.

Pazair enjoyed an excellent lunch: goose liver, herb salad and olive oil, fresh peas, pomegranates and pastries, the whole accompanied by a red Delta wine dating from the first year of Ramses' reign. The children ate on their own, but clamoured for cakes.

227

'Are you planning to start a family, Judge?' asked Silkis.

'My work keeps me very busy,' replied Pazair.

'Ah,' said Mahu, 'but having a wife and children is surely the goal of every man's life. There's no greater happiness.'

Thinking herself unnoticed, the little girl stole a pastry.

Her father seized her by the wrist. 'You shall have no games and no walk this afternoon.'

The child burst into floods of tears and stamped her feet.

'You're too strict,' protested Silkis. 'It's not so very serious.'

'Having everything you want and yet stealing is a terrible thing.'

'Didn't you do the same, when you were a child?'

'My parents were poor but I never stole a thing from anyone, and I won't let my daughter steal, either.'

The child wept even more bitterly.

'Take her away,' said Mahu.

Silkis obeyed.

'Ah, the trials of bringing up children! But there are more joys than pains, thanks be to the gods.'

After the meal, Mahu showed Pazair the batch of papyrus sheets he planned to supply him with. He proposed strengthening the edges and adding a few rolls of a lower quality and whitish colour, to be used for rough work.

The two men took a cordial leave of each other.

Mentmose's bald head turned red, betraying an anger he could scarcely contain. 'These are rumours, Judge Pazair, nothing but rumours.'

'And yet you did investigate.'

'Merely as a matter of routine.'

'And you found nothing?'

'Nothing at all. No one would dare steal wheat from a state grain store – it's a grotesque idea! And why are you bothering yourself with this matter?'

'Because the grain store is under my jurisdiction.'

Mentmose calmed down a little. 'So it is. I'd forgotten. Have you got proof?'

'The best of all: written evidence.'

Mentmose read the document. 'The checker noted that half the reserves had been used up. What's unusual about that?'

'The store is absolutely full – I saw it with my own eyes.'

Mentmose stood up, turned away and looked out of the window. 'This note is signed.'

'Yes, but it's a false name. It isn't on the list of accredited officials. You're best placed to find this elusive character, aren't you?'

'You have questioned the overseer of the granaries, I presume?'

'He claims not to know the real name of the man he dealt with, and to have seen him only once.'

'Do you think he's lying?'

'Perhaps not.' Despite Killer's presence, the steward had said nothing more, so Pazair believed he was telling the truth.

'There must be a lot of people involved.'

'There may be.'

'Judging by the evidence, the overseer's behind it all.'

'Perhaps, but I don't trust the evidence.'

'Hand the overseer over to me. I'll make him talk.'

'That's out of the question,' said Pazair.

'Then what do you suggest?'

'That a permanent and discreet watch is kept on the store. When the thief and his accomplices come for the grain you'll catch them red-handed, and then you'll be able to get the names of everyone involved.'

'But won't they have been alerted by the overseer's dismissal?'

'Quite. So he must continue in his post for the time being.'

'It's a complicated and risky plan.'

'I don't think so. But if you have a better one, I'll accept it.'

'I shall do what is necessary.'

26

Branir's house was the only haven of peace where Pazair's torments lessened. He had written a long letter to Neferet, declaring his love for her once again, and begging her to answer with her heart. He felt guilty for troubling her, but he could not hide his passion. Henceforth, his life was in Neferet's hands.

Branir laid flowers before the busts of the ancestors in the first room of his house. Pazair meditated at his side. Cornflowers with green calyxes and yellow persea flowers struggled against oblivion and enabled the sages to live longer in the paradise of Osiris.

Once the ceremony was over, master and pupil went up to the terrace. Pazair loved this time of day, when the light was dying, only to be reborn in the brightness of night.

Branir looked at him closely. 'You're shedding your youth like a worn-out skin. It was happy and peaceful, but now you must make a success of your life.'

'You know everything about me.'

'Even the things you don't confide to me?'

'It's pointless trying to hide anything from you. Do you think she'll accept me?'

'Neferet never play-acts. She will act in accordance with the truth.'

Pazair's throat tightened with strain. 'Perhaps I've gone mad.'

'There is only one act of madness: coveting what belongs to other people.'

'I was forgetting what you taught me: to increase one's intelligence through righteousness, deliberation and precision, never thinking of one's own happiness, but always acting so as to enable men to make their way in peace, temples to be built and orchards to blossom for the gods.* My love is burning me up, and I can't help feeding its flames.'

'That's good. Travel to the very ends of your being, to the point where you will never again turn back. May the heavens permit you never to stray from the right path.'

'I'm not neglecting my duties, though,' said Pazair.

'Any news of the Sphinx affair?'

'I've reached a dead end.'

'Is there no hope of progress?'

'Only if I find the fifth guard, or if Suti finds out something about General Asher.'

'That's a rather slender hope.'

'I know. But I shan't give up, even if I have to wait several years before I get any more clues. Don't forget, I have proof that the army lied. Officially, five guards were killed, but one of them lived and became a baker in Thebes.

'The fifth guard is alive,' declared Branir, as confidently as if he could see the man nearby. 'Don't give up, for misfortune is roaming the land.'

There was a long silence. Branir's solemnity had shaken Pazair. The old doctor had the gift of second sight; sometimes he perceived a reality which was as yet invisible to others.

'I shall soon leave this house,' said Branir eventually. 'The time has come for me to live in the temple, and end my days there. The silence of the gods of Karnak will fill my ears, and I shall converse with the stones of eternity. Each day will be

---

*These words were inscribed on stelae of the sages, placed inside temples.

more serene than the last, and I shall move towards old age, which prepares a man to appear before the court of Osiris.'

Pazair protested, 'But I still need you to teach me!'

'What advice can I give you? Tomorrow, I shall take up the staff of old age and walk towards the Beautiful West, from whence no man returns.'

'If I really have uncovered a formidable sickness afflicting Egypt, and if it is possible for me to fight it, your moral authority will be essential to me. Your actions could prove decisive. Please wait a little, I beg of you.'

'Whatever happens, this house will belong to you as soon as I have retired to the temple.'

Sheshi lit the fire with date kernels and charcoal, placed a horn-shaped cooking pot on the flames and kindled them with the aid of his bellows. He tried one more time to perfect a new method of fusing metal, by pouring the molten substance into special moulds. He had an exceptional memory, and never wrote anything down for fear of being betrayed. His two assistants, strong, tireless fellows, were capable of keeping the fire going for hours on end by blowing down long, hollow stems.

The unbreakable weapon would soon be ready. Equipped with swords and spears which could withstand any test, Pharaoh's soldiers would shatter the Asian enemy's helmets and pierce their armour.

Shouts and the sounds of a struggle interrupted his reflections. Sheshi opened the workshop door and came up against two guards, who held a man with white hair and red hands in an iron grip. He was panting like a worn-out horse, his eyes were streaming, and his kilt was torn.

'He got into the metal stores,' explained one of the guards. 'We spotted him, and he tried to run away.'

Sheshi recognized Qadash, but did not show the slightest surprise.

'Let me go, you brutes!' demanded Qadash.

'You're a thief,' replied the senior guard.

What crazy notion had Qadash taken into his head? For a long time he had dreamt of having celestial iron with which to manufacture his instruments, so that he would become an unrivalled tooth doctor. He had lost his head over that private dream, forgetting the conspirators' plan.

'I shall send one of my men to the office of the Judge of the Porch,' announced the officer. 'We need a judge here within the hour.'

For fear of drawing suspicion to himself, Sheshi dared not oppose this plan of action.

Dragged out of bed in the middle of the night, the Judge of the Porch's scribe did not consider it necessary to wake his master, who was very particular about his sleep. He consulted the list of judges, and chose the last name on it, a man called Pazair, who, since he was the lowest in the hierarchy, probably needed to learn his craft.

Pazair was not asleep. He was daydreaming of Neferet, imagining her close to him, tender and reassuring. He would tell her about his cases, and she would tell him about her patients. Together they would share the respective burdens of their work, and enjoy a simple happiness which was reborn with each day's sun.

Way-Finder started braying and Brave barked. Pazair got up and opened the window. An armed guard showed him the order issued by the Judge of the Porch's scribe. Pazair threw a short cape about his shoulders, and followed the guard to the barracks.

At the top of the stairs leading down to the basement stood two soldiers, their spears crossed. They moved them aside to allow the judge to pass, and Sheshi met him at the door of his workshop.

'I was expecting the Judge of the Porch,' said Sheshi.

'I'm sorry to disappoint you, but I was given the task. What has happened?'

'An attempted theft.'

'Do you suspect anyone?'

'The guilty man has been arrested.'

'Then I can hear the facts and proceed to the committal, and he can be tried without delay.'

Sheshi looked embarrassed.

'I must question him,' said Pazair. 'Where is he?'

'In the corridor, on your left.'

The culprit was sitting on an anvil, under armed guard. He started when he saw the judge.

'Qadash!' exclaimed Pazair. 'What are you doing here?'

'I was taking a walk near the barracks, when I was attacked and brought to this place by force.'

'That isn't true,' protested the guard. 'He got into a storeroom, and we caught him.'

'You're lying! I shall lodge a complaint against you for assault.'

'But there are several witnesses, and they all accuse you,' Sheshi reminded him.

'What does this storeroom contain?' asked Pazair.

'Metals, mainly copper,' said Sheshi.

Pazair asked Qadash, 'Are you short of metals to make your instruments?'

'No. This is all a silly misunderstanding.'

Sheshi went over to Pazair and whispered a few words in his ear.

'As you wish,' said Pazair, and the two of them went into the workshop.

'The work I'm doing here requires the utmost discretion,' said Sheshi. 'Could you arrange for the case to be heard in secret?'

'Certainly not.'

'But in special cases—'

'Don't say any more, please.'

'Qadash is an honourable, wealthy man. I can't understand why he did it.'

'What is the nature of your work here?' asked Pazair.

'It's to do with making weapons. I'm sure you understand.'

'There's no specific law for your line of work. If Qadash is accused of theft, he'll defend himself as he wishes and you'll have to appear.'

'And I'll have to answer questions?'

'Of course.'

Sheshi stroked his moustache. 'In that case, I'd rather not lodge a complaint.'

'That is your right.'

'Above all, it's in the interests of Egypt. Indiscreet ears, in court or elsewhere, would be disastrous. I'll leave Qadash to you – as far as I'm concerned, nothing has happened. As for you, Judge, do please remember that you're sworn to secrecy.'

Pazair left the barracks with Qadash. As they went, he told him, 'No charge has been brought against you.'

'Well I want to bring one.'

'Unfavourable witnesses, your unaccountable presence here at a strange time, the suspicion of theft: they all add up to a damning case against you.'

Qadash coughed, hawked and spat. 'Very well, I give up.'

'But I don't.'

'Pardon?'

'I don't mind getting up in the middle of the night, and investigating in whatever conditions I have to, but I will not be taken for a fool. Tell me exactly what you were doing there, or I shall charge you with insulting a judge.'

Qadash spoke with great embarrassment. 'Top-quality copper – perfectly pure. I've been longing for some for years.'

'How did you hear about this warehouse?'

'The officer in charge of the barracks is a client of mine – and a loose-tongued one at that. He boasted, and I took my chance. Barracks never used to be so well guarded.'

'You decided to steal.'

'No, I was going to pay! I was going to exchange the metal for several fat oxen – the soldiers love them. And my instruments would have been wonderful, so light and precise. But that little man with the moustache was so cold. It was impossible to come to an arrangement with him.'

'Not everyone in Egypt is corrupt.'

'Corrupt?' said Qadash. 'What on earth are you talking about? Just because two individuals do a deal, that doesn't necessarily mean it's an illegal one. You have a very pessimistic view of the human race.' And he went off, grumbling to himself.

Pazair walked on in the darkness. Qadash's explanation had not convinced him. A store of metals, in a barracks . . . the army again. And yet this incident seemed linked not to the soldiers' disappearance but to the distress of a soul in torment, a tooth doctor who could not accept that his skills were failing.

The moon was full. According to legend, a hare armed with a knife lived on it; he had a warlike spirit, and cut off the heads of the shadows. Pazair would happily have taken him on as a scribe. The night-sun waxed and waned, filling with light and then emptying itself of it; the airborne boat would carry his thoughts to Neferet.

Nile water was famous as an aid to digestion. It was light, and brought harmful humours out of the body. Some doctors believed that its healing powers came from the medicinal herbs that grew on the banks and passed on their virtues to the tide. When the annual flood was unleashed, it carried pieces of vegetation and mineral salts with it. The people filled thousands of jars with the water, which stayed fresh and did not spoil.

Nevertheless, Neferet checked last year's reserves. If she thought the contents of a vessel were tainted, she threw in a sweet almond: twenty-four hours later, the water would be clear and delicious. Some jars were three years old and still excellent.

Reassured, she turned to watch the washerman at work. At the palace, this task was given to a trusted man, for the cleanliness of one's clothes was considered essential – the same was true in any community, large or small. After washing and wringing out the clothes, the man had to strike them with a wooden beater, then shake them and hang them on a rope strung between two poles.

'Are you by any chance ill?' asked Neferet.

'Why do you ask?'

'Because you have no energy. The washing has been grey for several days.'

'Ah, this is a difficult job,' said the washerman. 'Women's soiled linens are the worst.'

'Water alone isn't enough. Use this cleanser and this perfume.'

Gruffly, disarmed by her smile, the washerman accepted the two jars.

Neferet went next to the grain stores. To stave off attacks by insects, she emptied wood ash into the stores, a cheap and efficient means of purification. A few weeks from the flood, she would safeguard the cereals.

While she was inspecting the last compartment in the granary, she received a new delivery from Kani: parsley, rosemary, sage, cumin and mint. Dried or reduced to powder, the herbs would be used as the basis for some of the remedies she prescribed. The potions had relieved the old man's pain, and he was so happy to be remaining among his own people that his health was improving.

237

In spite of the doctor's discretion, her successes had not gone unnoticed. Her reputation grew quickly through word of mouth, and many peasants from the west bank came to consult her. She never sent anyone away, and took as much time as was necessary over each case. After exhausting days, she often spent part of the night preparing pills, ointments and poultices, helped by two widows who had been chosen for their attention to detail. After a few hours' sleep, dawn brought another procession of patients to her door.

She had not imagined her career being like this, but she loved to heal. Seeing joy return to an anxious face rewarded her amply for her efforts. Nebamon had done her a service by forcing her to develop her skills among the most humble folk. Here, the fine words of a society doctor would have failed; the ploughman, the fisherman, the mother, all wanted to be cured quickly and cheaply.

When she grew tired, the little green monkey, which she had brought from Memphis, cheered her with her games. Mischief reminded Neferet of her first meeting with Pazair, so entire, so uncompromising, at once disturbing and attractive. What woman could live with a judge whose vocation took precedence over everything else?

When Neferet got back to her workshop, ten bearers were depositing baskets outside, while Mischief bounded from one to the next. Neferet looked in the baskets: they contained willow bark, natron, white oil, oliban, honey, terebinth resin, and large quantities of various types of animal fat.

'Is all this for me?' she asked in astonishment.

'Are you Neferet the doctor?'

'Yes.'

'Then this is yours.'

'But these things cost . . .'

'It's all been paid for.'

'Who by?'

'Don't know – all we do is deliver. Sign this receipt, please.'

Neferet duly wrote her name on a wooden tablet. She was stunned and delighted. Now she could make up complex prescriptions and treat serious illnesses without anyone else's involvement.

When Sababu entered Neferet's house at sunset, Neferet was not surprised. She said, 'I was expecting you.'

'You guessed?' asked Sababu.

'The balm for your rheumatism will soon be ready. I have all the ingredients.'

Sababu no longer looked like a pauper. Her hair was decorated with scented reeds, and she wore a necklace of lotus flowers fashioned from cornelian. Her linen robe, which was transparent from the waist down, openly displayed her long legs.

She said, 'I want to be treated by you, and only by you. The other doctors are charlatans and thieves.'

'Isn't that a bit harsh?'

'I know what I'm saying. Your price will be my price.'

'Your gift is magnificent. I now have enough expensive ingredients to treat hundreds of cases.'

Sababu smiled. 'Mine first, though.'

'Have you made your fortune?'

'I've set up in business again. Thebes is a smaller town than Memphis, and its spirit is more religious and less worldly, but the rich citizens like ale-houses and their pretty inhabitants just as much. I took on a few young women, rented a pretty house in the centre of town, paid the head of the city guards his due, and opened the doors of an establishment whose name was soon well known. You have the proof of that in front of you.'

'You're very generous.'

'Don't deceive yourself. I just want to be looked after well.'

'Will you follow my advice?'

'To the letter. I run the ale-house, but I no longer entertain clients.'

'I'm sure you have no shortage of invitations.'

'I am willing to give a man pleasure but not vice versa, so I'm inaccessible.'

Neferet blushed.

'Doctor, don't say I've shocked you?'

'No, of course not.'

'You give a great deal of love, but do you receive any?'

'The question's irrelevant.'

'Don't tell me,' said Sababu, amused, 'you're still a virgin. It'll be a lucky man who seduces you.'

'Lady Sababu, I—'

'Lady? Me? You're joking!'

Neferet said firmly, 'Close the door and take off your dress. Until you're completely cured, you must come here each day and I'll apply the balm.'

Sababu undressed and lay down on the massage slab. 'Doctor, you deserve to be truly happy, too.'

27

Strong currents made the river dangerous, so Suti slung Panther over his shoulder.

'Stop struggling,' he said. 'If you fall off, you'll drown.'

'You just want to humiliate me.'

'Do you want to find out?'

She stopped struggling. Suti waded into the waist-deep water, supporting himself on boulders as he made his way across.

The water got still deeper, and he told Panther, 'Climb on my back and put your arms round my neck.'

'I can nearly swim.'

'You can finish learning later.'

Once, he slipped and Panther cried out. When he resumed his swift and agile progress, she clung even more tightly to him.

'Make yourself light and kick your legs,' he said.

Suti had a moment of panic as a wild wave covered his head, but he withstood it and reached the opposite bank.

Once there, he drove a stake into the ground, tied a rope to it and threw the other end of the rope across to the other riverbank, where a soldier fixed it firmly in position. Had she wanted, Panther could have run away.

The survivors of the attack and General Asher's detachment of archers crossed the river. The last footsoldier, sure of his own strength, foolishly let go of the rope. Weighed down by his weapons, he hit a rock just below the surface, and sank beneath the water, unconscious.

Suti dived in.

As if delighted to have captured two victims at once, the current grew stronger. Swimming underwater, Suti spotted the soldier. He slid his hands under the man's arms, stopped him sinking any further and tried to lift him up. The drowning man came to his senses, elbowed his rescuer in the chest and was swept away by the water. Suti's lungs were burning, and he was forced to abandon him and fight his way back to land.

'It wasn't your fault,' said Panther as she rubbed him dry.

'I don't like death.'

'He was only a stupid Egyptian.'

He slapped her.

Shocked, she threw him a look of hatred. 'No one's ever treated me like that.'

'More's the pity.'

'Do they beat women in your country?'

'Women have the same rights and duties as men. Now that I think of it, you didn't deserve more than a smacked bottom.'

He rose threateningly.

'Get away from me!'

'Are you sorry for what you said?'

Panther's lips remained resolutely shut.

The sound of galloping horses diverted Suti. Soldiers came running out of their tents, and he snatched up his bow and quiver.

'If you want to go, go,' he told Panther.

'You'd find me and kill me.'

He shrugged.

'A curse on all Egyptians!'

The hoofbeats heralded not a surprise attack but the arrival of General Asher and his men. Already the news of the victory at the fort had spread.

The former pirate embraced Suti. 'I'm proud to know a hero. Asher will give you at least five donkeys, two bows, three bronze spears and a round shield. You won't be a simple soldier for long. You're brave, my boy, and that isn't common, even in the army.'

Suti rejoiced. At last he was approaching his goal. It was up to him to find a way of extracting information from the general's entourage and spot the fatal flaw. He would not fail; Pazair would be proud of him.

A huge man wearing a helmet hailed him. 'Are you the one they call Suti?'

'He's the one.' The pirate nodded. 'He enabled us to take the enemy fort and risked his life trying to save the man who drowned.'

'General Asher has promoted you to chariot officer. First thing tomorrow, you will help us to pursue that scum Adafi.'

'You mean he's been put to flight?'

'He's as slippery as an eel. But the rebellion's been crushed, and in the end we shall get our hands on that coward. Dozens of good men died in the ambushes he set. He kills at night like some deadly predator, corrupts the tribal chiefs, and thinks of nothing but stirring up trouble. Come with me, Suti. The general wants to decorate you himself.'

Although he loathed these ceremonies, in which one man's vanity simply exacerbated another man's boastfulness, Suti agreed. Seeing the general face to face would be compensation for the dangers he had run.

The hero walked between two ranks of enthusiastic soldiers, who banged their helmets against their shields and roared the victor's name. From a distance, General Asher did not look at all like a great warrior: he was short and stiff, more like a scribe who had been worn down by the minutiae of government.

Suti came to an abrupt halt a few yards from him.

Immediately, somebody gave him a shove in the back. 'Go on. The general's waiting for you.'

'Don't be afraid, my lad.'

White-faced, the young man advanced.

Asher took a step towards him. 'I am happy to meet the archer whose praises everyone is singing. Chariot Officer Suti, I hereby award you the Golden Fly for bravery. Keep this jewel. It is the proof of your courage.'

Suti bowed and accepted the award. His comrades crowded round and congratulated him. They all wanted to see and touch the decoration, which was coveted by every soldier. One or two of them noticed that the hero's thoughts seemed to be somewhere else, no doubt a result of high emotion.

When he returned to his tent, after a drinking session sanctioned by the general, Suti became the brunt of bawdy jibes. Surely beautiful Panther had different assaults in store for him?

Suti stretched out on his back. His eyes were open, but unseeing. Panther dared not speak, and huddled far away from him. She thought he looked like a demon who had been deprived of blood and was yearning to drain it from a new victim.

General Asher . . . Suti could not get the general's face out of his mind. It was the face of the very man who had tortured and murdered an Egyptian, a few yards from Suti's hiding place.

General Asher, a coward, a liar and a traitor.

The morning light shone through the bars of a high window, lighting up one of the hundred and thirty-four pillars in the immense chamber. The master builders had created the country's largest stone forest in the temple at Karnak, decorated with ritual scenes in which Pharaoh was shown making offerings to the gods. The vivid colours were revealed only at certain times; you had to live there for an entire year to follow the path of the sun's rays as it lit pillar after pillar, unveiling secret rites scene by scene.

Two men were conversing as they walked slowly along the central aisle, which was bordered by stone lotus flowers with outspread petals. The first was Branir, the second the High Priest of Amon, a man of seventy whose duty it was to govern the gods' sacred city, watch over its wealth and lead the priestly hierarchy.

'I have heard of your request, Branir. You, who have guided so many young people onto the path of wisdom, now wish to withdraw from the world and dwell within the inner temple.'

'That is my wish. My eyes are growing weak, and my legs are reluctant to walk.'

'Old age does not seem to handicap you so very much.'

'Appearances can be deceptive.'

'Your career is far from over,' said the High Priest.

'I have passed on everything I know to Neferet, and I no longer see patients. As for my house in Memphis, I have already willed it to Judge Pazair.'

'Nebamon has not exactly encouraged Neferet, has he?'

'He makes her undergo harsh tests, but he does not know her true nature. Her heart is as strong as her face is gentle.'

'Pazair is a native of Thebes, is he not?'

'Indeed.'

'You seem to have total trust in him.'

'He has fire within him.'

'Flames can destroy,' pointed out the High Priest.

'But if they are controlled they illuminate.'

'What role have you in mind for him?''

'Destiny will take care of that.'

'You understand people so well. To retire early would deprive Egypt of your gift.'

'A successor will emerge,' said Branir.

'You know, I'm thinking of retiring, too.'

'Your responsibilities are very heavy.'

'And they get heavier by the day. Too much administration,

245

not enough meditation. Pharaoh and his council have accepted my request. In a few weeks, I shall move to a little house on the eastern bank of the sacred lake, and devote myself to the study of the ancient texts.'

'Then we shall be neighbours.'

'I fear not. Your house will be much more impressive.'

'What do you mean?'

'I mean that you, Branir, are my designated successor.'

Denes and Nenophar had accepted Mahu's invitation. The man was but newly rich and his ambitions were all too clear but, nevertheless, the papyrus maker could no longer be called a nobody. His business acumen, his capacity for work and his skills had made him a man of the future. He had even received the approval of the palace, where he had influential friends. Denes could not allow himself to neglect a trader of this ilk, so he had persuaded his annoyed wife to attend the party given by Mahu to celebrate the opening of his new premises in Memphis.

The annual flood looked likely to be good. The fields would be properly irrigated, everyone would have enough to eat, and Egypt would export wheat to her protectorates in Asia. Memphis the magnificent overflowed with riches.

Denes and Nenophar travelled to the party in a superb high-backed chair carried by forty sturdy bearers. It was equipped with a stool on which their feet rested, and also boasted elegant carved arm rests and a canopy to protect them from wind, dust and dazzling sunlight. The bearers moved quickly, watched by open-mouthed passers-by. The poles were so long and there were so many pairs of legs that the ensemble was immediately nicknamed the 'Millipede'. The bearers sang, 'We prefer a full chair to an empty one,' as they thought of the large fees they would receive.

Dazzling other people justified the expense. Denes and Nenophar were the envy of the other guests, who had gathered around Mahu and Silkis. No one in Memphis could remember ever seeing such a wonderful chair. Denes swept away the compliments with a wave of his hand, and Nenophar deplored the lack of gilding.

All the business folk of Memphis were celebrating Mahu's admission to the narrow circle of men of power. The door was ajar. Now it was up to him to push it open and prove his worth decisively. The opinions of Denes and his wife would carry considerable weight; no one had entered the elite band of traders without their assent.

Mahu was nervous. He greeted the new arrivals immediately, and introduced them to Silkis, who had been ordered not to open her mouth. Nenophar looked her up and down disdainfully.

Denes surveyed his surroundings. 'Is this a warehouse or a trading house?'

'Both,' replied Mahu. 'But later, if all goes well, I shall expand and separate the two functions.'

'That's an ambitious project.'

'Don't you approve?'

'Gluttony isn't an asset in business. One can so easily get a stomach ache.'

'Fortunately, I have an excellent appetite and perfect digestion.'

Nenophar lost interest in the conversation and went off to talk with old friends. Her husband knew that she had given her verdict; she found Mahu unpleasant, vain and inconsistent. His high hopes would crumble like bad limestone.

Denes said to his host, 'Memphis is less welcoming than it seems; remember that. On your estate in the Delta you reign unchallenged. Here, you will encounter all the difficulties of a large city, and you may wear yourself out in useless activity.'

'You're pessimistic.'

'Follow my advice, dear friend. Each man has his limits. Don't go beyond yours.'

'To be frank,' said Mahu, 'I don't yet know what they are. That's why I'm so enthusiastic about this new venture.'

'There are several long-established makers and sellers of papyrus in Memphis, and they've always given complete satisfaction.'

'I shall try to surprise them by offering better-quality products.'

'Isn't that rather boastful?'

'I have confidence in my work and I don't understand your . . . advice.'

'I am thinking only of your interests. Accept reality, and you'll avoid many disagreeable experiences.'

'Perhaps you should be more concerned about your own interests.'

Denes's thin lips turned white. 'Precisely what do you mean by that?'

Mahu tightened the belt of his long kilt, which had a tendency to slip down. 'I've heard stories of offences and court cases. Your businesses no longer look as attractive as they used to.'

Their voices had risen, and many of the guests turned to listen.

'Those accusations are slanderous and uncalled-for,' said Denes furiously. 'My name is respected throughout Egypt, whereas no one's ever even heard of you.'

'Times are changing,' retorted Mahu.

'Your malicious gossip and your slanders don't even deserve a reply.'

'What I have to say, I say out loud for all to hear. I leave insinuations and illegal dealing to others.'

'Are you accusing me?' demanded Denes.

'Why? Do you feel guilty?'

Nenophar took her husband's arm. 'We've stayed here quite long enough.'

'Be careful, Mahu,' advised Denes angrily. 'One bad harvest and you'll be ruined.'

'I've taken precautions.'

'Your dreams are no more real than mirages in the desert.'

'Won't you be my first customer? I'll devise a range of products and prices especially for you.'

'I'll think about it.'

The opinions of those present were divided. Denes had got the better of many optimists, but Mahu seemed sure of his own strength. The duel was set fair to be exciting.

28

Suti's chariot headed down a difficult path which ran alongside the foot of a rocky cliff. For a week, General Asher's troops had been chasing the last few rebels in vain. In the end, thinking the region pacified, the general gave the order to return.

Though he himself was now flanked by an archer, Suti was silent and stern-faced as he concentrated on driving the chariot. Panther had been granted special treatment: she was riding a donkey, whereas the other prisoners had to endure a forced march. Asher had granted this privilege to the hero of the campaign, and no one found fault with it.

The Libyan girl still slept in Suti's tent, but she was bewildered by the transformation in him. Ordinarily so ardent and expansive, he had withdrawn into a strange sadness. In the end, unable to contain herself any longer, she said, 'You're a hero, you'll be celebrated, you'll be rich, and yet you look as though you've been defeated. I want to know why.'

'A prisoner has no right to want anything.'

'I shall fight you all my life, as long as you are fit to fight back. Don't tell me you've lost your taste for life?'

'Stop asking all these questions and be quiet.'

Panther took off her tunic.

Naked, she threw back her blonde hair and danced, turning

slow circles before him, displaying every facet of her body. Her hands traced her curves, brushed her breasts, her hips, her thighs. Her supple body swayed with an innate grace.

Sensual as a she-cat, she moved forward, but he did not react. She unfastened his kilt, kissed his body and lay down on top of him. She was delighted to see that the hero's vigour had not diminished. However much he might try to resist, he still desired her. She slid down her lover's body and kindled his lust with burning kisses.

Afterwards, as they lay quietly together, she asked, 'What will become of me?'

'In Egypt you'll be free.'

'Aren't you going to keep me with you?'

'One man wouldn't be enough for you.'

'Get rich, and I'll put up with it.'

'You'd be bored as a respectable woman. Besides, don't forget your promise to betray me.'

'You defeated me, and I shall defeat you.'

She continued to caress him with the low, seductive sound of her voice. Lying on her belly, with her hair tumbling about her shoulders and her legs apart, she beckoned him. Suti entered her with renewed ardour, only too aware that this devil-woman must be using magic to reawaken his desire like this.

'You aren't sad any more, are you?' she said.

'Don't try to read my heart.'

'Then talk to me.'

'Tomorrow, when I stop the chariot, dismount from your donkey, come to me and do as I say.'

'The right wheel's squeaking,' Suti told his archer.

'I can't hear anything.'

'I have very sharp hearing. That squeak might mean trouble. We'd better check.'

Suti was at the head of the column. He drove off the

roadway and turned the chariot slightly, so that it faced a path which led into a wood.

'Let's have a look.'

The two men dismounted from the chariot. Suti knelt down and examined the suspect wheel.

'It's bad,' he said 'Two spokes are on the point of breaking.'

'Can we repair them?'

'We'll wait until the army carpenters get here.'

The carpenters marched at the rear of the column, just behind the prisoners. When Panther dismounted from her donkey and went over to Suti, there were plenty of bawdy comments from the soldiers.

'Get in,' Suti told her.

He knocked the archer down, seized the reins and drove the chariot at top speed down the path and into the woods. No one had time to react. The hero's bemused comrades-in-arms wondered why he was deserting.

Even Panther was astonished. 'Have you gone mad?' she asked.

'I have a promise to keep.'

An hour later, the chariot halted at the place where Suti had buried his officer after the sand-travellers killed him. Although horrified, Panther helped him to dig up the body. Suti wrapped it in a large linen cloth and bound the ends tightly with cord.

'Who is he?' asked Panther.

'A true hero, who shall rest in his own land, close to his own people.' Suti did not add that General Asher would probably not have given him permission to do this.

As he was finishing his sombre task, the Libyan girl cried out. Suti swung round, but was unable to avoid the bear claws that tore open his left shoulder. He fell, rolled over and tried to hide behind a rock. The enraged bear stood six cubits tall. It was both heavy and agile, and it was hungry. It let out a terrifying roar which sent all the birds fluttering into the air in panic.

'My bow and arrows, quickly!' shouted Suti.

Panther threw them to him. She dared not leave the fragile protection of the chariot. Before Suti could use his weapons, the bear's paw came down a second time, and tore his back open. He fell face down on the ground, covered in blood, and lay very still.

Panther shouted again, attracting the bear's attention. It bore down on her; there was no escape.

Suti heaved himself to his knees. A red mist veiled his eyes. Summoning up the last of his strength, he drew his bow and fired at the brown shape. Hit in the flank, the bear turned, dropped down on to all fours and charged at its attacker. As he lost consciousness, Suti fired again.

The head doctor at the military hospital in Memphis had given up hope. Suti's wounds were so deep and so numerous that he ought not to have survived. Soon the pain would kill him.

According to Panther, he had killed the bear with an arrow in its eye, but had succumbed to a last swipe of its claws. Panther had dragged his bleeding body to the chariot and, with a superhuman effort, hauled it inside. Then she had lifted the officer's corpse aboard. Touching a dead body disgusted her, but Suti had risked his life to bring it back to Egypt.

Fortunately, the horses had proved docile. Instinctively they retraced their steps and guided Panther, rather than having to be driven. The corpse of a charioteer officer, a dying deserter and a foreign fugitive: that was the strange sight that had greeted General Asher's rearguard.

Thanks to Panther's explanations and the identification of the dead officer, the facts had been established. The officer, because he had died on the field of honour, had been post-humously decorated and then mummified in Memphis;

Panther had been put to work as an agricultural worker on a large estate; and Suti had been congratulated on his courage and condemned for his lack of discipline.

Kem tried to explain this complicated story to Pazair.

'Suti's here, in Memphis?' asked Pazair in amazement.

'The rebellion has been crushed, and Asher's victorious army has returned. The only thing they didn't do is catch the leader, Adafi.'

'When did Suti arrive?'

'Yesterday.'

'Then why hasn't he come home?'

The Nubian turned away, discomfited. 'He can't travel.'

The judge was annoyed. 'And what, exactly, does that mean?'

'He's wounded.'

'Seriously?'

'His condition is—'

'Tell me the truth.'

'His condition is critical.'

'Where is he?'

'At the military hospital – if he's still alive.'

'He's lost too much blood,' said the head doctor. 'Trying to clean and stitch the wounds would be madness. We'll have to leave him to die in peace.'

'Is that the best you can do?' demanded Pazair furiously.

'It's the only thing. That bear tore him to ribbons. His resilience is amazing, but he has no chance of surviving.'

'Can he be moved?'

'Of course not.'

Pazair made a decision: Suti was not going to die in a communal ward. 'Bring me a litter.'

'Surely you aren't going to move a dying man?'

'I'm his friend and I know what he wants: to die in his own

village. If you deny him that wish, you'll be responsible before him and before the gods.'

The doctor did not take the threat lightly. A discontented spirit would become a ghost, and ghosts took their revenge pitilessly, even on head doctors.

'Very well, then,' he said. 'But you must sign this form.'

During the night, Pazair dealt with twenty minor cases which would keep Iarrot busy for three weeks. If Iarrot needed to contact him, he was to send his messages to the main court in Thebes. Pazair would dearly have liked to consult Branir, but the old man was in Karnak, preparing for his retirement.

Just after dawn, Kem and two orderlies laid Suti on a litter, carried him to the river and laid him down in the comfortable cabin of a light boat.

Pazair stayed at his side throughout the voyage, holding Suti's right hand in his own. Once, for a few moments, he thought Suti awoke and gripped his hand slightly, but it was only an illusion.

Pazair found Neferet in her workshop, seeing her patients.

'You're my last hope,' he said. 'The army doctor refused to operate on Suti. Will you examine him?'

She explained to the patients waiting under the palm trees that she must leave to deal with an emergency. She selected a number of pots of remedies, and Kem carried them to the boat for her.

'What did the army doctor say?' she asked.

'His wounds are very deep.'

'How did he withstand the journey?'

'He was unconscious all the time, though there was a moment when I thought I felt him stir.'

'Is he strong?'

'As strong as a stele.'

'Has he had any serious illnesses?'

'No.'

Neferet's examination lasted more than an hour. When she left the cabin, she look grave but determined. 'I shall do all I can to fight this illness,' she said. 'The risks are very great, but if I do nothing he'll certainly die, whereas if I cleanse his wounds he at least has a chance.'

She began towards noon. Pazair acted as her assistant, and passed her the knives and drugs as she asked for them. To ensure that Suti remained unconscious, she used a preparation of silica mixed with opium and mandragora root; the mixture was reduced to powder and administered in small doses. When she started working on a wound, she dissolved the powder in vinegar. This produced an acid which she collected in a stone horn and applied locally, to reduce the pain. She checked how long the substances worked by consulting the clock she wore on her wrist.

Using knives and fine blades made from obsidian, which was sharper than metal, she cut into the flesh. Her movements were precise and steady. She reshaped the flesh, brought the edges of each wound together and stitched them with a very fine thread made from the intestines of oxen; the many stitches were then strengthened with adhesive linen strips.

After five hours, Neferet was exhausted but Suti was still alive. She had put fresh meat, fat and honey on the most serious wounds. First thing next morning, she would change the dressings, which were made from gentle, protective vegetable matter, and both prevented infection and hastened the formation of scar tissue.

Three days passed. Pazair did not leave Suti's bedside for a moment.

On the third day, Suti stirred, then awoke, and was able to take some water and honey.

'You're going to live, Suti!'

'Where am I?' he asked weakly.

'On a boat, near our village.'

'You remembered that I wanted to die here.'

'You aren't going to die, you're going to get well. Neferet operated on you.'

'Your betrothed?'

'A remarkable surgeon and the best doctor in the world.'

Suti tried to sit up, but he cried out in pain and fell back.

'You mustn't move,' said Pazair.

'Me, unable to move . . .'

'Be patient – just for a little while.'

'That bear tore me to shreds.'

'Neferet sewed you up again, and you'll soon get your strength back.'

Suti's eyes rolled and Pazair was afraid he was going to collapse, but he gripped Pazair's hand tightly.

'Asher,' he said, panting with rage. 'I've got to live so that I can tell you about that murderer.'

'And so you shall, but you must keep calm.'

'You've got to know the truth, Judge. You've got to see that justice is respected in this country.'

'I'll listen, but don't exhaust yourself – please.'

Reassured, Suti lay back again. He said, 'I saw General Asher torture and murder an Egyptian soldier. Asher was with Asiatic men, the rebels he claimed to be fighting.'

Pazair wondered if fever had made his friend delirious, but Suti spoke steadily, hammering home each word.

'You were right to suspect him, and I've brought you the proof you needed.'

'Not proof, a witness statement,' Pazair corrected him.

'Isn't that enough?'

'He'll deny everything.'

'My word's as good as his!'

'As soon as you're well enough, we'll think of a plan. Until then, not a word to anyone.'

'I shall live. I shall live so that I can see that coward

condemned to death.' Suti grimaced with pain. 'Are you proud of me, Pazair?'

'You and I speak with one voice.'

Neferet's reputation was spreading all over the west bank. Her successful treatment of Suti impressed her colleagues so much that some asked her to treat their most difficult cases. She agreed to do so, so long as she could benefit the village that had welcomed her, and obtain Suti's admission to the hospital at Deir el-Bahri. The authorities there agreed to accept him. He was not only a hero of the battlefield but also something of a medical miracle, whose case was becoming a shining light among doctors.

At the temple at Deir el-Bahri* people worshipped Imhotep, the greatest doctor of the Old Kingdom. A shrine had been hollowed out of the rock and dedicated to him. Doctors meditated there and sought their ancestor's wisdom, which was vital to the practice of their craft. A few patients were admitted to live in this magnificent place while they regained their strength; they strolled along the colonnades, marvelled at the relief carvings depicting Hatshepsut's exploits, and walked in the gardens, where they breathed in the aromatic resin of the incense trees brought from the mysterious land of Punt, in north-eastern Africa. Copper pipes linked pools to underground drainage systems and brought healing water, which was collected in vessels also made of copper. Suti drank about twenty cups a day, to prevent infection and other complications. Thanks to his prodigious vitality, he would heal swiftly.

Pazair and Neferet walked down the long, flower-lined ramp that linked the terraces of Deir el-Bahri.

'You have saved him,' said Pazair.

'I was lucky, and so was he.'

---

*It was built on the west bank by the great queen-pharaoh Hatshepsut.

'Will there be any lasting ill effects?'

'Only a few scars.'

'They'll just add to his charm.'

The burning sun was climbing to its zenith. They sat down in the shade of an acacia tree, at the bottom of the ramp.

'Have you thought about what I said?' asked Pazair nervously.

She was silent. Her answer would bring him either happiness or misery. Life had come to a halt in the noonday heat. In the fields, the peasants were eating their lunch in the shade of reed huts where they would stretch out for a long nap. Neferet closed her eyes.

'I love you with all my being, Neferet. I want to marry you.'

'A life together . . . Are we capable of such a thing?'

'I shall never love another woman.'

'How can you be so certain? The pains of love are soon forgotten.'

'If you knew me better. . .'

'I know how serious you are – that's what frightens me.'

'Are you in love with someone else?'

'No.'

'I couldn't bear that.'

'Are you jealous?'

'More than I'd thought possible.'

'You think I'm your ideal woman,' said Neferet doubtfully, 'faultless, endowed with all the virtues.'

'You aren't a dream.'

'Yes, you dream me. One day you'll wake up and you'll be disappointed.'

'I see you here and alive, I breathe in your perfume, you're close to me. That isn't an illusion.'

'I'm afraid. If you're wrong – if we're both wrong – the pain will be terrible.'

'You'll never disappoint me.'

'I'm not a goddess. When you realize that, you won't love me any more.'

'It's no use trying to discourage me,' said Pazair. 'The moment we met, the moment I first saw you, I knew you would be the sun of my life. You're as radiant as sunlight, Neferet – no one can deny the light that shines in you. My life belongs to you, whether or not you want it.'

'You're talking nonsense. You must think what it would be like for us living far apart. Your career will be in Memphis, but mine will be in Thebes.'

'My career doesn't matter.'

'Don't give up your vocation – you'd never let me give up mine, would you?'

'You have only to ask, and I will,' said Pazair.

'That would be absolutely untrue to your nature.'

'All I want is to love you more each day.'

'Don't you think you're being rather excessive?'

'If you refuse to marry me, I shall die.'

'Blackmailing me is unworthy of you.'

'That isn't what I meant. Please, Neferet, will you marry me?'

She opened her eyes and looked at him sadly. 'It would be wrong to deceive you.'

She walked lightly and gracefully away. Despite the heat, Pazair was frozen to the core.

29

Suti was not the kind of man who could endure the peace and silence of the temple gardens for long. The pretty priestesses did not take care of the patients, but remained far out of their reach, and Suti's only contact was with a gruff orderly, whose job was to change his dressings.

Within a month of the operation, he was bursting with impatience. When Neferet examined him, he could barely keep still.

'I'm better,' he insisted.

'Not completely,' she said, 'but you've certainly made a remarkable recovery. The stitches haven't given way, the wounds have scarred over, and there's no infection.'

'Then can I leave here?'

'Only if you take things slowly.'

He kissed her on both cheeks. 'I owe you my life, and I'm grateful. If you ever need me, I'll come running – you have my word as a hero.'

'You must take a jar of healing water with you and drink three cupfuls a day.'

'Can I start drinking beer again?'

'Yes, and wine, too – in small doses.'

Suti took a deep breath and stretched out his arms. 'It's so good to be alive again! All those hours of pain . . . Only women can wipe them out.'

'Aren't you ever going to marry one?'

'May Hathor protect me from that disaster! Me, with a faithful wife and a tribe of squalling brats? A mistress, and then another, and another – that's my wonderful fate. They're all different, and each one has her own secrets.'

'You seem very different from your friend Pazair,' Neferet remarked with a smile.

'Don't be deceived by him. He may look reserved but he's passionate, perhaps even more than I am. If he's summoned the courage to speak to you . . .'

'He has.'

'Don't take his words lightly.'

'He frightened me.'

'Pazair will love only once in his whole life. He's one of those men who fall madly in love and stay mad all their lives. Women can't understand them – a woman needs time to grow accustomed, to take time before committing herself. Pazair's a raging torrent, not a slow-burning fire, and his passion will never weaken. He's clumsy, and often too timid or too hasty, but his sincerity is absolute. He's never even had a flirtation or an amorous adventure, because he's capable only of one great love.'

'But what if he's mistaken?'

'He'll believe in his ideal right to the end. Don't hope for any concessions.'

'But can you understand why I'm afraid?'

'In love, reasoned argument's futile. I wish you happiness, whatever decision you make.'

Suti could understand why Pazair felt as he did. Neferet's beauty was radiant.

He had stopped eating, and sat at the foot of a palm tree like a grieving mourner, his head resting on his knees. He could no longer have told you if it was day or night. He looked so much like a block of stone that even the children did not taunt him.

'Pazair! It's Suti.'

There was no reaction.

'You're convinced that she doesn't love you.' Suti sat down next to his friend, and leant back against the tree. 'There'll never be another woman for you, I know. I can't share in your unhappiness, and I shan't try to console you. All you have left is your mission.'

Pazair was silent.

'Neither of us can let Asher win. If we give up, the court of the afterlife will condemn us to the second death, and we'll have no defence for our cowardice.'

Still the judge did not move.

'All right, then, starve to death thinking about her. I'll fight Asher by myself.'

At this, Pazair came out of his trance and looked at Suti. 'He'll destroy you.'

'Every man has ordeals to face. You can't bear Neferet's indifference. With me, it's the face of a murderer haunting my dreams.'

'I'll help you.' Pazair tried to stand up, but his head started spinning, and Suti had to steady him.

'I'm sorry,' said Pazair, 'but—'

'Don't say anything – you've told me often enough not to waste my breath. The important thing is to make you fit and well again.'

The two men took the ferry, which was as full as ever. Pazair had managed to nibble some bread and onions. The wind whipped at his face.

'Look at the Nile,' advised Suti. 'That's true nobility. Compared to the river, we're nothing.'

The judge gazed at the clear water.

'What are you thinking about, Pazair?'

'As if you didn't know.'

'How can you be sure she doesn't love you? I've spoken with her, and—'

'It's no use.'

'A drowned man may be blessed by the gods, but he's still drowned. And you've sworn to bring Asher to justice.'

'Without you, I'd give up.'

'Because you're no longer yourself.'

'Actually, it's only now that I really am myself. Now I know what real loneliness is.'

'You won't always feel like this.'

'You don't understand.'

'Time will heal you.'

'It won't change a thing.'

As soon as the ferry reached the bank, the other passengers disembarked in a noisy crowd, driving their donkeys, sheep and oxen before them. The two friends let them pass, then went ashore themselves.

'We must go back to Memphis,' said Suti.

'Why are you in such a hurry?'

'I want to see Asher again. Why don't you tell me what you've found out so far?'

In a flat voice, Pazair did so.

Suti listened closely. 'Who followed you?' he asked when Pazair had finished.

'I have no idea.'

'Are those the sort of methods Mentmose uses?'

'They may be.'

Suti thought for a moment, then said, 'Before we leave Thebes, let's go and see Kani.'

Pazair made no objection. He was indifferent, detached from reality. Neferet's refusal was gnawing away at his soul.

Kani now had several people working for him, and the part of the garden devoted to vegetables was a hive of activity. Kani himself was tending the medicinal plants. His suntanned skin was more deeply lined than ever, and he moved slowly, weighed down by the weight of a large yoke bearing two water pots. No one else was privileged to water his favourite plants.

When Pazair introduced Suti, Kani stared at him and asked, 'He's your friend?'

'Yes. You can talk freely in front of him.'

'I've kept on searching for the soldier. Carpenters, joiners, water carriers, washermen, peasants – I haven't missed out a single trade. There is one small clue: our man spent a few days repairing chariots before he disappeared.'

'That's a big clue,' Suti corrected him. 'It means he must be alive.'

'Let's hope so.'

'But he may have been murdered since then, of course.'

'Either way, I can't find him.'

'Go on looking,' said Pazair. 'He's still in the land of the living.'

Could anything be sweeter than a Theban evening, when the north wind brought coolness to the canopies and pergolas where people drank beer as they watched the sunset? Tiredness melted away, tormented souls were soothed, and the beauty of the goddess of silence filled the crimson western sky. Ibis soared through the gathering dusk.

'Neferet, I'm leaving for Memphis tomorrow,' said Pazair

'Because of your work?'

'Suti witnessed a crime. It's safer for you if I don't say any more than that.'

'Is it really that dangerous?'

'The army's involved.'

'Then you be careful, too,' said Neferet.

'What do you care about what happens to me?'

'Don't be bitter. I want you to be happy.'

'You're only person who can make me happy.'

'You are so uncompromising, so—'

'Come with me.'

'I can't. I'm not lit by the same flame as you. You have to accept that I'm different, that I can't do things in haste.'

'It's all very simple: I love you and you don't love me.'

'No, it is not all very simple. Day doesn't follow night with brutal suddenness, nor does one season succeed another abruptly.'

'Are you offering me a shred of hope?'

'If I promised you anything, I'd be lying.'

'You see?'

'Your feelings are so fierce, so impatient. You can't ask me to respond equally passionately.'

'Don't try to justify yourself.'

'I can't see clearly into my own heart, so how can I offer you anything with certainty?'

'If I leave alone, we'll never see each other again.'

With that, Pazair walked slowly away, hoping for words which did not come.

Pazair found that Iarrot had managed, by avoiding all responsibility, not to make any major errors. The district was quiet, and no serious crimes had been committed. Mentmose had sent a message summoning Pazair, so, after sorting out a few details, Pazair went to see him.

Mentmose's smile was broader than usual. 'My dear Judge,' he said, 'I'm delighted to see you again. You've been away?'

'An unavoidable absence.'

'The area under your jurisdiction is one of the most peaceful. Your reputation is bearing fruit: people know that you give no quarter where the law is concerned. But – and I don't wish to offend you – you look tired.'

'It's nothing.'

'Good, good.'

'Why did you want to see me?'

'On account of a delicate and . . . regrettable matter. I followed your plan to the letter regarding the grain store, although, if you remember, I doubted that it would work. Between you and me, I was right.'

'Has the overseer run away?'

'No, no – I have no complaint on his account. He wasn't there when the incident happened.'

'What incident?'

'Half the contents of the store were stolen during the night.'

Pazair gaped at him. 'Are you joking?'

'I'm afraid not. It is the sad truth.'

'But your men were watching the grain store.'

'Yes and no. There was a serious brawl not far away, and they had to intervene urgently – they can't be blamed for that. When they got back, they discovered the theft. And now, surprisingly, the state of the store matches the overseer's report!'

'Do you know who the thieves are?'

'We have no serious leads.'

'Any witnesses?'

'The area was deserted,' said Mentmose, 'and the theft was efficiently carried out. It won't be easy to identify the thieves.'

'I assume your best men are dealing with the matter?'

'You can rely on me for that.'

'Between ourselves, Mentmose, what is your opinion of me?'

'Well . . . I think you're a very conscientious judge.'

'Will you credit me with a little intelligence?'

'My dear Pazair, you underestimate yourself!'

'In that case, you will know that I cannot believe a word of your story.'

Silkis, who was in the grip of one of her frequent attacks of anxiety, was receiving attentive care from a specialist in disturbances of the mind, an interpreter of dreams. His consulting room was painted black and no light was permitted to enter. Each week, she lay down on a mat, told him her nightmares and asked for his advice.

The dream reader was a Syrian who had been settled in Memphis for many years. His clients were mainly noble ladies and well-off middle-class women, so his fees were very high – after all, using his grimoires, his 'keys to dreams',* and his practised flattery, he gave regular peace and comfort to the poor weak-minded creatures.

The interpreter insisted that the treatment must be open-ended; people never stopped dreaming. He alone could tell the meaning of the images and phantasms that disturbed a sleeping brain. He was very careful, and rejected the advances of most of his love-starved patients, yielding only to widows who had kept their looks.

Silkis gnawed her nails.

'Have you argued with your husband?' asked the dream reader.

'Yes, about the children.'

'What did they do wrong?'

'They told lies. But that's not such a terrible crime. My husband gets angry, I defend them, and voices are raised . . .'

'Does he hit you?'

'Sometimes, but I defend myself.'

'Is he pleased with the changes in your body?'

'Oh yes! He eats out of my hand most of the time. I can make him do what I want, as long as I don't interfere in his business affairs.'

'Are you interested in them?'

'Not in the least. We're rich – that's all that matters.'

'After the last argument, what did you do?'

---

*Some keys to dreams have been discovered; they indicate the nature of dreams and provide interpretations.

'What I always do. I shut myself away in my bedchamber and I cried. Then I went to sleep.'

'Did you have a long dream?'

'The same images as always. First, I saw a mist rising up from the river. Something – a boat, I thought – tried to pass through it. Then the sun made the mist melt away. The thing wasn't a boat, it was a gigantic phallus – and it was coming right at me. I turned aside and tried to hide in a house on the banks of the Nile. But it wasn't a building, it was a woman's sex, which attracted and terrified me at the same time.'

Silkis was panting.

'Be careful,' advised the dream reader. 'According to the key of dreams, seeing a phallus means there's going to be a theft.'

'And what about a woman's sex?'

'That means poverty.'

In great alarm, Silkis rushed to the warehouse, where she found Mahu talking to two embarrassed-looking men.

'Forgive me for disturbing you, my darling,' said Silkis, 'but I had to warn you. Someone's going to steal from you and we are in danger of ending up in poverty.'

'Your warning comes too late. These men are boat captains, and they have just told me there are no boats available to transport my papyri from the Delta to Memphis. Our warehouse will stand empty.'

30

Pazair tried to calm Mahu down. 'What do you want me to do?' he asked.

'I want you to take action against people impeding the proper flow of goods. Papyri are piling up, but I can't deliver them to the people who ordered them.'

'As soon as a boat's available—'

'There'll never be one.'

'Are you alleging deliberate ill-will?'

'If you investigate, you'll soon prove it. Meanwhile, every hour that passes brings me closer to ruin.'

'Come back tomorrow. I may have some evidence by then.'

'I shan't forget what you're doing for me.'

'Not for you, Mahu, for justice.'

The mission amused Kem, and amused Killer even more. Armed with a list of ship owners provided by Mahu, they asked each one why he had refused. Garbled explanations, regrets and obvious lies confirmed that Mahu was right. At the far end of a dock, at about the time when people took their afternoon nap, Kem turned his attention to a boat owner who was usually well-informed.

'Do you know Mahu?' asked Kem.

'I've heard of him.'

'There are no boats available to transport his papyri.'

'So it seems.'

'And yet yours is at the quayside, empty.'

Killer opened his mouth wide, showing his big, sharp teeth.

'Keep that animal under control!' said the man.

'Just tell me the truth and we'll leave you in peace.'

'Denes has hired all the boats for a week.'

Late that afternoon, Judge Pazair observed the proper procedures by questioning the ship owners himself and requiring them to show him their contracts of hire.

Every single one bore the name of Denes.

Sailors sang and shouted to each other as they unloaded food, jars and furniture from a sailing-barge. Carpenters were repairing a sail, stone cutters reinforcing a landing stage. Another cargo boat was preparing to leave for the south.

There were few oarsmen to be seen; almost all the deck was taken up with cabins for storing the goods. The helmsman, who steered using a special oar, was already in position. All that was missing was the man who stood at the bow, sounding the depth of the water at regular intervals with a long staff. Denes was standing on the bustling quayside, talking to the captain, when Pazair, Kem and Killer arrived.

'May I speak to you?' asked Pazair.

'With pleasure, but later.'

'Forgive me for insisting, but I'm in a hurry.'

'Not in such a hurry that you'd delay the departure of a boat, I hope.'

'I'm afraid I am.'

'Why?'

Pazair unrolled a papyrus a good two cubits long. 'Here is the list of offences you have committed: forced hiring, intimidating boat owners, attempting to control the hiring of boats, and impeding the proper movement of goods.'

271

Denes looked at it. The accusations were drawn up with absolute precision and according to the rules.

'I dispute your interpretation of the facts, which is unbalanced and overdramatic. If I've hired a lot of boats, it's because I've got some exceptionally large cargoes.'

'What are they?'

'Oh, various materials.'

'That's too vague.'

'In my line of work, it's wise to foresee the unforeseeable.'

'Mahu's business is suffering because of you.'

'There you are! I warned him that his ambition would lead to failure.'

'In order to break your control of hiring boats, which is incontestable, I am exercising the right of requisition.'

'As you wish. Take any barge from the western quay.'

'This one here will suit me very well.'

Denes stepped in front of the gangplank and shouted, 'I forbid you to touch it.'

'I shall pretend I did not hear that. Obstructing the law is a serious offence.'

The ship owner said more moderately, 'Be reasonable. Thebes needs this load.'

'Mahu has lost trade because of your actions, and justice requires that you offer him restitution. He is willing not to bring a complaint against you, so as not to jeopardize your future relations. However, because of the delay he has an enormous amount of stock to deliver. This barge will only just be big enough.'

Pazair, Kem and Killer climbed aboard. Not only did the judge wish to give Mahu justice, but he was also following his intuition.

Several cabins, made from planks with holes to allow free circulation of air, contained horses, oxen, bullocks and calves. Some were moving about freely, others were tied to rings fixed to the deck. Other cabins – simple shells made from light wood covered with a roof – contained stools, chairs and pedestal tables.

Aft, a large hold held some thirty portable grain stores.

Pazair called Denes over. 'Where did this wheat come from?'

'From warehouses.'

'Who delivered it to you?'

'Ask the cargo master.'

When questioned, the man produced an official-looking document bearing an indecipherable seal. Why, Pazair wondered, should he have taken care to look at it, since the goods were so ordinary? According to a province's needs, Denes transported grain all year round. The reserves in the state silos prevented any famine.

'Who gave the shipping order?' asked the judge.

The cargo master did not know. Pazair went back to Denes, who took him straight to his office in the port.

'I have nothing to hide,' insisted Denes edgily. 'All right, I tried to teach Mahu a lesson, but it was only a joke. Why are you so interested in my cargo?'

'That is an official secret.'

Denes' records were well kept, and he was only too eager to produce the relevant slate tablet.

The shipping order came from Hattusa, Ramses' diplomatic wife.

Thanks to General Asher, calm had returned to the Asian princedoms. Once again, he had proved his perfect knowledge of the terrain. Two months after his return, in high summer, while a favourable flood was depositing fertile silt upon the two banks, a magnificent ceremony was staged in his honour. For Asher had brought back a tribute of a thousand horses, five hundred prisoners, two thousand sheep, eight hundred goats, four hundred oxen, forty enemy chariots, hundreds of spears, swords, breastplates and shields, and two hundred thousand sacks of grain.

The elite troops, royal guard and desert guards were gathered before the royal palace, along with representatives of the four regiments of Amon, Re, Ptah and Set, comprising the chariot corps, footsoldiers and archers. Not a single officer was absent. The Egyptian armed forces were displaying their might and celebrating their most decorated senior officer. Ramses would hand him five gold collars and proclaim three days of celebration throughout the land. Asher was becoming one of the most important people in the state, the king's armed fist and the country's bulwark against invasion.

Suti, too, was at the celebration. The general had granted him a new chariot for the parade, without requiring him to purchase the shell and shaft as most officers had to; three soldiers would take care of the two horses.

Before the procession, the general congratulated Suti. He said, 'Go on serving Egypt like that, young man, and I promise you you'll have a brilliant future.'

'I wouldn't be able to enjoy it, sir.'

'I'm surprised to hear that.'

'Until we've captured Adafi, I shan't rest easy.'

'There speaks a brilliant and generous-spirited hero,' said Asher warmly.

'I keep wondering, how did he manage to escape? After all, sir, we were scouring the whole region for him.'

'He's a sly scoundrel.'

'It's almost as if he guessed our plans.'

General Asher's brow furrowed. 'You've answered your own question. There must be a spy in our ranks.'

'Sir, there can't be.'

'Take it as a fact. Don't worry: my staff and I will attend to the problem. You can be certain that Adafi won't stay free for long.'

Asher patted Suti's cheek, then turned his attention to another fellow.

He had shown no sign of being disturbed by the insinuation, and for a moment Suti almost wondered if he was wrong. But then he saw the horrible scene again, crystal-clear in his memory. He had been naive to hope the traitor's mask would slip.

Pharaoh's long speech was summarized and proclaimed in every town and village by heralds. As supreme commander of the army, he guaranteed peace and kept a careful watch on the borders. The four great regiments, twenty thousand strong, would protect Egypt from any threat of invasion. The charioteers and the footsoldiers, many of whom were Nubian, Syrian or Libyan, set great store by the happiness of the Two Lands, and would defend them against all attackers, even their own former countrymen. The king would not tolerate any lack of discipline, and the tjaty would carry out his instructions to the letter.

As a reward for his good and loyal services, General Asher was made responsible for instructing the officers who trained the troops who gathered secret information in Asia. His experience would be valuable: already a standard-bearer at the king's right hand, from now on the general would be consulted on all tactical and strategic options.

Pazair picked up legal papyri and put them down again, filed documents he had already filed, gave Iarrot contradictory orders, and forgot to take Brave for walks. Iarrot no longer dared ask him a question, because the answer was always oblique.

Every day Pazair was bombarded with demands from Suti, who was growing more and more impatient and could not bear to see Asher at liberty. The judge had no firm plan to offer, but he had ruled out doing anything in haste and had made his friend promise not to do anything rash. Attacking the general without proper preparation could only end in failure.

Suti could see that Pazair was not very interested in what he had to say. Lost in his own painful thoughts, he was slowly fading away.

Pazair had thought that his work would absorb him and make him forget Neferet, but he'd been wrong: instead, being far from her only increased his distress. Aware that time would make things worse, he decided to become a shadow. After bidding farewell to Brave and Way-Finder, he left Memphis and walked westwards, towards the Libyan desert. He had not had the courage to confide in Suti, for he knew what his friend's arguments would be and had not the strength to counter them. Giving love and not receiving it had made his life agony.

Pazair walked beneath the raging sun on the burning sand. He climbed a hillock and sat down on a stone, gazing into the vastness around him. The sky and the earth would close in upon him, the heat would dry him out, the hyenas and the vultures would destroy his remains. In neglecting his tomb, he would insult the gods and condemn himself to suffer the second death, which forbade resurrection; but to spend all eternity without Neferet would be the worst of all punishments.

Absent from his own body, indifferent to the wind and the biting grains of sand, Pazair sank into nothingness. Empty sun, unmoving light . . . it was not so easy to die. He kept absolutely still, convinced that he must soon sink into the final sleep.

When Branir laid a hand upon his shoulder, he did not react.

'This is a tiring walk, at my age. When I got back from Thebes I was planning to rest, but you've compelled me to come and find you in the desert. Drink a little of this.' He held out a goatskin water bag.

Pazair hesitated, then took it, put the spout to his parched lips and drank. 'Refusing would have been an insult, but I shan't yield to you on anything else.'

'You have great resistance, your skin is not burnt and your voice is almost steady.'

'The desert will take my life.'

'It will refuse to give you death.'

Pazair trembled. 'I shall be patient.'

'Your patience will be futile, for you are a liar.'

The judge started. 'You, my master, you—'

'The truth is often painful.'

'I haven't gone back on my word.'

'You've forgotten something. When you accepted your first post, in Memphis, you swore an oath to which a stone bore witness. Look at the desert around us. That stone has become a thousand, and each one reminds you of the sacred promise you made before the gods, before men and before yourself. You know very well, Pazair, that a judge is not an ordinary man. Your life no longer belongs to you. Spoil it, lay it waste, it is unimportant; but a man who breaks his sacred oath is condemned to wander among the hate-filled shades that rip each other apart.'

Pazair stared at his master. 'I cannot live without her.'

'You must fulfil your office as a judge.'

'Without joy and without hope?'

'Justice is nourished not by feelings but by righteousness.'

'I can never forget Neferet, even for a moment.'

'Tell me about your inquiries.'

The enigma of the Sphinx, the fifth guard, General Asher, the stolen wheat: Pazair related the facts, concealing neither his doubts nor his uncertainties.

'You, a new and inexperienced judge at the bottom of your profession, have been entrusted by destiny with matters of exceptional importance. They go far beyond you – and may involve the future of Egypt. Are you really so shameful as to neglect them?'

'Very well,' said Pazair wearily, 'I'll take action, since you demand it.'

'It's your office that demands it. Do you think mine is any easier?'

'You'll soon be enjoying the peace of the covered temple.'

'Not its peace, Pazair, but its entire life. Against my wishes, I have been appointed High Priest of Karnak.'

Pazair's face lit up. 'When will you receive the golden ring?'

'In a few months' time.'

For two days, Suti had been looking for Pazair all over Memphis. He knew his friend was desperate enough to end his own life.

At last Pazair reappeared in his office, his face burnt by the sun. Suti forced him to share a long drinking session, filled with talk about childhood memories.

Next morning they bathed in the Nile, but were unable to ease their pounding headaches.

'Where were you hiding?' asked Suti.

'I was meditating in the desert. Branir brought me back.'

'What have you decided?'

'Even if the road is dull and grey, I shall respect my oath as a judge.'

'Happiness will come one day, you'll see.'

'You know it won't.'

'We'll fight the battle together,' said Suti. 'Where are you going to start?

'Thebes.'

'Because of her?'

'I shall never see her again. I must investigate an illegal trade in wheat and also find the fifth guard. His testimony will be vital.'

'What if he's dead?'

'Thanks to Branir, whose pendulum is never wrong, I'm sure he's in hiding.'

'It may be a long search.'

'Watch Asher, study what he does, and try to find a weak spot.'

Suti's chariot threw up a cloud of dust. As he drove, he bellowed a bawdy song about women's infidelity. He was optimistic: Pazair might have lost his zest for life, but he'd never break his word. At the first opportunity, Suti would introduce him to a carefree damsel who would drive away his melancholy.

Asher would not escape justice. Suti must give him what he deserved.

The chariot passed between two boundary stones, marking the entrance to the estate. The heat was so oppressive that most of the peasants were resting in the shade, but in front of the farmhouse there was uproar: a donkey had just thrown off its load.

Suti halted, jumped down, and pushed away the donkey driver, who was brandishing a stick, ready to punish the animal. Suti steadied the frightened animal by holding its ears, and stroked it to calm it down.

'You should never hit a donkey,' he said.

'What about my sack of grain? Didn't you see him drop it?'

'It wasn't his fault,' cut in a young lad.

'Then whose was it?'

'The Libyan girl's. She likes sticking thorns in his backside.'

'That one!' said the donkey driver. 'She deserves the stick ten times over.'

'Where is she?' asked Suti.

'Near the pond. If you try and catch her, she climbs up into the willow tree.'

'I'll deal with it.'

As soon as Suti approached, Panther scrambled up the tree and stretched out on one of the largest branches.

'Come down,' he ordered.

'Go away! It's because of you that I'm reduced to slavery.'

'I almost died, if you remember, and I've come to set you free. Jump down into my arms.'

She did so without hesitation. Suti was knocked over, hit the ground hard and grimaced.

Panther traced his scars with her fingertip. 'Do other women reject you now?'

'I need a devoted nurse for a little while. You can massage me.'

'But you're all dusty.'

'I hurried, because I was so eager to see you again.'

'Liar!'

'You're right,' he said, 'I should have washed.'

He got up, scooped her into his arms, ran to the pool and dived in, locked in a passionate embrace.

Nebamon was trying on the official wigs his attendant had prepared. He didn't like any of them: too heavy, too complicated. It was becoming more and more difficult to follow the fashion. He was overwhelmed by the demands of rich ladies determined to preserve their charms by reshaping their bodies, and, as if that weren't enough, he had to preside over government commissions and to get rid of candidates who might want to succeed him. He wished he had a woman like Neferet at his side. His failure with her still rankled.

His private scribe bowed before him. 'My lord, I have the information you wanted.'

'Is she in poverty and distress?

'Not exactly.'

'Has she abandoned medicine?'

'Quite the reverse, my lord.'

'Are you mocking me?'

'She has set up a workshop in a small village, where she prepares her own remedies, she has carried out operations, and she has won the approval of the authorities in Thebes. Her fame is growing by the day.'

'That's insane! She has no money? How can she procure rare and expensive ingredients?'

The scribe smiled. 'I think you'll be pleased with me, my lord.'

'Why?'

'I followed a tortuous trail. Has the reputation of one Sababu reached your ears?'

'Didn't she keep an ale-house in Memphis?'

'The most famous of all. She left it suddenly, although it brought in a tidy profit.'

'What is the connection with Neferet?'

'Sababu not only receives treatment from her but also provides her with funds. The whore offers Theban customers pretty young girls, and then uses the money she makes money from this trade to support her favourite doctor. Isn't that an affront to morality?'

'A doctor financed by a prostitute . . . At last I have her!'

31

'Your reputation does you credit,' Nebamon told Pazair. 'Wealth doesn't impress you and you aren't afraid to attack the privileged – in short, justice is your daily bread and integrity is second nature to you.'

'That is the very least required of a judge.'

'Indeed, indeed; and that's also why I have chosen you.'

'Should I be flattered?'

'I'm counting on your probity.'

Ever since childhood, Pazair had disliked seducers, with their forced smiles and calculated attitudes. Nebamon annoyed him intensely.

Nebamon lowered his voice to a whisper, so as not to be heard by Iarrot. 'A terrible scandal is about to break, one which could devastate my profession and bring shame upon all doctors.'

'You will have to be more explicit.'

Nebamon gave a meaning look at Iarrot; Pazair nodded his consent, and the scribe withdrew.

'Complaints, courts, administrative slowness . . . Can't we avoid all these irritating formalities?'

Pazair said nothing.

'You want to know more, which is quite normal. May I count on your discretion?'

The judge waited.

'One of my pupils, Neferet, made bad mistakes, for which I punished her. At Thebes, she was supposed to be prudent, and defer to more competent colleagues. She has greatly disappointed me.'

'Are you saying she's made more mistakes?'

'Yes, and they're more and more serious. She treats patients without consulting someone more experienced, she provides out-of-season remedies, and she's set up a private workshop in which she makes the remedies herself.'

'Is that illegal?'

'No, but she had no money with which to do all this.'

'The gods must have looked kindly on her.'

'Not the gods, Judge Pazair. It was a woman of ill repute, Sababu, an ale-house proprietor from Memphis.'

Nebamon waited, grave-faced, for an expression of anger, but Pazair seemed unmoved.

'The situation is very worrying,' he went on. 'One day, someone will discover the truth and respectable doctors will be tainted.'

'Yourself, for example?'

'Absolutely, since I was Neferet's teacher. I can't tolerate such a risk any longer.'

'I sympathize, but I can't see what my role is in all this.'

'Discreet but firm action would get rid of this . . . unpleasantness. Sababu's ale-house is in your sector, and she's working in Thebes under a false identity, so you have ample reason to charge her. Threaten Neferet with very heavy penalties if she continues as she is – the warning will reduce her to her proper place as a village doctor. Of course, I don't expect you to help for nothing. A career has to be built: I am well placed to help you progress within the ranks of judges.'

'I'm aware of that.'

'I knew we'd understand each other. You're young, intelligent and ambitious, unlike so many of your colleagues, who are so insistent on the letter of the law that they lose sight of common sense.'

'What happens if I fail?'

'I'll bring a complaint against Neferet, you'll preside over the court, and between us we'll choose the jurors. But I hope we can avoid that – be as persuasive as you can.'

'I'll make every effort.'

Nebamon, relaxed now, congratulated himself on a job well done. He had judged the judge correctly. He said, 'I'm glad I knocked at the right door. Between people of quality, it's easy to smooth over difficulties.'

Divine Thebes, where he had known happiness and misery. Enchanting Thebes, where the splendour of dawn matched the magic of evening. Implacable Thebes, where destiny had brought him back in search of a truth that was as difficult to catch as a frightened lizard.

It was on the ferry that they met.

She was returning from the east bank, and he was crossing to the village where she practised. He had feared she'd avoid him, but she didn't.

He said, 'I meant what I said. This meeting should never have happened.'

'Haven't you forgotten me a little by now?'

'Not for a single moment.'

'You're torturing yourself.'

'What does that matter to you?'

'Your pain saddens me,' said Neferet. 'Do you really think it necessary to make it worse by seeing each other again?'

'I'm speaking to you now purely as a judge.'

'Why? Have I been accused of something?'

'Yes, of accepting gifts from a prostitute. Nebamon is demanding that you confine your activities to the village and that you refer all serious cases to your colleagues.'

'And if I don't?'

'He'll try to have you convicted of immorality – in other words, he'll try to stop you practising.'

'Is his threat one I should take seriously?'

'Nebamon is a man of considerable influence.'

'I escaped from him, and he can't bear to be defied.'

'Are you sure you don't want to give up?'

'What would you think of me if I did?'

'Nebamon's relying on me to persuade you.'

'He doesn't know you.'

'Fortunately for us. Do you trust me?'

'Unreservedly.'

There was a warmth in her voice which thrilled him. Was she emerging from her reserve, looking at him in a new, less distant way?

'Don't be afraid, Neferet. I'll help you.'

He accompanied her to the village, wishing the earthen track might never end.

Although still forced to take endless precautions because of the Nubian and his monkey, the shadow-eater felt reassured. Judge Pazair's journey seemed entirely private. Far from looking for the fifth guard, he was paying court to the lovely Neferet.

The shadow-eater was beginning to believe that the guard had died of natural causes, or else had fled so far to the south that nothing more would ever be heard of him; either way, the only thing that mattered was his silence. But the shadow-eater was cautious, and would continue to watch the judge.

Killer was uneasy.

Kem looked around, but could see nothing unusual. Peasants and their donkeys, workmen repairing the dykes, water carriers. And yet Killer could sense danger.

On the alert now, the Nubian drew closer to Pazair and Neferet. For the first time, he fully appreciated the judge's worth. The young man was forged from idealism, at once strong and fragile, realistic and dreamy; but righteousness guided him. He could not by himself wipe out the evil in human nature but he would fight it to the last, and in doing so he gave hope to the victims of injustice.

Kem would have preferred him not to embark on such a dangerous venture, which was sure to break him sooner or later; but how could he reproach him when so many poor souls had been murdered? As long as the welfare of simple folk wasn't scorned, as long as a judge didn't grant special privileges to the great merely because of their wealth, Egypt would continue to flourish.

Neferet and Pazair did not speak. He was dreaming of taking a walk like this one day when, hand in hand, they would be content to be together. They walked in step, as though they were a couple. He stole moments of impossible happiness, clung to a dream more precious than reality.

Neferet walked with a quick, light step; her feet seemed barely to brush the ground and she moved tirelessly. He revelled in the priceless privilege of accompanying her, and he would have offered himself to her as her humble, zealous servant, had he not been obliged to stay a judge in order to defend her against the coming storms. Was he imagining it, or did she seem less reticent towards him? Perhaps she needed this double silence. Perhaps, if he didn't speak of it, she would grow accustomed to his love.

They went to the workshop, where Kani was sorting medicinal plants.

'The crop was excellent,' he said.

'It may have been for nothing,' said Neferet sadly. 'Nebamon wants to stop me.'

'If poisoning people wasn't illegal . . .'

'He'll fail,' declared Pazair. 'I shall stand in his way.'

'He's deadlier than a viper,' said Kani. 'He'll bite you, too.'

'Is there any news?' asked Pazair.

'The temple priests have granted me a large piece of land to cultivate. I'm going to be their official supplier.'

'You deserve it, Kani,' said Pazair warmly.

'I haven't forgotten our investigation. I was able to talk to the scribe who keeps records of employees, and he said no ex-soldier from Memphis has been taken on in the workshops or on the farms in the last six months. Every ex-soldier has to register with the scribes or lose his rights, which would mean condemning himself to poverty.'

'Yes, but our man's so afraid that he prefers poverty to living in the light of day.'

'What if he's gone into exile?'

'No. I'm convinced he's in hiding somewhere on the west bank.'

Pazair was in the grip of warring emotions. One moment he felt light, almost joyful; the next he was sombre and depressed. Having seen Neferet, feeling her closer, more friendly, brought him back to life; admitting that she would never be his wife plunged him into despair. Fortunately, though, fighting for her, for Suti and Mahu, prevented him from dwelling on his feelings all the time. Branir's words had put him in his place: a judge's first duty was to others, and today it was his duty to see Hattusa.

It was a feast day in the Theban harem: they were celebrating the success of the Asian expedition, the greatness of Ramses, the consolidation of peace and the fame of General Asher. Weaving women, musicians, dancing girls, specialists in enamel, governesses, hairdressers and floral designers strolled in the gardens and chatted as they ate sweet pastries. In the shade of a pavilion, fruit juices were served. The guests admired one another's jewellery, and exchanged jealous remarks behind one another's backs.

Pazair felt out of place, but he managed to approach Hattusa.

In her beauty she outshone all the other women of the court. She was an expert in the arts of beauty, and showed great scorn towards those with less than perfect make-up. She aimed equally cutting remarks at the flatterers who surrounded her.

'Aren't you the little judge from Memphis?' she asked when she saw Pazair.

'If you will permit me to disturb you for a moment, my lady, I would be most grateful for a private audience.'

'What a lovely idea! These social events bore me. Let us walk to the lake.'

Everyone wondered who this modest-looking judge was, and how he could conquer the most inaccessible of princesses like this. Hattusa had probably decided to play with him, then throw him away like a broken doll. People had lost count of her extravagances.

White and blue lotus flowers mingled on the surface of the water, rippled by a light breeze. Hattusa and Pazair sat down on folding stools, beneath a sunshade.

'People will talk, Judge Pazair. We are hardly respecting etiquette.'

'I know that will please you.'

'Have you a taste for the splendours of my harem?'

'My lady, is the name Mahu familiar to you?'

'No.'

'What about Denes?'

'Again, no. Is this an interrogation?'

'I need your testimony, my lady.'

'These people don't belong to my household, as far as I know.'

'An order, issued by you, was sent to Denes, the largest ship owner in Memphis.'

'That means nothing to me. Do you think I interest myself in such details?'

'The hold of the boat, which was to unload here, was full of stolen grain.'

'I'm afraid I don't understand.'

'My lady, the boat, the grain, and the shipping order bearing your seal have all been seized.'

Hattusa's eyes flashed. 'Are you accusing me of theft?'

'I would be grateful for an explanation.'

'Who sent you?'

'Nobody.'

'You mean you're acting on your own initiative? I don't believe you.'

'Indeed I am, my lady.'

'People are trying to undermine me again, and this time they're using the services of an ignorant, compliant little judge!'

'Slandering a judge is punishable by strokes of the rod.'

'You're insane! Do you know to whom you're speaking?'

'To a lady of very high rank, who is as subject to the law as is the humblest peasant woman, and who is implicated in a theft of grain belonging to the state.'

'I couldn't care less.'

'Implicated doesn't mean guilty, my lady. That's why I'm asking for your explanation.'

'I shan't demean myself by giving one.'

'If you're innocent, what have you to fear?'

'How dare you cast doubt on my integrity!'

'My lady, the facts oblige me to do so.'

'You have gone too far, Judge Pazair, much too far.'

In fury, she rose to her feet and strode away. Courtiers scattered, worried by an anger whose consequences they were bound to suffer.

The most senior judge of Thebes, a ponderous, middle-aged man who was a close friend of the High Priest at Karnak, received Pazair three days later. He took time to examine the various documents pertaining to the case.

'Your work is exemplary in all respects,' he said when he had finished.

'As this is beyond my jurisdiction,' said Pazair, 'I'm leaving it to you to pursue. But if you think I ought to take action, I'm willing to convene a court.'

'What is your personal feeling about all this?'

'The illegal grain traffic has been proven. Denes doesn't seem to be involved.'

'What about Mentmose?'

'He probably knew something, but I can't tell how much.'

'And the lady Hattusa?'

'She refused to give me any explanation at all,' said Pazair.

'That's most unfortunate.'

'Her seal cannot be removed.'

'True, but who placed it there?'

'She did. It's her personal one, which she wears as a ring. Like all important people in the kingdom, she's never parted from it.'

'We're moving into dangerous territory, Judge Pazair. Hattusa may not be popular in Thebes – she's too haughty, too critical, too authoritarian – but even if he shares that opinion Pharaoh will be obliged to defend her.'

'Stealing food, the people's food, is a serious crime.'

'I agree, but I should like to avoid a public trial which might harm Ramses. As you yourself said, the investigation is not finished yet.'

Pazair tensed.

'Do not worry, my dear colleague; as the senior judge of Thebes, I have no intention of losing your case in the middle of a pile of dusty records. I should simply like a little more support for the accusation, since the accuser will be the state itself.'

'Thank you for making these details clear. As for the public trial . . .'

'It would be preferable, I know, but is your first desire for truth or for the head of the lady Hattusa?'

'I feel no special hostility towards her.'

'I shall try to persuade her to talk to you, and will send her an official summons, if necessary. We must let her be mistress of her own destiny. If she's guilty, she'll pay.'

Pazair thought the senior judge seemed sincere. With relief, he asked, 'Do you need my cooperation?'

'For the moment, no. In any case, you have been urgently recalled to Memphis.'

'By my scribe?'

'No, by the Judge of the Porch.'

32

Nenophar's anger showed no signs of abating. How could Denes have behaved so stupidly? He had judged his man badly, as usual, and had thought Mahu would crumble without putting up a fight. The result was catastrophic: a forthcoming court case, a cargo boat requisitioned, suspicion of theft and the triumph of that young crocodile of a judge.

'Your record is truly remarkable,' she said acidly.

Denes was undaunted. 'Have some more grilled goose – it's excellent.'

'You're leading us to public shame and failure.'

'Don't worry, our luck will change.'

'Luck perhaps, but not your stupidity!'

'One boat is out of action for a few days – what does that matter? The load has been transferred, and will soon arrive in Thebes.'

'And what about Mahu?' said Nenophar.

'He isn't lodging a complaint. We've reached an understanding. Instead of war between us, there'll be cooperation, and we'll both benefit from that. He isn't big enough to take our place, and he's learnt his lesson. We shall even be shipping a portion of his stock – at the right price.'

'There's still the accusation of theft.'

'It can't go any further, because there are plenty of

documents and witnesses to prove my innocence. Besides, I really wasn't involved. Hattusa used me.'

'And what about Judge Pazair's charges?'

'Ah, yes,' said Denes, 'them. They're awkward, I admit.'

'So we shall lose a case, lose our good name as well, and have to pay heavy fines.'

'We haven't reached that stage yet.'

'Do you believe in miracles?'

'If I organize them myself, why not?'

Silkis was quivering with joy. She had just received an aloe, an immensely long stem crowned with yellow, orange and red flowers. Its juice contained an oil with which she would rub her genitals in order to prevent inflammation, and which could be used to treat the skin ailment that had covered her husband's legs with red lumps. Silkis would also apply a paste made from egg whites and acacia flowers.

When Mahu heard that he had been summoned to the palace, he was stricken with an attack of itching. Braving the discomfort, he set off anxiously.

While she waited, Silkis prepared the soothing balm.

Mahu returned home in the early afternoon, and in reply to her anxious look he told her, 'We aren't returning to the Delta immediately. I shall appoint a local man to take charge there.'

'Has our papyrus-making authorization been withdrawn?'

'Quite the reverse. I was most warmly congratulated on my management and expansion of the business to Memphis. The palace has actually been watching my activities for two years.'

'Then who's trying to harm you?'

'Nobody. It seems that the head of the Granaries secretariat has been following my rise and wondered how I would react to success. As he's seen me working harder and harder, he's called me to his side.'

Silkis was entranced. The head of the Granaries secretariat fixed taxes, collected them in kind, oversaw their redistribution in the provinces, headed a body of specialist scribes, inspected provincial collection centres, drew up lists of revenues and sent them to the Double House, where the kingdom's finances were administered.

'Called you to his side? You mean . . . ?'

'I've been appointed principal treasurer of the granaries.'

'That's wonderful!' She threw her arms round his neck. 'Are we going to be even richer?'

'Probably, but business will take up a lot more of my time. I'll be spending short periods in the provinces and will have to do as my superior orders. You shall take charge of the children.'

'I'm so proud! You can rely on me.'

When Pazair reached his office, he found Iarrot sitting next to Way-Finder in front of the door, which had been sealed shut.

'Who did this?' asked Pazair.

'Mentmose himself, on the orders of the Judge of the Porch.'

'Why?'

'He refused to tell me,' said Iarrot.

'That's against the law.'

'What could I do? I couldn't fight him.'

Pazair went immediately to see the Judge of the Porch, who kept him waiting for over an hour before receiving him. When he was admitted, the Judge's opening words were, 'So here you are at last, Judge Pazair. You're away from your office a great deal.'

'On business matters.'

'Well, you're going to have a rest. As you have no doubt seen, you are suspended from your office.'

'May I ask why?'

'Because of your youthful carelessness. Being a judge doesn't place you above rules and regulations.'

'Which ones have I broken?'

The Judge's voice became fierce. 'The rules of taxation. You have failed to pay your taxes.'

'But I haven't received any notification,' protested Pazair.

'I took it to your office myself three days ago, but you weren't there.'

'But I have three months in which to pay.'

'In the provinces, but not in Memphis. Here, you have only three days, and that time has expired.'

Pazair was dumbfounded. 'Why are you doing this?'

'Out of simple respect for the law. A judge must set an example, and you have not done so.'

Pazair swallowed the anger bubbling up inside him – attacking the Judge of the Porch would only make matters worse. But he couldn't help saying, 'You're persecuting me.'

'No grand words, now. I must compel late payers to set their affairs in order, whoever they may be.'

'I'm ready to settle my debt straight away.'

'Let's see now . . . Two sacks of grain.'

Pazair was very relieved that the amount was so low.

'But the fine, that's a different matter. Let's say . . . one fat ox.'

Pazair rebelled. 'That's disproportionate!'

'Your office obliges me to be severe.'

'Who's behind all this?'

The Judge of the Porch pointed to the door of his office. 'Go.'

Suti had promised himself that he would gallop to Thebes, break into the harem and make the Hittite confess. From what Pazair had said, she must be the one behind this ridiculous punishment. Ordinarily, there was no arguing with taxation, and complaints were as rare as fraud. By attacking Pazair from this angle, and using the rules applying to large towns, she had reduced the judge to silence.

Pazair, aware of how his friend felt, said, 'I strongly advise you against heroics. You'd lose your position as an officer, and would have no credibility during the trial.'

'What trial? You no longer have the authority to convene one.'

'Do you think I've given up already?'

'Almost.'

'Almost . . . yes, you're right, but not altogether. This attack is too unjust.'

'How can you stay so calm?'

'Hardship helps me think,' said Pazair, 'and so does your hospitality.'

As a charioteer officer, Suti had a house with four rooms, fronted by a garden where Way-Finder and Brave slept all they liked. Panther had, without enthusiasm, taken charge of the cooking and cleaning – fortunately, Suti often interrupted her to lead her off into other, more entertaining activities.

Pazair hardly left his room. He went over the various aspects of his main cases again and again, indifferent to the amorous exploits of his friend and his beautiful mistress.

'Thinking, thinking,' grumbled Suti. 'And what do you get from all this thinking?'

'Thanks to you, we may perhaps be moving forward a bit. Qadash tried to steal copper from a barracks where Sheshi has a secret workshop.'

'Making weapons?'

'Without a doubt.'

'Isn't he one of General Asher's favourites?'

'I don't know. But Qadash's explanation didn't convince me. Why was he wandering around there? According to him, the officer in charge of the barracks told him about Sheshi – that should be easy for you to check.'

'I'll take care of it.'

Pazair fed his donkey, took his dog for a walk, then ate the midday meal with Panther.

'You scare me,' she confessed.

'Why? I'm not exactly terrifying, am I?'

'You're so serious all the time. Haven't you ever been in love?'

'More deeply than you can imagine.'

'Good. You're different from Suti, but your friendship means everything to him, and he's told me about your problems. How are you going to pay the fine?'

'Frankly, I'm wondering that, too. If I have to, I'll work in the fields for a few months.'

Panther was scandalized. 'A judge, working as a peasant?'

'I grew up in a village. I don't mind sowing, ploughing and reaping.'

'Well, I'd steal the ox. After all, taxation is the biggest thief of all.'

'Temptation is always there – that's why we have judges.'

'And you're honest?'

'I try to be.'

'Why are those people trying to destroy you?'

'It's to do with power.'

'Is there something rotten in the kingdom of Egypt?'

'We're no better than other men, but at least we know it. If rottenness exists, it will be cleansed.'

'By you?'

'With Suti's help. And if we fail, others will replace us.'

Panther rested her sulky chin on her fist. 'In your place, I'd let myself be corrupted.'

'When a judge commits a crime, it's a step towards war.'

'My people like fighting, yours don't.'

'Do you think that's a weakness?'

The black eyes flamed. 'Life's a battle I want to win, and I don't care how I do it or what it costs.'

Suti drained half a pitcher of beer with gusto. He was sitting astride the low garden wall, enjoying the last rays of the setting sun. Pazair sat cross-legged on the ground, stroking Brave.

'Mission accomplished,' said Suti. 'The commander of the barracks was flattered to welcome a hero of the last campaign. What's more, he has a loose tongue.'

'What are his teeth like?'

'Excellent – he's never been Qadash's patient.'

Suti and Pazair shook hand jubilantly. They had just uncovered a magnificent lie.

'And that's not all,' said Suti.

'Don't keep me in suspense.'

Suti grinned.

'Do I have to beg?'

'A hero must have a modest triumph. The warehouse contains top-quality copper.'

'I know.'

'What you don't know is that, immediately after being questioned, Sheshi had an unmarked chest moved elsewhere. It must have contained something very heavy, because four men could only just carry it.'

'What men? Soldiers?'

'Sheshi's personal guards.'

'Where did they take it?'

'I don't know. But I shall find out.'

'What would Sheshi need in order to make unbreakable weapons?'

'The rarest and hardest material is iron.'

'I agree. If we're right, that's the treasure Qadash was after. A tooth doctor with iron instruments . . . he thought they'd give him his skills back. All we have to do now is find out who told him about the hiding place.'

'How did Sheshi behave when you questioned him?'

'He was remarkably discreet. He didn't even lodge a complaint.'

'That's rather odd. He ought to have been delighted that a thief had been caught.'

'Which means . . .'

'. . . that they're accomplices.'

'But we've no proof,' said Pazair.

'Sheshi told Qadash about the iron, and he tried to steal part of it for his own use, but got caught. Sheshi didn't want him to appear in court because he'd have had to testify.'

'The workshop, the iron, the weapons – everything points to the army. But why should Sheshi, who's always so close-mouthed, confide in Qadash? And how does a tooth doctor get involved in a military conspiracy? It's absurd.'

'We may not have got everything right, but we're on the right track.'

'No, I think we're straying off the track.'

'Don't be a defeatist,' said Suti. 'The key person is Sheshi. I'll watch him day and night, I'll question his household, I'll break through the wall that this discreet, unassuming man has built round himself.'

'If only I could do something.'

'Just be patient for a while.'

Pazair looked up. Hope shone again in his eyes. 'Have you thought of something?'

'I shall sell my chariot.'

'You can't. You'd be dismissed from the army.'

Suti punched the wall. 'We've got to get you out of this mess – and soon. What about Sababu?'

'You mustn't even think of such a thing! A judge's debt paid by a prostitute? The Judge of the Porch would strike me from the roll of judges.'

Brave stretched out his paws and looked up at his master with trusting eyes.

33

Brave loathed water, so he kept a safe distance from the riverbank. Having run until he was out of breath, he paused, sniffed around, ran back to his master and then ran off again. The area around the irrigation channel was deserted and silent. Pazair thought of Neferet and tried to interpret every small sign in his favour. Had she or had she not shown a new kindness towards him? At the very least she had agreed to hear him out.

Behind a tamarisk tree, a shadow moved. Brave took no notice so, reassured, Pazair continued his walk. Thanks to Suti, the investigation had moved forward; but would he be able to take it any further? A junior judge with no experience was at his superiors' mercy: the Judge of the Porch had reminded him of that fact in the most brutal way.

Branir had comforted his pupil and told him that, if necessary, he would sell his house to enable Pazair to pay his debt. It had to be paid. The Judge of the Porch's actions must not be taken lightly, because he was stubborn and relentless, and quite happy to attack young judges in order to shape their characters.

Brave stopped in his tracks, sniffing the wind.

The shadow emerged from its hiding place and walked towards Pazair. The dog growled, but his master held him back by his collar.

'Don't be afraid, there are two of us.'

Brave nuzzled Pazair's hand.

It was a woman, a slender woman, her face concealed by a piece of dark cloth. She walked confidently and stopped a couple of paces from Pazair.

Brave froze.

'You have nothing to fear,' she said, and she removed her veil. It was Hattusa.

'The night is mild, my lady,' said Pazair, 'and conducive to meditation.'

'I wished to see you alone, away from all witnesses.'

'Officially, you're at Thebes.'

'You're very perceptive.'

'Your vengeance had the desired effect, my lady.'

'My vengeance?'

'I have been suspended, as you wished me to be.'

'I don't understand,' she said.

'My lady, please don't make fun of me.'

'On the name of Pharaoh, I have done nothing against you.'

'To use your own words, I went too far, didn't I?'

'You made me angry, it's true, but I admire your courage.'

'Are you saying you acknowledge that I had reason to do what I did?'

'One piece of proof will be enough for you. I have spoken with the senior judge of Thebes.'

'And what was the result?'

'He knows the truth, and the incident is closed.'

'It isn't for me, my lady.'

'Is your superior's opinion not good enough for you?'

'In this case, no.'

'That's why I'm here. The senior judge assumed – rightly, it seems – that my visit would be necessary. I'm going to tell you the truth, but first I require your promise of silence.'

'I cannot accept any restrictions.'

'You're so inflexible,' complained Hattusa.

'Were you hoping for a compromise?'

'You don't like me very much, and neither do most of your fellow countrymen.'

'You should say, "our fellow countrymen". You're Egyptian now.'

'None of us can ever forget our origins. I'm concerned with the fate of the Hittites who were brought here as prisoners of war. Some have virtually become Egyptian, others find it difficult to survive. It's my duty to help them, so I used wheat from the store in my harem for them. My steward told me our reserves would be exhausted before the next harvest. He suggested an arrangement with one of his colleagues in Memphis, and I gave my assent. Therefore I take full responsibility for that transfer.'

'Was Mentmose informed, my lady?'

'Of course. Feeding hungry people didn't seem criminal to him.'

What court would convict her? It would accuse her only of an administrative offence, which in any case would be blamed on the two stewards. Mentmose would deny everything, Denes would be exonerated, and Hattusa wouldn't even appear before the court.

'The senior judge of Thebes and his counterpart in Memphis have put the documents in order,' she added. 'If you feel the procedure is illegal, you are free to act. The letter of the law was not respected, I grant you, but surely the spirit is more important?'

She was fighting him on his own ground.

'My poor compatriots don't know where the food they receive comes from, and I don't want them to find out. Will you grant me that privilege?'

'It seems to me that the case has been dealt with in Thebes.'

She smiled. 'They say your heart is made of stone. Are they wrong?'

'I wish it were.'

Reassured, Brave started trotting about and sniffing the ground.

'One last question, my lady: have you met General Asher?'

She stiffened, and her voice became harsh. 'The day he dies, I shall rejoice. May the demons of hell devour the man who slaughtered my people.'

Suti was living the good life. Following his exploits, and because of his wounds, he had been granted several months of rest before returning to active service.

Panther played the submissive wife, but the wildness of her lovemaking proved that her temperament had scarcely softened. Each evening the joust began again; sometimes she was the radiant victor, and complained of her partner's softness. The following evening, Suti would make her surrender. The game enchanted them, for they took pleasure together and knew how to provoke each other while skilfully stimulating each other's bodies. She repeated that she would never fall in love with an Egyptian, and he declared that he loathed barbarians.

When he announced that he was going to be away for an unspecified time, she threw herself at him and hit him. He flattened her against a wall, prised her hands off him, and gave her the longest kiss they had ever shared. She quivered like a she-cat, rubbed herself against him, and made him want her so violently that he took her standing up, without letting her go.

'You shan't go away,' she said.

'It's a secret mission.'

'If you go, I shall kill you.'

'I'll come back.'

'When?'

'I've no idea.'

'You're lying! What is this mission?'

'It's secret.'

'You haven't any secrets from me.'

'Don't presume too much.'

'Take me with you. I can help you.'

Suti had not considered that possibility. Spying on Sheshi would undoubtedly be long and boring; besides, in some circumstances it would indeed help if there were two of them.

'If you betray me, I shall cut off one of your feet.'

'You wouldn't dare.'

'Once again, you're wrong.'

Picking up Sheshi's trail took only a few days. In the mornings, he worked in the palace workshops, alongside the best inventors in the kingdom. In the afternoons, he went to an outlying barracks, not emerging until dawn. Suti heard only good things about Sheshi: he was hard-working, skilful, discreet, modest. The only criticisms were that he was too quiet and self-effacing.

Panther soon got bored. There was no movement and no danger, and she had to be content with waiting and watching. The mission offered little of interest. Suti himself grew discouraged. Sheshi saw no one and was wholly absorbed in his work.

The full moon lit up the Memphis sky. Panther slept, draped across Suti. This would be their last night's watch. Suddenly, Sheshi appeared in the barracks' doorway.

Suti shook Panther awake and whispered, 'There he is.'

'I'm sleepy.'

'He seems worried about something.'

Sulkily, Panther looked. 'It's nearly dawn,' she said. 'He's just going to the workshop.'

Sheshi came out into the courtyard, mounted a donkey and let his legs hang down slackly. The beast moved off.

'It's finished for us,' said Suti. 'Sheshi's a blind alley.'

But Panther suddenly looked astounded. 'Where was he born?' she demanded.

'In Memphis, I think.'

'Sheshi's no Egyptian.'

'How do you know that?'

'Only a sand-traveller would ride a donkey like that.'

Suti's chariot halted in the courtyard of the frontier post, which was not far from the marshes of the town of Pitom. He entrusted his horses to a groom and ran to see the scribe in charge of immigration.

It was here that sand-travellers who wished to come and live in Egypt underwent detailed questioning. At certain times, no one was allowed in. In many cases, the request sent by the scribe to the authorities in Memphis was rejected.

'I'm Charioteer Officer Suti.'

'I've heard of you.'

'Can you give me some information about a sand-traveller who became a naturalized Egyptian, probably a long time ago?'

'That's rather irregular. Why do you want to know?'

Suti looked down in embarrassment. 'An affair of the heart. If I could persuade my betrothed that he isn't of Egyptian stock, I think she'd come back to me.'

'Very well,' said the scribe with a smile. 'What's his name?'

'Sheshi.'

The scribe consulted his records.

'I have one Sheshi,' he said eventually. 'He is indeed a sand-traveller, originally from Syria. He arrived at the frontier post fifteen years ago, and as Egypt and her neighbours were at peace, we let him enter.'

'There was nothing suspicious about him?'

'He had no dubious associates, and he'd never been in any military action against Egypt. The commission gave a favourable answer after three months' investigation. He took the name of Sheshi and found work in Memphis as a metal worker. The checks carried out during his first five years in Egypt didn't reveal any irregularity. It looks as though he's forgotten his origins, but I wish you luck anyway with your betrothed.'

Pazair and Branir were sitting on the terrace of Branir's house, with Brave asleep at his master's feet. With his last scruple of strength, Pazair had again refused Branir's offer to sell the house, even though the old man had tried hard to persuade him. Selling the house would be too great a wrench for Branir.

They sat in silence for a while, then Pazair asked, 'Are you certain the fifth guard is still alive?'

'If he were dead, I'd have felt it when I used my pendulum.'

'He's given up his pension and taken refuge in anonymity, so he'll have to work to survive. Kani was methodical and thorough, but he couldn't find him.'

Pazair went to the edge of the terrace and gazed down at Memphis. Suddenly the great city's peace seemed threatened, as if some sly danger were spreading out across it. If Memphis were stricken, first Thebes would yield, then the entire country. Feeling ill, he sat down again.

'You feel it too, don't you?' said Branir.

'It's horrible.'

'And it's getting stronger.'

'Are we the victims of some illusion?'

'You felt the evil in your flesh. At first, a few months ago, I thought it was just a nightmare. But it came back more and more often, and each time it was stronger and more oppressive.'

'What is it?'

'A plague whose nature we don't yet know.'

Pazair shivered. The feeling of illness faded, but his body retained the memory of it.

A chariot drew up outside the house, and Suti leapt out and raced up the steps to the terrace.

'Sheshi's a naturalized sand-traveller! Do I deserve a beer? Forgive me, Branir, I didn't greet you properly.'

Pazair handed his friend a drink, which he gulped down gratefully.

'I had time to think as I was travelling back from the frontier. Qadash is Libyan, Sheshi's a Syrian sand-traveller, Hattusa's a Hittite – foreigners, all three of them. Qadash has become a respectable tooth doctor, but he takes part in lewd dances with his countrymen. Hattusa hates her new life and keeps all her affection for her own people. Sheshi, the loner, takes part in strange research. There's your conspiracy! And Asher is behind them, manipulating them.'

Branir said nothing. Pazair wondered if Suti really had just given them the solution to the puzzle that had been tormenting them.

After a few more moments' thought, Pazair said, 'You're jumping to conclusions. How can there be a link between Hattusa and Sheshi, or between her and Qadash?'

'The link is their hatred of Egypt.'

'She hates Asher even more,' said Pazair.

'How do you know?'

'She told me, and I believe her.'

'Don't be so naive, Pazair. Those objections are childish. Be objective, and you'll soon see the truth. Hattusa and Asher devise the plots and then Qadash and Sheshi put them into action. The weapons Sheshi's developing won't go to the army.'

'Do you mean there'll be a rebellion?'

'Hattusa wants an invasion, and Asher's organizing it.'

Suti and Pazair both turned to Branir, eager to hear his opinion.

'Ramses' power hasn't weakened,' said the old man. 'Any attempt of that kind seems bound to fail.'

307

'And yet preparations are being made for it,' said Suti. 'We must act now – nip the conspiracy in the bud. If we start legal action, they'll take fright and know they've been unmasked.'

'But,' said Pazair, 'if our accusations are deemed to be unfounded and defamatory, we'll be heavily punished and they'll have free rein. We must strike hard and accurately. If we had the fifth guard with us, General Asher's credibility would be destroyed.'

'Are you going to wait for disaster to strike?' demanded Suti.

'Give me a night to think.'

'A night? Take all year if you want! You can't convene a court any more.'

'I'll say it once more, and this time,' said Branir, 'Pazair cannot refuse. I shall sell my house, and Pazair must pay his debts and return to office as soon as possible.'

Pazair walked alone through the darkness. Life had taken him by the throat, forcing him to concentrate on the ins and outs of a conspiracy whose seriousness seemed to grow from one hour to the next. All he wanted to think about was the woman he loved, who was out of his reach. He could renounce happiness, but not justice.

His suffering was making him more mature; a force, deep inside him, refused to be extinguished. A force he would use to serve those he loved.

The moon, the 'Fighter', was a knife which cut through the clouds, or a mirror which reflected the beauty of the gods. He asked it for power, praying that his gaze might be as all-seeing as that of the night-sun.

His thoughts returned to the fifth guard. What trade would a man pursue if he wanted to go unnoticed? Pazair ran through the occupations of the people who lived on the west bank of Thebes, and eliminated them one by one. From butcher to seed sower, all had links with the general population, and Kani would have found out about him sooner or later.

Except one.

Yes, there was one trade, at once so solitary and so visible that it formed the most perfect mask.

Pazair lifted his eyes to the sky, a lapis-lazuli vault pierced with doors in the form of stars, through which the light passed. As if he had managed to gather in that light, he now knew where to find the fifth guard.

34

Mahu's new office was huge and light, and he would have four specialist scribes permanently at his disposal. He was positively radiant in a brand-new kilt and a short-sleeved linen shirt which didn't really suit him. He had enjoyed his success as a trader, but wielding public power had attracted him ever since he learnt to read and write. Because of his modest birth and scant education, it had seemed out of reach. But his hard work had proved his worth in the eyes of the government, and he was determined to use his energies in its service.

After greeting his staff and emphasizing his preference for order and punctuality, he turned to the first matter assigned to him: a list of people who were late paying their taxes. Mahu always paid his on time, so he read the list with a certain amusement. A land owner, an army scribe, a man who ran a carpenters' workshop and . . . Judge Pazair! The tax scribe had noted the amount owing and the size of the fine, and Mentmose himself had affixed the seals to the judge's door.

Mahu went to see Iarrot and asked where the judge was living. When he reached Suti's house, he found only Suti and Panther there. Pazair had just left for the port, from which light boats sailed between Memphis and Thebes.

Mahu was just in time to catch him. 'I have learnt of your difficulties,' he said.

'It was an oversight on my part.'

'It's blatantly unjust. The fine is grotesque in comparison with the offence. Seek redress through the courts.'

Pazair shook his head. 'I'm in the wrong. The case would last a long time, and all I'd gain would be a reduction in the fine and countless enemies.'

'The Judge of the Porch doesn't seem to like you very much.'

'It's his custom to put young judges to the test.'

'You helped me when I was in difficulties; I'd like to do the same for you. Will you let me pay your debt?'

'I appreciate your offer, but I can't accept it.'

'Then will you accept a loan – interest free, of course? At least let me not make a profit out of a friend.'

'But how can I repay you?'

'Through your work. In my new position as head of the Granaries secretariat, I shall often need to call upon your skills. I'll leave you to calculate how many consultations are worth two sacks of grain and a fat ox.'

'I think we'll be seeing a lot of each other,' said Pazair.

'Here's a document showing you can pay all that's due.'

Mahu and Pazair embraced warmly.

The Judge of the Porch was making preparations for the following day's audience. A sandal thief, a disputed inheritance, compensation for an accident: simple cases which could be sorted out quickly. Then came an entertaining visitor.

'Pazair! Have you changed your profession, or have you come to pay what you owe?' The Judge laughed at his own joke.

'The latter.'

Still laughing, the Judge looked more closely at Pazair, who was perfectly serious.

'That's good, you have a sense of humour. This career isn't for you, you know. Later, you'll thank me for my severity. Go back to your village, marry a good peasant woman, give her

311

two children, and forget about judges and justice. It's too complex a world. I know men, Pazair.'

'I congratulate you.'

'Ah, so you have returned to your senses.'

'Here is confirmation that my debt has been paid.'

The Judge stared at the document in utter amazement.

'The two sacks of grain have been deposited outside your door, and the fat ox is recovering its strength in your official stables. Are you satisfied?'

Mentmose looked ill-tempered. His face was red, his features pinched, his voice nasal and his impatience evident.

'I'm receiving you simply out of good manners, Pazair. Today, you're no more than a citizen outside the law.'

'If that were so, I'd no longer be permitted to disturb you.'

Mentmose looked up. 'What does that mean?'

'Here is a document signed by the Judge of the Porch. Everything is now in order with the tax authorities. He even considered that my fat ox exceeded the norm and granted me a tax credit for next year.'

'How did you . . . ?'

'I should be obliged if you would remove the seals from my door with all possible speed.'

'Of course, my dear Judge, of course! Naturally I tried to defend you in this unfortunate matter.'

'I don't doubt it for a moment.'

'Our future collaboration . . .'

'Augurs extremely well. There's just one thing: as regards the stolen wheat, everything has been settled. I'm fully informed about the matter now – but of course you knew all about it before I did.'

Restored to office, and with his mind much eased, Pazair boarded a fast boat for Thebes. Kem accompanied him, and Killer slept beside them.

'You've surprised me,' said the Nubian. 'Most people would have been crushed by what you've been through.'

'I was lucky.'

'Force of will, more like. A will so strong that people and events bend to it.'

Pazair smiled. 'You credit me with powers I haven't got.'

The boat sailed on, taking him closer to Neferet. Nebamon would soon demand results, but she would never rein in her activities. A confrontation was inevitable.

The boat berthed at Thebes late in the afternoon. Pazair sat down on the bank, away from passers-by. The sun was sinking, tingeing the Peak of the West rosy pink; the flocks were returning from the fields, to the melancholy sound of flutes.

The last ferry carried only a few passengers. Kem and Killer stood at the back. Pazair went over to the ferryman. The man wore an old-fashioned wig which hid half his face.

'Stay as you are,' ordered the judge.

The ferryman remained hunched over the tiller.

'We need to talk; you're safe here. Answer without looking at me.'

Who paid any attention to the ferryman? Everyone was in a hurry to get to the other bank, talking, dreaming, never glancing at the man in charge of the ferry. He was content with little, lived apart, and had no contact with the general population.

'You're the fifth soldier, the only survivor of the Sphinx's honour guard.'

The ferryman didn't protest.

'I'm Judge Pazair and I need to know the truth. Your four comrades are dead, probably murdered, and that's why you're in hiding. There must be something mortally serious behind so many killings.'

'How do I know you're who you say you are?'

'If I wanted to kill you, you'd already be dead. Trust me.'

'That's easy for you—'

'No it isn't – far from it. Now tell me, what terrible event did you witness?'

'There were five of us, five ex-soldiers. We guarded the Sphinx at night. It was a risk-free job, completely honorary, before we retired. I and a colleague were sitting outside the wall that surrounds the stone lion, and as usual we'd fallen asleep. He was woken by a noise and he woke me. I was sleepy, and I calmed him down. But he was anxious and insisted, so we went to see. We walked inside the wall and found the body of one of our men by the Sphinx's right flank, then another on the other side.' He stopped a lump in his throat. 'And then there were these terrible moans – I still hear them. I found our commander lying between the Sphinx's paws. There was blood flowing from his mouth, and he could hardly speak.'

'What did he say?'

'He'd been attacked and he'd defended himself.'

'Who attacked him? Did he say?'

'A naked woman, and several men. "Foreign words in the darkness": those were his last words. My comrade and I were afraid. Why all the violence? Should we warn the soldiers on guard at the Great Pyramid? My comrade was against it, because he thought it would cause trouble for us – we might even be accused ourselves. The three others were dead . . . He said it was better to keep quiet, pretend we'd seen nothing, heard nothing. In the end I agreed, and we went back to our posts. When the day guard relieved us at dawn, they discovered the bodies. We pretended to be horrified.'

'Were you punished at all?' asked Pazair.

'No. We were just sent into retirement in our home villages. My comrade became a baker, and I was planning to repair chariots. But when he was murdered, I had to go into hiding.'

'He was murdered? Why do you say that?'

'He was a very careful man, especially with fire. I'm certain he was pushed. The tragedy at the Sphinx is pursuing us. We weren't believed. Someone thinks we know too much.'

'Who questioned you at Giza?'

'A senior officer.'

'Has General Asher contacted you at all?'

'No.'

'Your testimony will be decisive during the trial.'

'What trial?' asked the ferryman.

'The general approved a document certifying that you and your fellow guards were killed in an accident.'

'Good, that means I no longer exist.'

'If I could find you, others will. But if you testify, you'll be free again.'

The ferry arrived at the riverbank.

'I . . . I don't know. Leave me in peace.'

'It's the only way – for your comrades' memory and for yourself.'

'Tomorrow morning, on the first ferry, I'll give you my answer.'

The ferryman jumped onto the bank and wound a mooring rope round a stake. Pazair, Kem and Killer went ashore and walked off.

'Watch that man all night,' said Pazair.

'What about you?'

'I'll sleep at the nearest village, and come back at dawn.'

Kem hesitated. He didn't like the idea. If the ferryman had talked, Pazair was in danger, and Kem couldn't guard both men at once. He decided to guard Pazair.

The shadow-eater had watched the ferry cross the river, bathed in the setting sun. The Nubian was at the back, the judge next to the ferryman. That was strange. Side by side, they looked at the other bank. There were few passengers, and plenty of room, so why this closeness, unless it was so that they could talk?

A ferryman . . . the most visible yet unnoticeable of trades.

The shadow-eater jumped into the water and crossed the

Nile, swimming with the current. When he reached the other side, he remained crouching in the reeds for a long time, watching. The ferryman slept in a wooden hut.

Neither Kem nor Killer was anywhere to be seen, but the shadow-eater waited a little longer, to be certain that no one was watching the hut. Then he sneaked inside and slipped a leather strap round the neck of the sleeping man who awoke with a start.

'If you move, you die,' growled the murderer.

The ferryman was helpless. He raised his right arm in submission.

The shadow-eater loosened the strap a little, and said, 'Who are you?'

'The . . . the ferryman.'

'One more lie and I'll strangle you. Are you an ex-soldier?'

'Yes.'

'Where did you serve?'

'In the Asian army.'

'What was your last posting?'

'The Sphinx's honour guard.'

'Why are you hiding?'

'I'm afraid.'

'Afraid of what?'

'I . . . I don't know.'

'What is your secret?

'I haven't got one!'

The leather strap bit into his flesh.

Half-choked, he managed to say, 'An attack, at Giza. Killings. The Sphinx was attacked, and my comrades died.'

'Who was the attacker?'

'I didn't see.'

'Did the judge question you?'

'Yes.'

'What did he ask?'

'The same as you.'

'And what did you tell him?'

'He threatened me with court, but I didn't say anything. I don't want any problems with the law.'

'Then what did you tell him?'

'That I was a ferryman, not a soldier.'

'Good.'

The leather strap was removed and, greatly relieved, the soldier rubbed his painful neck. The shadow-eater knocked him out with savage blow to the forehead, then dragged him out of the hut and down to the river. He held the ferryman's head under the water for a long time. When he left, the corpse was floating beside the ferry. Just another run-of-the-mill drowning accident.

Neferet was preparing a potion for Sababu. As the prostitute was now taking proper care of herself, her illness had abated. Full of energy again, and free from the burning attacks of rheumatism, she had asked Neferet's permission to make love with the porter at her ale-house, a strapping young Nubian.

'May I disturb you?' asked Pazair.

'I was coming to the end of my day's work.'

Neferet looked drawn.

'You work too hard,' he said.

'It's just tiredness, that's all. Is there any news of Nebamon?'

'He hasn't shown his hand yet.'

'It's probably the calm before the storm.'

'I'm afraid you may be right.'

'And how is your investigation going?' asked Neferet.

'It's taking great strides forward, although for a while I was suspended by the Judge of the Porch.'

'Tell me about it.'

He told her of his misfortunes while she washed her hands and tidied her workshop.

'You're surrounded by friends. Our master Branir, Suti, Mahu – that was great good luck.'

'Do you feel lonely here?'

'The villagers do all they can to help, but I can't ask anyone for advice. Sometimes it's a heavy burden.'

They sat down on a mat outside, facing the palm grove.

'You look worried,' said Neferet.

'I've just found a vital witness. You're the first person to know.'

Neferet did not look away. In her eyes he saw interest, if not affection.

'You might be prevented from making more progress, mightn't you?'

'I don't care. I believe in justice as you believe in medicine.'

Their shoulders touched. Pazair held his breath. As if she were unaware of this chance contact, Neferet did not draw away.

'Would you go so far as to sacrifice your life to find the truth?' she asked.

'If I had to, without hesitation.'

'Do you still think of me?'

'Every moment of every day.'

His hand brushed Neferet's, rested on it, lightly, imperceptibly.

'When I'm tired,' she said, 'I think of you. Whatever happens to you, you seem indestructible and you keep on going.'

'That's only on the surface – I'm often full of doubts and fears. Suti accuses me of being naive. For him, the only thing that counts is adventure. As soon as he's threatened with routine, he's ready to commit any kind of madness.'

'Do you dislike it too?'

'No. It's an ally.'

'Can a feeling last for years and years?'

'A whole lifetime, if it's more than a feeling, a commitment of the whole being, a certain paradise, a communion nourished by daybreaks and sunsets. If love fades, it's really no more than a conquest.'

She leant her head on his shoulder, her hair brushing his cheek, and said, 'You have a strange power, Pazair.'

It was only a dream, as fleeting as a shooting star in the Theban night, but it lit up his life.

He spent a sleepless night in the palm grove, gazing up at the stars. He tried to preserve the brief moment when Neferet had lowered her guard before sending him away and closing her door. Did it mean she felt a degree of tenderness for him, or had it been simply the result of tiredness? At the idea that she might accept his presence and his love, even without sharing his passion, he felt as light as a spring cloud and as ardent as a swelling flood. It was almost dawn before he slept.

When he awoke, Killer was sitting a few paces away, eating dates and cracking open the kernels.

'Killer? What are you—'

'I decided to make sure you were safe,' said Kem from behind him.

'To the river, quickly!'

Day was breaking when they got there. A crowd had gathered on the bank.

'Stand aside,' ordered Pazair.

A fisherman had brought in the body of the ferryman, which he had found floating down river.

'Perhaps he couldn't swim,' said a woman.

'He must have slipped,' said another.

Ignoring these and other comments, Pazair examined the body.

'This was murder, not an accident,' he declared. 'There is the mark of a ligature on his neck, and a bruise from a violent blow on his forehead. He was strangled and knocked unconscious before being drowned.'

319

35

Pazair was in a cold rage. The ferryman's body, which had been carried to the nearest guard post, had been the subject of a misleading report by a petty local official who, for fear of being demoted, refused to admit that a crime had taken place on his territory, and declared that the ferryman had drowned. According to him, the injuries on the man's neck and forehead were accidental. Pazair could do nothing but express his grave reservations.

Before leaving for the north, he had seen Neferet for only a few moments. Many patients had been occupying her attention since early morning, so the pair had restricted themselves to a few polite words and an exchange of looks, in which he was sure he saw encouragement and support.

Laden with papyrus, brushes and palettes, Way-Finder guided his master and his master's friends through the outskirts of Memphis. If he made a mistake Suti could correct it, but the animal lived up to his name. Kem and Killer completed the procession, which headed for the barracks where Sheshi had his workshop. Early in the morning, he worked at the palace; the coast was clear.

Suti was jubilant. At last his friend had decided to take action.

In the barracks, which was some distance from the main

military establishments in Memphis, there was no sign of life. Not one soldier at weapons drill, not one horse being exercised.

Suti went off to talk to the sentry stationed at the entrance; he found there was none. Cautiously, they entered the building, which was rather dilapidated.

Two old men were sitting on a stone wall. Pazair went over to them and asked, 'Which army corps is stationed here?'

The older man guffawed. 'The regiment of veterans and walking wounded, my lad! We've been billeted here until we're packed off to the provinces. Farewell Asian roads, forced marches, inadequate rations. Soon I'll have a little garden, a housekeeper, fresh milk and good vegetables.'

'Who's in charge here?'

'He's in that building over there, behind the well.'

The officer, when Pazair found him, looked very weary. 'We don't get many visitors,' he said.

'I'm Judge Pazair, and I wish to search your storehouses.'

'Why?'

'A man named Sheshi has a workshop here.'

'Sheshi? Don't know him.'

Pazair described him.

'Oh, him,' said the officer. 'He comes here in the afternoon and spends the night here, that's right. Orders from on high. I just carry them out.'

'Open up the room for me.'

'I haven't got a key.'

'Take me there.'

A stout wooden door prevented anyone entering Sheshi's underground workshop. On a slate tablet, Pazair noted down the year, month, day and time of his visit, together with a description of the place.

'Open the door,' he told the officer.

'I have no authority to do that.'

'I'll take full responsibility.'

Suti helped the officer to force the wooden lock with a spear, and Pazair and Suti entered, while Kem and Killer stood guard.

The workshop looked well equipped, with its hearth, furnaces, stocks of charcoal and palm bark, moulds and copper tools. Everything was tidy and clean. After a quick search, Suti found the mysterious chest that had been brought here from the other barracks.

'I'm as excited as a virgin with his first girl!' he crowed.

'Just a moment,' said Pazair.

'We can't stop now, not when we're so close to our goal.'

'I'm writing my report: condition and location of suspect object.'

Hardly had Pazair finished writing when Suti removed the lid from the chest.

'Iron,' he said, 'iron ingots – and not just any iron, either.' He felt the weight of an ingot, pressed it, licked it and scratched it with a nail. 'This doesn't come from the volcanic rocks in the Eastern desert. It's the legendary iron they used to tell tales about in the village: sky-iron.'

'From rocks that fall from the sky,' agreed Pazair.

'It's worth a fortune.'

'This is the iron the priests use in the House of Life to make the metal ropes up which Pharaoh ascends to the heavens. How can Sheshi possibly have got it?'

Suti was fascinated. 'I knew of it, but I never thought I'd actually hold it in my hand.'

'It doesn't belong to us,' Pazair reminded him. 'It'll be needed in the trial. Sheshi must explain where it came from.'

At the bottom of the chest lay a carpenter's adze made of sky-iron. An adze was used to open a mummy's mouth and eyes when the mortal body had been brought back to life through resurrection rituals and was transformed into light. Neither Pazair nor Suti dared touch it. If it had been dedicated to the gods, it was endowed with supernatural powers.

'We're being ridiculous,' said Suti stoutly. 'It's only metal.'

'You may be right, but I'm not taking any risks.'

'Then what do you suggest we do?'

'Wait here until Sheshi arrives.'

When Sheshi saw the door to his workshop standing open, he spun round and tried to run away. He ran straight into the Nubian, who pushed him inside. Killer went on calmly eating raisins, which Kem knew meant that none of Sheshi's allies was lurking nearby.

'I'm glad to see you again,' said Pazair. 'You have a taste for moving about.'

Sheshi's gaze fell on the chest. 'Who gave you permission to do that?' he demanded.

'It has been confiscated.'

Sheshi exercised all his self-control and stayed icily calm. 'Confiscation is an unusual procedure,' he remarked.

'So are your activities.'

'I have the use of this workshop in addition to my official one.'

'You seem to like working in army barracks.'

'I'm developing the weapons of the future, so the army authorized me to work here. If you check, you'll find that these premises are known about and my work is encouraged.'

'I'm sure it is, but you won't succeed by using sky-iron. That is for temple use only – and so is the adze hidden at the bottom of the chest.'

'It isn't mine.'

'Were you aware of its existence?'

'No. Somebody must have put it there without my knowledge.'

'That's not true,' cut in Suti. 'You ordered the chest's transfer yourself. You thought you'd be safe from prying eyes in this forgotten corner.'

'Have you been spying on me?' said Sheshi angrily.

'Never mind that,' said Pazair. 'Where did you get this iron?'

'I refuse to answer your questions.'

'In that case, you're under arrest for theft, receiving stolen goods, and obstructing an official investigation.'

'I shall deny everything, and you'll have no case.'

'Either you come with us calmly, or I shall tell Kem to bind your hands.'

'I shan't run away.'

The interrogation meant that Iarrot had to work overtime while his daughter, the finest dancer in her class, was giving a performance in the main square. To make matters worse, he had little to do, because Sheshi wouldn't answer any questions and remained stubbornly silent, sitting upright on a mat.

Pazair asked patiently, 'Who are your accomplices? One man alone could not have stolen iron of this quality.'

Sheshi looked at him through half-closed eyelids. He seemed as impregnable as a fortress on the King's Walls.

'Who entrusted you with this precious material? And why? When your research bore fruit, you dismissed the men who worked for you, using Qadash's attempted theft as an excuse to accuse them of incompetence. That meant there were no further checks on your activities. Did you make that adze, or did you steal it?'

Still the man did not answer. Suti would have liked to beat him, but Pazair would have intervened.

'You and Qadash have been friends for a long time, haven't you?' said Pazair. 'He knew about your treasure, and tried to steal it. Unless, of course, it was all a charade so that you could appear to be a victim and remove all inconvenient witnesses from your workshop.'

Sheshi kept silent. He knew Pazair could not use violence on him.

'Despite your silence, I shall find out the truth.'

The prediction did not worry Sheshi.

Pazair asked Suti to tie the suspect's hands and attach them to a ring fixed into the wall. When that had been done, Pazair turned to Iarrot.

'I'm sorry,' he said, 'but I must ask you to watch him.'

'Will it take long?'

'We'll be back before nightfall.'

The palace at Memphis was a government institution made up of dozens of departments, where a multitude of scribes worked. The inventors answered to an overseer of royal workshops, a tall, dried-out man of around fifty, who was openly astonished by the judge's visit.

'My assistant is Charioteer Officer Suti, who bears witness to my accusations,' said Pazair.

'What accusations?'

'One of your subordinates, Sheshi, has been arrested.'

'Sheshi? That's impossible! There must be some mistake.'

'Do your people use sky-iron?'

'Of course not,' exclaimed the overseer. 'It's so rare that it's reserved for ritual use in temples.'

'Then how do you explain the fact that Sheshi has a large quantity of it?'

'There must have been a mix-up.'

'Does he have specific duties?'

'He works directly for those in charge of making weapons, and it's his duty to check the quality of the copper used. I can vouch for Sheshi's honesty, the thoroughness of his work and his worth as a man.'

'Do you know that he has a secret workshop in an isolated barracks?'

'He had proper authorization from the army.'

'Signed by whom?' asked Pazair.

'By some of the senior officers who get specialists to develop new weapons. Sheshi's one of the specialists.'

'But the use of iron was not provided for.'

'There must be a simple explanation.'

'If so, he won't tell us what it is.'

'Sheshi's never been talkative,' said the overseer. 'He's a rather taciturn fellow.'

'Do you know where he hails from?'

'He was born in the Memphis region, I think.'

'Could you check that?'

'Is it important?'

'It might be.'

'I must consult my records.'

The search lasted more than an hour.

'I was right,' said the overseer. 'Sheshi comes from a small village to the north of Memphis.'

'Given the nature of his work, you checked, of course.'

'The army took charge of that, and found nothing unusual. The controller's seal was affixed, according to the rules, and the department employed Sheshi without any worries. I expect you to release him in the very near future.'

'The charges against him are multiplying. To theft, he's added lying.'

'Judge, aren't you being rather excessive? If you knew Sheshi better, you'd know that he's incapable of dishonesty.'

'If he's innocent, the trial will prove it.'

Iarrot was sobbing on the doorstep under the cynical gaze of Way-Finder. Suti took the scribe by the shoulders and shook him. Pazair looked inside his office and saw that Sheshi was gone.

'What happened?' he asked.

'He came here, he demanded my statement of charges, he saw two shortened paragraphs which made it illegal, he threatened me with reprisals, freed the suspect. He was right, so I had to give in.'

'Who are you talking about?'

'Mentmose.'

Pazair read the statement of charges. Iarrot had indeed failed to note down Sheshi's titles and offices, or to state that the judge himself was conducting a preliminary enquiry without the involvement of a third party. The case was therefore null and void.

A ray of sunlight filtered through the crossbars of a stone-framed window and lit up Mentmose's head, which was shiny with perfumed lotion.

Smiling, he greeted Pazair with forced enthusiasm. 'We live in a wonderful country, don't we, my dear Judge? No one can be subjected to the severity of an excessive law, since we watch over the citizens' well-being.'

'"Excessive" seems to be a fashionable word. The overseer of the palace workshops also used it.'

'He can hardly be blamed. While he was consulting his records, he sent word to me of Sheshi's arrest. I went immediately to your office, convinced that a regrettable mistake had been made. That was indeed the case, so Sheshi was freed immediately.'

'My scribe's failings are not in question,' admitted Pazair, 'but why are you so interested in Sheshi?'

'His work is of great value to the army. Like his colleagues, he's under my direct supervision, so he cannot be questioned without my agreement. I'd like to think you were unaware of that fact.'

'The accusation of theft removes Sheshi's partial immunity.'

'The accusation is unfounded.'

'A procedural error doesn't alter the validity of the complaint.'

Mentmose grew solemn. 'Sheshi is one of our finest experts in weaponry. Do you really think he'd risk his whole career in such a stupid way?'

'Do you know what the stolen object is?'

'What does it matter? I don't believe Sheshi stole it. Stop being so eager to gain yourself a reputation for righting wrongs.'

'Where have you hidden Sheshi?'

'Beyond the reach of a judge who exceeds his rights.'

Suti agreed with Pazair: the only option was to convene a court and put their all into it. Evidence and arguments would be decisive, provided the jurors had not been bribed by the opposition – Pazair could not reject the jurors wholesale, on pain of being removed from the case. The two friends were convinced that the truth, if proclaimed at a public trial, would penetrate even the dullest of minds.

When Pazair told his plan to Branir, the old doctor said, 'You're taking a lot of risks.'

'Is there a better way?'

'You must do as your heart tells you.'

'I think it's necessary to strike high, so as not to lose myself in secondary details. By concentrating on what is vital, I'll be better able to combat lies and cowardice.'

'You'll never be content with half-measures; you must have the full light of day.'

'Am I wrong, Branir?'

'This trial really needs a mature, experienced judge, but the gods have entrusted you with the task and you have accepted it.'

'Kem's guarding the chest of sky-iron. He's covered it with a plank and Killer's sitting on it. No one will get near it.'

'When will you convene the trial?'

'Within a week at the latest – because of the exceptional nature of the case, I shall speed up the procedures.' Pazair hesitated for a moment, then asked, 'Do you think I've identified the evil that's prowling round us?'

'You're getting close.'

'May I ask a favour of you?'

'Of course.'

'Despite your new appointment, will you be a juror?'

Branir gazed up at his patron planet, Horus, Bull of the Sky,* which was unusually bright tonight. 'Need you ask?'

*Saturn.

36

Brave could not get used to Killer's presence under his roof, but as his master tolerated it so did he. Kem spoke little, saying only that this trial was madness: however bold he might be, Pazair was too inexperienced to succeed. Although he understood the Nubian's disapproval, the judge continued to prepare himself, while Iarrot provided him with forms and registers, duly checked – the Judge of the Porch would be quick to exploit any irregularities.

Nebamon's arrival was hardly discreet: he was very elegantly dressed and wore a perfumed wig.

'I should like to speak with you privately, Judge,' he said. He seemed annoyed.

'I'm very busy.'

'It's urgent.'

Pazair abandoned a papyrus relating the trial of a nobleman accused of farming lands which did not belong to him; in the name of the king, despite his position at court – or, rather, because of it – his possessions had been confiscated and he had been sentenced to exile. He had appealed against the sentence, but it stood.

The two men walked into a quiet side street shaded from the sun. Little girls were playing with their dolls; a donkey passed, laden with baskets of vegetables; an old man was asleep on the doorstep of his house.

'We have misunderstood each other, my dear Pazair,' said Nebamon.

'Like you, I deplore the fact that Sababu continues in her distasteful profession, but there are no legal grounds for charging her. She pays her taxes and doesn't disturb public order. I have even heard it said that certain well-known doctors frequent her ale-house.'

'And what about Neferet? I asked you to persuade her to obey me.'

'And I said I'd do my best.'

'What a brilliant result you've achieved! One of my Theban colleagues was about to give her a post at the hospital in Deir el-Bahri, but fortunately I intervened in time. Do you realize how much offence she causes to approved doctors?'

'Well, at least you recognize her skills.'

'However gifted she may be, Neferet is on the fringes of medicine.'

'That isn't the impression I got.'

'I'm not interested in your impressions,' said Nebamon crossly. 'When one is trying to build a career, one must bow to the wishes of influential men.'

'You're right.'

'I'll give you one last chance, but don't disappoint me.'

'I don't deserve another chance.'

'Forget your initial failure and do something.'

'I'm wondering . . .' said Pazair.

'What about?'

'My career.'

'Follow my advice, and you'll have no further worries.'

'I'm content to be a judge.'

'I don't understand.'

'Leave Neferet alone,' said Pazair.

'Have you lost your mind?'

'Don't ignore my warning.'

'You're being very stupid,' said Nebamon. 'You're wrong

331

to support a young woman who's going to fail most abjectly. Neferet has no future – and anyone who links his fate with hers will be swept away.'

'Your bitterness has clouded your mind.'

'No one has ever spoken to me like that! I demand an apology.'

'I'll try to help you.'

'Help *me*?'

'I can feel you sliding down towards failure.'

'You will live to regret those words!'

Denes was watching a cargo boat unloading. The crew were in a hurry, as they were due to leave again for the south the following morning, taking advantage of a favourable current. The cargo of furniture and spices was directed to a new warehouse which Denes had just acquired. Soon, he would buy up one of his fiercest competitors and swell the empire that he would bequeath to his two sons. Thanks to his wife's relatives, he was constantly strengthening his links with senior levels of government, so he wouldn't encounter any obstacles to his expansion.

The Judge of the Porch took a rare walk along the quayside. Leaning on a walking stick, because of an attack of gout, he approached Denes.

'Don't stand here, Judge, or they'll knock you over.'

Denes took the Judge by the arm and led him towards the part of the warehouse where the goods had already been stacked.

'Why this visit, Judge?' he asked.

'Dramatic events are in the offing.'

'Am I involved?'

'No, but you must help me to avert a disaster. Tomorrow, Pazair is presiding over the court. I could not refuse him, because he convened it according to all the rules.'

'Who's being charged?'

'He's kept the names of the accused and accuser secret. But rumour has it that state security is involved.'

'Then rumour's wrong,' said Denes. 'How could that little judge handle a case of such magnitude?'

'Beneath his reserved exterior, Pazair is a ram. He charges straight ahead, and no obstacle stops him.'

'Are you worried?'

'The man's dangerous. He carries out his duties as though they were a sacred mission.'

'You've known judges like him before, and they soon crumbled.'

'But this one is harder than granite,' said the Judge. 'I have already had occasion to put him to the test, and he's unusually resilient. In his place, a young judge who was preoccupied with his career would have withdrawn. Believe me, he's going to cause problems.'

'You're too pessimistic,' said Denes.

'Not this time.'

'Well, how can I help?'

'It's my task to appoint two jurors, since I have allowed Pazair to preside beneath the Porch. I have already chosen Mentmose, whose good sense will be vitally important to us. With you as well, I shall feel much more confident.'

'Tomorrow's impossible for me – there is a cargo of precious vases arriving, and I must check every single one. But my wife will be more than able to do what you want.'

Pazair took the summons to Mentmose himself.

'I could have sent my scribe, but our friendly relations oblige me to be more polite.'

Mentmose did not invite him to sit down.

'Sheshi will appear as a witness,' continued Pazair. 'As you're the only person who knows where he is, please bring him to the court. Otherwise, we'll have to send town guards out to look for him.'

'Sheshi's a reasonable man,' said Mentmose. 'I wish you were – then you'd give up this trial.'

'The Judge of the Porch considered it could be upheld.'

'You'll wreck your career.'

'A lot of people seem to be concerned about my career at the moment. Should I be worried?'

'When you've failed dismally, Memphis will laugh at you and you'll have to resign.'

'If you're chosen as a juror, don't refuse to hear the truth.'

'Me, sit on a jury?' Mahu was astonished. 'I'd never have dreamt—'

'This is a very important trial, and its outcome is uncertain.'

'Do I have to do it?'

'Not at all. The Judge of the Porch is appointing two jurors, as am I, and four will be chosen from among leading citizens who have already officiated.'

'I confess I'm worried. Playing a part in a legal decision seems more difficult than selling papyrus.'

'You'll have to pronounce on the fate of a man.'

Mahu took a long time to think. Eventually, he said, 'I'm moved by your trust in me. I'll do it.'

Suti made love with a fury which surprised Panther, even though she was accustomed to his ardour. He was insatiable and could not tear himself away from her, bombarding her with kisses and caresses.

Skilled in love, she knew how to be tender after the storm. 'Such violence,' she said, 'like a traveller who's about to leave. What are you hiding from me?'

'It's the trial tomorrow.'

'Are you afraid?'

'I'd prefer to fight with my bare fists.'

'Your friend scares me.'

'What do you have to fear from Pazair?'

'He'll spare no one, if the law demands it.'

'You haven't betrayed him, have you, without telling me?'

She threw him onto his back and lay across him. 'When will you stop being suspicious of me?'

'Never. You're a wild panther, the most dangerous of all species, and you've sworn a thousand times to kill me.'

'Your judge is more dangerous than I am.'

'You're the one who's hiding something, aren't you?'

She rolled onto her side, away from her lover. 'Perhaps.'

'I haven't interrogated you very well.'

'You know how to make my body speak.'

'But you're still keeping your secret.'

'If I didn't, would I be worth anything in your eyes?'

He threw himself on her and held her fast. 'Have you forgotten you're my prisoner?'

'Believe what you like.'

'When will you run away?'

'As soon as I'm a free woman.'

'That decision's up to me. I have to declare you as such to the authorities.'

'What are you waiting for?'

'Nothing. I'll do it straight away.'

Suti dressed in haste, putting on his finest kilt, and the collar on which hung the Golden Fly, and hurried to the government office.

He arrived just as the scribe was about to leave, long before the office was supposed to close. 'Come back tomorrow,' said the scribe.

'That's out of the question.'

Suti's tone was threatening. Moreover, the Golden Fly indicated that this powerfully built young man was a soldier, and soldiers often quickly resorted to violence.

'What do you want?' asked the scribe.

'An end to the conditional freedom of the Libyan woman

Christian Jacq

Panther, who was granted to me during the last Asian campaign.'

'Do you guarantee her morality?'

'It's perfect.'

'What kind of work does she plan to do?'

'She's already worked on a farm.'

Suti completed the necessary formalities, wishing that he had made love to Panther one last time; his future mistresses might not be her equal. This would have happened anyway, sooner or later. It was better to cut the bonds before they became too strong.

On his way home, he recalled some of their amorous jousts, which had equalled the exploits of the mightiest conquerors. Panther had taught him that a woman's body was a paradise filled with moving landscapes, and that the pleasure of discovery could be constantly renewed.

The house was empty.

Suti wished he hadn't hurried. He'd have liked to spend the night before the trial with her, to forget tomorrow's battles, to sate himself on her perfume. He'd console himself with some old wine.

'Fill another cup,' said Panther, stealing up behind him and sliding her arms round his chest.

Qadash broke the copper instruments and threw them at the walls of his consulting room, which he had virtually destroyed. When he received the summons to appear before the court, a destructive madness had taken hold of him.

Without the sky-iron, he could no longer operate, because his hand shook too much. With the miraculous metal, he would have been like a god, rediscovering his youth and his skill. Who would respect him now? Who would boast of his marvellous work? People would talk of him in the past tense.

Could he delay his downfall? He must fight, refuse to become decrepit. Above all, he must disprove Judge Pazair's

336

suspicions. If only he had the judge's strength, his dynamism, his determination! Making an ally of him was just a fantasy. The young judge must fall, and justice with him.

In a few hours, the trial would start. Pazair walked along the riverbank with Brave and Way-Finder. The dog and the donkey were content to wander along in the dusk after a good dinner, though they never lost sight of their master. Way-Finder walked in front, and chose the route.

Tired and tense, Pazair was assailed by questions. Was he wrong? Had he burnt his boats? Was he taking a path which led to the abyss? But these were shameful thoughts. Justice would take its course, as imperious as the course of the divine river. Pazair was not its master but its servant. Whatever the result of the trial might be, the veils would be lifted.

What would become of Neferet if he was dismissed? Nebamon would attack her even more determinedly, to prevent her practising. But fortunately Branir was watching over her. The future High Priest of Amon would admit her into the medical team at the temple, out of Nebamon's reach.

Knowing that she was protected from a miserable fate gave Pazair the courage he needed to confront the whole of Egypt.

37

The trial opened with the customary ritual words: 'Before the gate of justice, in the place where all complaints are heard, where truth is distinguished from lies, in this great square where the weak are protected and saved from the powerful.'*
The court of justice backed onto the pillared gateway of the Temple of Ptah, and had been enlarged to accommodate a large number of dignitaries and common folk, all of them curious about the trial.

Judge Pazair, assisted by Iarrot, stood in the middle of the chamber. To his right was the jury. It was made up of Mentmose, Nenophar, Branir, Mahu, a priest from the Temple of Ptah, a priestess from the Temple of Hathor, a landowner and a carpenter. The presence of Branir, who was regarded by many as a true sage, proved the gravity of the occasion. The Judge of the Porch sat on Pazair's left. He represented the legal hierarchy, and was there to ensure that the proceedings were conducted in the proper manner. The two judges, dressed in long white linen robes and plain, old-fashioned wigs, unrolled a papyrus relating the glory of the golden age when Ma'at, the harmony of the universe, had reigned unchallenged.

'I, Judge Pazair, declare this court in session. The accuser

*This text was inscribed on the gate itself.

in this case is Charioteer Officer Suti, and the accused is General Asher, standard-bearer to the king and instructor to officers in the Asian army.'

A ripple of disbelief ran around the assembled throng. If their surroundings had not been so austere, many would have believed that this was a joke.

'I am Charioteer Officer Suti.'

The young man made a good impression on the crowd. He was handsome and confident, and did not look like a crank or an embittered soldier who had fallen out with his superior.

'Do you swear to tell the truth before this court?'

Suti read the words on the papyrus Iarrot handed him. 'By the everlasting names of Amon and Pharaoh – whose power is more terrible than death – I swear to tell the truth.'

'Set forth your case,' said Pazair.

'I accuse General Asher of felony, high treason and murder.'

Exclamations of amazement and disbelief rose from the watching throng.

The Judge of the Porch cut in. 'Out of respect for Ma'at, I demand silence in court. Anyone who fails to observe it will be expelled immediately and heavily punished.'

The warning was effective.

'Officer Suti,' Pazair went on, 'have you any evidence to support these charges?'

'The evidence exists.'

'In accordance with the law,' said Pazair, 'I carried out an investigation. During it, I uncovered a number of strange facts, which I believe to be linked to the main accusation. I therefore put forward the theory that there is a conspiracy against the state and a threat to Egypt's safety.'

The tension increased. Those leading citizens who were seeing Pazair for the first time were astonished by the gravity of such a young man, by his firmness and the weight with which he spoke.

'I am General Asher.'

However famous he might be, Asher had had to appear before the court: the law did not permit substitutes or representatives. The small, rat-faced man came forward and took the oath. He had donned full fighting kit: a short kilt, leg protectors and a coat of mail.

'General Asher, how do you respond to your accuser?'

'Officer Suti, whom I appointed to his post myself, is a brave man – I decorated him with the Golden Fly. During the last Asian campaign, he achieved several remarkable things and he deserves to be recognized as a hero. I consider him a gifted archer, one of the best in our army. His accusations have no basis in truth. I reject them. No doubt this is simply a fleeting lapse of reason on his part.'

'So you consider yourself innocent?'

'I am innocent.'

Suti sat down at the base of a pillar, facing Pazair and a few paces from him. Asher did likewise, on the other side, near the jurors, who could easily see his facial expressions and the way he conducted himself.

'The role of this court,' said Pazair, 'is to establish the truth. If the crime is proved, the matter will be referred to the tjaty's court. I summon Qadash the tooth doctor.'

Qadash took the oath nervously.

'Do you admit that you tried to steal from an army workshop directed by the inventor Sheshi?'

'No, I do not.'

'Then how do you explain your presence there?'

'I had gone there to buy top-quality copper. The transaction didn't go well.'

'Who told you where the copper was?'

'The officer in charge of the barracks.'

'That is not true.'

'Yes, it is. I—'

'The court has his written statement. On that point, you

have lied. Moreover, you have just repeated this lie after taking the oath, and have therefore committed the offence of perjury.'

Qadash trembled. A harsh jury would sentence him to forced labour in the mines; if they were lenient, the punishment might be a season working in the fields.

'I challenge your previous answers,' continued Pazair, 'and I ask you again: who told you about the copper?'

Qadash stood frozen to the spot, his mouth hanging open.

'Was it Sheshi?'

Qadash dissolved into tears. At a sign from Pazair, Iarrot led him back to his seat.

'I summon Sheshi the inventor.'

For a moment, Pazair thought Sheshi was not going to appear. But he had proved 'reasonable', as Mentmose put it.

The general asked permission to speak. 'I really am astonished. Surely this has become an entirely different trial?'

'In my opinion,' said Pazair, 'these persons are very much part of the matter we are dealing with.'

'Neither Qadash nor Sheshi has ever served under me.'

'Have a little patience, General.'

Thwarted, Asher watched Sheshi out of the corner of his eye. He seemed relaxed.

'Is it true that you work for the army in a workshop, developing new weapons?' asked Pazair.

'Yes,' said Sheshi.

'In reality, you have two jobs: one official, out in the open, in a palace workshop; the other much more discreet, in a workshop hidden in a barracks.'

Sheshi gave a brief nod.

'Following Qadash's attempt at robbery, you moved to new premises, but you did not bring charges against Qadash.'

'It seemed the most discreet solution.'

'As a specialist in metal alloys and foundry procedures,

341

you receive materials from the army and keep an inventory of your stocks.'

'Of course.'

'Why have you been hiding ingots of sky-iron, which is reserved for religious uses, and an adze made of that metal?'

The question stunned the audience. Neither sky-iron nor sacred adzes ever left the precincts of the temple, and stealing them was punishable by death.

'I'm unaware of the existence of this treasure,' said Sheshi.

'Then how do you explain its presence in your workshop?'

'Someone is trying to do me harm.'

'Have you many enemies?'

'If I were convicted, my research would be interrupted and Egypt would suffer.'

'But you aren't a native Egyptian, are you?' said Pazair. 'You were born a sand-traveller.'

'I had forgotten.'

'You lied to the overseer of the workshops, and told him you were born in Memphis.'

'There was a misunderstanding. I meant that I felt like a true native of Memphis.'

Pazair turned to Asher. 'As was its duty, the army checked and corroborated your statement. Were the officials carrying out those checks not under your authority, General?'

'It's possible,' murmured the general.

'Therefore you authorized a lie.'

'I didn't do it myself. It was an official under my command.'

'In law you are responsible for your subordinates' errors.'

'I admit that, but it's too trifling a matter to punish. Scribes make mistakes every day when they write their reports. Besides, Sheshi has become a true Egyptian. His profession proves the trust placed in him, and he has shown himself worthy of that trust.'

'The facts can be read another way. You have known

Sheshi for a long time. You first met during your earliest campaigns in Asia. His gift for working with metal interested you, so you made it easy for him to enter Egyptian territory, glossed over his past, and helped him set out on his career making weapons.'

'That is pure speculation,' retorted Asher.

'The sky-iron is no speculation. What did you plan to use it for, and why did you obtain it for Sheshi?'

'That is a complete fabrication.'

Pazair turned to the jury. 'I would ask you to note that Qadash is Libyan, and Sheshi is a sand-traveller of Syrian origin. I believe that these two men are co-conspirators, with links to General Asher. They have been plotting for a long time, and were planning to take a decisive step forward by using sky-iron.'

'That's only your theory,' objected the general. 'You have not one shred of proof.'

'I admit that I have established only three reprehensible facts: Qadash's false testimony, Sheshi's false declaration, and your department's administrative shortcomings.'

The general folded his arms arrogantly. Thus far, Pazair was making himself look ridiculous.

'Now for the second part of my investigation,' Pazair went on, 'the matter of the honour guard at the Great Sphinx at Giza. According to an official document signed by General Asher, the five ex-soldiers forming the honour guard died in an accident, when they fell from the Sphinx. Do you confirm that, General?'

'I indeed placed my seal upon the report.'

'That version of the facts doesn't correspond with reality.'

Disconcerted, Asher unfolded his arms. 'The army paid for the funerals of those unfortunate men.'

'For three of them,' said Pazair, 'the head guard and two men from the Delta. I was unable to establish the exact cause of death. The other two were sent into retirement in the

Theban region. They were certainly alive after the alleged accident.'

'That's very strange,' agreed Asher. 'May we hear what they have to say?'

'They are both dead now. The fourth soldier died in an accident – or was he in fact pushed into his own bread oven? The fifth was afraid and took refuge in the guise of a ferryman. He drowned – or should I say someone drowned him?'

'I object,' declared the Judge of the Porch. 'According to the report sent to my office, the local authorities believe it was an accident.'

'Whatever it was, at least two of the five soldiers did not die by falling from the Sphinx, as General Asher would have us believe. Moreover, the ferryman spoke to me before he died. His fellow guards were attacked and killed by an armed band comprising several men and a woman. They spoke in foreign tongues. That's the truth that the general's report concealed.'

The Judge of the Porch frowned. Although he detested Pazair, he could not cast doubt on a judge's words, spoken before the court and revealing a new fact of enormous importance.

Even Mentmose was shaken; the real trial was beginning.

The general defended himself vehemently. 'Each day I sign many reports without checking the facts myself, and I have very little to do with ex-soldiers.'

'The jurors will be interested to learn,' said Pazair, 'that Sheshi's workshop, where the chest containing the sky-iron was stored, was situated in a veterans' barracks.'

'What does that matter?' snapped Asher. 'The accident was investigated and verified by the army, and I simply signed the necessary document so that the funeral ceremonies could be organized.'

'Then you deny, under oath, that you knew of the attack on the honour guard at the Sphinx?'

'Yes, I certainly do deny it. And I also deny all responsibility, direct or indirect, in the deaths of those five unfortunate men. I knew nothing of this tragedy or subsequent events.'

The general defended himself with a conviction which would be looked upon favourably by the majority of the jury. True, the judge had brought a tragedy to light, but Asher could be blamed only for a second administrative error, not for one or more murders.

'Without calling into question the bizarre features of this case,' interposed the Judge of the Porch, 'I think that an additional investigation is essential. But we must surely cast doubt upon the statements made by the fifth guard, who may have made up a story to impress the judge.'

'A few hours later, he was dead,' Pazair reminded him.

'A sad coincidence.'

'If he was indeed murdered, someone wished to prevent him saying more, and to prevent him appearing before this court.'

'Even if we accept your theory,' said Asher, 'how am I involved? If I had checked, I would have seen, as you did, that the honour guard didn't die in an accident. At the time, I was busy preparing for the Asian campaign, and that was necessarily my first priority.'

Pazair had hoped, but without too much optimism, that the general would be less confident, but he was managing to parry the attacks and turn the most incisive arguments to his favour.

'I am Suti.' He rose, solemn-faced.

'Do you maintain your allegations?'

'I do.'

'Explain why.'

'During my first mission in Asia, after the death of my officer, who was killed in an ambush, I wandered through a troubled region, trying to find General Asher's regiment. I thought I was lost when I witnessed a terrible scene. An Egyptian soldier was tortured and murdered a few paces from me; I was too exhausted to help him, and his attackers were too numerous. One man carried out the interrogation, then slit the soldier's throat. That criminal, that traitor to his country, is General Asher.'

The general kept his composure. The shocked spectators held their breath. The jurors became suddenly grim-faced.

'Those scandalous words have no basis in truth,' declared Asher in a voice which was almost serene.

'Denying it is not enough,' said Suti hotly. 'I saw you, you murderer!'

'Please remain calm,' Pazair told him. 'This testimony proves that General Asher is collaborating with the enemy, and that is why the Libyan rebel Adafi remains uncaptured. His accomplice warns him in advance of our troop movements, and is planning an invasion of Egypt with him. The general's guilt leads us to believe that he is not innocent in the Sphinx affair. Did he have the five soldiers killed to try out the weapons made by Sheshi? An additional investigation will no doubt demonstrate this, linking together the various elements I have set out.'

'My guilt has not been proved in any way,' declared Asher.

'Do you cast doubt upon the words of Officer Suti?'

'I believe he's sincere, but he's wrong. According to his own testimony, he was utterly exhausted. No doubt his eyes deceived him.'

'The murderer's face is engraved in my mind,' declared Suti, 'and I swore that I would find him again. I didn't know then who he was. I identified him as General Asher at our first meeting, when he congratulated me on my exploits.'

'General, did you send out scouts into enemy territory?' asked Pazair.

'Of course,' replied Asher.

'How many?'

'Three.'

'And were their names registered at the Foreign Affairs secretariat?'

'That's the rule.'

'Did they all return alive from the last campaign?'

For the first time, the general looked uneasy. 'No. One of them died.'

'The one you killed with your own hands because he had realized what you were doing.'

'That's untrue. I'm not guilty.'

The jurors noticed that his voice was trembling.

'You, who are laden with honours,' said Pazair, 'who train officers, have betrayed your country in the most contemptible manner. It is time to confess, General.'

Asher gazed into the distance. This time, he was close to yielding. 'Suti is mistaken.'

'Send me back there with officers and scribes,' suggested Suti. 'I'll recognize the place where I buried the poor man. We'll bring back his body, he'll be identified, and we shall give him a worthy tomb.'

'I order an immediate expedition,' declared Pazair. 'General Asher will be held in the main barracks at Memphis, under close guard. He is to have no contact with the outside world until Suti returns. We shall then continue the trial and the jury will reach its verdict.'

38

The echoes of the trial could still be heard in Memphis. Some people already believed General Asher to be the worst kind of traitor, and praised Suti's courage and Judge Pazair's skill.

Pazair would have loved to consult Branir, but the law forbade him to speak to the jurors until the end of the case. He declined several invitations from leading citizens and locked himself away in his house. In less than a week, the expedition would return with the body of the scout murdered by Asher, and the general would be convicted and sentenced to death. Suti would be promoted to a senior rank. Above all, the plot would be dismantled and Egypt saved from a peril which came both from outside and from within. Even if Sheshi slipped through the net, the goal would have been reached.

Pazair had not lied to Neferet. He had not stopped thinking about her for a moment. Even during the trial, her face had haunted him. He had had to concentrate on every word so as not to sink into a dream in which she was the only heroine.

He had entrusted the sky-iron and the adze to the Judge of the Porch, who had immediately handed them over to the High Priest of Ptah. Working with the religious authorities, Pazair must establish where they came from. One thing worried him: why had no one reported their theft? Their exceptional quality hinted at a rich and powerful shrine, which was certainly the kind most likely to own them.

Pazair had granted Iarrot and Kem three rest days. Iarrot was eager to return home, where a new domestic drama had just broken out. His daughter was refusing to eat vegetables, and living solely on pastries. Iarrot could accept the whim, but his wife could not.

The Nubian did not leave the office. He didn't need rest and considered himself responsible for Pazair's safety. A judge might be untouchable, but it was vital to be careful.

When a shaven-headed priest tried to enter the building, Kem barred his way.

'I must give a message to Judge Pazair,' said the priest.

'Give it to me.'

'I must give it to him in person.'

'Wait here.'

Although the man was thin and unarmed, the Nubian felt uneasy.

He went into Pazair's office and told him, 'A priest wants to speak to you. Be careful.'

Pazair smiled. 'You see danger everywhere.'

'At least keep Killer with you.'

'As you wish.'

The priest entered, and Kem remained behind the door. Killer munched unconcernedly on a date stone.

'Judge Pazair, you're expected tomorrow at dawn, at the great gate of the Temple of Ptah.'

'Who wants to see me?'

'I have no other message.'

'What is the reason for this meeting?'

'I repeat, I have no other message. Please shave off all your bodily hair, abstain from sexual relations, and meditate before the ancestors.'

'I'm a judge. I have no intention of becoming a priest.'

'Do as I ask. May the gods protect you.'

Kem watched while the barber finished shaving Pazair.

'There you are,' said the man, 'smooth enough to enter holy orders. Are we losing a judge and gaining a priest?'

'It's simply a matter of cleanliness. Don't the nobility do the same on a regular basis?'

'You've become one of them, true enough. I like that. In the streets of Memphis, people can't stop talking about you. Who would dare attack all-powerful Asher? Today, tongues are loosening. Nobody liked him. There are rumours that he tortured recruits.'

Yesterday worshipped, today scorned. Asher had seen his destiny turned upside-down in a few hours. The most sordid rumours were circulating about him. Pazair took the lesson to heart: no one was safe from human baseness.

'If you aren't becoming a priest,' ventured the barber, 'you must be going to see a lady. Lots of women like well-shaven men who look like priests – or who *are* priests. All right, love isn't forbidden to them, but it must be exciting to consort with men who see the gods face to face. I have a jasmine and lotus lotion here; I bought it from the best perfume maker in Memphis. It will give your skin a pleasant scent for several days.'

Pazair accepted it. In so doing, he ensured that the barber would spread throughout Memphis the news that the most unbending judge in the city was also a charming lover. All that remained was to find out the name of the chosen woman.

After the barber had left, Pazair read a text dedicated to Ma'at. She was the venerable ancestor, the source of joy and harmony. Daughter of the Light, Light herself, she showed favour to those who acted in her name.

Pazair asked her to keep his life on the path of righteousness.

Cloistered priests, dressed in white linen, emerged from their dwellings on the edges of the lake, from which they took water to wash themselves each morning. In procession, they laid vegetables and bread on the altars, while the High Priest, acting in the name of Pharaoh, lit a lamp, broke the seal on the innermost shrine where the god lay, wafted incense, and spoke the words 'Awaken in peace.' At the same time, other high priests were carrying out the same ritual in other temples.

In one of the chambers of the inner temple, nine men had gathered. The tjaty, the bearer of the Rule, the overseer of the Double House, the official in charge of canals and director of water dwellings, the overseer of writings, the overseer of fields, the director of secret missions, the scribe of the land registry and the king's steward formed the council of the nine friends of King Ramses.

Each month, they met in this secret place, far from their offices and their staff. In the peace of the shrine, they enjoyed the quiet they needed for reflection. They felt the weight of their task more and more heavily since Pharaoh had issued his unusual orders, as if the empire were in peril. Each man must carry out a systematic inspection within his own department, to ensure the honesty of his most senior colleagues. Ramses had demanded swift results. Irregularities and laxness must be thoroughly dealt with, and incompetent officials dismissed. Each of the nine friends had noticed, during conversations with Pharaoh, that the king was preoccupied or even worried.

After a night of fruitful conversations, the nine men parted. A priest whispered a few words in Bagey's ear, and the tjaty headed for the doorway to the pillared hall. A young man was awaiting him there.

'Thank you for coming, Judge Pazair,' said Bagey. 'I'm the tjaty.'

Pazair, already impressed by his majestic surroundings, was even more impressed by this meeting. He, an insignificant judge from Memphis, had been granted the immense privilege of speaking alone with Tjaty Bagey, whose legendary strictness frightened even the most senior officials.

Bagey was taller than Pazair, with a long, austere face and a muffled, slightly hoarse voice. His tone was cold, almost abrupt.

'I wanted to see you here, so that our conversation would remain secret. If you consider it against the law, withdraw now.'

'Please continue, Tjaty. I'm listening.'

'Are you aware of the importance of the trial you are conducting?'

'General Asher is a great man, but I believe I have demonstrated that he is a criminal.'

'Are you certain of that?'

'Suti's testimony cannot be contested.'

'But he is your closest friend, is he not?' said Bagey.

'That's true, Tjaty, but our friendship doesn't influence my judgment.'

'That fault would be unforgivable.'

'I believe the facts have been established.'

'Isn't that for the jury to decide?'

'I shall bow to their decision.'

'In attacking General Asher, you're calling into question our defence policy in Asia. The morale of our troops will be damaged.'

'Tjaty, if the truth had not been discovered,' said Pazair, 'the country would have faced a much more serious danger.'

'Have there been attempts to impede your investigation?'

'The army threw obstacles in my way, and I'm certain that murders have been committed.'

'The fifth guard?'

'All five guards died violently, three at Giza, and the two survivors in their villages. That's my belief. It's for the Judge of the Porch to pursue the investigation, but . . .'

'But?'

Pazair hesitated. This was the tjaty himself standing before him. To speak lightly would be fatal; to hide his thoughts would be tantamount to lying. Those who had tried to mislead Bagey no longer served in his government.

'But, Tjaty, I am not altogether certain that he'll conduct it with the necessary determination.'

'Are you daring to accuse the most senior judge in Memphis of incompetence?'

'I have a feeling that the fight against darkness no longer attracts him. His experience makes him foresee so many worrying consequences that he prefers to remain in the background and not venture onto dangerous ground.'

'That's a harsh criticism. Do you think he's corrupt?'

'No, Tjaty, merely linked to important people he doesn't want to annoy.'

'We are a long way from justice.'

'It is not justice as I understand it, that's true.'

'If General Asher is convicted, he'll appeal,' said Bagey.

'That's his right.'

'Whatever the verdict, the Judge of the Porch will not remove you from this case and will ask you to pursue the instruction on points which are unclear.'

'Forgive me, Tjaty, but I doubt that.'

'You're wrong, for I shall give him the order. I want everything out in the open, Judge Pazair.'

'Suti got back yesterday evening,' Kem told Pazair.

'Then why isn't he here?'

'He's been detained at the central barracks.'

'That's illegal!'

Pazair hurried to the barracks, where he was received by the scribe who had commanded the expedition.

'I demand an explanation,' said Pazair.

'We went to the scene of the incident. Officer Suti recognized the place, but we searched in vain for the scout's body. I believed it fitting that Suti be placed under arrest.'

'That decision is unacceptable, as long as the current trial hasn't ended.'

The scribe agreed that that was true, and Suti was immediately freed.

The two friends embraced.

'Were you tortured?' asked Pazair.

'No. My travelling companions were all convinced of Asher's guilt, and our failure has plunged them into despair. Even the cave had been laid waste, to wipe out all traces.'

'And yet we told no one about it.'

'Asher and his allies took precautions. I was as naive as you, Pazair. We shan't be able to defeat him on our own.'

'For one thing, the trial is not lost yet; and for another, I have full powers.'

The trial recommenced the following day.

Pazair summoned Suti to give evidence.

'Please tell the court about your expedition to the scene of the crime.'

'In the presence of sworn witnesses, I saw that the corpse had gone. Someone had carefully destroyed the place.'

'That's grotesque.' Asher sniffed. 'The officer made up a story and now he's trying to justify it.'

'Do you maintain your accusations, Officer Suti?' asked Pazair.

'I did indeed see General Asher torture and murder an Egyptian.'

'Where is the body?' sneered Asher.

'You had it removed.'

'You think that I, general of the Asian army, would act like the vilest of criminals? Who could possibly believe that? The facts can be made to tell a very different story: you killed your chariot officer because you yourself are the sand-travellers' accomplice. And you are anxious to put the blame on someone else to vindicate yourself. Since there is no proof of either version of the story, the trick rebounds on its author. I therefore demand that you be punished.'

Suti clenched his fists. 'You're guilty and you know it. How dare you give instruction to our best troops when you viciously murdered one of your own men and led our soldiers into ambushes?'

Asher lowered his voice. 'The jurors will enjoy these increasingly ludicrous fabrications. Soon, no doubt, I shall be accused of wiping out the whole army.' His mocking smile won over the spectators.

'Suti is speaking under oath,' Pazair reminded him, 'and you recognized his worth as a soldier.'

'All the praise for his heroism has turned his head.'

'The disappearance of the body doesn't wipe out his testimony.'

'No, but you will agree, Judge, that it reduces its scope considerably. I, too, am testifying under oath. Is my word worth less than Suti's? If he did indeed see a murder, he has the wrong murderer. If he'll make a public apology to me here and now, I shall forget his fleeting madness.'

Pazair turned to Suti. 'Officer Suti, are you agreeable to that suggestion?'

'When I emerged from the hornets' nest that almost killed me, I swore to bring this most contemptible of men to justice. Asher is skilful: he fosters doubt and suspicion. And now he wants me to recant. I shall proclaim the truth to my last breath.'

'Faced with the blind stubbornness of a soldier who has lost his mind,' said Asher, 'I, general and royal standard-bearer, affirm my innocence.'

Suti wanted to rush at him and make him eat his words. But a hard stare from Pazair held him back.

'Does anyone here present wish to speak?' asked Pazair.

No one said a word.

'Then I invite the jury to consider its verdict.'

*

The jury sat in a chamber at the palace, the judge presiding over discussions which he was not allowed to enter into on either side. His role was to ensure that everyone had a chance to speak, to avoid confrontations and to maintain the dignity of the court.

Mentmose spoke first, with objectivity and moderation. A few specific points were added to what he had to say, but his conclusions were retained with no great changes. Less than two hours later, Pazair read the verdict and Iarrot noted it down.

'Qadash the tooth doctor is found guilty of perjury. Because the lie was not a serious one, and in view of his age and brilliant past, Qadash is sentenced to give one fat ox to the temple and a hundred sacks of grain to the veterans' barracks he disturbed by his intrusion.'

Qadash sighed with relief.

'Does Qadash wish to appeal or to reject this judgment?'

He rose. 'I accept it, Judge Pazair.'

'Sheshi is acquitted of all charges.'

The man did not even smile.

'General Asher is found guilty of two administrative errors, which did not prejudice the conduct of the army in Asia. Moreover, his excuses were found to be valid. He is therefore only given a warning, so that this kind of failure doesn't happen again. The jurors do not consider that the murder was properly and definitively established. General Asher is therefore not considered to be a traitor or a criminal, but Officer Suti's testimony cannot be qualified as defamatory. Since the jurors could not make a clear pronouncement because of the doubt surrounding several vital facts, the court asks that the investigation be continued, in order to establish the truth as quickly as possible.'

39

The Judge of the Porch was kneeling by a flower bed, watering a clump of irises which grew between some hibiscus bushes. He had been a widower for five years, and lived alone in his villa on the south side of the city.

He looked sternly up at Pazair, and asked, 'Are you proud of yourself, Judge? You have sullied the reputation of a general respected by everyone, sown confusion in people's minds, and have not even obtained victory for your friend Suti.'

'That was not my goal.'

'Then what was?'

'The truth.'

'Ah, the truth! Don't you realize it's harder to grasp than an eel?'

'But I unearthed the elements of a conspiracy against the state.'

'Stop talking nonsense. Why don't you help me to my feet and water the narcissi – gently, mind. That will make a change from your usual ruthlessness.'

Pazair did as he was bidden.

'Have you calmed our hero down?'

'No, he's as angry as ever.'

'What did he expect? To overthrow Asher with one mad gesture?'

'I believe Asher's guilty,' said Pazair, 'and so do you.'

'You're very indiscreet. That's yet another fault.'

'Did my arguments give you cause for concern?'

'At my age, nothing disturbs me any more.'

'I think the contrary is true.'

'I'm tired,' said the Judge, 'and no longer fit to carry out long investigations. Since you have begun, you can continue.'

'Am I to understand that—'

'You understand perfectly. I have taken my decision, and I shan't change my mind.'

The news was soon all round the palace and the official buildings: to everyone's surprise, Pazair was not being removed from Asher's case. Although he had not succeeded, the young judge had impressed many dignitaries by his thoroughness. Favouring neither the accuser nor the accused, he had not tried to hide the gaps in the evidence. Some had forgotten his youth and stressed his promising future, although it might be compromised because of who the accused was.

Undoubtedly Pazair had been wrong to give so much credit to the testimony of Suti, the hero of a day and a fanciful fellow. But if most people, after reflection, believed the general innocent, all agreed that Pazair had brought to light some disturbing facts. Even if the deaths of the five guards and the theft of the sky-iron were not linked to some imaginary conspiracy, they were nevertheless scandalous episodes which ought not to be forgotten. The state, the legal hierarchy, dignitaries and the common people all expected Judge Pazair to reveal the truth to them.

Suti did calm down somewhat when he learnt that Pazair was to continue his enquiries, and he tried to forget his disappointment in Panther's arms. He promised his friend that he wouldn't do anything without their first agreeing on a strategy. Although he had retained his status as a charioteer officer, he wouldn't be taking part in any missions before the final verdict.

The dying sun turned the desert sand and the stones in the quarries to gold; the workmen's tools had fallen silent, the peasants were returning to their farmhouses, and the donkeys were resting, relieved of their burdens. On the flat roofs of the houses in Memphis, people were enjoying the cool air while eating cheese and drinking beer.

Brave was stretched out on Branir's terrace, dreaming of the piece of grilled beef he had just eaten. In the distance, the pyramids on the Giza plateau formed triangles of absolute purity, marking the edges of eternity in the dusk. The country was falling peacefully asleep, as it did every evening in Ramses' reign.

'You overcame the biggest obstacle,' said Branir.

'It was a paltry success,' objected Pazair.

'You have been recognized as an honest, skilful judge, and you now have a chance to pursue the investigation without hindrance. Who could ask for more?'

'Asher lied, even though he was speaking under oath. Not just a murderer but a perjurer, too.'

'The jury didn't censure you. Neither Mentmose nor Nenophar tried to vindicate the general. They have set you on the road to your destiny.'

'The Judge of the Porch would have liked to remove me from the case.'

'Perhaps, but he has confidence in your abilities, and the tjaty wants reliable information on which to base his actions.'

'I may not be able to find any, because Asher took care to destroy the proof.'

'Your path will be long and difficult, but you can reach the goal. Soon, you'll have the support of the High Priest of Karnak and you'll have access to temple records.'

Pazair nodded. He was determined to investigate the

theft of the sky-iron and the adze as soon as Branir took office.

Branir went on, 'You are your own master now. Distinguish justice from iniquity, and resist the advice of those who fail to do so in order to mislead people. This trial was only a skirmish; the true battle has yet to be fought. Neferet, too, will be proud of you.'

In the stars' light shone the souls of the sages. Pazair thanked the gods, who had permitted him to meet one in the world of men.

Way-Finder was a silent, thoughtful donkey. He rarely made a sound, but when he did, his braying was piercing enough to wake a whole street.

Pazair awoke with a start.

It was scarcely past dawn, but his donkey had definitely called to him. The judge opened the window.

Outside the house stood a crowd of some twenty people, among them Nebamon.

Nebamon shook his fist and shouted, 'Here are the finest doctors in Memphis, Judge Pazair! We are lodging a complaint against our colleague Neferet, for preparing unsafe medicines, and we demand her expulsion from the medical profession.'

Pazair reached the west bank of Thebes at the hottest time of the day. He requisitioned a town-guard chariot, whose driver was sleeping in the shade of an awning, and ordered him to drive quickly to Neferet's village. The sun reigned unchallenged, halting time in its tracks.

Neferet was neither at home nor at her workshop.

'Try the canal,' recommended an old man, rousing briefly from his doze.

Pazair abandoned the chariot, walked alongside a field of wheat, crossed a shady garden, set off along a path and at last reached the canal, where the villagers often bathed. He scrambled down the steep slope, passed through a curtain of reeds, and saw her.

He should have called to her, closed his eyes, turned away, but no words emerged from his lips and he was frozen to the spot by her entrancing beauty. She was naked, and swimming with natural grace, letting the current bear her along. She dived and resurfaced, and he saw that she was wearing a cap made from reeds and a necklace of turquoises.

When she saw him, she went on swimming. 'The water's wonderful,' she called. 'Come in and have a swim.'

Pazair took off his kilt and walked towards her, not even feeling the cool of the water. She reached out her hand to him and he took it, his whole being aflame. A wave brought their bodies into contact. When her breasts touched his chest, she didn't draw away. He dared to press his lips against hers and slip his arms round her.

'I love you, Neferet.'

'I shall learn to love you.'

'You're the first, and there will never be anyone else.'

Clumsily, he kissed her. Arm in arm, they returned to the riverbank and stretched out on a sandy beach, hidden in the reeds.

'I'm a virgin, too,' said Neferet.

'I want to offer you my life. First thing tomorrow, I shall ask for your hand in marriage.'

She smiled, conquered, abandoning herself to the moment. 'Make love to me. Make love to me now.'

He lay down on top of her, gazing into her blue eyes. Their souls and bodies united under the midday sun.

Neferet listened to her father's and mother's views. Neither of them was opposed to the marriage, but they wanted to see their future son-in-law before making their decision. True, she had no need of their consent, but she respected them and their approval meant a great deal to her. Her mother had a few reservations. Wasn't Pazair too young? And there were still doubts about his future prospects. Not to mention the fact that he was late, on the very day when he was asking for her daughter's hand.

Their concerns transmitted themselves to Neferet. A horrible thought entered her head: what if he had already stopped loving her? What if, contrary to everything he had said, he had wanted only a brief affair? No, that was impossible. His passion would be as everlasting as the mountain of Thebes.

At last he entered the modest dwelling. Neferet remained distant, as the solemnity of the moment required.

'Please forgive me; I lost my way in the maze of little streets. I confess I have no sense of direction – usually, my donkey guides me.'

Neferet's mother was astonished. 'You have a donkey?'

'Yes. His name is Way-Finder.'

'Is he young and in good health?'

'He's never been ill in his life.'

'What else have you got?'

'Next month, I shall have a house in Memphis.'

'Being a judge is a good job,' declared Neferet's father.

'Our daughter is young,' pointed out her mother. 'Couldn't you wait?'

'I love her, and want to marry her this very second.'

Pazair's manner was serious and determined. Neferet gazed at him with the eyes of a woman in love. Her parents yielded.

Suti's chariot hurtled through the gates of the main barracks in Memphis. The guards dropped their spears and threw themselves aside to avoid being run over. Suti jumped down from the moving vehicle, leaving the horses to continue galloping round the great courtyard. He ran up the staircase that led to the senior officers' quarters, where General Asher was staying. He dealt the first guard a sharp blow to the back of the neck, punched the second in the belly, and kicked the third in the testicles. The fourth had time to unsheathe his sword and wound him in the left shoulder; but the pain only intensified Suti's rage, and he knocked out his opponent with a double-fisted blow.

General Asher was sitting on a mat, with a map of Asia spread out in front of him. He turned to look at Suti. 'What are you here for?'

'To kill you.'

'Don't be a fool.'

'You may escape justice, but you won't escape me.'

'If you attack me, you won't leave this barracks alive.'

'How many Egyptians have you killed with your own hands?'

'You were exhausted,' said Asher, 'and your eyes deceived you. You made a mistake.'

'You know that isn't true.'

'Then let us come to an arrangement.'

'An arrangement?'

'A public reconciliation would be the most effective thing. I shall be confirmed in my position, and you'll be promoted.'

Suti rushed at Asher and grabbed him by the throat. 'Die, filth!'

Soldiers rushed in and surrounded the madman. They dragged him off the general, and rained blows upon him.

Asher was magnanimous enough not to lodge a complaint against Suti. He could understand his attacker's reaction, although he had the wrong culprit. In his place, he would have done the same. This behaviour cast Asher in a favourable light.

As soon as he returned from Thebes, Pazair did everything he could to free Suti, who was being held in the main barracks. Asher even agreed to waive the punishments for insubordination and insulting a superior officer if Suti resigned from the army.

'You'd better accept,' Pazair advised him.

'I'm sorry. I forgot my promise. Please forgive me.'

'With you, I'm always too soft-hearted.'

'You'll never be able to beat Asher.'

'I'm stubborn and determined, remember.'

'Yes, but he's cunning.'

'Forget the army.'

'I hate the discipline, anyway. I have other plans.'

Pazair dreaded to think what they might be. He said, 'Will you help me prepare for a celebration?'

'What are you celebrating?'

'My marriage.'

The conspirators met at an abandoned farm, making sure that none of them had been followed.

Since they had looted the Great Pyramid and stolen the symbols of Pharaoh's legitimacy, they had been content to observe. Recent events, however, had forced them to take decisions.

Only Ramses knew that his throne rested on shifting sands. As soon as his power faltered, he must celebrate his festival of regeneration, which would mean admitting to the court and the country that he no longer possessed the Testament of the Gods.

'The king's stronger than we thought.'

'Patience is our best weapon.'

'Yes, but time is passing.'

'What risks do we run? Pharaoh is bound hand and foot. He takes protective measures, and hardens his attitude towards his own government, but he can't confide in anyone. His character's strong but it's crumbling. The man's doomed – and he knows it.'

'We've lost the sky-iron and the adze.'

'That's just a tactical error.'

'I'm afraid. We should give up, put them back.'

'Don't be stupid.'

'We can't give up, not when we're so close.'

'Egypt's in our hands. Tomorrow, the kingdom and its riches will belong to us. Are you forgetting our great plan?'

'All conquests require sacrifices, this one more than any other. We mustn't let remorse stop us. A few corpses along the way are unimportant compared to what we're going to accomplish.

'Judge Pazair's a real danger, though. We're here now because of him.'

'He'll get bogged down.'

'Don't fool yourself. He's the keenest investigator in Egypt.'

'He doesn't know anything.'

'His conduct of his first major trial was masterly, and his instinct's often acute. He's already gathered damaging evidence; he might put us at risk.'

'When he arrived in Memphis he was alone, but now he has considerable support. If he takes one more step in the right direction, who is there to stop him? We should have prevented his rise to power.'

'It isn't too late.'

40

Suti was waiting for Neferet when the boat arrived from Thebes.

'You're so beautiful!' he exclaimed.

She laughed. 'Don't make me blush in front of a hero.'

'Now that I've seen you, I'd rather be a judge. Give me your travelling bag. I think Way-Finder will be happy to carry it.'

She asked anxiously, 'Where's Pazair?'

'He's cleaning the house and he hasn't finished yet, which is why I've come to meet you. I'm so happy for you both.'

'Are you fully recovered?'

'You're the best healer in the world. I've got all my strength back, and I'm planning to use it well.'

'And wisely, I hope?'

'Don't worry,' said Suti. 'And don't let's keep Pazair waiting. Since yesterday he's talked of nothing but headwinds, probable delays, and I don't know what other disasters that might stop you coming. Being that much in love stuns me.'

Way-Finder led the way.

The judge had given Iarrot a day's holiday, decorated the front of his house with flowers, and purified the interior. A delicate scent of oliban and jasmine filled the air.

Neferet's green monkey and Pazair's dog glared at each other, while he took her in his arms. The local inhabitants were always on the alert for unusual events, and soon realized what was going on.

'I can't help worrying about the patients I've left behind in the village,' said Neferet.

'They'll have to get used to another doctor. In three days' time, we're moving into Branir's house.'

'Do you still want to marry me?'

His answer was to lift her up and carry her across the threshold of the little house where he had spent so many nights dreaming of her.

Outside, there were shouts of joy. Since they were now living under the same roof, Pazair and Neferet had officially become man and wife.

After a night of celebration involving everyone in the district, they slept entwined until late morning. When he awoke, Pazair gazed at her lovingly. He had not thought that he could ever be so happy.

Eyes still closed, she took his hand and laid it upon her heart. 'Swear to me that we shall never be parted.'

'May the gods make us one and inscribe our love in eternity.'

Their bodies were so attuned that their desires were in perfect harmony. Beyond the pleasure of the senses, in which they revelled with adolescent fervour and hunger, they were already experiencing a spiritual union that would endure for all time.

'Well, Judge Pazair,' said Nebamon, 'when is the trial to begin? I understand that Neferet has returned to Memphis. She's therefore ready to appear before the court.'

'Neferet has become my wife.'

Nebamon frowned disapprovingly. 'That's very unwise. Her conviction will tarnish your name. If you value your career, you must divorce her quickly.'

'Are you still determined to make these accusations?'

Nebamon burst out laughing. 'Has love turned your brain?'

'Here is the list of medicines Neferet made in her workshop. The plants were supplied by Kani, gardener to the temple at Karnak. As you will see, everything she made is on the official list of permissible medicines.'

'You aren't a doctor, Pazair, and the testimony of this fellow Kani won't be enough to convince the jury.'

'Do you think Branir's testimony will?'

Nebamon's smile froze on his lips. 'Branir no longer practises. He—'

'He is the future High Priest of the temple at Karnak, and will testify in Neferet's favour. He is well known for thoroughness and honesty. He has examined the drugs that you call dangerous, and has found nothing amiss.'

Nebamon was furious. Branir's unrivalled prestige meant that his support would be of enormous benefit to Neferet. He said, 'I underestimated you, Pazair. You're a good tactician.'

'I simply use the truth to counter your wish to do harm.'

'Today you've won, it seems, but tomorrow you'll be brought down to earth.'

That night, while Neferet was asleep upstairs, Pazair worked late on a case in his office. He heard Way-Finder bray, which meant someone was coming.

He went to the door. There was no one about, but on the doorstep he found a scrap of papyrus. On it was scrawled: *'Branir is in danger. Come quickly.'*

Pazair dropped the papyrus and ran.

The surroundings of Branir's house seemed peaceful, but although it was late the door stood open. Pazair crossed the first room and saw his master sitting with his back against the wall and his head sunk on his chest. A blood-spattered spike of mother-of-pearl was embedded in his neck.

Pazair's heart stood still. Overwhelmed, he could hardly take in the truth: someone had murdered Branir.

Mentmose strode in, followed by several guards who surrounded Pazair.

'What are you doing here?' demanded Mentmose.

'I got a message saying Branir was in danger.'

'Show it to me.'

'I dropped it in the street, outside my house.'

'We'll check.'

'Why are you so suspicious?'

'Because I'm accusing you of murder.'

Mentmose woke the Judge of the Porch in the middle of the night. The Judge was astonished to see Pazair standing between two guards.

'Before making the facts public,' declared Mentmose, 'I want to consult you.'

'Why have you arrested Judge Pazair?'

'For murder.'

'Whom has he killed?'

'Branir.'

'That's absurd,' cut in Pazair. 'He was my master, and I venerated him.'

'Why are you so certain, Mentmose?' asked the Judge.

'We caught him almost in the act. He'd pushed a mother-of-pearl spike into Branir's neck – there wasn't much bleeding. When my men and I entered the house, he was standing over his victim.'

'That's a lie,' protested Pazair. 'I had just discovered the body.'

'Did you summon a doctor to examine the body?' asked the Judge.

'Yes. Nebamon,' said Mentmose.

Despite the terrible sadness in his heart, Pazair tried to think clearly. 'It's strange that you happened to be there at that time, with a squad of guards, Mentomose. How do you explain it?'

'A night patrol. From time to time, I go out with my men – it's the best way of knowing their difficulties and resolving them. We were lucky enough to catch a criminal red-handed.'

'Who sent you, Mentmose?' said Pazair. 'Who set this trap?'

His guards seized Pazair by the arms. The Judge took Mentmose aside and asked, 'Answer me, Mentmose: were you there by chance?'

'Not entirely. An anonymous message reached my office that afternoon. At nightfall, I stationed myself near Branir's house. I saw Pazair go in and followed almost immediately, but it was already too late.'

'Is his guilt certain?'

'I didn't see him stab his victim, but there's not much doubt about it.'

'Nevertheless, that small doubt is important. After the Asher scandal, such a drama . . . And accusing a judge, a judge serving under me!'

'Let justice do its duty,' said Mentmose. 'I've done mine.'

'One point is still unclear. What was his motive?'

'That's of minor importance.'

'By no means.' The Judge of the Porch seemed troubled.

'Detain Pazair secretly,' suggested Mentmose. 'Officially, he'll have left Memphis for a special mission in Asia, in connection with the Asher case. That's dangerous country – he might well meet with an accident, or be killed by bandits.'

'Mentmose, you wouldn't dare . . .'

'We've known each other a long time, Judge. Our only guide is our country's interest. You wouldn't want me to find out who sent the anonymous message. This little judge is causing a lot of trouble, and Memphis likes calm.'

Pazair interrupted them. 'You're wrong to attack a judge. I

shall return and find out the truth. By the name of Pharaoh, I swear that I shall return!'

The Judge of the Porch closed his eyes and his ears.

Mad with worry, Neferet had alerted everyone in the district. Some had heard Way-Finder braying, but no one had any idea where Pazair had gone. Suti could find out nothing, and Branir's house was locked up. The only thing left to Neferet was to consult the Judge of the Porch.

'Pazair has disappeared,' she said.

The Judge looked astonished. 'The very idea! Don't worry, he's on a secret mission in connection with his investigation.'

'But where is he?'

'Even if I knew, I couldn't tell you. But he didn't give me any details, and I don't know where's he's gone.'

'He didn't say anything to me,' said Neferet.

'I'm glad to hear it. If he had, he would have deserved a reprimand.'

'But he left in the middle of the night, without a word.'

'No doubt he wanted to avoid a painful parting.'

'We were going to move to Branir's house the day after tomorrow. I wanted to speak to Branir, but he's on his way to Karnak.'

The Judge's voice grew solemn. 'My poor child, haven't you heard? Branir died last night. His former colleagues are going to organize a magnificent funeral.'

41

The little green monkey no longer played, the dog refused to eat, and the donkey's large eyes brimmed with tears. Devastated by the death of Branir and the disappearance of her husband, Neferet had lost the heart to do anything.

Suti and Kem came to her aid. They ran from barracks to barracks, from government office to government office, from official to official, to find out even the tiniest piece of information about Pazair's mission. But doors closed in their faces, and lips were sealed.

In her despair, Neferet realized just how much she loved Pazair. For a long time she had repressed her feelings, for fear of becoming involved too lightly, but his persistence had made them grow, day after day. She had become one with Pazair; parted, they would wither. Without him, life lost its meaning.

Accompanied by Suti, Neferet laid lotus flowers on the shrine at Branir's tomb. The master would never be forgotten. He was the guest of the sages, in communion with the reborn sun, which would give his soul the energy it needed to journey continually between the afterlife and the darkness of the tomb, where it would continue to shine forth.

Suti was too much on edge to pray. He left the shrine picked up a stone, and flung it into the distance.

Neferet laid a hand on his shoulder. 'He'll come back, I'm sure.'

'Ten times I've tried to corner that damned Judge of the Porch, but he's more slippery than an eel. "Secret mission" – those are the only two words he knows. And now he's refusing to see me.'

'What are you going to?'

'Go to Asia and find Pazair.'

'But you don't know where he is.'

'I still have friends in the army.'

'And have they helped you?'

Suti lowered his eyes. 'Nobody knows anything. It's as if Pazair had vanished in a puff of smoke. Can you imagine how distressed he'll be when he learns of Branir's death?'

Neferet felt cold.

They walked away from the burial ground with heavy hearts.

Killer devoured a chicken leg greedily. Kem was worn out. He refreshed himself by washing in warm, scented water and putting on a clean kilt.

Neferet brought him a meal of meat and vegetables.

'I'm not hungry,' he said.

'How long is it since you had any sleep?'

'Three days – maybe more.'

'And you've learnt nothing?'

'Nothing at all. I've done everything I can, but my informers are all silent. I'm certain of only one thing: Pazair has left Memphis.'

'Then he must have gone to Asia.'

'Without telling you?'

From the roof of the High Temple of Ptah, Ramses gazed down upon the city, which was sometimes feverish and always joyful. Beyond its white walls lay the lush fields, fringed with deserts where the dead lived. After conducting ten hours of rituals, the king had chosen to be alone, to savour the invigorating evening air.

At the palace, at court, in the provinces, nothing had changed. The threat seemed to have moved further away, carried off by the river. But Ramses remembered the prophecies of the old sage Ipu-Ur, announcing that crime would spread, that the Great Pyramid would be desecrated, and that the secrets of power would fall into the hands of a few madmen, who were prepared to destroy a thousand-year-old civilization to serve their own interests and their madness.

As a child, reading the famous text under the guidance of his teacher, he had rebelled against this pessimistic vision; if he reigned, he would drive it away for ever! In his foolish vanity he had forgotten that no one, not even Pharaoh, could drive evil out of men's hearts.

Today, more alone than a traveller lost in the desert, despite the hundreds of courtiers who surrounded him, he must fight darkness so dense that it would soon hide the sun. Ramses was too clear-headed to be beguiled by illusions; this battle was lost in advance, since he did not know his enemy's face and so could not take action against him.

A prisoner in his own land, a victim doomed to the worst of all downfalls, his spirit haunted by an incurable evil, the greatest of Egypt's kings sank into the end of his reign as though into the murky waters of a marsh. His final dignity was to accept destiny without cowardly complaints.

When the conspirators met, they were smiling broadly. They congratulated themselves on their ruse, which had produced an excellent result. Fortune did indeed smile upon victors. If there had been a few criticisms about an individual's behaviour, or an incautious act, they were no longer relevant in this period of triumph, this prelude to the birth of a new state. The bloodshed was forgotten, the last traces of remorse wiped away.

Everyone had done his part, and no one had succumbed to Judge Pazair's assaults. By not yielding to panic, the group of conspirators had shown its unity, a precious treasure which must be preserved in the future, when power was distributed.

All that remained was to carry out one formality, so as to rid themselves of the ghost of Judge Pazair for ever.

In the middle of the night, Way-Finder's bray warned Neferet of a hostile presence. She lit a lamp, pushed open the shutter and looked down into the street. Two soldiers were knocking at her door.

They looked up at her. 'Are you Neferet?'

'Yes, but—'

'Please come with us.'

'Why?'

'Orders from our superiors.'

'And if I refuse?'

'We'll have to use force.'

Brave growled. Neferet could have called for help, woken her neighbours, but she calmed the dog, threw a shawl round her shoulders, and went downstairs. The presence of these two soldiers must be linked to Pazair's mission. What did her safety matter, if she was at last going to get some reliable information?

The trio crossed the sleeping town swiftly, and went to the central barracks. Once there, the soldiers handed Neferet over to an officer, who took her without a word to General Asher's office.

He was seated on a mat, surrounded by papyri, and his attention remained on his work.

'Sit down, Neferet,' he said.

'I would rather stand.'

'Would you like some warm milk?'

'Why have you summoned me at this peculiar hour?'

Asher's voice became aggressive. 'Do you know why Pazair went away?'

'He didn't have time to tell me.'

'He's so stubborn! He couldn't accept his defeat, and he wants to bring back this famous corpse – which doesn't exist! Why does he continue to pursue me with his hatred?'

'Pazair is a judge. He wants to find out the truth.'

'The truth was brought out during the trial, but he didn't like it. All that mattered was for me to be dismissed and dishonoured.'

'I'm not interested in your grievances, General,' said Neferet. 'Have you anything else to say?'

'Indeed I have.' Asher unrolled a papyrus. 'This report is marked with the seal of the Judge of the Porch; it has been checked. I received it less than an hour ago.'

'What does it say?'

'Pazair is dead.'

Neferet closed her eyes. She wanted to wither away like a lotus flower, to die in a single breath.

'There was an accident on a mountain path,' explained the general. 'Pazair didn't know the area but, with his usual imprudence, he set out on a mad venture.'

The words seared her throat, but Neferet had to ask, 'When will you bring his body home?'

'We're still searching for it, but I haven't much hope. In that region, the rivers are wild and the gorges inaccessible. I condole with your pain, Neferet. Pazair was a man of virtue.'

'Justice doesn't exist,' said Kem, laying down his weapons.

'Have you seen Suti?' asked Neferet anxiously.

'He'll wear out his feet with walking, but he won't give up until he finds Pazair – he's still convinced that he isn't dead.'

'And if . . . ?'

The Nubian shook his head.

'I shall continue the investigation,' she declared.

'It's no use.'

'Evil must not win.'

'It always wins.'

'No, Kem. If that were so, Egypt wouldn't exist. It was justice that founded this country, and it was justice that Pazair wished to see reigning. We have no right to surrender to lies.'

'I shall be at your side, Neferet.'

Neferet sat beside the canal, at the place where she had met Pazair for the first time. Winter was approaching, and the wind tugged at the turquoise hanging at her throat. Why had the precious talisman not protected him? Hesitantly, she rubbed the precious stone between her thumb and index finger, thinking of Hathor, the mother of turquoises and queen of love.

The first stars appeared, their light springing forth from the otherworld; she suddenly felt certain that her beloved was with her, as if the frontiers of death had been broken down. One wild thought became a hope: the soul of Branir, Pazair's murdered master, must be watching over his disciple.

Yes, Pazair would return. Yes, the Egyptian judge would drive away the darkness, and light would be reborn.